Oddjobs 3:
You Only Live Once

by Heide Goody and Iain Grant

Pigeon Park Press

Published by Pigeon Park Press

www.pigeonparkpress.com

Cover artwork and design by Mike Watts – www.bigbeano.co.uk

SUNDAY

Morag Murray raised her phone and compared the Facebook picture to the path ahead. Those two rotting trunks rose out of the swampy ground at an unmistakeable angle.

"That direction," she said.

Kathy Kaur led the way through the nature reserve, along a walkway of wire-bound planks laid over marshy ground.

"Stay on the path," said Rod needlessly.

Morag followed the pair of them. A bubble popped in the mud beneath her.

"Is this place always like this?" she said.

"Like this?"

"Like the Bog of Eternal Stench."

"Moseley Bog," said Kathy. "Clue's in the name. Technically it's a fen, not a bog."

"Really?"

Kathy waved her phone. "According to Google."

The wooden walkway led upward to a dry patch of ground in the woodland. They'd been walking for no more than ten minutes and she'd already got herself turned around and couldn't say which direction the car park was in. Near the edge of the clearing, half in and half out of the bog, a fallen log had been carved into a fat crocodile. One almond eye looked at her.

Nature walks weren't a usual part of Morag's job. In the two plus months since she'd transferred down from Scotland to the Birmingham consular mission to the Venislarn, she'd been through drains and down abandoned nuclear bunkers, stood above the highest rooftops in the city and trodden more canal towpath than any city had a right to possess. Woodlands were a rarity. Working Sunday mornings was also rare, but the list of crackpot calls that needed checking out had spilled over into the weekend. Today's outing had started with a social media page called 'Fairy Wishes Wood', a secret group that the mission's tech support expert Professor Sheikh Omar had stumbled upon. Morag had first dismissed it as a cutesy little fairy fan page favoured by stay-at-home mums of the elf-on-a-shelf, dreamcatchers and Disney princesses variety. But then Omar had prompted her to read the testimonial posts of people who'd left 'offerings' for the fairies.

The testimonials had reminded Morag of the magical threats that used to appear in chain letters, those carrot-and-stick exhortations of the 'one woman passed on the chain letter and won the lottery the next day, another woman refused and her house exploded' variety. Below the picture she was using for navigation, a poster had commented, 'Made an offering to the fairy yesterday and my sciatica hasn't given me any trouble since.' The poster had finished off with a range of heart and smiley emojis. The reply comments were all hearts and hugs and Tinkerbell gifs.

The consular mission didn't have any interest in fairies. Fairies were, to the best of Morag's knowledge, not real; but, the mission did have an interest in creatures that accepted 'offerings' from members of the public. There were no registered Venislarn in the area, but it was quite possible a minor god had taken up residence.

Moseley Bog was a patch of damp, overgrown woodland surrounded by the manicured suburbs of Hall Green and Moseley. Narrow, plank walkways led into the dim, wet heart of the wood. Trees, rotting and blooming with equal vigour, crowded the walkways, blocking the bright morning sky. The sounds of the city did not penetrate here.

"Scuse me," said a voice behind Morag and she stepped aside to allow a shaven-headed man pushing an old woman in wheelchair to come through.

"Nice day for it, innit?" he said as he passed.

There was a loud ratchetting sound above. Morag looked up. "What was that?"

"A woodpecker," said Kathy.

"Sounded like something hammering."

"A woodpecker," agreed Kathy.

Morag was no longer the new girl at the mission. Since her arrival in Birmingham, two of her colleagues had been killed by the Venislarn. In both cases there hadn't been a body to bury. Omar had been given the tech support role vacated by the mad-rather-than-bad Ingrid Spence. And Dr Kathy Kaur had replaced Vivian

4

Grey on the response team. Vivian Grey had been a very difficult woman to like but she was nonetheless sorely missed, especially by Nina, the youngest member of the team. Kathy Kaur wouldn't find it easy filling Vivian's shoes—her severe and practical shoes—but she did at least seem to share Vivian's fierce intelligence and near matchless knowledge of all things Venislarn. There, however, the similarities ended. Where Vivian had been as coldly efficient as a chest freezer, Kathy was warm, playful and very much alive. Morag wasn't one to use the word 'sensual' (she was Scottish) but, if she did, she might use it to describe Kathy.

"Woodpecker," said Morag doubtfully.

Rod was looking across the field of standing water.

"How far does this go down?" he said.

"This?" said Morag.

"How big a creature could live under the surface?"

"In reality, hardly anything," said Kathy. "Although they found a wandering *mi'nasulu* in here years ago. The bog isn't deep, but a Venislarn could have created a whole pocket universe down there."

Morag gave the carved crocodile a gentle kick. "You thinking there's a monster croc in the mud?"

Rod frowned. "That's a dragon."

"Really?"

"Assume so." He pointed off in some non-specific direction. "Tolkien grew up here. They have a festival each year and you can't move for elves and wizards and..."—he tutted—"the ones with the faces."

"Orcs," said Kathy.

"Orcs, aye."

"Nerd stuff," said Morag.

Rod pressed on.

"Hey, Rod," said Kathy, "ever tell you, you sound like—"

"Is this going to be the Sean Bean thing again?" said Rod unexpectedly curt.

"All right, Mr Grumpy!" said Kathy and looked back at Morag.

Morag shrugged. "He's heard it before."

"Doesn't like the comparison?"

Morag couldn't understand why. It wasn't just Rod's accent. With his broad shoulders and soldier's physique he would have made a good Boromir too "He's just grumpy today," she said. "He's dealing with some bad news."

"Bad news?"

Morag nodded. "Let's just say, I hope we don't find ourselves in a situation where he'd need to use a firearm."

"I thought he'd requisitioned a new one."

"Lois lost the forms. Again. Also, the Sean Bean thing: he doesn't like being reminded of Sean Bean's survival rate."

"Ah."

Kathy thought.

"Anyroads, we going to find this thing or not?" said Rod, further down the walkway, almost invisible in the encroaching shrubbery.

Morag and Kathy moved to catch up.

"The path forks here," said Rod.

Morag scrolled through dozens of posts on the 'Fairy Wishes Wood' group. There were plenty of photos of trees and offerings but few that offered a clue to an exact location. People had mostly left offerings of food and reported minor miracles: lost things found, workplace promotions, driving tests passed.

"We might find some offerings next to trees," suggested Morag. "Fruit. Cakes. Sweets."

"Kebab," said Rod, pointing.

Morag made a noise. "More likely dropped by a drunkard. Can't see any self-respecting god demanding doner kebabs from the faithful..." She stopped. There was a whole heap of them, arranged in various states of decomposition and consumption around the base of tree.

"It's like a floral tribute to the dead," said Kathy.

The sight made Morag simultaneously hungry and queasy. She'd bought a chicken salad sandwich for breakfast, but it had rapidly disagreed with her and she'd thrown most of it in the bin. She told herself the chicken was probably off because that was better than the alternative.

"I don't like kebabs," said Kathy.

"Well, not tree kebab," admitted Morag.

"Beer," said Rod and, brushing a stand of tall grasses, stepped off the path.

6

"Hey, you said stay on the path," said Kathy.

Morag followed them, stepping into black mud that rose past her heels. "*Muda*," she swore in Venislarn.

There was indeed beer. And vodka and gin and bottles of wine... arranged, mostly unopened, around another tree. All of them had labels or scraps of paper tied to them. Morag knelt to read the labels as Rod moved on to a tree where sunglasses had been left as offerings, and then to another festooned with various hats and scarves. The offerings had been categorised and sorted with an obsessive-compulsive neatness.

Morag turned over a label. *I want to pass my English and Science GCSEs.* Another read, *Aston Villa to win the FA cup.*

The wind whistled and tree boughs creaked above. A shadow crossed Morag but when she looked up it had passed.

"You know any Venislarn that take material goods in exchange for wishes?" she said.

"No," said Kathy. "I think this is just local superstition, physical offerings as prayers."

"A clootie well."

"Like the one at Munlochy?"

Morag was pleased and impressed. "You've heard of it? I grew up round there."

"Beautiful bit of Scotland." She took a deep breath and looked round. "Yeah, local superstition. There are no Venislarn here."

"What do you think did this then?" said Rod.

He held a hat that had fallen to the ground near the hat tree. It was a cowboy hat made of stiffened leather. As Rod brushed the muck away, Morag saw that a wedge-shaped chunk had been bitten out of the brim. There was blood and hair and what might have been a shard of skull bone caked to the edge of the bite mark.

Kathy took the hat and measured the bite with her fingers. "That's a big mouth."

"Badger?" suggested Morag.

Kathy blinked. "You think a badger did this?"

"A big badger?" Morag looked at the hat. "I've seen that hat before."

"A hat like that?"

7

"Bugger," said Rod. He had moved on, further from the path, into the deepening thicket. "Come look at this."

Thin branches slapped Morag's face and mud squelched over the tops of her shoes. "This better be good."

"No, it's definitely bad," he replied. A trio of dog leads were tied to a thin tree. The collar of one was ripped. Dark, dried blood spattered them all and the exposed roots of the tree. There were little hand-written wish labels in the dirt.

"What kind of wish is worth a dog sacrifice?" said Morag and then realised Rod wasn't even looking at the dog leads. He pointed to a pair of narrow tyre tracks in the mud, cutting across from a different section of the path.

"We're happy that a badger didn't do this?" he said.

"Yes," said Kathy.

"Fair enough, because I reckon those are wheelchair tracks."

The trees above creaked in the wind. Morag couldn't feel any wind.

"What do you reckon the going rate is for a grandma, these days?" said Rod.

Nina Seth walked from the bus stop on Rotton Park Road, the folder of documents under her arm. The houses here were tall and grand properties, looming over high front hedges. This area, on the border of Edgbaston and Soho, was less than two miles from Nina's own, far more modest home. She had never known that she and Vivian Grey had lived so near to each other.

Vivian's house stood on the corner of Rotton Park Road and Jacey Road. Pebbled concrete steps ran from the pavement to the door. Nina let herself in with the keys she had taken on her previous visit. The house was cold and silent.

Vivian was dead, seven weeks dead. Her husband was dead too. He'd already been dead. Dead some time, although the when and the where and the how had never been disclosed. The Greys had never had children, there was no other living family, no close friends to be found.

It was a sunny morning, but the old house was dark. Nina flicked the hallway light on and went through to the back room that was part dining room, part study, part old lady cave.

Vivian had been an unpleasant and hard-edged thing, like an ancient cracker found in the back of a cupboard. She had been the only person—the only thing even—that Nina had ever truly been frightened of. Nina wasn't sure why she now grieved for a woman she had never liked—it wasn't even as though Vivian had been a mentor; Vivian wouldn't have considered Nina worth the bother—but Nina grieved nonetheless.

Fuelled by this inexplicable sense of loss, Nina had insisted she be one of the consular mission staff deployed to Vivian's home to check that there weren't any Venislarn artefacts, consular documents, incriminating journals or other items of interest lying about the place. There hadn't been. Like the woman's desk in the mission office, there was barely any evidence that a real human being, with hopes or hobbies, passions or personality, had ever lived here. The place was functionally furnished in a lifeless modern style. Even the flowers in the vase on the mantelpiece were fake. Nina had expected stuffy armchairs, tablecloths and doilies.

There were only two items left in the house that suggested a real human life had once been lived here and was now ended: a photo of a donkey next to the vase on the mantelpiece, and a key from Vivian's desk drawer.

The framed picture of the donkey was the only photograph in the house. There wasn't even one of the mysterious and late Mr Grey. The donkey was only partially explained by Vivian's will which was curt to the point of apathy and simply declared that the entire estate be sold and the proceeds given to the Donkey Sanctuary in Sutton Park.

The reading and execution of a will seemed profoundly wrong to Nina. Vivian was dead, yes. That was the official line, yes. But Vivian hadn't died. There wasn't a body. She had crossed over into a Venislarn hell, *Kal Frexo leng*-space, and had been trapped there when the doorway closed. It was impossible to live in hell but dead? No.

The papers Nina carried with her represented everything Professor Omar had been able to locate in the Vault library on the topic of *Leng*-space. Omar was Nina's least favourite human being on earth, but he'd recognised her loss and she'd recognised his professional respect for Vivian and, in the truce that currently existed between them, he'd provided her with all he could. None of it helped, none of it would bring her back.

Nina put the papers on the dining table and took the key out of her pocket. It was old, as long as Nina's smart phone and five times as heavy. The teeth on one end and the semi-circular crest on the other topped by what looked like a giraffe chewing an arrow were equally ornate. It had sat at the back of a drawer in Vivian's office desk and fitted no lock in the consular mission office.

Vivian didn't believe in keeping things that had no use. There would be a lock to match the key and Nina felt, without logic or reason, that finding it was something she had to do. She started in the back room—looking at the bureau, the cabinet, the back door— and proceeded through the house, downstairs and then up, searching for a keyhole to match the key. She tried the keyholes on already unlocked doors. She investigated the wardrobe. She shifted furniture and probed for secret doorways or spooky wooden chests that might be worthy of the key. She spent too long trying to get access to the loft, balancing on a chair on tiptoes and prodding with a pole until the extendable ladder came down, only to find the loft was home to nothing but dusty insulation, dead spiders and a box of Christmas decorations that looked like it hadn't been opened in decades. She went to the bottom of the garden and broke into the shed, more to express her annoyance than in any real hope of finding the hole to fit the key.

Dusty, angry and nursing a knee bruised in her attack on the shed door, Nina flopped into a chair in the back room and scowled at the picture of the donkey. She picked up the folder of information on *Leng*-space and flicked through the pages of photocopied notes. She hadn't exactly read it all, although she had skimmed through it *really hard*. Nina wasn't a huge fan of reading. Her English GCSE—if it had taught her anything at all—had taught her that any book worth reading would have been adapted into a Hollywood movie.

Nina had entered the fiery pink landscape of *Leng*-space, briefly. She had seen some of its residents. But that wasn't enough. She'd seen the trailer, but she hadn't stayed for the full, immersive CGI-ed IMAX 3D extended edition movie. She couldn't picture Vivian beyond those first and final moments. She couldn't comprehend—and she needed to—what seven weeks in hell would be like for Vivian.

And then Nina remembered she knew someone who might better understand what that particular hell was like. He'd spent a week there and had come back in one piece: Pupfish.

Rod hurriedly followed the wheelchair tracks as they jigged and curved along the edge of the bog. Kathy spat and shouted as he accidentally let a branch swing back into her face.

"Rod!"

"Sorry," he said.

"Rod!"

"Sorry!"

"Look up," she hissed.

In the canopy above, a broad silhouette moved from bough to bough, shredding leaves from branches as it passed. It didn't leap or climb. It insinuated itself from tree to tree. A claw here, a prehensile tail there, an unfurling of a membranous wing.

"A dragon," he said.

"Definitely not a badger," said Kathy.

Rod thrust ahead. The thing was moving in the same direction as the tyre tracks. Rod's ankle caught on a trailing bramble. He ripped forcefully through it and came up suddenly beside the wheelchair. It was positioned in the shade of a stout tree around which several weeks' worth of cake-making and home baking were scattered and trampled. Whatever this wish-granting 'fairy' was, it was a messy picnicker.

The grey-haired woman in the chair looked at Rod.

"You've got mud on your shoes," she said.

There was a card-and-string luggage label hanging from the button of the woman's cardigan, the kind that should say, *Please, look after this bear. Thank you.* What it actually said was, *A new PlayStation. And a milion pounds, please,* spelt wrong.

"Jesus," sighed Rod.

"Oh, it'll come off with some soapy water and a bit of elbow grease," said the woman optimistically.

Kathy and Morag came through behind him.

"Okay, it's not a badger," said Morag.

11

The Venislarn creature descended the tree trunk, claw over tentacle over claw. It was nut brown, as big as a man and moved on an indeterminate number of limbs hidden beneath the cowl of its giant wings. It looked like the child of an octopus and a bat; the mammalian jaw at the end of a sinuous neck was lined with canine fangs. The teeth glistened with drool.

"Hypothetically," said Rod, not taking his eyes off the thing, "*if* I had a gun..."

"I wasn't going to bring that up," said Morag.

"But *would* I have been allowed to shoot it?"

"It's a *Bondook* shambler," said Kathy as it approached, hungrily eyeing the four humans. "It's just an animal. Fair game."

"Buggeration," said Rod.

"What kind of animal is that?" said the old woman. "I've not got my varifocals with me."

"I've seen a baby one of those," said Morag. "Nina and I confiscated it off some Gandalf wannabe who thought it would make a good pet. What was his name? Nina would remember. Strange Ken or...?"

"Mystic Trevor," said Rod, thumbing the blade out from his penknife.

"That's right," said Morag. "Mystic Trevor. That's his—ah. I now remember where I've seen that hat before."

"Mystery solved then," said Kathy. "Wizard wants pet. Pet gets confiscated. Wizard gets another pet. Pet eats wizard."

"Stupid locals mistake pet for woodland sprite," said Morag.

"Pet eats Rod," said Rod. "I've got a knife and a pepper spray disguised as mouth spray."

The shambler's amber eyes fixed on Rod and from its wide throat came a staccato growl—fifty-percent rattlesnake, fifty-percent bronchial cough.

"It doesn't sound well," said Morag.

The shambler coiled its tentacles beneath it. If it could spring forward, snake fast, he'd barely have a chance at all.

"It's been eating a diet of kebabs and party cakes," said Kathy.

"And people," Rod pointed out. "People. You going to move the old lady out of the way while I try to fend it off?"

"No need," said Kathy.

"Harsh. Grey lives matter too."

Rod raised the pepper spray in a slow and unthreatening manner. If he could get a blast in its mouth—and it was offering a big enough target—it might be distracted long enough for him to thrust his knife into a vital organ. He wondered where a *Bondook* shambler's vital organs were.

"*Iyuzha gha'bho*," said Kathy loudly.

The shambler tumbled forward, curling its wings about itself as it fell. When it hit the ground, it was a tightly wrapped and immobile parcel of leathery brown, the size of a beanbag.

"It's like a big conker," said the woman in the wheelchair, neither impressed nor afraid.

"Do we kill it now?" said Rod. He was still doubtful he could.

"That wasn't a spell of binding," said Morag. "Was it?"

"A command word," said Kathy. "Most of the shamblers are hand-reared by Carcosans."

"You just told it to 'sit'?" said Rod.

Kathy waggled an eyebrow cockily. "It's all about tone of voice, really."

At midday on *Daganau-Vei*, the *samakha* youths were noisily racing coracles, living their lives a quarter mile at a time. As she crossed a footbridge, Nina watched a human girl on the buoy in the middle of the canal drop the tatty handkerchief that served as a start flag and the boys in their souped-up and pimped-out circular boats kicked and paddled for all they were worth. Mackerel the Knife might have outfitted his craft with hydrofoil spoilers trimmed with blue down-lighters that glowed underwater and he might have purchased (or more probably stolen) an Olympic standard kayak oar but he was simply no match for Death Roe, who powerfully propelled his craft with his size thirteen webbed feet.

These rowdy teens were not true *samakha*. They were the offspring of the human women foolish enough to sell themselves as wives to the true *samakha* and the god who owned this section of urban canal. There were a few true *samakha* visible if you knew where to look. One of the fishmen lay just below the surface of the water. Lidless eyes watched them from the darkness of an alleyway. High up, in the vertical shanty town the locals had built against the existing canalside buildings, a hunched shape with a serrated dorsal fin gazed down. The true *samakha* observed, perhaps with the disdain of all parents, perhaps with blunt incomprehension.

Nina spotted a fish-boy she knew, one of the Waters Crew. She spoke to him, got some fishy backchat from him before he pointed to a fast food place down by the waterside. The lit sign over the front door had half the letters missing. The inside was *samakha* burger bar chic, plastic chairs and laminate tables covered with mould and warped by damp. In the glass fronted display counter, a green-shelled thing with claws had crawled off the salad bed on which it had been placed and was attacking a pizza on the next tray over. Hragra, the fishman in an apron behind the counter, picked up the scavenging crab-thing and put it back where it belonged.

The only patron in the place was the *samakha* youth Pupfish. He sat at a table, webbed hands wrapped around an empty bottle of Dr Pepper, staring at nothing.

Nina looked at the choices of chairs available and decided to remain standing.

"What's up, Pupfish?"

He looked up, seeing her for the first time.

"Hey, Nina," his fishy face brightening just for a minute before switching to suspicion. "What you doing here?"

"Just chilling."

"Aight. Cos if this is about—ggh!"—he gave an involuntary gill-gasp—"the thing with the thefts from the market then I don't know."

"It's not about the thefts," said Nina, who knew nothing about any thefts but would be sure to look into it. "I came to ask you what you remember about what happened to you in *leng*-space. I expected to see you out there on the canal, racing. Or at least watching the racing."

Pupfish gave a despondent shrug. "Don't fancy it. Not in the mood. And I can't be at home, homes."

"No?"

Pupfish's mouth turned down in a miserable frown and, given that his fishy mouth was naturally downturned, it was a wretched thing to look at.

"Ggh! What do you want?" he said.

14

"You and Allana, the human girl, you were snatched by Priests of *Nystar*. You spent two days in hell before I found you."

"Felt like longer, yo," he said.

"But you survived. I need to know, is it possible to survive there?"

He sat back. "We did. It wan't easy though. You call it hell but it ain't no fire and brimstone, you know."

Nina held her folder of notes. "There are creatures there."

"Fasho. It's like the jungle. An' I don't mean the concrete jungle. I mean like—ggh!—with trees and shit, 'cept the trees are trying to eat you and the shit too. We got ambushed by a pack of *dendooshi*."

"*Dendooshi* are the wolf creatures."

"Big-ass wolves, Nina. Taller 'n you."

"Most things are."

He cracked an almost grin at that. He started ticking things off his glistening fingers. "You got the priests of *Nystar* and then these evil mushroom things."

"*Ix'kwir*?"

"Them. We rested under one for... I don't know. Time is like a dream there—ggh!—you get me? It nearly had Allana."

"But you survived," insisted Nina. "How long could someone survive in there?"

Pupfish gave her a straight look, as straight as he could with eyes on the sides of his head. "Your friend, Mrs Grey. She's been gone a long time. She—ggh!—she's a tough bitch."

"She is."

He shook his head. "Thing is, dog, it's hell. You can't die there. Ggh! You might wanna die but you can't. And, thing is, even if you do survive... My girl, Allana, she says she's all right, but she wakes up screaming in the night. The doctors have got her on these—ggh!—tablets but I don't know if they working. She's messed up."

Having a gangsta fish-boy for a boyfriend probably wasn't doing her health or sanity any good either but Nina didn't say that.

"You two still an item?" she said.

"Fasho," he said. "It's not easy. I can't go to hers. Her mom don't like my kind. And I can't bring her back to mine. My mom..." He looked like he was going to be sick. "Fluke's moved in with us."

Nina knew Fluke, one of the Waters Crew gang, a wannabe gangsta with a man-crush for dead rappers.

"He's moved in with you?" she said and then understood. "He's moved in with your mom? You mean...?"

Fluke was Pupfish's age. They had been best friends.

"That's *bhul-detar*," she said.

"Fucked up don' even begin to cover it," he said, looking like he was going to throw up.

Over by the counter, the crab-thing had vaulted the divide into the pizza tray again and snatched up a chunk of dried pineapple topping before Hragra the proprietor flipped it back onto the salad.

"And I'm—ggh!—gonna lose Allana if I don't have a place to bring her to," said Pupfish. "I'm tryin' do it right, ya feel me?"

"I do," she said.

"I bring her stuff, to show I'm still... you know. I was gonna get her a pet, one of them *dnebian* land-squids."

"Just what a girl wants."

"They scent-bond to the first thing they smell after they hatch. I know where to get one from."

"I don't think a land-squid is gonna be to her taste."

Pupfish pulled an unhappy face. "I even got her this big-ass bunch of flowers from—"

He stopped.

"From the market?" suggested Nina and smiled.

"*Adn-bhul* truckload cos the bitches love flowers, right?"

She shrugged. "Most of them, yeah. Vivian didn't like flowers. She said she could never see the point of giving someone a plant's severed reproductive organs."

"Ggh! She was a tough woman, that one."

A thought struck Nina, almost like a physical assault. She backed into a table. "*Kos-kho bhul!*" she gasped.

"What?" said Pupfish.

"The flowers!" she said. "She hated flowers."

She turned to the door. The crab-thing was climbing the divide again to get to the pizza.

"*Zek'ee*, Hragra," she said to the proprietor, "just kill that thing or chuck it a slice."

She ran out and across the bridge. Down on the water Daganua-Pysh, the god of the deeps, had eaten one of the coracle racers. And his coracle.

Carrying the shambler back to the car park was no easy task. It was heavy and the wrong kind of round. Rod fashioned a harness from his belt and the length of climbing cord woven into his utility bracelet and lugged it on his shoulder like Atlas. While Kathy collected *Bondook*-chewed hats and other items of evidence, Morag dragged the old woman out the way she'd been brought in and tried to work out what to do with her.

"The man who brought you here..." she said.

"That's our Georgina's eldest," said the woman. "He said he was going to get us ice creams."

"Is that so? Do you live with him?"

"I've been staying with our Laura. That's Laura who's not Jim's youngest but the other one."

"Right. And where do you live?"

This question gave the woman some pause for thought and they were nearly back at the car park when the woman finally decided it was "one of those Wimpey homes. Or Barratt homes. Barely enough room inside to swing a cat."

Rod juggled the shambler ball onto one shoulder while he opened the boot of his car and then dropped it inside. Kathy appeared. She had found a box somewhere and loaded it with her finds.

"This dog collar has got the owner's details on it," she said. "Some of this other stuff we can trace if we need to."

"The bottle of vodka?" said Morag.

Kathy made a playful face. "I've got an uncle who likes this stuff. It's his birthday next week."

Rod grimaced. The bottle was unopened but there felt something wrong about drinking spirits that had been presented as a sacrificial offering to a Venislarn. Kathy read his expression.

"I didn't say I liked the uncle," she said. She nodded to the older woman. "I'm going to put a call in to social services. It might be unwise to return her to the family home."

"I can hear you, you know," said the woman.

"You two, log the shambler into the Vault for now. I'm sure we'll end up transferring it to the Menagerie in Dudley. I'll wait here for social services and then I'm going to call in on this Mystic Trevor. Does he live close to here?"

"Should be on file. Otherwise, Nina will know," said Rod.

"Where is she?" said Morag.

"Some personal errands," he said.

"I'll call her in a bit," said Kathy. She looked at the sky. "It's a nice day."

Rod closed the boot. Morag stamped the worst of the mud off her shoes and climbed into the passenger seat.

"She's a wee bit bossy, isn't she?" said Morag when the doors were closed.

"Who?" said Rod. "Kathy?"

"Uh-huh."

"Aye. Is she? I'm never sure."

"Not sure if she's bossy?" said Morag.

Rod reversed out of the parking spot.

"If I think a woman's bossy," he said, "is it because she's bossy or is that my male privilege getting all defensive?"

"I just said she was bossy. I didn't ask for your gender politics credentials."

"You asked me what I thought."

"Shouldn't have bothered. You've still got the hots for Kathy. You'd take her side in anything."

"No need to get snippy," he said, amiably enough.

"I've got mud up to my shins, and I didn't sign up for this job to deal with idiot Brummies who'd sell their grandma for a games console. I think I've got a right to be snippy."

He laughed. "You think your life's hard, huh?"

Morag rubbed her bloated, groaning belly and told herself it was just the chicken sandwich.

"We have noticed that you've been Mr Grumpy-pants today."

"You did, huh?" he said, edging through the car-crowded streets of Sparkbrook. Every other shop was either a restaurant or a dessert shop. Morag wondered if it would be too cheeky to ask Rod to stop off so she could buy a cookie-dough dessert or an ice-cream waffle.

"Lois will find your requisition paperwork again at some point," she said.

"Got freshly filled forms here," he said and tapped his jacket pocket. "It's not that. Did you not hear what they've got me doing this afternoon?"

"Did I hear someone mention a Hollywood production company was coming to town?" she said.

Rod snorted derisively. "Don't know about Hollywood but they've got me—me!—on liaison duty for some movie they want to film in the city."

"*Muda*. It's not that *samakha*/human teenage angst romance thing Chad and Leandra were pitching? You know, *Twilight* but with fishes."

"No, thank God. Chad dropped that as soon someone told him it was too similar to that *Shape of Water* movie. Although he said they'd totally stolen the idea from him. I've no idea what this movie is supposed to be but can you imagine, having to babysit movie stars and creative types for the week?"

For Rod 'creative types', were in the same category as sponging royals, lager drinkers and people who called their evening meal 'supper'.

"What did you do to deserve such a high honour?" said Morag.

"No idea," he said miserably. "But Chad was insistent."

"Ah," she said, understanding. "So, this is nothing to do with you getting Leandra fired for selling dangerous texts to the Mammonites? A little payback perhaps?"

Rod pushed the car aggressively through a gap in the traffic. "That Leandra was lucky she was just sacked. If it wasn't for her stupidity..."

"I know," said Morag.

If Leandra hadn't passed pages of the Bloody Big Book to the Mammonites they wouldn't have been able to open a doorway to *Kal-Frexo Leng*-space and Vivian would still be alive.

Morag patted Rod's tree trunk leg.

"Oh, I know, mate."

Nina took a uCab taxi back to Vivian's house. She was too restless to wait for a bus. She felt a strange urgency, as though the vase of fake flowers would spontaneously do something if she didn't get there in time.

She ran up the concrete steps, let herself in. Mantelpiece, donkey photo, vase, flowers.

"You hated flowers," she said.

She grabbed the flowers by the stems and pulled them out. Nina wasn't good with names of flowers, real or fake. If they weren't daffodils, dandelions or daisies she was essentially stumped. She had half-expected to find a note tied to them, or something inserted into a hollow stem. There was nothing.

"But you hated flowers," she said.

She turned her attention to the vase. She couldn't see anything inside it. She tipped it up. Maybe another key would fall out. A trinket. A Venislarn charm. Something. There was nothing.

"Give me something, woman."

She looked at the vase. It was decorated with a raised image of a woman in a big costume drama dress, walking and talking, against a powdery blue background. The pottery felt thin, as delicate as eggshells. She looked for Venislarn markings or script. There was none to be found, no markings at all but an uneven row of blurred letters stamped into the base of which the letters 'gwood' were the only ones legible.

"It's just a vase."

Her phone rang. It was Kathy Kaur.

"Yo," she said.

"Are you busy at the moment?" said Kathy.

Nina peered closer at the plant-like garlands around the rim of the vase, hoping to distinguish something special in them.

"It's just an *adn-bhul* vase," she said, unable to quite accept it.

"Pardon?" said Kathy.

"Nothing," said Nina with a huff and set the vase back above the fireplace. "What were you saying?"

"Mystic Trevor," said Kathy.

"An arsehole," replied Nina.

"Do you know where he lives?"

"He's a registered occultist. He should be on file."

"He moved. Landlady said he killed her pet guinea pig."

"Can't help you," said Nina and then mentally backtracked. "Wait. Rumour was he used to work for Omar."

"Work?"

"Snitch. Trevor would feed him the word on the street. Omar would give him scraps from his table."

"Thanks," said Kathy.

"Why'd you ask?"

"We think he's dead."

Nina grunted. She had no feelings one way or the other about that.

Across the globe, there were hundreds of consular missions to the Venislarn, or at least offices with similar names performing similar functions. The governments of the world had responded as one to the news that the earth was under occupation by alien horrors who intended (but were in no hurry) to drag the human race into an everlasting hell of torture and terror with zero chance of reprieve or release. Multilaterally, world governments agreed to keep the existence of the Venislarn out of the media. Dissenters and conspiracy theorists were discredited as hoaxers or silenced by other means. The world had become a global hospice, one in which the populace weren't aware of their terminal condition or even of those government employees who doled out palliative care and regrettable acts of euthanasia. In the United Kingdom, funding was distributed to those regions that had suffered the most critical incursions and acts of destruction. That funding had given Birmingham various facilities including a consular mission office twelve storeys high from top down to basement Vault, wrapped in shiny occult metals and designs and positioned in a prime city centre location. Even dull-witted locals were capable of noticing such a building, so it was rebadged as the Library of Birmingham and opened its doors so infrequently that none but the most persistent of book-borrowers bothered to visit its 'public' spaces.

Rod and Morag rode up to the seventh floor with a tightly wrapped *Bondook* shambler between them on the lift floor. Morag had her hands on her stomach and a vaguely pained look on her face.

"You all right?" he said.

"Huh?" she said, coming back from wherever her mind had wandered.

"You look like you've got a tummy ache."

"A dodgy breakfast," she said.

"You do eat junk," he pointed out.

Rod wasn't a keen observer of human beings, but he thought Morag had put on weight recently. However, he was neither a body fascist nor an idiot and had no intention of sharing that observation with a female colleague and friend.

"It was a chicken sandwich," she said. "A chicken *salad* sandwich."

"Maybe you've got a salad intolerance," he said. "Lots of Scots have that, don't they?"

She gave him a glare that was halfway to becoming a smile and took her hands away from her stomach. The door pinged.

Rod dragged the shambler sphere into the reception area and gave a half-hearted wave to Lois Wheeler, who manned the reception desk behind a glass screen.

"Lost anyone's weapons requisition forms today?" he said.

"That an attempt at humour, bab?" she said and fluttered her long false lashes at him.

"The poor man's pining for his pistol," said Morag.

"He can joke all he likes," said Lois, "but if he's not polite, he might not get this lovely present I've got tucked away down here for him."

She pointed below the counter directly in front of her. Rod's heart leapt with fear as he instinctively and irrationally assumed she was pointing at her own groin.

"By which you mean, stored in the safe under the desk?" said Morag who had apparently jumped to the same interpretation.

"That I do," she said.

"It's come?" said Rod, surprised and delighted. "It's here?"

"Yes, bab."

"But you said you'd lost the forms."

"Mislaid."

"Same thing."

"But I had a nice word with the quartermaster, and I explained that once you had refilled the forms I could present you with your present."

Rod grinned and tried not to look like a six-year-old on Christmas morning. Despite what others might believe, he didn't love his gun. Rod loved all of his tools and gadgets. The loss of his pistol (into the belly of an angry spider monster) had affected him no more keenly than if he had lost his Leatherman multitool, his zipline tie or his taser-pen. But a gun was a tool and he was one of the few people in the mission who both knew how to use one and were permitted to do so and he simply couldn't order a new one over the internet. He'd checked.

"Smashing," he said. "Let's have at it then."

"Forms," said Lois. "Specifically, GAT3B."

Rod half-opened his mouth to argue but he stopped himself. He had the forms in his pocket and silence was the wise option here. He pulled them out and passed them through the parcel tray below the reception screen.

"Let's take a look," she said and unfolded the documents. "What's that anyway?" she said, nodding at the curled up shambler.

"We were bringing it in for Omar," said Morag.

"You should have taken it down to the Vault."

"We did, but he's not down there."

"No, the professor's up here somewhere."

"And we didn't want to leave a *Bondook* shambler in the Vault unattended," Morag pointed out.

"Oh, then it belongs in the Menagerie in Dudley."

"Possibly so," said Rod, fingers twitching in anticipation of being given a firearm again.

"They've got three of them in the Menagerie," said Lois. "The cutest little one. It sits up and begs on command. *Warz-iz!* And it gets up on its back paws or whatever it has and—oh."

"Oh?" said Rod, fearing there was something wrong with his paperwork but then saw Lois was looking past him.

The shambler on the floor was waking—had woken. Its wings pushed at the climbing cord wrapped around it, snapping through what it couldn't shake off.

"Did you just tell it to sit up and beg?" said Morag.

"Didn't mean to," said Lois.

The shambler didn't sit up or beg. It stretched and then lashed out, suddenly filling the small reception area with tentacles, leathery wings and the woody musk of an angry apex predator. As its head swung her way, Morag retaliated with the only object to hand: a cylindrical waste bin. Morag clonked the creature on the side of the head. It snarled, whipped out a tentacle and took her legs out from under her. She fell heavily against the stone wall, smacking her head.

Rod rushed the shambler and barged it bodily against the lift door. The creature's eye rolled madly at him. Display spines along its cheek ridge fluttered angrily. Limbs tensed and extended and Rod was thrown away across the reception.

"Gun!" he said, holding out his hand.

"Hang on," said Lois.

"For what?"

Morag was slumped in the corner, eyes closed, mumbling woozily. The shambler ignored her and leapt at Rod. He punched it in the throat and wrestled it while it was momentarily distracted. Wingspan and tentacle-length, it was bigger than him, but it was lighter – a big dog with wings that were a hindrance in this small room. Rod had the strength to hold its head and its front claws back but, limb for limb, it outnumbered him. Tentacles seized his legs, trying to unbalance him.

"Gun, Lois!"

"There's a bit you haven't filled out here," she said.

He threw her a stunned look.

"Are you kidding me?"

The *Bondook* shifted in his grip. It twisted and snapped at him.

"'What happened to previously-issued firearm,'" read Lois.

"It was swallowed by a bloody huge spider!" he said.

24

"'Reason for not reclaiming previously issued firearm.'"

"Again! Swallowed by a bloody huge spider!"

"Right. I'll just jot that in. Oh. It says, black ink only. I had a pen somewhere."

"Buggering hell, Lois! I'm not winning here and Morag's down!"

"'m all right," mumbled Morag, hand to her head. "You need to tell it to sit."

Bondook shambler drool dripped from its jaws onto Rod's wrist. He could feel the ache growing in his upper arms, the monster levering against him, muscle overpowering muscle.

"Now, I just need you to sign the form here," said Lois.

"Are you bloody kidding me?" he yelled.

"There's no need to shout!"

With an animal roar, he pushed back, bounced the shambler's head off a wall, pounded it with a reception chair and bolted for the reception glass. He grabbed the form from the tray, scribbled something on it and thrust it back.

"I don't mean to be a stickler," said Lois, "but I promised the quartermaster."

The shambler was making a mess of extricating itself from the chair. One of its wing spurs was caught between two legs and it staggered lopsidedly as it rounded on Rod. Lois placed a locked gun case in the parcel tray. Rod fumbled with the cylindrical keys. The shambler charged. Rod swung the case two-handed into the beast's head and then finally unlocked the case while the shambler was recovering.

He pulled the Glock 21 pistol from the foam inset along with the magazine. He looked in the magazine.

"Ammo!" he swore.

"Did you requisition any?" said Lois.

The shambler lunged. Rod turned with its attack, clubbed it with the useless pistol, then grabbed its jaws and forced them closed. He held on grimly, but this was not a long-term strategy. He was forced to dance left and right to avoid a disembowelling swipe from its claws.

"Morag! What's 'sit!' in Venislarn?"

"*Usk'hulen*," she said.

The shambler did not sit.

"That's not what Kathy said!" he shouted.

Morag struggled to get to her feet. "I don't remember what Kathy said.

"Oogle-boogle something," said Rod.

"*Oozma bento?*"

The shambler forced its jaws open a fraction and snarled.

"Not that," said Rod.

"*Ogwin b'yoch?*"

A stray claw tore down his upper thigh, an inch from some delicate bits he would be very sad to lose.

"Not it either!"

"*Hespikh chen terexx?*"

"Not even trying now!"

Greased by shambler spit, the snout snapped open in Rod's hands.

"*Iyuzha gha'bho!*" called out the voice of Professor Sheikh Omar.

The shambler collapsed like a reverse Jack-in-the-box and dropped into its spherical form with an audible 'fwap!' of folding wings. Rod staggered away.

"*That's* the one," he said, taking a deep and cleansing breath.

"It's all in the tone my dears," said Omar, emerging from the admin offices. "Maurice says I have a little bit of the Barbara Woodhouse in me."

Professor Sheikh Omar, formerly of Birmingham University's department of Practical Theology, was the proverbial poacher turned gamekeeper – the game in question being the inscrutable terrors that were primed to consume this world. Previously, he had been a poker of things best not poked and a trader in the occult equivalents of weapons-grade uranium. For the past two months, however, he had toiled among the white hats to ensure that only the right people did the poking and the weapons-grade occultism was safely locked away. He had taken to his new role like a kid to a candy store.

"What are you playing at, Rodney?" he said.

"I wasn't playing."

Morag rubbed the back of her head and inspected her fingertips for blood. Omar hurried—as much as he ever hurried—over to her and put a supportive hand under her elbow. Omar had a hairline that had receded almost all the way to the back of his head, NHS glasses from the 1960s and mannerisms straight out of the camper variety of Agatha Christie story.

"And putting Morag in danger in her condition," chided Omar. "For shame."

Rod picked up his new pistol and the empty magazine and inspected them for damage.

"Her condition?" said Rod.

"The human condition."

"I'm fine," said Morag.

"We will see," he said darkly.

The door from the office opened and the consular mission chief, Vaughn Sitterson, appeared. Vaughn was a boss who didn't make much of a mental impression on people and seemingly preferred it that way. Rod had never seen the man look anyone in the eye or speak to an individual directly.

"There is an unacceptable level of noise out here," he said to no one in particular. His gaze, careful to avoid any actual people, fell on the comatose Venislarn creature.

"We brought the professor a *Bondook* shambler," said Rod.

"You always know exactly what to get me, Rodney," said Omar.

"It doesn't belong up here," said Vaughn.

"And it will have to wait for my attentions," said Omar. "I have an appointment in Moseley at the abode of the probably late and definitely lamentable Mystic Trevor. Dr Kathy is waiting for me and, for reasons that I don't yet fully grasp, Nina is joining us also in order to show me some pottery." He scowled at Rod playfully. "Pottery. That's not some colourful piece of drug-culture argot, is it?"

"This," Vaughn waved a limp hand in the general direction of the shambler, "needs resolving."

"Pop it in the Vault for now, Rod," said Omar. "On a wheeled trolley for preference. Heavy weights and I never got on."

Rod strained to keep the shambler ball in his arms whilst pressing the lift button.

"Rod can't be delayed too long," said Vaughn. "He has a working lunch meeting with Chad from marketing and the director of this feature film project."

Rod groaned.

"Free lunch," pointed out Morag. "That's not bad."

"Swap?" he said.

With the address for Mystic Trevor from Omar, Kathy had knocked on the door and received no reply. Forcing entry into premises generally necessitated police assistance and so Nina felt no guilt for getting Ricky Lee to pick her up on the way and drive her over there. Chief Inspector Ricky Lee was the city police-Venislarn liaison and he and Nina had an on-off colleagues-with-benefits things going on that never threatened to get serious and was all the better for that. Nina had relegated Ricky's pet sergeant to the back seat. Nina sat in the front with Vivian's really uninteresting vase in her lap.

Mystic Trevor's flat was above a hairdressers on a tiny parade of shops. Kathy, Morag, Omar and a pair of uniformed cops were already waiting in the badly tarmacked alley round the side when Nina's personal chauffeur pulled up.

"The gang's all here," said Kathy.

"Some of us just want to be certain he's dead," said Nina.

"Some of us want to check for any evidence of salacious wrongdoings," said Omar.

"His or yours?"

"Ouch," said the professor bashfully.

Ricky freed his pet sergeant, who had been child-locked in the back of the car, and led the coppers up the external metal stairs at the rear of the property. They earned their fee for the day by doing some grade A police-style thumping on the door and a bit of classic police-style shouting.

"You gonna kick it in or what, Ricky?" said Nina.

"Or I could unlock it using the keys I borrowed from the landlord downstairs," he said, dangling a key fob.

"That's clever."

After a brief squabble over whether the police should go in first (because there might be a dangerous or volatile individual inside) or the consular mission team should go in first (because the individual wasn't necessarily going to be human), Nina and Ricky entered together. A sour, grimy smell filled the flat. In the kitchen, there was a saucepan on the hob in which a layer of baked beans had completely dried out. The milk on the side had separated into liquid and solid, grey and yellow.

"Why do single men's flats stink?" said Nina.

"A lot of people's houses stink," said Ricky.

"I'm a single girl. My house don't stink."

"You live with your mum."

"Old people. Their houses stink as well."

They checked out the bedroom and bathroom and living room. Two homes with dead or missing owners in one day, Nina thought. A feeling of sadness filled both spaces. But whereas Vivian's house had been sparsely furnished and almost unmarked by its inhabitant, Trevor's squalid flat was very much lived in. It was full of the junk and mess and bits and bobs that maybe meant a great deal to Trevor but, now, it was all just pointless tat. Indeed, although there were plenty of unidentifiable objects and dark crevices, none of which Nina intended to touch or put her hand in, there was a distinct lack of things that were of immediate threat. Ricky joined his officers in the fresh air on the stairway and let the consular team in.

"This place stinks," said Morag.

"That's what I said," said Nina.

"Turns my stomach."

"Then maybe you should sit this one out, Miss Murray," said Omar with uncharacteristic gentleness.

"I'll manage," she said, peevishly.

Kathy picked through the piles of scrunched up lilac printer paper on the living room windowsill.

"Tell you what does smell," she said. "Any of you ever cut open a *zenif* tumour?"

Omar laughed. "Oh, that's but sweet perfume compared to the *lediron* fruit of *Forrikler*."

Morag leaned close to Nina.

29

"Are they seriously playing 'I've smelt something worse than you'?"

Nina shrugged. "I'm gonna trump 'em all with our bathroom at home after my dad had been in it."

Kathy pulled out a dog-eared book from the windowsill, spilling paper on the floor. She shook the remains of an orange peel from the book and showed the title to Omar.

He made a noise of almost amusement.

"The *Simon Necronomicon*? This man was a dabbler," said Kathy.

"A dangerous dabbler."

Morag, who was looking paler than her usual semi-skimmed paleness, sat down in an armchair.

"You all right?" said Kathy.

"Dodgy breakfast," she said. She pressed her foot reflexively up and down on the carpet. "This floor's wet."

"Damp?" said Kathy.

On the coffee table between two armchairs was a large enamel teapot with green edging and an elegant elephant trunk spout. To Nina's eyes, it looked like it had come from a World War Two army canteen. The table around it was stained brown and shiny. Morag ran her fingers up the coffee table leg and along the visibly sticky top.

"Massive tea spillage," she said and then made a surprised noise as her fingers touched the base of the teapot. "It's still warm."

"How warm?" said Kathy and came over to feel it herself. She picked up the teapot. It came away with a sticky peeling sound, leaving a ring of brown dried tea on the table. "It's actually hot, like it's just been made."

"Are you really getting excited by the man's teapot?" said Nina.

"Mystic Trevor has been gone for several days but his tea remains hot. That is unusual."

"Magical kitchenware," mused Omar. "I have seen such pieces before."

Nina was struck by an idea and dashed out and down to Ricky's car. She returned to find Omar, braving the almost-certainly-dead man's bedroom in the search for banned materials. Nina followed him in. He drew back the curtains to let some light into the filthy scene.

"Can you take a look at this?" said Nina and presented him with the vase from Vivian's.

Omar's eyebrows rose and he took it with deliberate delicateness.

"Didn't have Trevor down as a collector of fine things," he said.

"So, it's important?" she said, hopeful.

"Important?"

"Magical. Venislarn."

He chuckled knowingly, like she was a child with a stupid question to be humoured. She felt a flash of anger for the bastard she'd not felt for a while.

"It's Wedgwood," he said and tapped the markings on the base.

"I took it from Vivian's. I thought it might be important."

He adjusted his specs and straightened his back, emphasising the difference in their heights.

"Ah, Miss Seth, you seem to have mistaken me for the *Antiques Roadshow*."

"It's a clue," she insisted. "You see, she hated flowers. And then there's this." She pulled out the key with the ornate teeth. "I can't find where it belongs."

"And where did you uncover that?" he said.

"Back of a drawer. Vivian's drawer. She hated flowers but she had some at home in this vase."

Omar nodded. "I see."

"Yes?"

He tapped the window with the back of his fingertips.

"That conveniently fluffy cloud up there. When you look at it, what do you see?"

Nina looked out. "Dunno. A horse? Like a horse's head?"

"I see a cloud," said Omar.

"Yeah, well that's cos you're a smug *vangru* who just has to be cleverer than everyone else."

He put a hand on her arm. She flinched even though he meant nothing by it.

"I'm making a point, Nina," he said. "We see patterns and designs where there are none – a side effect of our amazing brains."

31

"Yeah? And?"

"And... Vivian is gone. She is trapped in *leng*-space and is, in every sense that counts, dead. There is no mystery to that, no clues to be followed and no resurrection to be found." He sighed with a decent impression of genuine human sadness and looked at the key in her hand. "It's just a key. That deer with the arrow in its mouth—"

"I thought it was a giraffe."

"That is part of the coat of arms of the Boulton family. Matthew Boulton?"

"As in the college?" she said.

"As in the industrialist. It's just a key. This..." he said and handed the vase back to her, "is a lovely piece of jasperware. Could be very old but it's not my field. Josiah Wedgwood and Boulton were friends, I believe. Met at Soho House a few times in the seventeen hundreds."

Images of primary school trips flashed through Nina's mind. "The old museum place?"

"Handsworth. Your neck of the woods."

Nina recalled a large, white and astoundingly dull old house, twiddly bits of furniture, roped off areas and lots of Do Not Touch signs. The twin smells of furniture polish and boredom suddenly came back to her.

"Perhaps our Mrs Grey was a local history buff," suggested Omar. "There's so much about her we did not know."

Nina opened her mouth to say something about the donkey photo and then stopped. He'd only laugh at her again. Without further conversation, she turned and walked out. Coming out of the back door and onto the narrow metal landing above the stairs was like surfacing from a fog.

"So?" said Ricky Lee.

"I'm just seeing pictures in clouds, apparently."

He frowned. "I meant the flat. Is he dead? Any indication of where he is?"

Nina shook her head. "I don't think he's been home for several days. I think there's a half-eaten wizard in Moseley Bog."

"Right," he said, suddenly dropping into policeman mode, and turned to his pet sergeant. "Take the local uniforms, rustle up some PCSOs and search the bog."

"Some of that bog is deep," said the sarge.

"And at that point we'll call in a dive unit or the fire service."

The pet sergeant nodded and went downstairs to repeat her boss's orders to the uniformed coppers.

"What's this about clouds then?" Ricky said to Nina. There was a smile on his face. When Ricky smiled, he always looked like a fool, sometimes a kissable fool.

"I thought this was something," she said, holding up the vase. "Omar says it's just an old vase. Wedgwood?"

"Old?" said Ricky and took it from her. "Made to look old maybe."

"Oh, you're the expert now are you?"

"No, but I can recognise a mobile phone when I see one."

"What?"

He put a finger on the raised image of the woman. "What's she holding up to her ear if it isn't a phone?"

Nina looked. He was right.

The Malmaison Hotel, where Rod was due to have his first brush with Hollywood, occupied a corner chunk of the Mailbox building, ten minutes' walk from the consular mission office.

The Mailbox's name came from the fact that it had originally been built as the Birmingham Royal Mail sorting office. Rod wasn't sure why Birmingham needed a sorting office big enough to house several jumbo jets. There were also well-founded rumours that the Mailbox had its own private tunnels through which mail used to be carried, and a now disused rail link to New Street station. Rod had asked to see them once but had been fobbed off with stories of unsafe ceilings and renovation works.

The Mailbox, like Birmingham generally, seemed to be under constant renovation. After the sorting office was closed some twenty years ago, it was bought up and redeveloped to include hotels, shops, restaurants and office spaces. Within a decade, the front half was closed and redesigned yet again to create an upscale roofed shopping mall, its marble-like floors and walls giving it more the air of a classical temple than of a simple shopping centre. Now, less than a handful of years further on, the Mailbox was under further redevelopment.

Apparently, the ostentatious classical look was neither ostentatious nor classical enough for the punters and, while the shops and offices at the higher, waterfront level continued to operate as normal, the shops towards the front were emptied, stripped out and were going to be renovated once again.

Rod rarely went in the Mailbox. Its restaurants were over-priced, the beer doubly so and, being next door to the Cube and the Venislarn Court, it was popular with those Venislarn who could pass for human and those humans who swarmed round the court like flies.

Rod entered the Malmaison brasserie with the distinct feeling that socially, culturally and economically, he did not belong. The diners, the glasses, even the cutlery, all seemed to scream that he was a scummy northerner, the wrong kind of middle class, and wouldn't he be happier dining at the pie and ale pub round the corner? Which, of course, he would.

Rod adjusted his tie, tried to remind himself that he had faced down scarier situations than this, and looked round for the people he'd come to meet. One of the waiting staff approached and, as she asked if he had a reservation, he saw Chad, half out of his chair, waving at him.

"I'm with that... individual," said Rod, gave the woman a smile and went over.

Chad looked like the kind of man who practised smiling in the mirror. He clasped Rod's hand and shook it as though Rod were his long-lost brother.

"Rod Campbell!" He turned to the woman and the man sitting on the red couch on the other side of the table. "Guys, *this* is the guy. This *is* the guy. I was saying, wasn't I? This is *the* guy."

Rod wondered if Chad was going to throw in a 'this is the *guy*' just for completeness. Chad held out a dramatic impresario's hand to the woman and the man.

"This is Tammy Barfield-Jones from Skyscape Media who are producing this project and this—I'm sure no introductions are needed—is Bryan Birdsong Jr, our director."

Rod shook their offered hands.

"Heard so much about you," said Tammy the producer and there was a twinkle in her eye that suggested Chad had indeed done a lot of talking about him.

"I'm the guy, apparently," said Rod.

"Rod," said Bryan the director, tasting the name. "Rod? Like Rod Steiger, yeah?"

"This," said Chad and simultaneously placed a hand on Rod's chest and back to make a deeply weird Rod-sandwich, "this is a decorated war veteran, special forces special ops kind of guy, lots of hush-hush missions, fighting to protect our freedoms from the Iraqis back in the day. This guy's a killing machine, could take down a man with a drinking straw."

One drink in the company of these Americans and Chad had already started pronouncing 'Iraqis' as 'eye-raqis'. Iraqi or eye-raqi, Rod hadn't seen any of them trying to steal British or American freedoms while he was posted to the Gulf. He'd never killed anyone with a drinking straw but, right now, he was prepared to give it a try.

Rod said nothing, extricated himself from Chad's hands and sat down.

Bryan picked up his menu. He looked like he knew a free meal when he was getting one and never turned it down.

Tammy leaned towards Rod. Compared to Bryan, she looked like someone who knew the value of decent cardio exercise. Rod reckoned she was either a good ten to fifteen years older than him or had just spent too much time in the California sun.

"I gather you SAS types don't like talking about your combat experience," she said.

"Aye, you have no idea how little I want to talk about it," said Rod.

She smiled at that. "I'm simply glad you're able to work with us on this. Have you read the briefing notes?"

Rod was shaking his head when Chad cut in.

"Rod's a man of action, not words, am I right? But with him on board as technical advisor and action consultant, you've got the best of the best right here."

"Action consultant?" said Rod. "I thought this was just Venislarn liaison work, making sure your film crew stay within the rules and regulations."

Bryan chuckled. For a moment, Rod thought he was laughing at something on the menu. "We don't want to leave you on the bench, Rod. This movie—"

"Motion picture event," said Tammy.

"Tentpole motion picture event," said Chad.

"—this movie, we're just artistes recreating something that you live, day to day. We want you in the thick of it."

"Champion," said Rod, weakly. He looked at the menu. "I reckon I'm gonna need a beer."

Morag was feeling both nauseated and starving and was considering popping downstairs to the greasy spoon on the parade of shops and ordering a big plate of everything. She wondered how Rod was getting on with his working lunch and what haute cuisine hell he was currently enjoying.

But Nina had gone, dragging Chief Inspector Ricky Lee away on what she said was a 'vital mission' which, knowing them might just have been code for 'recreational car-sex'. Nina had gone and there was still a job to be done in Mystic Trevor's flat and Omar was accumulating a box full of very low level but nonetheless prohibited Venislarn items. None of it was any more dangerous than items in Trevor's cutlery drawer and none of it more horrific than the thing growing in Trevor's microwave.

The oddest item was the message on Trevor's answerphone. Morag was surprised that anyone still owned a telephone with an answerphone, let alone left messages on them. She played it several times over. The caller sounded like a young woman.

"Hi. Hi, it's Khaleesi-*Qalawe*. From the chapter. We've not heard from you and I needed to check we were still on for communion on Tuesday the twelfth. *Shala'pinz Syu* is still coming, right? Give us a call."

There were Venislarn words in there. *Shala'pinz Syu* sounded suspiciously close to the name of an August Handmaiden of *Prein* Morag had briefly and explosively met. *Qalawe* wasn't a name. It was an adjective with no human equivalent, describing the relative closeness or divergence of two realities. Khaleesi?

"Omar," she called to him wherever he was hiding. "Khaleesi? Have you ever come across the word or name 'Khaleesi'?"

There was a muffled reply from the kitchen. Morag went through. Kathy and Omar were searching the cupboards.

"What did you say?" said Morag.

"*Game of Thrones*," said Kathy. "Khaleesi. It's from *Game of Thrones*, isn't it?"

"I wouldn't know. Nerd stuff."

"Tits and dragons. What's not to like?"

"Maurice is a fan," said Omar.

"Of tits or dragons?" said Kathy.

"The production design and the music, Dr Kaur. He's quite the medievalist. He wanted to install an authentic medieval loom in the back bedroom. And he's an accomplished lute-player. It's the tiny fingers, you know. Not that I pay him any compliments; it would only encourage the chap."

"Right," sighed Morag, who really couldn't muster any interest in either Maurice's medieval music or some TV show. "I'm going to take a breather."

She went outside and, following her basest desires, went straight round to the greasy spoon café. It was called The Hungry Hobb but she could see the faint outline of an 'I' and a 'T' that had once been on the end. The window was plastered with posters and flyers for local bands. The air inside was thick with the smell of cooking fat.

Morag inspected the menu board. A large model of a skinny man-creature with lank hair squatted on the counter. It might have been a hobbit; Morag wasn't au fait with such things.

A woman poked her head through the serving hatch.

"What can I get you, love?"

"I'll have a Hungry Hobbit breakfast," said Morag.

"It is quite large," said the woman. "Three eggs, three sausages, three bacon, black pudding, two hash browns, beans, tomatoes, mushrooms, fried slice and toast."

"You saying it's too big for me?" Morag replied, challengingly.

"One Hungry Hobbit it is."

"And a mug of tea," said Morag.

Morag took her tea and sat at a window table. She stared out at the passing traffic and tried not to think about what was going on inside her.

Nearly two months ago, Professor Sheikh Omar had told her she was pregnant. There hadn't been a pregnancy test, there hadn't been any pissing on little sticks (unless pissing on sticks was part of some ritual Omar and Maurice, his magician's assistant, had performed). Omar had simply stated it to her as fact. And, unfortunately, the facts fitted.

Morag had had unprotected sex with Drew – a handsome naturist in service to *Yo-Morgantus*, Venislarn prince and secret ruler of Birmingham. Mere hours later, an August Handmaiden of *Prein* had pinched off his head and his genitals in a ritual sacrifice in the city cathedral. Before the week was out, the Handmaiden herself had been killed, not exactly by Morag's hand but close enough to count as revenge.

Omar had said she was pregnant. *Yo-Morgantus* had made enough veiled comments that Morag was convinced he also knew and might even have planned for it to happen. But she hadn't the nerve to consider the implications. She was suffering something that was a decent approximation of morning sickness. She'd missed a period and was now seriously overdue on the next, but she didn't want to think about it. No pissing on little sticks for her.

The plate laden with sausages, bacon, eggs and beans landed heavily on the table in front of her. Morag gave the woman a nod of thanks. Yes, the breakfast was indeed quite large, too large, but she'd made a minor deal out of it at the counter and set to work eating it.

Halfway through her second sausage, Morag's gaze drifted across the flyers in the window and snagged on the word 'chapter'. The flyer was printed on lilac paper, the same shade she'd seen in Mystic Trevor's flat.

HAVE YOU ALWAYS FELT LIKE AN OUTSIDER?
DO YOU FEEL YOU HAVE A GIFT? — SECOND SIGHT, TELEPATH,
EMPATH, ECT. (DEVELOPED OR UNDEVELOPED)
DO YOU HAVE MEMORIES OF YOUR LIFE ON THE ASTRAL PLANE
BEFORE THIS MORTAL LIFE?
DO YOU SUFFER FROM PHANTOM LIMB SYNDROME FOR LIMBS
OTHER THAN THE FOUR HUMAN LIMBS YOU WERE BORN WITH?
DO YOU FEEL AFFINITY FOR ALIEN WORDS AND LANGUAGE? (EVEN
IF YOU DON'T UNDERSTAND THEM)

MAYBE YOU BELONG TO A DIFFERENT TRIBE. JOIN THE CHAPTER, FIND YOUR TRUE SELF, COMMUNE WITH THE *EM-SHADT JOYIP.*

Morag ripped the flyer off the window.

"Did the man from upstairs ask to put this up?" she asked.

The woman at the counter squinted short-sightedly.

"Wore a cowboy hat," prompted Morag.

"Yeah, I think so. Used to come in here a lot. Not seen him for a while."

"I bet you haven't." She stood up, folding the flyer.

"Used to come in with this dragon puppet thing. It was dead realistic. You not eating that?"

"Sorry," said Morag.

"I told you it was large," the woman said as the door swung closed behind Morag.

She ran round to the stairs, had to push past the copper who momentarily failed to recognise her and burst into the kitchen.

"Dramatic entrance," said Kathy.

"Venislarnkin," said Morag.

"What?"

"Really?" said Omar.

Morag nodded, out of breath and held up the flyer.

"What are Venislarnkin?" said Kathy.

Morag smiled. It was nice to find something Kathy didn't already know about.

Rod looked at his meal and tried to remember what he'd ordered. He speared something on his fork and ate it cautiously. Next to him, Chad was tucking happily into... something, something gluten-free, cruelty-free, locally-sourced and chakra-balancing apparently.

"At its heart, *Man of War* is about raising awareness," said Tammy. "It's about opening people's eyes to a new way of looking at the world."

"You want to put the Venislarn on screen," said Rod.

"Not just on screen but portray them..."

39

"Sympathetically," suggested Chad.

Tammy's mouth twitched. "We want to go behind the slime and the horror. Get to what's deep inside them. We're making an issues film here. If Spielberg can make people think aliens are cute and cuddly with *E.T.*, we can do the same thing for the Venislarn hordes," she said.

"Spielberg's an issues movie god," said Bryan. "Cut him and he bleeds issues movies."

"*The Colour Purple, Schindler's List.* You Brits should be all over this," said Tammy. "Issues movies. Think of this as being like *I, Daniel Blake* but with tentacles."

"Classy," said Rod.

"It will be. It's got a lot of heart," said Tammy.

"And a very commercial soundtrack," put in Chad.

"A stylish, espionage thriller feel," said Bryan.

"And a helicopter chase," said Chad.

"And set in Birmingham?" said Rod.

"We love Birmingham," said Tammy, pronouncing the 'h' in 'ham'. "It's friendly and welcoming and real easy to work with."

"Spielberg loved it," said Bryan.

"And it makes an ideal stand-in for Philadelphia," said Bryan.

"Philadelphia?" said Rod.

"Or Detroit. We haven't made a firm decision on that yet."

"We can decide a lot of these things in post-production," said Tammy. "Right now, we need to focus on the Birmingham scenes. We're on a tight schedule. The crew's already set up for the shoot at the Mailbox tomorrow."

Rod saw Chad's hand tighten on his wine glass.

"Any particular reason for the, um, tight schedule?" said Chad with forced nonchalance. "Any key deadlines we're trying to meet?"

The Americans gave him uncomprehending looks.

Rod laughed loudly.

"Chad here wants to know if the film's being released before or after the end of the world."

"Ah," said Tammy. "We're working to the schedule our financiers have given us. As for the Soulgate..."

"None shall know the day or the hour," said Bryan. He emptied the last of the wine into his own glass and called loudly to a waiter for another bottle.

"I'm just thinking it would be a shame to make this beautiful film and have everything... end before it got to awards season," said Chad.

Bryan snorted softly. "The Oscars are rigged. I'll tell you that much."

"But they love issues movies," said Tammy enticingly. "And Taylor Graham is one of Hollywood's anointed."

"Is he?" said Rod, wondering if he was supposed to have heard of him.

"We're doing a high-level read through later," she said. "You'll meet the key cast and some of the crew."

"The ones who *know*," said Bryan.

"Know as in...?"

"Know that this is more docu-drama than fantasy."

Rod thought about this. "So, you're making a movie—"

"Motion picture event," said Tammy.

"—about the Venislarn and some of the people working on it know that it's about the Venislarn, the real Venislarn, and some of the people have no idea?"

"That's the situation, Rod," said Bryan.

"Well, there's no way that can go wrong, is there?"

"Our thoughts exactly," said Bryan, raising his glass and entirely failing to spot the sarcasm.

Ricky Lee cut through the slow lane-hoggers on the ring road by the Central Mosque before entering the underpass that led to Five Ways. The afternoon traffic was light. There was no need for him to put his lights and siren on, but he would have done if Nina had asked.

Nina studied the vase in her hands.

"Do you think she looks a bit like me?" she said.

Ricky gave it the briefest glance.

"Don't know. I've never seen you in one of those dresses with an enormous bustle."

41

She ran her thumb over the woman's face and the minutely sculpted hand holding a rectangular object to her ear.

"It's a phone, isn't it?"

"Looks it."

"And Omar said this could be from the seventeen hundreds. And they didn't have phones then?"

"Are you asking me?" said Ricky. "Was that a non-rhetorical question?"

"Hey. I'm just asking."

He smiled. "No, Nina. They didn't have phones back then."

"I suppose this could be from later... When were the Tudors?"

"Earlier. And, no, there weren't any phones in Victorian England, before you ask." Ricky was struggling to keep a straight face. "There weren't even mobile phones when I was a boy, least none that weren't the size of a breeze block."

"Yeah, but you're *adn-bhul* ancient, man."

"I'm nine years older than you."

"Ancient."

He slipped through an orange light on Five Ways island and dropped down onto the road for Ladywood and Handsworth.

"Okay," he said, "for the benefit of those of us who have no grasp of history, let me be clear: you are holding a vase that definitely looks old. Could be two hundred and fifty years old, yeah. Mobile phones like that have been around for ten, fifteen years at best. Either that's a modern vase that's been aged somehow, or it's an authentic eighteenth-century Wedgwood and we're mistaking something else for a mobile phone."

"Or there's some messed up *muda* going on," said Nina.

"Right," said Ricky. "We're five minutes from Soho House museum. We'll find out."

Nina sat in thought.

"I saw this clip on YouTube from a real old film, that guy with the moustache."

"Hitler?"

"The funny one."

"Charlie Chaplin?"

"Right. And there's this woman walking past in the background, a film extra. And she was talking on a mobile phone."

Ricky nodded. "I've seen it. Odd one that." He switched lanes. "Born round here he was."

"Who? Charlie Chaplin?"

"Well, not Hitler."

Nina felt an odd sense of embarrassment at bringing Ricky to her old stomping ground. If he turned right at these lights, they'd go right up to the Shree Geeta Bhawan temple where the more pious members of her family still performed puja. Straight ahead were the dessert shops and cafes where she met her cousins on her days off. If she thought about it, she could find the homes of fifty to sixty family members in the side roads. And here was Ricky Lee in the middle of it all. It felt like she was bringing a boyfriend home for her mother's approval and she couldn't help thinking the area she'd grown up in was a bit of a shithole. She had to fight down the impulse to say, "If I'd know you were coming round, we'd have tidied up."

Ricky turned off the high street just before the high white domes of the Guru Nanak gurdwara and the feeling lessened. She let out a small sigh of relief.

"You all right?" said Ricky.

She nodded and pointed ahead. "My old primary school's down there."

Ricky steered into the car park for Soho House. It looked like a child's drawing of a posh house: a tall, white box with large, evenly spaced windows and some twiddly bits of scrolled stonework near the roof. To the left of the house, across the rear gardens, was the car park and visitors centre.

"Let's go ask some questions," said Ricky.

The visitors centre was mostly given over to a gift shop: books, souvenirs, tour guides and mementos. Nina felt a child's overwhelming desire to waste some money on an over-priced novelty rubber or a plastic slinky spring printed with an image of Soho House.

"Two adults, is it?" said the tank top-wearing man at the cash till.

Ricky showed him his police ID.

"We'd like to speak to someone who could perhaps help us with this."

Nina held up the pottery in both hands and did some catwalk model swivels to really show it off.

"Oh," said the tank top man and picked up the little walkie-talkie on the counter. "Julie. We've got some people here."

"What people?"

"The police, Julie."

There was a pause. "I'll be right there."

Tank Top put the radio down. "She'll be right here."

"We got that," said Nina.

Tank Top gestured to a guidebook. "Would you like to purchase one to take round with you?"

"Um, we'll pass."

Ricky picked a cheaply printed black and white book from the display rack and dropped it on the counter in front of Nina. "Maybe you'd like this."

The title, *A Children's Guide to Soho House and the Industrial Revolution,* was written in a friendly Comic Sans font.

"Ha ha," she said.

Nina flicked through. She gave the tank top guy a guilty look.

"I might just hold onto this for the moment," she said.

"Right, what's this then?" said a short, middle-aged woman, brushing her hands together as she came through the far door. She wore a long cardigan and a chunky necklace of wooden beads.

"The police wanted to speak to someone about a vase," said Tank Top.

"Chief Inspector Ricky Lee," said Ricky.

"Julie Fiddler," the woman replied.

Nina felt a gut punch of surprise and the blood drained from her face. Ricky turned to introduce Nina.

"And this is —"

"Nina Seth," said Mrs Fiddler and shook her hand like they were playing at being grownups.

"Oh, you know each other?"

Nina's lips didn't want to work. "Mrs Fiddler was my year six teacher at primary school," she managed to say.

Mrs Fiddler's smile was thin, knowing and amused. She glanced down and Nina was too slow in hiding the children's guidebook.

"Yes, that's about right," said Mrs Fiddler. "Do you want to come through?"

Fine net curtains diffused rosy afternoon light into a conference room at the Malmaison Hotel. A large horseshoe-shaped table dominated the room, but for the moment people's attention was focused on a small table of refreshments in a corner. There was fizzy mineral water and the obligatory plastic pod coffee machine, but no tea. Rod mashed down on a handle to puncture a pod of *darjeeling fantasy*, then watched with grim resignation as an indicator light flashed and the machine spit liquid into a cold porcelain cup. A tall American with the lean physique of a mixed martial arts fighter and the cheekbones of a runway model stood nearby, awaiting his turn with the machine. He smiled at Rod and said "capable of producing all manner of excellent coffees and coffee-flavoured teas."

Rod grunted in appreciation and sat at the far end of the horseshoe, sipping his foul-smelling simulacrum of a cup of tea and taking notes as film industry people introduced themselves.

There were those who recited their entire CV, dropping names Rod had never heard. And there were those who acted as though they were so well known any introduction would be pointless. Apparently, the Hollywood madness was contagious. To Rod's disappointment, the Brits were bigger braggarts and name-droppers than the Americans and, lacking practice at self-aggrandisement, they sounded even more needy. Chad spoke for four minutes straight, and the phrase 'client-centric cross-platforming' was the nearest thing to actual English he said in all that time. The Americans didn't seem to notice it was all nonsense; perhaps they were dazzled by his British accent.

When it came round to the young American who had stood behind Rod at the coffee machine, the man cracked a white smile and said, "I'm Taylor Graham."

There was instant laughter as he made to introduce himself further. He waved it down with good humour.

"I'm an actor," he said. "Done a number of little movies. Arthouse pieces. Still learning."

There was more laughter and Taylor joined in. So, this was the movie star. The man looked to be in his twenties, but he laughed with the confidence and self-ease that most people didn't find until middle age.

A career in the army had taught Rod that men who had to show they were alpha dogs weren't really alphas at all. Rod was happy knowing he was the best man he could be without having to tell people. But there was something about this young, tall handsome and self-assured specimen (probably his youth, height, good looks and self-assurance) that Rod found instantly threatening.

Rod pushed the babyish feelings of jealousy aside as the ritual of introductions rolled slowly on. A thoroughly miserable and grey-eyed man (whose credits included *BMX Bandits 4*, *Bikini Bloodbath 3* and a 'beautiful little coming of age piece that those bastards have kept in development hell for two decades') was the writer on this film. The way people looked at him, the stony deference they showed him, it was like writers were a necessary but despised part of the process, the sewage workers of tinsel town.

And then it was Rod's turn.

This was hell.

"Hi, I'm Rod Campbell," he said. "I'm from the Birmingham consular mission. I'm just here as liaison. Here to answer any questions you have." He nodded, introduction over.

"Oh, don't be shy," called out producer Tammy. "We're very lucky to have Rod here as a technical and action consultant. He's not only dealing with the Venislarn day-to-day in Birmingham, he's also a decorated veteran of the Gulf War."

There was spontaneous—hideous, cringeworthy and spontaneous—applause from around the table. A couple of people, definitely non-military personnel, threw him salutes—admiring, not-even-a-little-bit ironic salutes. Rod hid his face in his cup of tea and grimaced.

"How's your tea?" said Taylor Graham.

"Diabolical," said Rod and there was laughter even though he hadn't said anything funny.

"That simply won't do," said Tammy.

"Get this man a proper cup of tea!" laughed Taylor, hammering a nail in the coffin of Rod's self-esteem.

Tammy spoke sharply to the little man by her side. He immediately stood and went to the door.

"Hey, it's fine," said Rod. "It's just tea. Don't make any fuss on my account."

"It is not a fuss," said Tammy firmly. "If we can't get a decent 'brew' for a patriot who risked his life for his country, then we have failed you, sir."

Rod squirmed. "Well... as long as I'm not causing trouble or nowt."

"Can I just say," said a woman across the table.—Rod glanced at his notes. *Jarmane (Charmaine?)* ~~Zocky-lee~~ *Zoccoli, design philosophy conceptualist (WTF?)*—"I just love your accent."

There were various noises of agreement.

"Er, thank you?" said Rod.

"So refined, but reminds me of... Who does it remind me of?"

"Sean Bean," said someone else.

"Yes. That's it. Oh, I love Sean Bean."

"*Game of Thrones*. Oh! A masterclass."

"We all love Sean," said Tammy with wildly unnecessary solemnity.

Rod had been wrong. This wasn't hell. Hell couldn't hold a candle to this place.

As they crossed from the visitors' centre to the house, Ricky gave Mrs Fiddler an abbreviated version of the truth – one that didn't involve dark gods from the dawn of time or consular mission employees that had been banished to hell.

"And are these items stolen?" asked Mrs Fiddler. "Do you believe this vase to be a forgery?"

"We're just trying to determine why or how Mrs Grey came to have them in her home," said Ricky. "They may or may not prove relevant to another, on-going investigation."

"Do you think it is a forgery?" said Nina.

Mrs Fiddler hummed musically. "Because of the image of the woman clearly holding a mobile phone? Are you familiar with the concept of OOPArts, Nina?"

"I am," said Nina, eliciting a nod of surprised respect from her former teacher. There were dozens of anachronistically impossible objects in the Vault. Certain Venislarn seemed to just pump them out as by-products of their incomprehensible daily lives.

"We come across more than our fair share in the museum business. Some are easily explained but that doesn't make them easy to caption and put in display cases. We even have some here in storage."

"We're really just looking for some background on these pieces," Ricky emphasised.

"Very well." She stopped on the steps of the house, beneath the semi-circular portico. "How much do you know about Matthew Boulton and the Lunar Society?"

"Pretend we know nothing," said Ricky.

"Yeah, yeah," said Nina. "Pretend."

Julie Fiddler smiled. "Then let's do the primary school tour." She gave Nina a look. "Again."

The glazed double doors rattled and stuck momentarily and then opened. Inside, a tiled hallway led to a long dining hall: marble pillars, richly patterned carpet, sagging golden drapes and twiddly wooden chairs around an equally twiddly table with a deep conker shine.

"Matthew Boulton was born in 1728 and was the son of a Birmingham toymaker," said Mrs Fiddler, adding quickly to forestall any questions, "a toymaker in those days was any manufacturer of small metal items. Buttons, buckles, medals, et cetera. Upon his father's death, Matthew took over and was such a successful salesman that his products were requested by the Prince of Wales, the future George III. In 1761, he leased this site. This was all just Staffordshire countryside back then, two miles outside of the town of Birmingham."

Nina itched to ask what had happened to bring the house and the town together. She wasn't sure if it was continental drift or if they had put the house on rollers and wheeled it closer to town for convenience. She suspected neither answer was right.

Mrs Fiddler led them past a narrow set of stairs and along a door-lined corridor.

"Boulton built his manufactory on this site. Yes, a factory. One of the earliest factories in the modern world. Silverware, ormolu, ornate pieces of Sheffield steel."

They entered a room filled with glass cabinets. Nina's gaze swept over the gaudy candlesticks, impractical jugs and peculiar goblet things that were more sculpture than cup.

"This stuff gold?" she said, pointing.

"Ormolu," said Mrs Fiddler. "Milled gold applied with a mercury-based process. Ormolu."

"Ormolu," said Nina automatically and wondered if Mrs Fiddler still carried round sheets of gold star stickers for good learners. Nina was a grown up now but that didn't mean she was going to turn down a gold star sticker if one was available.

"Soho House became Boulton's home. Although it was bigger back then, nearly twice its current size. A whole wing has been demolished. It was not long after Boulton's arrival that this house became the main meeting point for the Lunar Society."

"And what was that?" said Ricky. "I can't say I've ever heard of it."

"No. Few have. Odd really, considering it was at the very heart of the English Enlightenment and the Industrial Revolution. Its members included Boulton, Josiah Wedgwood, James Watt, Benjamin Franklin -"

"The kite and lightning guy," said Ricky, seemingly for Nina's benefit.

"Hundred-dollar bill, sure," she said.

Mrs Fiddler continued listing names. "Joseph Priestley, James Keir, John Baskerville, William Small, Erasmus Darwin."

"The evolution guy?" said Nina.

"His grandfather." Mrs Fiddler laughed, gently but unexpectedly. "You're interested in OOPArts? Erasmus Darwin was an inventor, mostly windmills and canal lifts and the like. But he drew plans, in 1779 I think, for a hydrogen-oxygen rocket engine. A rocket engine. And it would have worked in principle."

Nina shrugged. "What? And no one else had invented rockets before then?"

Mrs Fiddler looked at her levelly. "It would be another hundred years before anyone else thought of the idea, a hundred and fifty before anyone would build one."

"Why does no one know this stuff?" said Nina. "About the, what was it, the Lunar Society?"

"Well, some of us might have if we'd paid more attention in school. But, no, the Lunar Society were always at the edge of what you could call mainstream history."

Ricky clicked his fingers. "A secret society? Like the Illuminati."

"Nothing quite so Dan Brown as that, chief inspector," said Mrs Fiddler. "The Lunar Society was a very informal group and mostly existed through personal correspondence rather than actual meetings. There are no group records, no meeting minutes and certainly no secret rituals."

"But with a cool name like the Lunar Society you'd think..."

"Yes, you would." Mrs Fiddler made her way out of the display room, took aside a barrier cord, and led them down a staircase into the cellars. "The name comes from the fact that they met on nights when there was a full moon the men—sadly, it was all men—needed the light of the moon to see them home after a long evening of discussing the latest inventions, industrial innovations and their own forays into scientific experimentation." She stopped at the foot of the stairs to turn on a light. "Picture a band of forward-thinking businessmen and inventors whose thirst for knowledge and discovery brought them into each other's orbits and, more specifically, into the orbit of this house. This way."

"What's down here?" said Ricky.

Mrs Fiddler produced a set of keys and unlocked a door. The room beyond was dusty but not dirty. The muck of ages was kept at bay with freshly painted walls and tough institutional flooring. It was filled end-to-end with boxes, crates, display pieces and all manner of junk.

"Our vault of oddments," said Mrs Fiddler.

"We've got a Vault," said Nina, poking at a box that contained nothing but teaspoons.

"All the items that aren't currently on display or loan elsewhere and, among them..." She pulled down a plain cardboard box, lifted aside the tissue paper and lifted out a vase that was the twin of the one they had brought with them, in size and manufacture if not design – no mobile phone here.

"Very similar," said Ricky.

Mrs Fiddler hummed in agreement. "Crafted and fired by Josiah Wedgwood himself in the late seventeen eighties. Same biscuit finish on both. I'd wager that only a true expert would be able to say whether your vase is a forgery."

"So, it's real?"

While Mrs Fiddler ummed and ahhed over the thing's authenticity, Nina progressed through the untidily stacked pieces of furniture, houseware and tools. Everything just needed a price tag and it would be like a tiny oldy-worldy IKEA. A tall clock filled a recess between a battered chest of drawers and a stack of mouldy linen. The clock looked like brass or gold.

"Ormolu," said Nina to herself and mentally debated asking for that gold star sticker.

The barrel around the clock face was decorated with a fiddly design of anchors and stylised leaves and positioned on the top was a reclining woman dressed in only a sheet who looked like she was wondering where the rest of her clothes had gone or how she was going to get down from the clock. The clock face was divided not into twelve hours but twenty-four and was criss-crossed with curving lines, spirals and astrological symbols.

"What's going on with this clock?" she said.

Mrs Fiddler looked round Ricky and squinted. "It's a sidereal clock."

"What's that?"

"Measures time not based on a solar day but on the shorter sidereal day. A star clock."

"Star clock, huh?"

"Boulton himself built that one but it doesn't work. Never has. There's a functioning one upstairs in the parlour. Much grander than that thing." Mrs Fiddler turned back to her discussion with Ricky.

Nina was about to move on when she noticed the keyhole just below the clock face. The whole damn house was full of keyholes but none of the ones she'd seen so far had an engraved deer biting an arrow next to it. She took out the key she had found in Vivian's desk drawer. It looked approximately the right size. Then again there were thousands of keyholes that were *approximately* the right size for this key.

51

She couldn't go trying the mystery key in all of them, she told herself.

But she could try it in this one.

Taken with her own reasoning, she inserted the key. It seemed to fit. She tried to turn it. The lock resisted and then something gave way with a 'clunk'. For a second, unsure if that was a good clunk or an 'oh, God, I've snapped something I shouldn't have' clunk, she waited, glancing guiltily over to Mrs Fiddler.

Then the clock began to tick.

"Score," said Nina to herself.

The ticking of the clock reverberated loudly in the enclosed cellar. It resonated more loudly than she thought a clock of this size ought to. It was a grandfather clock tick, a Big Ben tock. Nina put an ear to the clock. The sound seemed to be coming from lower down within the body of the clock and, as she listened, it filled out with other ticks and whirrs as though other pieces of the mechanism were coming to life, a complex but ordered drum solo of mechanical motion.

"Have you done something, Nina?" said Mrs Fiddler.

Nina stepped back from the clock. The ticking continued to grow in volume and scope, expanding, impossibly, beyond the frame of the clock.

"Where's that sound coming from?" said Ricky. "Is it in the walls?"

"A trick of the acoustics?" said Mrs Fiddler. "Nina?"

"I tried the key," she said to Ricky.

Ricky closed his eyes briefly. "Always sticking X into Y. Fingers in holes. Noses in other people's business."

Mrs Fiddler nodded. "There was that time in year four when you took a pack of wax crayons and—"

"Enough of that," said Nina, cutting her off. And, abruptly, the ticking sound stopped.

No, she realised, it hadn't stopped. It had moved off, to a distance, out to the very cusp of audibility.

"I would thank you, Nina, to not mess with the historical artefacts," said Mrs Fiddler.

"Okay, okay. Point taken. But the key did fit."

Mrs Fiddler made a noise that didn't approve of Nina's rationale.

"And it's clearly not broken," Nina added. She nodded ahead. "So, what's through that door?"

Mrs Fiddler looked at the door at the far end of the room, whirled back to the door they'd come in and did a double take back and forth several times until her wooden beads rattled.

"What?" said Nina.

"I've worked her for eight years," said Mrs Fiddler in a hoarse whisper.

"Yes?"

"And in all that time, this room has only had one door."

Nina frowned. "Really?"

Mrs Fiddler nodded in dumb shock.

"And when was the last time you counted them?" said Nina.

Morag and Kathy returned to the consular mission offices with plastic tubs of the most promising effects of Trevor's life. The teapot sloshed around as Morag carried it. She emptied it into the sink in the response office kitchenette and put it on the side.

It took Morag very little time to track down her first Venislarnkin.

The hashtag on the flyer put up by the late and far-from-great Mystic Trevor led her to a Facebook group. Among the many members was one Khaleesi-*Qalawe*, the woman who'd left a message about 'communion' on Trevor's answerphone. She didn't match any human registered as a Venislarn associate on the mission's records. An image search of her profile picture showed it was part of a larger photograph taken at a tattooist and body-modification shop in South Yardley.

Kathy and Morag got into Kathy's car and drove the three miles to the tattooist shop.

As they drove, Kathy held up an open packet of bourbons.

"Car biscuit?"

"What's a car biscuit?" said Morag.

"It's a biscuit you eat in the car."

Morag took one, then a second. Processed sugars were one thing her pregnant body was more than happy to handle.

"I must have led a sheltered life," said Kathy. "I've never heard of Venislarnkin."

"Just an off-shoot of the otherkin community," said Morag.

"Which is?"

"We live in a time when what we feel we actually are doesn't have to correspond with our physical selves. People are born male but instinctively know that they're female."

"Sure," said Kathy. "Gender isn't determined by something as simple as X and Y chromosomes."

"Right. Well, that philosophy has been extended further. Perhaps an individual has never felt happy as who they are and identifies, on a deeply personal level, as something else – something non-human. Venislarnkin are people who, despite being born human, identify as being one of the Venislarn."

"*Cod-zhu!*"

"No, not a word of a lie," said Morag.

"But that's... that's just stupid."

"Is it? Is it stupid and utterly ridiculous? Or are you just being prejudiced, hmmm? Regardless, if these people intend on 'communing' with *Shala'pinz Syu* that won't end well, will it? Turn here."

Studying the map on her phone, Morag pointed to the right. Kathy turned at the Tesco superstore and headed down a street of terraced housing and pokey little shops.

"*Shala'pinz Syu*. That's one of the twelve August Handmaidens of *Prein*, right?" said Kathy.

"Correct," said Morag, in the precise tones of someone who knew that as a fact and definitely not someone who had just had her vague suspicions confirmed by her more learned colleague. "And there are ten, not twelve."

"Really I'm sure there were twelve."

"There were," said Morag.

The August Handmaidens of *Prein* were difficult to encapsulate in a few words. 'Sadistic crab monsters' came close, but that didn't do justice to their perverse taste in human lovers or their hideous-beyond-reckoning physical forms.

Kathy parked up outside the Inkorporeal Arts tattoo shop.

"This place isn't registered with us," she said, as she got out.

"No. They either have no idea of any links to the Venislarn or they're operating illegally."

"Excellent," said Kathy. "I'll lead."

Kathy didn't need to say that, thought Morag. She always assumed she was in charge. Morag wondered whether it was innate arrogance or an attitude picked up in medical school. Most doctors in Morag's experience suffered from an irritating superiority complex. Kathy's predecessor, Vivian Grey, had dominated situations through iron will and the fearsome persona of an older woman who had earned her authority. But Kathy dominated people through a combination of supreme confidence and blinding intelligence – and, if those failed, by intimidating them with her terrifying cleavage. Gay, straight, male, female—Kathy's several acres of underwired décolletage were sufficiently distracting and disconcerting to break anyone's will.

Whatever the case, it worked on the poor man behind the counter at Inkorporeal Arts. They didn't need to show any identification or misleadingly imply they were police officers. He just rolled over, broke out his book of client tats and implants and showed them. Maybe he was just proud of his work. Maybe he thought data protection laws were for other people.

"Khaleesi has been coming here for years," he said. "A lot of great tattoos." He flicked through the pages of photos. "That octopus tentacle wrapped round her arm in a spiral, shoulder to wrist, came out really well. She's really got this Under the Sea thing going on. And I don't mean she's got a tattoo of Ariel. She..." He flicked again. "We did some subdermal gill implants a few months back."

Morag put her fingertips on the picture and peered closely. There were steep, frilled ridges below the jaw and behind the ears.

"Are those actual gills?" she said.

"Not actual gills, obviously," the man grinned. "This is a body-mod shop, not the island of Dr fucking Moreau. It's just subdermals. Metal, yeah? I'm really pleased with it though."

"We need to speak to Khaleesi," said Kathy. "Do you have contact details?"

The man looked twitchy for the first time.

"I thought you said you'd found her online. You can message her."

55

"We want something more physical," said Kathy. "An address?"

The man took a step back, stroking his chin. "I don't know about that, but..." He glanced at the clock on the wall. "This time of day she's always down at Stechford swimming pool. Doing her breathing exercises."

"Breathing exercises?"

"You know." He held his nose and puffed out his cheeks as though holding his breath. "The whole Under the Sea thing."

Beneath Soho House, Nina opened the new door at the end of the storeroom. She did the old 'fling it wide and adopt a karate stance' she used if she ever thought there was an intruder in the house at night. She wasn't going to take chances with any Venislarn *muda* or fucking Aslan leaping out at her.

There were no Venislarn horrors and no CGI Jesus-lion. There were flaky plaster walls, wooden stairs leading down into darkness and a round, old-fashioned light switch.

"Uh-huh," she said. "Mrs Fiddler?"

"Yes?" said the primary school teacher turned museum guide.

"When you said that this door was never here before..."

"Yes?"

"Have you ever been tested for dementia?"

"Nina Seth, that was a very poor attempt at humour."

"Sorry, miss."

Ricky peered down the stairs. "Venislarn?" he said to Nina.

"Not exactly their style," she said. She tried the light switch. Nothing happened. "You got a torch?"

He unclipped a pencil torch from his belt.

"This is impossible," said Mrs Fiddler. "It can't be here."

"Which is more likely?" said Nina. "A door appearing out of thin air or you... you know, having a brain tumour or something?"

"But there's only one basement level under the house. We're in it. And those stairs go down!"

As Ricky made to go first, Nina put an arm in front of him.

"I'll go first. Who knows what we might meet? Don't want face-suckers from *Hurhk-doi Han* chewing on your good looks. What would your wife say?"

Ricky reluctantly put the torch in her hand. "I don't see how it's any better if you go first."

"You only live once," she said and led the way.

"That's not an actual answer," said Ricky, following her, with Mrs Fiddler cautiously bringing up the rear.

"YOLO."

"You can't just say that and expect—"

"YOLO."

They brought Rod tea on a proper tea tray, with a proper teapot and a teacup and saucer like he was some spoilt brat who needed pampering to avoid a tantrum. And the monstrous trouble he felt he had caused would have been half worth it if it hadn't been bloody Earl Grey.

"That better for you?" said Tammy.

"Oh, aye," said Rod. "Champion."

He took a sip of the horribly flowery tea and did his best to smile in appreciation.

"Back to the story," said the director, Bryan. "This is a special-effects-driven movie-event, but with a characterful, small-movie heart. It's about relationships, which is something we can all relate to."

"We can all relate to relationships," agreed Chad.

"The central relationship—I'm not going to use the word bromance, but it's a bromance, right?—is between Agent Jack Steele, played by Taylor Graham, and the *samakha* prince, "Fin" *Yaghur*, played by Langford James – one of the finest motion capture actors working today."

"Thanks, Bryan," said a lanky man whose drawn out American twang suggested the southern states to Rod.

"This," said Bryan, "is a relationship that transcends race, transcend species. It really speaks to our times."

"Yeah, I was wondering actually," said Langford James, "if, given that, I should play my character as African-American."

Everyone looked at the definitely white actor. Tammy tried to articulate what a lot of people were thinking.

"African-American, as in...?"

"Black, Tammy."

"And you would do this through—I don't know?—an accent?"

Langford pulled back, affronted. "I'm not sure what a 'black' accent is, Tammy," he said frostily. "I'm talking about acting choices."

"You're looking for dialogue changes?" said Bryan.

"Not at all. I'm merely suggesting that to present Fin as an outsider, which is surely what he is, I could play him black."

"Your character," said Tammy slowly, "is a CGI fish monster."

"Exactly."

"Black?"

"It's a thought."

"And we'll stick a pin in that," said Bryan. "Jack Steele is a top agent for the government. He's Ethan Hunt and Jason Bourne and James Bond all rolled into one. He's cool. He always gets his man... or monster. He works alone. That is, until a shadowy underworld organisation intent on breaking the fragile peace between humans and Venislarn forces him to team up with Fin. Fin's avenue into this story is the death of his uncle and the theft of a mysterious Venislarn magic gizmo. It looks like the work of humans and he sets out on a path of revenge, coming to the human city to follow clues. A Venislarn mystic—we've hopefully got Morgan Freeman to voice the part—claims to know who the thieves are but is killed as Fin arrives. Fin kills one of the assassins and trails the others back to their base." Bryan held up his hands to indicate the building around them. "The corporate headquarters of evil industrialist Vlad Botticelli."

"It's going to look amazing," said design philosophy conceptualist Jarmane.

"Meanwhile," continued Bryan, "suave super-agent Jack Steele is following up his own end of the case. The local consular mission has been overrun by a swarm of *Dineer.*"

"*Dinh'r,*" said the sullen writer.

"*Dinher.*"

"*Dinh'r!*"

Bryan looked to Rod for assistance. Rod sat up, uncomfortable.

"Well, I've met them. I've fought them. One of them swallowed my last pistol. I don't know how to pronounce their names. I just called them 'bloody big spiders.'"

This drew a warm laugh from the assembled movie folk.

"The mission is overrun by bloody big spiders," said Bryan, "and in what is assumed to be a Venislarn attack, a mystical artefact is stolen. Jack Steele's department determines that Vlad Botticelli could have had access to the vault access codes and sends Jack undercover to check out the industrialist. Jack arrives at Botticelli's charity gala with a tux, a ready quip and all the secret gadgets he needs to get the job done. And this is where our heroes meet. Of course, the odd couple partnership causes some friction—yes, some laughs—and provides all the sparks we need. We've got the forces of authority and their 'cold war' enemy, the Venislarn, going—"

"I could play him Russian," said Langford.

"What?"

"Fin. Russian. Give it some old school soviet tones."

"I don't think that's really—"

"Or in a wheelchair? Disability rights are really big right now. They're treated like an invisible underclass and that could really resonate."

"You want the motion capture demon fish to be in a wheelchair."

"Just being creative here," said Langford.

"I think there's a time for creativity," said Taylor Graham.

Langford gave an irritable shake. "What character are you playing in this movie, Taylor? Aw, that's right. You're playing yourself. Taylor Graham. That's what you did in your last ten movies."

"C'mon, guys," said Tammy. "Can we just get to the read through?"

"I'm trying to explore the options," said Langford.

"Really?" said Taylor. "Let's ask the expert. Rod?"

Rod truly didn't want to engage in any of this.

"Yes?" he said warily.

"You met any *samakha* in wheelchairs?"

"Um."

"You've met some *samakha*, right?"

"Yeah. A few. Er, no I don't think I've ever seen one in a wheelchair."

"What about soviet Russian ones?"

"Well, not in Birmingham."

"African-American *samakha*?"

Tammy continued. "Rod has gotten us clearance to film with the local Venislarn authorities and it's a real pleasure to know we have the support of—"

Rod raised his hand tentatively.

"I've not personally cleared this with the Venislarn court." He looked to Chad and only got a genially blank gaze in return. "I just need to check that's happened."

"Chad assured us it had all been done," said Tammy.

"Absolutely," said Chad. "That's totally doable."

"Doable or done?"

Chad smiled broadly. "I know that Lord *Morgantus* will have no objections to this film production," he said with confidence.

"We've been planning this shoot for weeks," said Bryan.

"And all we need to do is get that final say-so," said Chad. "Just needs signing off. It's fine. All fine." He looked to Rod. "Your colleague. The Scottish one."

"Morag?"

"Right? She's got *Yo-Morgantus*'s ear, or whatever... ear-thing he has. She can pull us some strings, can't she?"

Rod woke his phone and walked out, scrolling for Morag's contact number.

After the first hundred downward steps, Mrs Fiddler stopped saying that these stairs were impossible and spontaneously started her tour guide spiel about the house and its owner. That kept her going for the next few hundred steps.

Half-listening, Nina ran her fingers over a bubble of dried plaster on the wall.

"—and that allowed him the finances to purchase this site," said Mrs Fiddler.

"Wait," said Nina, "so Boulton only got his wealth because he married two women for their money."

"Certainly, the initial investment for the manufactory," said Mrs Fiddler. "He married Mary Robinson in 1749 and invested her dowry. When his wife died ten years later, he married her sister Anne."

"Sly bugger," said Ricky.

"By all accounts, he loved them both very deeply. Consecutively, not concurrently."

"And you always imagine these ancient history types to be stuck up prigs and holier than thou," said Nina.

"The Lunar Society were mostly free thinkers. Their progressive views on matters of science, philosophy and religion often put them at odds with the establishment. There were even riots."

"How long are each of these steps, do you reckon?" said Ricky.

"Eight inches deep, I'd say," said Mrs Fiddler. "Maybe seven inches high."

"Convert to metric," said Ricky and muttered to himself.

"I've counted three hundred and eighteen steps so far."

"What are you guys thinking?" said Nina.

"That we're at least sixty metres away from where we started, horizontally," said Ricky. "Can't be underneath the house anymore."

"And at least fifty metres down," said Mrs Fiddler. "But it doesn't feel like we're in a tunnel, does it?"

Nina put her hand to the wall.

"This far underground, should we be feeling hotter or colder?" said Ricky.

Nina looked back up the stairs. The door to the storeroom was just a patch of white light now, a blob, not even a rectangle.

"This is certainly very trippy," said Mrs Fiddler.

"Bet you took a lot of LSD in your hippy days, huh?" said Nina.

Even in the glimmer of torchlight, Nina saw the look of patiently restrained exasperation on Mrs Fiddler's face.

"For your information, Nina Seth, I was four years old during the Summer of Love. I'm not quite sure how old you think I am."

"Ninety?"

Nina poked three holes in a bubble of plaster to make two eyes and a surprised little mouth.

"Apologies for Nina here," said Ricky. "She has a very weak grasp of timescales or anything that happened more than six months ago."

"Yes," said Mrs Fiddler. "I assume that the department or whatever you work in doesn't deal with antiquities and the like. No offence."

61

"None taken," said Nina who couldn't see anything to be offended about.

They continued down, towards a growing light. The steps bottomed out in a short corridor with a door at its end. Nina opened it. There was a wide and dark space beyond.

Nina shone Ricky's torch. The beam picked out the floorboards – a whole forest's worth of wooden flooring – and a plaster ceiling ten feet above them, but no far wall.

Ricky whistled.

"Echo!" shouted Nina and enjoyed the sound of it.

She thought about it for a second and then shouted, "*San-shu carra pi em-shadt! Skeidl hraim! Pet hrifet!*"

Ricky frowned. He didn't have her gift for Venislarn.

"I just asked any Venislarn present to not eat us," she said. "Basically, cos we're cool." Translating it gave her pause for thought. She turned to Mrs Fiddler. "This place could be dangerous."

Mrs Fiddler hummed in agreement, apparently unconcerned. "We're a hundred metres below the city of Birmingham in an enormous hall with a roof that has no visible means of support. You don't need to tell me."

"Other dangers, Mrs Fiddler," said Nina.

The woman's eyes had a sly quality. Nina remembered as child suspecting that Mrs Fiddler was psychic, that she knew your innermost thoughts.

"This is the most exciting historical find in the region since the Staffordshire Hoard," said Mrs Fiddler and then wrinkled her nose. "No, screw the Staffordshire Hoard. This is the find of the century and you aren't about to tell me to go back for my own safety."

"Perhaps we should *all* go back for our own safety," suggested Ricky. "That's a big room. We could get lost."

"Pff," said Nina and made to step forward but Ricky caught her elbow.

She locked gazes with him.

"Why did we come here?" he said in an annoyingly reasonable tone.

"Because Vivian had a key," said Nina, "and... that means something. Something out there."

"And what would Vivian advise right now, huh?"

Nina thought about it and ignored the obvious and possibly correct answer and said, "She would tell us to not let our fears and emotions stop us doing the job."

Mrs Fiddler stepped past her and into the wider hall. "Wedge something under the door, chief inspector," she said decisively. "The light will guide us back if we get lost."

Nina smiled. "Yeah. Door wedge, chief inspector. Let's go exploring."

Morag and Kathy sat in the cafeteria and spectator area of Stechford leisure centre, nursing coffees and waiting for Khaleesi to come out from the changing rooms. Morag's phone rang.

"Hello?"

"It's Rod. You free to talk?"

"Uh-huh."

"You sound somewhere echoey."

"Kathy and I are at the swimming pool."

There was a pause. "Did I miss an e-mail or something?"

"We're waiting for a woman who thinks she's a Venislarn or a fish or something."

"Of course," he said. "Sounds obvious now you've said it. I needed to check something with *Yo-Morgantus*."

"Uh-huh?"

"And I know you're his favourite."

She tutted realising. "This is a ginger thing, right?"

Yo-Morgantus, the god king and secret ruler of Birmingham, had a fondness for redheads. In much the same way that the English aristocracy had a fondness for partridges and pheasants.

Kathy tapped Morag's elbow and stood. A woman with pink gills beneath the ends of her damp blue hair had just come out from the changing area, a sports bag under her arm.

"This film crew I've been assigned to," said Rod, "we need to double-check that Lord *Morgantus* is fine with them filming in the city."

Kathy had intercepted the young woman and drawn her aside to a cafeteria table.

"Surely, that would have been sorted out weeks ago," said Morag. "Look, I've gotta go."

"But I need to check."

By the look on Khaleesi's face, the conversation with Kathy had gone badly from the start.

"I'm kind of busy here," said Morag.

"But when you're done..." said Rod.

"Yep, will check in with you after."

She ended the call and walked briskly over to Kathy, who was failing to engage Khaleesi in calm conversation.

"—and haters just keep on hating even though it's no business of theirs what therianthropes do with their lives," said Khaleesi hotly. "What harm's it doing you? What harm? Do you feel threatened?"

Morag inserted herself smoothly into a vacant chair.

"Hi, I'm Morag," she said. "You're a friend of Trevor's, right?"

Khaleesi glared daggers at her.

"And who are you?"

"We got the phone message. You needed to ask Trevor about tomorrow night's communion, yeah?"

Her expression softened a little and Morag saw how young this woman was. Probably still a teenager, either still living at home or a resident of bedsit-land. Those gill implants had probably cost her a month's rent. "You know Trevor?" she said.

"I did," said Morag honestly. "We knew each other in a professional capacity." She lingered conspiratorially on the word 'professional'.

Khaleesi's gaze narrowed, intrigued. She waved dismissively at Kathy. "She said we couldn't meet tomorrow, that it wasn't 'right'."

Kathy pointed a finger. "What I said was—"

"I heard you first time, shape-fascist."

"*Jur-kalla fek muda khi umlaq!*" hissed Kathy under her breath.

"Ignore what she said," said Morag, causing Kathy to swear some more. "I hear you're getting better at holding your breath."

"Breathing underwater," Khaleesi corrected her.

"Of course. Yeah." Khaleesi's gill were infection pink. Morag wondered how long she'd been told to wait for them to heal before going back in the water and how long she'd actually waited. "What's your record?"

"Three minutes, twelve seconds."

"Impressive." Morag felt around for the correct terminology. "And what... kintype? What kintype do you identify as?"

"I am a *yon-bun* dweller," said the girl with evident pride.

Kathy made a light cough. Morag kicked her under the table.

"Good for you," said Morag brightly. "Now, your chapter is planning to meet with one of the Venislarn tomorrow night. Trevor set that up for you, did he?"

"He did. We're very excited."

"And he charged you for it, naturally."

"There are costs," nodded Khaleesi. "He did explain."

"Costs?" said Kathy.

"Transportation through the *lo-frax* field isn't cheap and there are tariffs on the *randhu gefit ta-ta,* aren't there?"

It was nonsense. It was that perverse kind of nonsense which was so close to the truth that it seemed doubly nonsensical for not being quite right.

"We paid membership subs to belong to the chapter too," said Khaleesi, "but they were very reasonable rates."

"I'm sure they were," said Morag. "Trevor was all about doing things by the book, I bet. Now, did he happen to mention an organisation that dealt with registration and documentation of anyone having dealings with the Venislarn?"

"He gave us some forms to fill out," the girl said doubtfully.

"Forms," said Morag. "Well that's just lovely. I'm guessing they just got lost in the post because Kathy here and myself, we're from the consular mission and we've got no paperwork with your name on it."

"Or any of your friends from the chapter," said Kathy.

"But..." Khaleesi's expression flickered from surprise to concern to suspicion. "We're not paying any more money."

Morag smiled cheerily. "We don't need a single penny. We just need you and your friends to come down to our office and spend a few minutes—"

"Hour tops," said Kathy.

"—talking to us about your... experiences as Venislarn."

"Venislarnkin," said Khaleesi.

"That."

Morag thought they had sold it to her and then Khaleesi said, "Registration's just another form of hating though."

"The actual Venislarn submit to registration," said Kathy softly.

"Really?" said Khaleesi.

"Even *yon-bun* dwellers. You know, if you and your friends come in—all of them—then I could even show you some *yon-bun* pictures and data, stuff I know that Mystic Trevor never had access to."

Khaleesi's eyes sparkled. Sold, to the woman with blue hair and gills.

With the promise that he would confirm the Venislarn court's approval of the film shoot and that he would be on set at six the following morning, Rod walked the several hundred metres from the production team's hotel to the Library of Birmingham and the consular mission offices. This involved a detour around the building site that now covered Centenary Square. There was nothing to be seen of the redevelopment at the moment except building site hoardings (beneath the company's arm and hammer logo, the assurance that 'Forward Management are committed to considerate building practices') and the top of a cement storage silo.

Once in the Library, Rod hurried to the response team office. He did not consider himself one of life's moaners—he much more saw himself as a tireless stoic—but he hankered to relay his views on the excruciating meeting he'd had to sit through.

To Rod's disappointment, there was no one in the office. But he found a large enamel teapot in the kitchenette which was still warm to the touch. He gave it an experimental sniff to check it was not over-stewed and then poured himself a cuppa. It steamed lightly in his mug. With milk, it was the perfect pale orangey-brown. Not since the days when Vivian deigned to make her colleagues cups of tea had he tasted so fine a cup.

Mug in hand, he went wandering. In meeting room two, chairs had been set out in rows and the blinds had been drawn while a video played on the projector screen for the benefit of the dozen or so young adults in the audience. Rod instantly recognised the video which went by the unofficial title of the *So, You Want to Give Yourself to the Venislarn!* It was fifteen minutes of photos and footage of Venislarn, nothing more mind-melting than Abyssal Rating one with a voice-over from some soothing Shakespearean actor type. Every time he saw it, the unpleasant visuals and incongruous narration put Rod in mind of the Public Safety Announcement films shown on TV when he was kid—*don't pick up spent fireworks! don't swim in abandoned quarries! don't play near farm machinery!* They'd terrified him as a child and left mental scars that had not yet healed. This video was having a similar and desired effect on most of the room.

Some watched the film with wide-eyed dread. Some watched only through their fingers. Others had turned away. Two had put their heads in their hands and one of them was sobbing loudly, which Rod regarded as a positive result.

"Remember," said the voice-over, "giving yourself to the *em-shadt* Venislarn is your choice. No one can legally stop you from, for example, becoming a bride sacrifice to *Yo-Creyakhtor*, a *ghist-rashall* of *Yoth-Sheol-Niggurauth* or a willing host for the spawn of the *Penvith Lhoma*."

At the accompanying visual for this last one, a woman gave a strangled squeal of terror and a man threw up, unfortunately missing the sick bag he had been provided. Kathy Kaur detached herself from the shadows beside the projector screen and slid over to Rod.

"As you can see," she whispered, "we're having the best time here."

Rod frowned questioning as he sipped his brew and waved a finger over the congregation.

"Venislarnkin," whispered Kathy. "Mystic Trevor had sold this lot a dream of communion with the Venislarn host and, as best as I can work out, took payment from both sides. I think we may have 'inadvertently' put some of them off the idea."

One of the audience whimpered, "I want my mom."

"Where have you been this afternoon?" said Kathy.

Rod made a disgusted noise. "Trapped in a room with the worst kind of morons."

"No. Where have *you* been?" she smiled. "Have you seen Nina around? We could do with a hand, processing this lot."

Rod shook his head. "Is Morag here?"

"Room Eight, doing interviews and forms."

Rod went down to Room Eight and peered through the vertical pane in the door. Morag sat across the table from a young woman with bright blue hair and something seriously wrong with her neck. Rod tapped on the door. Morag looked up and waved him in.

"Not intruding?" he asked.

"Don't think so," said Morag. "Khaleesi here is just filling out the final declaration that she wants to sign herself over to the Venislarn. I've given her all the statutory warnings and advice and all she needs to do is put her signature in that book."

The blue-haired girl sniffed snottily and wiped tears from her red-rimmed eyes with the heel of her palm.

Rod leaned in close to Morag. "Have you had a chance to check about filming permissions with *Yo-Morgantus*?"

"Funnily, some of us have been busy," said Morag.

"I've had a tough afternoon too, you know," he replied.

She looked at his cup of tea. "Wining and dining with the Hollywood set, sure. Listen, when Khaleesi has made her decision here, I'll get onto it."

Khaleesi sniffled miserably.

"It's just... it's just so difficult," she said, her voice cracking.

"I know," said Morag. "You've had your heart set on this for so long and now you've discovered that being the plaything of evil gods from beyond the stars might not be as fun as it sounds."

Khaleesi picked up the pen in a trembling hand.

"I don't know," wailed Khaleesi. "I can't decide."

Morag patted her hand reassuringly and slipped the forms away from her grasp. "Then don't," she said. "Put it off for another day."

"Or a week," said Rod.

"Or a month."

There was a rap at the door. Lois Wheeler popped her head round.

"Morag. Just a reminder. You need to be up at the Cube this afternoon."

"Yeah, I know. Campbell here keeps pestering me to go."

"I mean you've been summoned."

"By Lord *Morgantus*?"

"Demanding your immediate presence," said the receptionist.

Rod left her to wrap up and went back into the office. There was enough tea in the pot for another cup.

Nina raised the torch. Again, it illuminated only wooden floorboards, plaster ceiling and nothing whatsoever to either side. Whichever way she turned it was the same: floor and ceiling.

"Is this some kind of illusion?" she suggested.

"It's not normal, if that's what you mean," said Ricky.

"We've been walking nine and a half minutes since the door," said Mrs Fiddler. Nina looked at her. Mrs Fiddler tapped her watch. "In the absence of landmarks, time is a good aid to navigation."

Nina shone the torch away to the side and looked back the way they'd come. The light from the doorway was still visible, a yellow-white beacon in the dark.

"Nine minutes at this pace," said Ricky, thinking allowed. "Nearly half a mile?"

"I would point out that that's impossible," said Mrs Fiddler, "if it were not for the evidence of our senses."

"There's something ahead," said Nina.

It was a long, low shape on the floor that as they neared, resolved itself to be a skeleton. It was human, adult, grey-brown in colour and it was laid out and complete, apart its head.

"The skull's been crushed," said Ricky.

"I think we can see that," said Nina.

"Not just crushed," said Mrs Fiddler. "Pulverised."

The top half of the skull had been reduced to powdery fragments. Ricky crouched to look at it closer. He produced a pair of latex gloves from his pocket, put them on and gently lifted and inspected the material.

"At a guess. This is old. Very old. But it's a body," he sighed.

"I guess that means paperwork for you, huh?" said Nina.

He gave her an irritated look and took several photos with his phone.

"Turn the torch off, please," said Mrs Fiddler.

"Too gruesome for you?" said Nina.

The old teacher lady scoffed. "Just turn it off a second, please. I thought I saw something."

Nina flicked it off. The darkness was complete. Automatically, she blinked, her eyes unwilling to accept that they were open and there was nothing to see.

"Okay, this is stupid," she said and turned round to look back at the distant door they had come through to reassure her brain she hadn't gone entirely blind.

"I'm sure I saw something," said Mrs Fiddler.

"Stare into the dark long enough and your eyes will imagine there's something there," said Ricky.

"There," said Mrs Fiddler.

"Uh-huh," said Nina. "Now, are you perhaps pointing something out to us? Because, you know, it's dark and..."

She flicked the torch back on. Mrs Fiddler was indeed pointing. Nina aligned herself with her outstretched hand and turned it off again.

"See it?" said Mrs Fiddler and leaned in close. She smelled of hand cream and boiled vegetables.

"I see it," said Ricky.

Nina stared furiously. After a while, she decided she could perhaps see something.

"The light?"

"The light," said Ricky.

It was tiny or possibly very distant and off to a slight angle from the direction they had been walking.

"Let's go check out the light," said Nina.

"Let's go back and come back when we're properly equipped," said Ricky.

"Fortune favours the bold," she argued.

"In my experience, that's never true," he replied. "Fortune generally favours the cautious and those who follow health and safety guidance."

Nina wasn't listening. She was already striding forward.

The exact date at which the Venislarn invaded the earth was a matter of debate and conjecture. There had clearly been a time when there had been no need for organisations such as the consular missions, and there had been a number of spectacular and barely concealable incursions that had marked some sort of 'start' to the

Venislarn presence, and yet... The Venislarn were new, old and ancient and did not play fair with the rules of time or causality. Whatever their plans, this invading army was now kicking back and enjoying itself in anticipation of the glorious bloodbath and pain-fest that would be the Soulgate. They had metaphorically goose-stepped down the Champs-Élysées and were now enjoying the finest Parisian cafes in the summer sun. In Birmingham, the Venislarn slummed it in style, occupying the top floors of one of the most illustrious tower blocks in the city.

The Cube sat at one end of Gas Street Basin, literal spitting distance from the high-end shops and restaurants of the Mailbox and the finest bars and clubs that stretched along the most fashionable bit of canal waterfront. The Venislarn rarely descended to visit any bars or restaurants but it suited their tastes to know that if they fancied popping out for a human snack they would find deliciously self-entitled prize specimens on their doorstep.

Morag entered the lobby of the Cube and headed straight for the bank of lifts. The corpulent concierge made a wordless noise at her from his desk and pointed at a specific lift.

The doors slid open. The lift contained an August Handmaiden of *Prein*. The Handmaiden's bone white carapace filled the top half of the carriage. The Handmaidens had no faces of their own, so they had adorned themselves with the likenesses of tortured children to give people something to look at. One of the screaming baby protuberances faced Morag at head height.

The Handmaiden tilted its shell and a new baby face rotated into place.

"Going up?" The Handmaidens had mouths directly below their bodies, but they weren't shaped for speech. The Handmaiden's voice—speaking with the clear, received pronunciation of an Edwardian governess—came from nowhere at all.

"I'll wait for the next one," said Morag.

Armoured crab legs shifted aside to create a pocket of room in the lift.

"This is your lift," said the Handmaiden.

Morag hesitated, which was an under-reaction if anything. Getting into a confined space with this Venislarn monster was inadvisable but she could see with total prescience what would happen if she refused. *Yo-Morgantus* had sent this lift and this creature for her. If this was his will then obeying would be far less painful than disobedience.

She squeezed, pressing herself through the copse of thin legs to stand in the corner. A claw slowly reached down, passed Morag's nose and pressed the button for the top floor. The door slid shut.

As they rode up, Morag involuntarily looked up at the underside of the monster that stood over her. Its belly was unarmoured and a mottled grey colour, apart from its mouth, which was membranous pink and sharply toothed.

The Handmaiden didn't speak for the duration of the journey. Any 'quiet word' or specific threats Morag had expected from the Handmaiden failed to materialise. Threats would have been less unnerving than thirty seconds in silent and close proximity to an over-sized crustacean, breathing its air, watching its mouth twitch.

When the lift dinged on the top floor, the Handmaiden of *Prein* left first, scraping its shell on the doorframe as it pushed through. Morag followed.

Much of the court was gathered in a single room (if the word 'room' can be used to describe a cathedral-like space that defies the spatial boundaries of the building that contains it, and if the word 'court' is meaningfully applicable to a menagerie of gods and monsters). The Handmaiden of *Prein* stepped over the outstretched pseudopod of a lounging *draybbea* and around a mud pool in which something was either wallowing or drowning. Morag stepped close behind, happy to avoid bumping into any of *Yo-Morgantus's* vile courtiers or, just as bad, any of his human slaves who were, to an individual, red-haired and butt-naked.

Morag suspected a day would come when *Yo-Morgantus* would insist she join the red-headed naturist set. She would hardly be able to refuse, she thought, watching a fibrous tendril unfurl from above. Thousands of translucent strands hung from the ceiling vents. Morag knew they depended from the god's bloated and immobile body itself, a football field-sized sack of fatty gels that floated in a cavity above the ceiling. Lord Morgantus used these mind-stinging tendrils to exert his will over the court. They were also his primary means of communication, tapping into any red-haired human mouthpiece he chose.

One such mouthpiece, a young woman with resting bitch face and a perky-and-don't-I-just-know-it body, walked out across the hall of horrors to meet Morag.

"Brigit," said Morag with unconcealed contempt.

Brigit raised a hand to touch a dangling tendril and her expression spasmed.

"*San-shu chuman'n, Yo-Morgantus,*" said Morag and bowed her head.

Brigit looked to the Handmaiden. "*Tendhu, Shala'pinz Syu.* Be about your business. We will discuss your petition later."

The Venislarn angled a frozen baby face directly at Morag for a moment before stalking off on segmented legs.

"*Shala'pinz Syu?*" said Morag. "I would like to talk about her if—"

"That is not why I summoned you," said Brigit. "Walk with me."

There was a superior sneer in her voice to back up the one on her face. Her mind might have belonged to *Yo-Morgantus* but Morag suspected the attitude was all her own.

Morag did as instructed, walking with Brigit deeper into the hall.

Something splashed at Morag's feet. A *royogthrap* loomed over them, dangling a wet and tasty morsel above its mouth before shooting out its stomach to snatch it from its own claw. A bone-feathered *blevit* creature crawled across the larger being's body to snatch up any dropped crumbs.

"Do you know what your failing is?" said Brigit.

"Mine?" said Morag. "I drink too much and never know when to back down from a fight."

"Your failing, collectively," said Brigit. "Humanity's."

Morag shrugged and walked on. "I've got this weird feeling you're going to tell me."

There was a set of double doors at the furthest end of the hall. Two naked gingers stood stiffly to attention at either side, so still that Morag thought for a moment they were taxidermy specimens.

"You believe that you and the Venislarn are engaged in a rational transaction. Servant and master. Conqueror and vassal state."

Brigit reached out with perfectly manicured nails and pinched one man's nostril until it bled. The man didn't move a millimetre.

"These two are under the belief that the first of them to move or make a noise will be skinned alive and his worthless hide used as a piñata," said Brigit.

"And is that true?" said Morag.

Brigit pushed through the door.

"You know why we're doing that to them?" she said.

"Is there a reason?" said Morag.

Brigit shook her head, not in answer but at Morag's question. "Give and take. Plead and appease. You think you can deal with us. You think you can know our motives."

They were in a corridor with windows overlooking the city centre along its length. In daylight, away from the nightclub dungeon atmosphere of the hall, Brigit's nakedness seemed laughable.

"Is this going to be an entirely cryptic meeting?" said Morag. "I feel I should be taking notes."

Brigit spun and slapped Morag with the flat of her hand. Morag stumbled back in surprise more than anything else. She had to sit hard on her natural instinct to come back at Brigit with fists flying. Morag shook with rage.

"We do as we wish," said Brigit. "We take nothing because it is already ours. There is a film crew in the city. We tolerate their presence. There are twenty-eight souls offered to us as sacrifice by a human called Trevor. We will accept those."

Morag put a hand to her stinging cheek. "Those kids. They don't know what they agreed to."

"And there it is," said Brigit, "the belief that we are engaging in a rational transaction. Do we demand those twenty-eight souls as payment for allowing the filming to take place? Tell yourself that if you like."

"But several have decided—cos they're not stupid—that they don't want to be involved anymore. We went through the agreed registration documents and they have decided not to proceed."

Brigit blinked. "Do I look like a lawyer, Morag Murray? Do I look like a Mammonite, clinging to a piece of paper like it's been

74

signed in blood? Twenty-eight. That's the number. I don't care where you get them."

Morag tried to hold her temper, but it really wasn't working. "Is that you saying that, Brigit? Or is that Lord *Morgantus*?"

Brigit put her hands on the window sill and looked out over the city. "Ownership."

"*Azbhul!*" hissed Morag. "Talk straight. You sound like the second Matrix movie."

"*Yo-Morgantus* owns Brigit, body and mind," said the naked ginger. "He owns the city. They are one and the same. There is no distinction."

Brigit came towards Morag, hands reaching for her blouse. Morag's first thought was that she was going to be attacked, her second was that she was going to be subjected to some seriously unwanted sexual advances.

"Do not resist," said Brigit.

In the corner of her eye, Morag saw a tendril drop from a ceiling vent and twist, like a jellyfish sting in an ocean current. If it touched her then her compliance was guaranteed. Twice *Yo-Morgantus* had accessed her mind in the past: once to show her another man's memories and once to replay a childhood memory of her own. That was, at least, her recollection of those instances. But if *Yo-Morgantus* could read, write and edit thoughts with a touch, there was no knowing what moments he had erased, what beliefs and ideas he had planted. She couldn't even be certain that the childhood memory—the grisly discovery of a dying otter on the shores of the Moray Firth—was even real.

"*Yo-Morgantus* owned the man you knew as Drew," said Brigit. "He owned the man. He owned his seed." Brigit unbuttoned the lower half of Morag's blouse and slid her hand inside, across Morag's stomach. Morag's mental chart of top ten instances of unwanted touching had suddenly got a new number one. "This," said Brigit and gently pressed the flesh. "This belongs to us."

"I might not even be pregnant," said Morag but she didn't even believe that herself.

Brigit's fingers explored Morag's abdomen, as though she could somehow sense a tiny foetus through skin, muscle and fat.

"You came to us some weeks ago," said Brigit, "when your colleagues were taken prisoner by the Mammonites and *Yoth Mammon* threatened to return from *Kal Frexo Leng*-space. You begged me to intervene. You said you would do anything to save your friends and the city."

"I did."

Brigit cupped the flesh below Morag's bellybutton. "This is what you will do. You will nurture our investment in you. You will nurture our *kaatbari*. We will protect our investment and, as long you nurture it, we will protect you. Tomorrow, we will find you new accommodation in the city, something more suited to your honoured role. We will provide guardians for you and your unborn."

"I don't—"

Brigit removed her hand from Morag's stomach. "What you want doesn't matter."

Morag backed away, clumsily buttoning up her blouse.

"The twenty-eight souls." She huffed. "They're not souls, they're human beings. People."

Brigit reached up a hand and the winding tendril above her obligingly touched her.

"*Shala'pinz Syu* will meet them as arranged. Here. Tuesday. Midnight."

"Please," said Morag wretchedly. "I beg you to reconsider. I'll beg again."

Brigit looked down her nose at Morag.

"Not this time," she said.

Morag stumbled out through the hall of Venislarn unholy horrors. She stabbed repeatedly at the call button for the lift. The lift was empty, and Morag spent the ride down punching the wall and screaming Scots obscenities at the universe.

Out on the canal and the towpath that led back to Centenary Square and the Library, she put in a call to the team office. Kathy picked up.

"How many idiot Venislarnkin do we have at the Library?" said Morag.

"Twenty-eight," said Kathy, "but I was just about to let a whole lot of them go, having sufficiently put them off going to the dark side."

"Well, don't."

"Oh?"

"Trevor promised twenty-eight human sacrifices to the Venislarn and *Yo-Morgantus, Shala'pinz Syu,* whatever, intends to collect on Tuesday night."

"You told him that most of them have changed their minds?"

Morag massaged her brow with her fingers. "Yeah. He really doesn't care. He wants his twenty-eight souls."

"Souls?" said Kathy. "Did he want people or souls?"

"Does the exact wording matter?"

"Soul—*fraxasa*—and people—*yoch'i'di*—are two very different things."

"Yes, I know that, thank you, doctor," said Morag.

"The point is, I recall a rumour that the mission tech bods at the Think Tank were working on synthesising artificial *fraxasa*."

"Artificial souls?"

"That's what I heard. Let me check it out with Professor Omar."

"Is he there?" said Morag.

"Just walked in."

"Put him on."

"I can ask him."

"Put him on. Please."

On the canal, ducklings swam behind their mother, V-trails merging in her larger wake, making confetti of the first evening lights.

"Department of minor miracles and intercessions," sang Omar. "How may I help you?"

"I want a scan."

"Ah, no greeting. No how-do-you-dos."

"I said I want a scan."

"And I seem to recall you telling me and my sensitive friend Maurice that there was, I quote, 'no *adn-bhul* way are you coming anywhere near me with KY jelly and an ultrasound.'"

"Morgantus knows," said Morag tersely.

"Of course, he does."

"He says it's the *kaatbari*."

Omar didn't reply.

"Well?" demanded Morag.

"Hmmm," said Omar.

"Hmmm? What the *bhul* does 'hmmm' mean?"

"It means we had always suspected this might be the case."

"We?" Morag shouted. "We certainly did not! At no point did *we* discuss the possibility that I might be pregnant with the Venislarn anti-Christ!"

"By 'we', I meant Maurice and myself."

"Oh! Right! And when were you planning on sharing those suspicions with me, eh?"

"Preferably, after you allowed us to take an ultrasound scan."

Morag was tempted to throw her phone in the water. "Scan! Now!"

"I will endeavour to make the preparations, Miss Murray."

"And not a word to anyone."

Omar chuckled. The *vangru* was actually laughing. "I've always been adept at keeping things secret from the authorities, my dear."

The light was, according to Mrs Fiddler's timekeeping, another twelve minutes' distance from the point they had first spotted it. It came from something lying on the ground next to a door in a wall and a second skeleton. The skeleton was humanoid, but it was not human. It was huge, several metres in length with arm bones like sapling trees.

"At last," said Ricky. "A wall, an actual wall. I was starting to get a bit... Is it possible to get agoraphobic when you're indoors?"

"Uh, that's not any creature I know," said Mrs Fiddler, pointing at the large skeleton. "Are you both seeing this?"

"Could be a *Kobashi*," said Nina. "Though I've never seen one in the flesh before. Or in the bone, I mean."

"Kobashi?"

"Monster demon ape." The light came from a slender, multi-pronged item, like an avant-garde egg-whisk. Dots of occult light glowed at the ends of the prongs. It was an avant-garde egg-whisk with fairy lights. "I don't know what this is."

She picked it up, expecting the lights to fade, but they didn't.

"Door," said Ricky.

"It is," said Nina and opened it. Inside was a parlour, old-fashioned like some Sherlock Holmes thing. There was a pair of plump leather armchairs, a posh old patterned rug, red velvety curtains, a fireplace and a huge mantelpiece covered in ornaments.

"Ridiculous," said Mrs Fiddler softly. "A fireplace? An actual chimney? This far below ground."

The three of them entered. Ricky knelt in the hearth and tried to look up the chimney. Mrs Fiddler ran her fingers over a bell jar containing a stuffed owl.

Nina went straight to the curtains, compelled to fling them aside, to confirm to herself there was nothing behind them but more wall, more floral pattern wallpaper. But she was wrong. There was a window, a sliding sash window. There was another curtain immediately beyond the glass. Nina found the brass catch and slid the window up. It ran smoothly on well-oiled runners. She pulled aside the curtain beyond and looked into another room.

It was study or a small library. It was lit, like the parlour, with an old-fashioned ceiling light. Brown books crowded brown shelves. There was a sloping desk. It took Nina a while to realise what was most odd about the room, apart from the fact that its one window looked directly into another room...

Nina, a girl who was afraid of nothing, felt a slight chill.

"I used to have this dream when I was a kid," she said. "I'd wake up in my bedroom, or at least think it was my bedroom, and then I'd look around and everything would seem normal until I realised that there was no door and no window."

There was no door in the study. No exit.

"It was just walls all the way round," said Nina. "And I knew that beyond the wall was just more wall, forever and ever."

She pulled herself back and shut the sash window.

Mrs Fiddler toyed with her beads nervously. "It's like a cancer."

"Cancer?" said Nina.

"Cancer," she said, "and I speak from experience here, is what happens when your body's cells forget their instructions and multiply at random, pumping out unneeded cells that should normally benefit the body but, instead, write over the systems of the body with their uncontrolled growth. This"—she dropped, shaking, into an armchair—"is a building with cancer, mad and without purpose."

"Okay," said Ricky. "Executive decision by the police. It's time to go."

Nina didn't argue. She tapped Mrs Fiddler lightly on the shoulder. The older woman sniffed as though waking and looked up at Nina.

"Time to go, Mrs Fiddler."

Nina's old teacher nodded silently and got up. The three of them left the parlour and Nina felt a deep sense of agreement when Ricky firmly shut the door behind them.

"Home," said Ricky and pointed at the almost invisibly tiny light of the door that was their way out.

The distant light winked for a second and then went out.

"Oh, wow," said Ricky, tired more than worried. "If only someone had suggested we go back earlier."

"I'm not the one who used a defective door wedge," replied Nina.

Kathy loomed over the rear of Rod's computer.

"Whatcha doing?" she asked in a sing-song voice, her exquisite and expressive eyebrows arched playfully.

Kathy had her coat over her arm as though she was leaving for the day. Rod looked at his watch. Yes, it was that time. He ran a hand down his face.

"Oh, just some research. Background reading."

Kathy swung round the desk to look, almost plonking her backside in his lap. Rod, who had been brought up with the unwritten understanding that one didn't go near ladies' backsides without permission, tried to distance himself without appearing to distance himself. He sipped his fourth cup of tea of the afternoon to try to emphasise his nonchalance.

"IMDb?" said Kathy, looking at the screen. "Background reading?"

"Now Morag's got it cleared with *Morgantus*, I've got this movie thing tomorrow. Down at the Mailbox."

"Opportunity to man-crush with movie star Taylor Graham, huh?"

"Never heard of him before today," said Rod.

It was true, he hadn't, but after reading up on him one could be forgiven for thinking the American was the most accomplished, desirable, and philanthropic individual on earth.

"Do I detect a hint of jealousy?" said Kathy, straightening up and putting her backside safely out of Rod's panic zone.

"Jealous? No." He made a disagreeable noise which came out sounding forced and false.

"You have nothing to worry about," she said, her eyebrow arched in wry amusement.

It was at moments like this that Rod unavoidably remembered how attractive Dr Kathy Kaur was. Before she had joined the response team, back when she was a doctor over at the Restricted Ward of the hospital, he had regarded her as a potential lover. The role of 'Rod's potential lover' wasn't a huge or demanding one. It simply meant that he considered her as, yes, sexually desirable. And, yes, if the situation arose—the proper situation—then, yes, he would definitely think about asking her out – yes, if the stars were right and, yes, if he could build up the courage to ask a confident, intelligent and distractingly shapely woman like Kathy out. And, yes, it probably was going to amount to nothing unless she made the first move and, yes, that was incredibly unlikely but, no, it didn't stop her being one of a number of women—yes, he was honest enough to admit she was one of a series of candidates—that he very much liked. Now that they were working closely together, the awkwardness of that fact—especially if she rejected him (or did not reject him) and it all went sour—meant the chances of him making any kind of move were nil.

"Drink?" she said.

"Eh?"

She nodded at his mug of tea.

"End of the working week. Maybe a proper drink to round things off."

"We're back in tomorrow," he pointed out.

"And we've been in every day since last Monday. Some day has to be the last day of the week."

Rod couldn't agree more but tried to play it cool. "Yeah, I'm sort of tea'd out. That pot in the kitchen is deceptively large."

Kathy frowned. "The big cream and green teapot?"

He nodded. "Someone's been paying attention to Vivian's tea-making lectures."

Kathy moved to the kitchenette with an urgency that made Rod follow. She scooped up the big barrel of a pot and poured tea out into the sink. It only took a second or two to empty it.

"That's a waste of good tea," said Rod.

"This came from Mystic Trevor's flat," she said, set it on the countertop and removed the lid.

Rod peered in beside her. In the dark, stained base of the pot, tea swirled and steamed, the water level rising.

"A magically refilling teapot," said Rod, who was partly astounded that such a wonderful item existed and partly worried that he'd drunk the contents.

"And did it taste like tea?" said Kathy.

"A right nice cuppa."

Kathy gazed at it in thought, hand on chin, hips tilted. "And you feel...?"

"Fine."

She nodded. "Then I suspect a magic teapot can wait until the morning for further analysis. Grab your coat, Campbell. Let's get that drink."

A call and a uCab and Morag found herself outside a private medical clinic among the old brick walls and leafy avenues of Edgbaston. Maurice was waiting outside in the dusk. He was Jeeves to Omar's Wooster, that is, if Wooster had been an amoral occult genius and Jeeves had been fond of pastel knitwear and golfing slacks.

"Where is he?" she said. "Or doesn't this warrant his attention?"

"He's inside, talking to the doctor," said Maurice kindly and gestured like a stage magician for her to go in.

Maurice's manner was always gentle, always kind. That was probably what he brought to the partnership of Omar and Maurice. Professor Sheikh Omar generated a lot of tension and anger in those around him. Maurice had the undeniable skill of absorbing and dissipating those tensions, that anger. He was, despite the company he kept, surprisingly likeable.

Morag went inside. The reception area was more like the lobby of an upmarket boutique hotel. Regular clients here could easily see where their medical insurance premiums went. Morag was more used to NHS waiting rooms, the wipe-clean plastic chairs and the faint whiff of disinfectant. This was the world of other people, richer people, as alien to her as the Venislarn.

She sat down in the opposite corner to the one other person in the waiting room, a pale woman. Maurice offered to fetch Morag a cup of water and, when she declined, went off in search of his Omar.

"Here for a scan?" said the pale woman, in the tones of someone who had had no one to talk to for a long time and ached to chat.

"Yeah," said Morag and looked at the magazines on the coffee table nearby. There appeared to be a choice between *Warwickshire Life*, *Worcestershire Life* and *Shropshire Life*. Morag simply could not decide. There was a single issue of *Yachting Monthly* on the bottom of the pile and she went for that in an instant.

"Is this your first one?" said the pale woman.

"Scan?"

"Baby."

"Definitely my last," said Morag. "Quite possibly the very last baby."

"Oh, it's not that bad, is it?" The woman's smiled flickered—on, off—as though she feared it might cause offence. "I know that having a baby feels like the end of the world."

"Funny you should say that..."

"I'm Niamh," said the woman.

"Morag." Morag's foul mood relented. "And you? First?"

The woman smiled and nodded enthusiastically. "Three-month scan. It feels like I've been pregnant forever. Can't believe I've got this thing for another six months yet."

Morag didn't know what the gestation period of Venislarn anti-Christs was. She hoped it was measured in years, not months, to give her time to consider her options.

"I'm going to ask Dr Fazook to tell me the gender, if he can tell. What are you hoping for? Boy or girl?"

"Human," said Morag. The woman laughed dutifully. "Actually," said Morag, "I'm hoping it's trapped wind." A smaller laugh. "Or ovarian cancer. Anything but a baby."

That put a dent in the woman's wilful chumminess but not enough to kill the conversation.

"You're frightened?"

"Terrified."

"That's understandable."

"This isn't a world I want to bring a child into. Any child. But particularly this child."

"It's not that bad," said Niamh.

Morag thought of the Venislarn and the apocalyptic Soulgate and the millions of babies that would spend eternity writhing in hell.

The creak of a door and Maurice was there, gesturing for her to come through. Morag put back the *Yachting Monthly* and went to see what the end of the world looked like.

Rod and Kathy sat in the restaurant bar of the Rep Theatre and had a drink to mark the seamless boundary between one working week and the next. The Rep was right next to the Library of Birmingham and picked only because they wouldn't have far to walk back to collect their cars afterwards.

The view from their window table was unimpressive. Centenary Square was a building site, ten-foot-high wooden panels concealed the works going on across the length of the square. In the slit of sky visible above the barriers, the city skyline of grand old buildings, office blocks and skyscrapers was dotted with construction cranes near and far.

"One day, I'd like to think this city will be finished," said Kathy, "and all the cranes and diggers will move off somewhere else."

"It's been the same the ten-plus years I've been here," said Rod.

"I've lived here near enough all my life," she said, shaking her head. She stirred her straw around the remains of her gin and tonic. "You know, something that takes this long to put right probably isn't worth saving."

Rod laughed. "Fine words from a doctor."

She pulled a deeply unladylike face. "I was never interested in palliative care. I like to fix things and have them stayed fixed."

"Nothing stays fixed," said Rod.

She grunted in agreement. "That's the difference between humans and animals," she said.

"Eh?" he said, feeling he'd missed something.

"People, we patch them up again and again, always fighting a defensive battle, always losing ground. You're over forty, you know what I mean."

"Cheers, thanks."

"The warranty on these bodies runs out but we do our best." She rolled her shoulder. He'd seen her do that often. A couple of months back, she'd been stabbed in that shoulder by a nearly-human-but-not-nearly-human-enough Mammonite. "The pain is worth it to win the battle. But animals, pets and so on, if they're in pain we put them out of their misery. If Fido or Tiddles is in enough pain to affect their quality of life, then..." She mimed holding a shotgun to an invisible animal on the floor.

"Wow," said Rod. "I'm guessing you didn't have many pets as a kid."

She smiled. "My dad didn't allow them. I pestered him for a puppy or a guinea pig for years, but he stood firm. And then after he died, it just didn't seem appropriate for me to get a pet. If your dad dies one day and you buy a cockapoo the next, it looks suspiciously like you're trying to replace him."

Rod vaguely knew that Kathy's dad was dead. If a person talks about a loved one in the past tense for a sufficient length of time, one comes to certain conclusions.

"He worked in construction, didn't he?" said Rod.

She looked surprised.

"I do pay attention to things people say sometimes," he said.

"Um, yeah. Sort of," said Kathy. "He was in construction. One of these big companies that manage and renovate old buildings. Um, that one actually."

She was pointing out of the window at the logo for Forward Management on the building site hoarding.

"Oh, so this is his fault?" said Rod and jerked a thumb out the window at a city that was constantly half-built. As the words came out of his mouth, he wondered if making jokes about the livelihood of dead dads was less than appropriate, but she laughed.

"In his day, Forward Management were always about fixing things for good and then leaving well alone," she said. "We had that in common."

While Rod had been staring out the window, Kathy had gathered her things. She made to stand. "Have a good weekend," she said.

"It's Sunday," he said.

"And it's back to work tomorrow, so enjoy it while you can."

He grunted.

"And you're ringing," she said, getting up.

His phone, face down on the table, was flashing and buzzing.

"Night, Rod," she said with a smile and left.

Rod tried to say goodbye to Kathy and answer the phone at the same time but simply ended up answering the phone with a "Good night."

"Good night?" Rod recognised the voice of Ricky Lee's pet sergeant.

"Sorry," said Rod. "Trying to do two things at once. Can't multitask."

"I didn't mean to interrupt, Rod," she said. "I wanted to know if you've heard from the chief inspector this afternoon?"

"Er, no? I think he went off with Nina on some errand."

"Yes. Is she there?"

"No. I've tried to get hold of her a few times myself."

"It's just the end of shift and I've not heard from him. I would have expected him to text or radio the control room."

Nina was hardly as considerate. She was happy to maintain radio silence for days on end unless she needed something or had juicy gossip to share.

"I'm sure they're fine," said Rod.

"I suspect they're fine," said the sergeant.

"And Nina and Ricky, they..." He wondered how to phrase what he wanted to say.

"Rod, I'm perfectly aware of what Ricky and Nina get up to when they think no one's looking," said the sergeant. "He's not as cunning as he thinks he is, and I'm a cop."

"Yes," said Rod flatly. "That. So, maybe…"

"He'd still check in with me. The man's got some grasp of professional and safe working practices."

"Fair enough," he said. "Look, let me try to get hold of Nina and, either way, I'll get back to you."

"Thank you," said the sergeant and rang off.

Rod sighed and started texting.

Nina thought Mrs Fiddler's tiny, primary school teacher mind had been blown by the insanely improbable architecture of the underground space they had uncovered, but all it took was a mathematics problem to bring her back.

"I found it infuriating when pupils, and parents," said Mrs Fiddler, "made the same old complaint about maths lessons— 'When will we ever use algebra?' 'What's the point of learning trigonometry?'—unable to see that it's all applicable to the real world and we often use those mathematical skills without even realising it."

"Yeah?" said Nina, who didn't have a clue what she was on about.

Mrs Fiddler gave her a look. Nina remembered that look. It was the look of a teacher who was not going to let a student off answering a question by saying 'I don't know.' She waited and then gave a little sigh.

"Look at the floorboards," Mrs Fiddler instructed.

Nina and Ricky dutifully looked.

"We have the angle of the floorboards to work from," said Mrs Fiddler. "We followed them straight for nine minutes and then came off at that angle"—she made a drawing motion along the floor—"for twelve minutes. What's that, about twenty-five degrees?"

"Yes?" said Nina.

"About that," said Ricky.

"So, we have the length of two sides of a triangle, measured in time rather than length but it will do. And we have the angle between them. A hundred and fifty-five degrees. Now, what kind of triangle is this, Nina?"

"Er, a big one."

Ricky laughed.

"Ricky?" said Mrs Fiddler.

He stopped laughing. "Well, it's not a right-angle triangle."

"No. So...?"

"And not the one with all sides the same. Isosceles? No."

"It's an oblique triangle, isn't it?" said Mrs Fiddler.

"I was getting there," said Ricky.

The look she gave him was patient but unimpressed. No gold star stickers for Ricky.

"With an oblique triangle, where we know the length of two sides and the angle between them, we can use the law of cosines. Now, I must admit we might need a calculator for this bit..."

Rod wished he'd not bothered going round to Nina's house on the way home to check if she was there. Establishing she had not yet returned home was one thing. Stopping Mrs Seth getting into an absolute flap about what might have happened to her little girl was something else entirely.

"I'm sure she's fine," Rod assured her, trying to back away from the doorstep but being held in place by English politeness and Nina's mum's endless wittering.

"... and then sometimes she's out at all hours. In town with boys and wotnot, the pubbing and the clubbing, and I know what's going on there, don't think I don't."

"Aye, I'm sure you do," said Rod. "And maybe that's where she is."

"Oh, you know what she gets up to, do you?"

Mrs Seth, a tiny woman, no taller than Nina although considerably rounder, gave Rod a gimlet-like stare.

"I wouldn't know anything about anything," he said. "We're just colleagues."

"But you think she's gone missing?"

"I just..." He broke off, no idea what he could say to make this conversation stop. "I'll catch up with her tomorrow."

"And if she doesn't come home tonight? What then? What then?"

Rod's phone buzzed in her pocket.

"Ah!" he said, seizing on it. "This might be her!"

He stepped away, finger raised in a 'one moment' gesture to Mrs Seth and took the call. It wasn't Nina. It was Ricky's pet sergeant.

"Found them?" he asked.

"Them?" said Mrs Seth. "You've lost more than one?"

"Not found them, no," said the sergeant, "but we've found the chief inspector's car. It's at Soho House."

Rod turned around and considered the local geography. He was in Handsworth. "I could be there in five minutes."

"What's she doing there?" demanded Mrs Seth.

"Seems one of their tour guides has gone missing too," said the sergeant, "but they didn't think it was a police matter for some reason."

"Missing? In a house?" said Rod. "How hard do they have to look?"

Dr Fazook was a neat little man with oddly feminine hands. While he introduced himself, Professor Omar loomed over his shoulder as though he were somehow operating the man from behind. From the look on Fazook's face, he had already been told the score by Omar or something very much like the score. Fazook asked her to undo her blouse, loosen her trousers and lie down on the bed.

"Now, I am just applying the gel," said Fazook, and squirted a blob of the clear gel onto her stomach. The tube made a soft 'pfft!' sound. "Pardon me," said the doctor and smiled, content that his little joke had amused him if no one else.

Morag put her head back and tried to relax. Her gaze flicked from Fazook to Omar to Maurice – all three gathered in a huddle at the business end of the bed.

"Just so you know," she said, "I'm not having you three present at the birth, standing there like bloody wise men."

She couldn't help but notice that Omar had produced a Venislarn talisman, a *Nahl'i'yet-Khlar*, and muttered prayers as he gripped it tightly.

89

"Now, if you care to look at the little screen," said Fazook. "We'll see what we can find."

"Come on ovarian cancer!" she murmured under her breath.

Fazook moved the scanner across her abdomen, firmly and deeply but not unpleasantly, driving a path of lubricating gel before it. Twenty seconds later, he had locked onto something.

"There it is."

Morag stared.

"It's... it's a baby."

Fazook chuckled. "It certainly is."

On the ultrasound scanner screen was the grainy, constantly shifting stereotypical baby scan image: a big blob head, a big blob body and a number of lines that could easily be arms and legs. Omar had stopped praying.

"I was expecting tentacles," said Morag. The men laughed. "No. Seriously. I thought... *Shey muda corvei*," she sighed. "It's going to be born human?"

"Of course, it's human," said Fazook.

"The *kaatbari*? The *adn-bhul* anti-Christ..."

Fazook tapped her hand reassuringly. "You are pregnant with a perfectly normal and perfectly healthy little baby."

Morag did not know how to feel anymore. She was certain she was feeling something and it was a big feeling but she didn't know what it was. She was pregnant, undeniably pregnant. If she didn't choose to terminate it, she was going to be a mum. She didn't know what she felt about that either.

"And it's normal," she said.

"Good solid heartbeat. No sign of problems. I can tell you the gender, if you like, if we can just see the angle of the dangle. Let me—"

He froze suddenly, the scanner jabbed in her belly. On the screen, the blob baby slowly turned its head to look into the scanner. It twitched and loomed, pressing itself towards the imager. There was no seeing the expression on its face. It hardly had a face to express with. Nonetheless, it was looking at them all through the scanner.

"Is *that* normal?" whispered Morag.

"No," Fazook whispered back.

Omar started praying again.

It turned out that Mrs Fiddler's calculations weren't very far off. Walking at the angle suggested by Mrs Fiddler brought them eventually to a wall with a varnished skirting board. Nina knocked on the wall. It felt like concrete. It made a dull, leaden sound. Nina was reminded of childhood nightmares and walls that were just wall forever and ever, plaster and brick for infinity.

"The door can't be far," said Mrs Fiddler.

"Left or right?" said Ricky.

"Toss for it," said Nina.

"Right," said Mrs Fiddler. "Don't right-handed people—right-footed people that should be—don't they drift to the left when trying to walk in a straight line?"

"Is that true?" said Ricky.

"I'm sure I saw it in a film once about plane crash survivors lost in the desert."

They found the door within a minute. The door wedge Ricky had made from a piece of folded cardboard was on the floor, a dozen feet into the insanely huge room.

"Must have been flung there by the closing door," he said.

Nina made a doubtful noise and opened the door. Rod and Ricky's pet sergeant were in the corridor on the other side.

"There you are!" said Rod, sounding very much like the irritable mother hen he frequently was.

"Yes," said Nina. "We are here, obviously."

"What is this place?" said the sergeant.

"And are you all right?" said Rod.

"It was horrible," said Nina with feeling. "There was maths and everything."

"You did very well," said Mrs Fiddler and pressed something onto Nina's lapel. It was a gold star sticker, exactly like the ones she used to hand out at primary school.

"Oh, wow," said Nina. "You actually carry those with you at all times?"

"You never know when someone might need one."

"A gold star?" said Ricky, unimpressed.

"You're just jealous," said Nina.

"No, I'm not. I'm…" He pouted and then looked contritely at Mrs Fiddler. "Do I get one?"

It had gone nine o'clock and Rod had a woman in his flat. It had been a long time since that had happened.

The woman in question, though, was Nina Seth and while Rod was an unfussy man when it came to women, Nina definitely fell into the category of women he cheerfully considered off-limits. It wasn't that they were colleagues. It wasn't that she was barely half his age (and certainly acted half his age). It wasn't that he found her sexual candour and confidence unsettling (which he did). It was a range of factors which had turned their relationship into one that was a bit teacher-and-student or master-and-apprentice, although even that wasn't quite right because Nina had no master and was hardly willing to learn from anyone. As far as their relationship went, he existed to guide and protect her, and she existed to ignore and deride him. Strangely, it seemed to work; they were, for want of a more accurate word, friends, and he had a real fondness for her, even when she had come round to ransack his supplies.

"What exactly are you after?" he said.

"Explorer gear," she said.

"Crampons? Pitons?"

Rod turned on the light to what was notionally his second bedroom but was actually his equipment store and workshop.

Nina looked at the plastic boxes that lined the shelves. "Let's pretend I know what those words mean," she said. "There's a massive unexplored space under Soho House."

"An apparently infinite cellar."

"I didn't say that but yeah."

"And that's where you found that wand."

Nina regarded the glowing pronged item. "It's not necessarily a wand."

"What is it then?" he asked.

"I don't know but it's definitely Venislarn or something like it. I need to go back down there."

"Why?"

She waved the wand at him. "Because there's something going on. And Vivian knew about it. Or knew there was something worth investigating. And that's what we do. We investigate."

"Okay," said Rod. "Not why but shouldn't we seek guidance on this? An impossible space has opened up beneath the city. Vaughn needs to know, and he needs to decide what is done about it."

Nina waved Rod's concern away. "It's okay. I messaged him on Instagram. He knows."

Rod was agog. "Right, I don't know which is more unbelievable, that Vaughn has Instagram or that you think that's the best way to communicate with our boss."

"I need gear," she said and pulled out a box.

He took the box from her. "Those are emergency flares."

"Cool."

"Not in your hands," he said. "It sounds like you're going to need surveying equipment."

"Night vision goggles, those long-distance microphone things with umbrellas on..."

"Surveying, not surveillance." He pulled out a tub and passed her a small black device.

She put down the mouldering brown book she'd brought with her from Soho House and took the gadget. She pressed the button on the side and red laser lines shot out at either end. "Like I'm a mini Darth Maul," she said.

Rod didn't know who that was. "I'm assuming Darth Maul was really into measuring the distances between two walls," he said and pointed at the digital readout which changed as Nina turned and angled the lasers. "I've even got one of these."

He passed her a chunkier device with a 360-camera attachment. He turned it on and held the 360-camera aloft. A patchy but hi-definition 3D model of the room appeared on the screen.

"Now, that is cool," she said.

"Aye, it is," he agreed.

"It's like them thingies off *Aliens*," she said.

He frowned. "Motion detectors?"

"Right."

He went to another tub and took out a piece of kit that looked like a supermarket price scanner. "Good to two hundred metres, depending on conditions. Ooh, and check this out." He passed her a similar looking item. "You know what that is?"

"A tech nerd's best friend."

"Subsurface radar."

"Which is?"

"The ability to see through walls."

"You are kidding me."

"Nope."

"This is like some next-level James Bond *muda*."

"It's just the tools you'd want for the job," he said but couldn't help smiling. It was so rare for someone to appreciate his love of quality gadgetry. "And I'm a bit suspicious about the construction methods used in that space you explored."

"No one built it," said Nina. "It just is."

He shook his head. "Ignoring the fact that such a space can't exist without support beams holding the roof up, I want to know what the walls are made of."

"Why?"

"Let's say walls are made of concrete."

"Do we have to?"

"Then those walls are probably going to be made using ordinary hydraulic cement."

"Words. Just words," she told him.

He maintained his patience. "Cement drying is an exothermic hydration reaction. That means it soaks up liquid and produces heat as it dries. Quite a lot of heat."

Nina closed her eyes and pretended to snore.

"A supposedly infinite cellar with concrete walls would create enough heat to boil you where you stood."

"But we were fine," she said. "Look, I just want to borrow stuff, so we don't get lost down there."

He dropped the smile. "You're not borrowing this 'stuff'."

"But..."

"If I can get out of this film crew babysitting malarkey later in the week then I'll happily accompany you."

"But..."

He put as many things as possible back in tubs and onto high shelves that were out of her reach. "You and expensive gear do not have a good record," he said.

"That's not true."

"That night scope I loaned you?"

"It was dark. I couldn't see where I was going."

"That wearable GPS tracker watch?"

"We know where it is."

"At the bottom of the canal."

"You said it was waterproof to fifty metres or something."

"We'll see when someone finds it."

She huffed. "Well, what can I have?"

Rod looked about. He found his cheapest compass and put it in her hand.

"Really?" she said. "This?"

He gave her a torch. She turned it over. "Is it a special torch?"

"It's a torch."

"Doesn't double as a taser or fire targeting lasers?"

"It's a torch. May I also recommend paper, pencil and a tape measure?"

"Meanie."

"Just protecting my property."

She tutted and answered her ringing phone.

"Hi mom. Yes, yes. I'll be home soon." She paused and then looked at Rod. "Oh, did he? That's nice? Yeah, we got our wires crossed. He didn't need to worry. *You* don't need to worry." Nina's frown deepened. "Pubbing and clubbing? Is that what he said?"

Rod made gestures of denial.

"What *does* he think I get up to?" said Nina. "Boys? And wotnot?"

"I said nothing of the sort," Rod whispered but the telephone conversation had slipped into a rather terse Hindi but Nina's angry gaze was directed purely at Rod.

"Maybe take the laser measurer," he suggested, passing the device back to her.

He expression did not lessen one jot.

"The motion detector?" he suggested and passed that to her too. He suspected he wasn't going to get out of this lightly.

MONDAY

The Mailbox was a huge cuboid building in the centre of the city. Its grand front entrance, at the top of a flight of stone steps, overlooked the screwed up tinfoil edifice of New Street train station, with the A38 flyover between them, like a cordon to keep these two titanic buildings apart. Its rear led out through overpriced restaurants and waterside bars to Gas Street canal basin, only a stone's throw from the Cube and the Venislarn court.

It was here at the Mailbox that the film company had taken up residence.

Private security had checked Rod's ID at the front steps and waved him through, making sure to point him in the direction of the catering rooms and admin space. The vast atrium, several storeys of marbled gantries and balconies overlooking the central space, was clearly what the moviemakers had come to use. In their ridiculous Venislarn-meets-spies movie, this space, stripped of shop fronts and display windows, could serve as a grandiose company headquarters, a supervillain's lair or, just possibly, an abandoned shopping mall.

The army of technicians involved in the film production were housed in blocked off shop spaces to the sides of the atrium. Different factions had put up screens or taped off areas to mark their territory. There was a genuine buzz of activity in the air, but Rod couldn't be sure what anyone was doing. He briefly glimpsed Producer Tammy before being led away by a fresh-faced and enthusiastic youngster, a sort of Tammy-lite. Tammy-lite recited a checklist that included the euphemistic 'filming permissions gained from the temporal authorities' and handed him a daily brief that featured shooting schedules and a list of people he was supposed to 'liaise' with.

Thirty minutes later, he was perched on a folding chair holding a plate piled with Danish pastries and a cup of tea that almost passed for tea. All around him, people hurried with a loud and very public energy although nothing in particular seemed to be happening. Rod wondered if he too ought to be doing something. It took him five minutes to twig, and then he laughed.

The woman in another folding chair looked across.

"Everything okay, hun?" she asked. Next to her, another woman with tattoos running down both her exposed arms, slouched back and snoozed under a baseball cap.

"Sorry," he said. "My first time on a film set."

"And that's funny?"

"It puts me in mind of being in a warzone."

"No one knows what they're doing, and it costs ten million dollars a day?"

"That too, maybe," he said. "I was thinking it's all 'hurry up and wait.'"

"Exciting and boring at the same time."

"Exactly," he said. "And I should just hunker down and do nothing unless someone needs me."

The woman smiled. "And you worked that out on your first day? Well done. I'm Skye. Prosthetics finals and motion-capture application."

"Oh aye? Great," said Rod.

"It means that if a fake tentacle needs its make-up touched up, that's me. And you know when motion capture guys have ping pong balls and dots stuck all over them?"

"Yes?"

"I stick 'em on."

"Got it. Well, I'm Rod. I'm..." He had no idea if Skye knew the Venislarn movie wasn't a hundred percent make-believe. "Blummin' heck, I don't know what I'm meant to be doing. I'm a local liaison."

Skye clicked her fingers. "You're the ex-SAS guy."

"If you like."

Skye slapped the shoulder of the snoozing woman next to her. The woman didn't stir. "Jayda here is our armourer and is in charge of the gadget shop."

"Gadget shop?"

"Oh, yeah," said Skye. "More doohickeys and thingamabobs than James Bond on this production. You read the script?"

"I don't even really know what this film is about," said Rod.

Skye laughed. "Oh, between you and me and anyone else who gives a damn, this film is the biggest pile of horseshit you could ever imagine. Pardon my French. Let me give you the lowdown."

Rod turned to face her more properly. He was abruptly conscious that he had a plate still stacked with three Danishes.

"Pastry?"

She waved them away. "I have a five-minute rule with movie set finger food."

"Rule?"

"Yeah. I either get some within five minutes of craft services setting it out or not at all. Because the grips and drivers will pick through that stuff, and those boys aren't the kind who wash their hands after hitting the head. No, you enjoy your urine cakes."

"Thanks," said Rod and put the pastries aside.

"So, backstory," said Skye. "This film is set in a world where our daily lives are controlled by dark and terrible gods. It's like our world is the foam on a cup of coffee and underneath it's all just monsters and torture. It's like all the shit Clive Barker and David Cronenberg thought was too fucked up to use and they gave Stan Winston a billion dollars to bring it to life."

Rod recognised only one out of the three names and wasn't even sure about that one, but he nodded anyway.

"Taylor Graham plays this superspy character who works for the government agency that keeps all this stuff secret from the public," continued Skye, "because, you know, the public can't cope with the truth. So far, it's basically an R-rated *Men in Black* but with different monsters, right?"

"Aye," said Rod.

"You've got these two sides, the humans and the monsters. Opposing forces. A kind of a cold war situation. And maybe it's all a big metaphor. Maybe this hell that keeps threatening to blow up and consume the world is meant to represent nuclear Armageddon or something. I don't think the writers thought that far ahead. So, into this contrived scenario comes this third force, a secret organisation, determined to bring the status quo to an end."

"Okay?"

"They begin to play the two sides off each other. A terrorist attack here, an assassination there. Did I say it was contrived?"

"You did."

"Contrived and derivative," said Skye. "Standard movie plot. You get two people who should be enemies and to make them team up for some buddy-cop nonsense, you create an even greater enemy for them to fight against. And so, Taylor gets to team up with Langford's character, who is basically a fish."

"A fish?"

"Right," she said. "As I said, steaming pile of horseshit. Forget that it's James Bond meets *Finding Nemo*, I've had it up to here with movie scripts where there's a massive secret that the government are keeping hidden from the public. I don't buy any of that conspiracy bull."

"No?" said Rod, sipping his tea.

"If the government can't keep the president's sex scandals under wraps, how are we expected to believe that they can keep a shadow world of gods and monsters from us?"

"Good point."

"We're just not that stupid," said Skye.

Morag poured out another cup of tea in the office kitchenette, sniffed it, poked it, poured milk in and considered its colour.

"Are we expecting company?" said Kathy.

There were half a dozen mugs of hot tea on the counter.

"It's a magically refilling teapot," said Morag.

"It is," said Kathy.

"Although it only fills up an inch or two. And..." She lifted it up above her head to look at the underside. "Venislarn runes painted onto the bottom."

"*Khelleq... ash n'tarh...* It's a detection spell mixed with some conjuration phrases."

"Possibly beyond the abilities of Mystic Trevor," said Morag. "The important question is—"

"What's it for?" said Kathy.

"—is it safe to drink?" said Morag.

Kathy shrugged, took one of the mugs and noisily slurped. "Only one way to find out."

When Kathy didn't immediately drop dead, Morag took a cup for herself. It certainly didn't taste deadly. In fact, it was a near perfect cuppa.

"But you have to drink up or bring it with you," said Kathy. "I told the professor we'd be over at the Think Tank before ten."

100

"Where they make artificial souls."

"*Fraxasa*, yes."

Morag drank half a cup and poured all the others down the sink. If they now had a magic teapot in the office, she could afford to be wasteful.

They walked to the multi-storey car park where Kathy had parked. As Kathy drove down the ramps to the exit, she offered Morag a bourbon from the packet in the well of the dashboard and took one for herself.

With one hand on the steering wheel, Kathy posted a bourbon between her lips and didn't bite until she had put the biscuit packet down and freed up her hand.

"I'll start that diet one day," she said.

"Diets are over-rated," said Morag.

Kathy jiggled a little to indicate her own body. "You'd think going to the gym four times a week and doing energetic martial arts training would be enough to stay in shape. It's almost like my body wants me to starve myself."

Kathy wove the car through the mess of roadworks that was Paradise Circus and somehow came out pointing in the right direction.

"So, what martial arts do you do?" said Morag.

"Hmm?"

"Judo? Aikido?"

"Bartitsu."

Morag coughed. "Bartitsu?"

"Yes."

"Bar? Tit? Su?"

"Yes."

"You just made that up."

"It's a British martial art. It's a sort of down and dirty fist and stick fighting technique. I belong to a club."

"Bartitsu?"

"You can repeat it as often as you like," laughed Kathy. "It's a real thing. It's the fighting technique Sherlock Holmes used."

Morag looked at her. "You are aware he's a fictional character? Bartitsu?"

"Oh, shut up," said Kathy. "We're here."

101

In a cellar storage room beneath Soho House, Nina cleared space on a table and put down her rucksack of explorer's gear. It landed with a solid clunk.

"Someone came prepared," said Mrs Fiddler.

"I'm a professional," said Nina.

"It's a Thomas the Tank Engine rucksack," the old teacher pointed out.

"It's what I could find."

"That policeman not with you today?"

"No," said Nina, trying not to pout. "Apparently, he has 'proper' police work to do today."

Nina wondered if Mrs Fiddler had eavesdropped on Nina's rather loud telephone conversation with Ricky in the car park. Ricky did have proper police work to do. He also had an ultimatum from his wife about what would happen if he came home late again with a cock-and-bull story as to why. So, she had come alone today. The wand they had found yesterday was safely in her underbed drawer at home. Technically, she should have delivered it to the Vault and Professor Sheikh Omar, but she wasn't quite ready to share this personal investigation with him after his dismissive attitude yesterday.

"We will try to do our best without your policeman friend, shan't we?" said Mrs Fiddler.

Mrs Fiddler had come dressed for a school trip. Her blousy clothes of yesterday had been replaced with practical trousers and jumper. There was a pair of stout boots on her feet, as though she expected to be climbing a mountain.

"I don't expect you to come with me," said Nina.

"Are you telling me not to come with you?" said Mrs Fiddler.

"Do I need to?"

Mrs Fiddler gave her a thoughtful look. "You don't work for the police, do you?"

"No."

"But it's some sort of governmental investigative body?"

"Some sort."

"And I suppose if you were unwilling to accept the Birmingham Museum Service's assistance and got all uppity about it, there would be a number I could ring, some noises I could make about the lack of proper warrants or permissions? Something of that ilk?"

"School teachers are meant to be nice people," Nina told her.

"I retired," said Mrs Fiddler. "And I brought my own rucksack. I've got provisions for a full day. Sandwiches, cake bars, emergency Kendall mint cake, lots of water."

"We're not going on a picnic."

"What have you brought?"

"Wham bars."

"Wham bars?"

"And Boost."

"Boost?

Nina half-lifted a heavy bottle of energy drink out of her bag to show her. "It's got sugars. It's got caffeine. Everything you need. It's a no brainer."

"No brainer," echoed Mrs Fiddler.

Nina returned the bottle to the bag and retrieved Vivian's key. The wall at the far end of the storeroom was currently blank, with no door or any sign there had been one there the day before. Nina supposed it had vanished at some point in the night after she had removed the key.

"Be sure to video this," said Nina.

"With what?"

Nina sighed and passed her phone to the woman. Working with the elderly was going to be a challenge.

Nina went to the ornate ormolu star clock by the wall, inserted the key into the hole and gave it a firm twist to the right. The clock began to tick.

"Filming?" said Nina.

"How do I do that?" said Mrs Fiddler.

"You're not filming?"

The sounds of the ticking expanded, seemingly moving off into spaces beyond the physical form of the clock.

"I don't know where the camera function is," said Mrs Fiddler.

"It's the one that looks like a camera."

"I can't see one that looks like a camera."

Nina glanced at the wall. The door had not yet magically appeared. The ticks and tocks had become creaks and whirrs and clunks within the house generally. She hurried to Mrs Fiddler and looked at the screen.

"Swipe," she said. "Swipe. Next screen."

She snatched the camera from the useless woman, found the correct icon herself and started filming. Still no door.

The ticking sound was fading, travelling away, like a marching band leaving town.

"Any moment now," said Nina.

The ticking stopped.

"Any moment now."

A door did not appear. Not even a small one. Nina waited a full minute, camera held to capture the moment, but a door didn't appear.

With such an early start, Rod had expected the film crew to be shooting from the off: setting up, shooting and moving on, possibly with someone shouting, "Come on, folks! We're losing daylight!" every now and then. In truth, there seemed to be nothing but setting up and much of that seemed fixated with the light. Black sheets on high scaffolding to block the light, mirrored surfaces to reflect it, hazy white canvasses to diffuse it.

Rod hung with Skye the tentacle make-up artist and Jayda the armourer who were experts at managing on-set boredom. Jayda's technique, clearly learned from a past career in the US Army, was to sleep, whenever and wherever was possible. Skye passed the time by applying makeup and prosthetics to anyone willing to submit to her skills. By mid-morning, she had stuck a third ear to a runner's forehead, had given the second assistant director's second assistant some very convincing facial blisters and had grafted a prosthetic penis onto the back of the shoulder of a sleeping Jayda. It was small, floppy and disturbingly realistic.

"Isn't she going to be upset when she wakes?" asked Rod, while Skye painted a realistic gunshot wound onto his upper cheek.

"Pissed," agreed Skye happily. "But I do it all the time. My record is four," she said, pointing out spots on her own body that were apparently prime penis-location sites. "And I used Krazy Glue that time. She couldn't pull 'em off."

"Dare I ask," said Rod. "Why do you own so many fake... um..."

"A personal hobby," said Skye, layering flaps of fake skin around Rod's fake wound.

"A personal hobby," said Rod, careful to not make a question of it.

Skye nodded and picked up a bottle of fake blood to touch up Rod's injury. "Yeah. They're a technical challenge, particularly if you want them to look right when they jiggle." She did a little shake in case Rod didn't know what 'jiggle' meant. "I build them all up from plaster casts."

"Right," he said. "And when you say plaster casts...?"

Skye finished dabbing blood in Rod's wound and turned to her shelf of materials and tools. She tapped a tub of plaster of Paris. "Yeah, plaster casts. Maybe later, if there's time, we can add yours to the collection."

Rod suddenly realised that, behind the pots and bottles on the shelf, there was a row of white plaster ornaments. All of them were standing to attention. The largest ones leaned over the tops of the pots. Less proud ones could be seen peering through the spaces between.

Rod stood abruptly, panicked.

"No, ta. That's a... a really kind offer. But I, I..."

Skye laughed. It was a warm laugh, genuinely amused and perhaps meant to put him at ease but, right now, she was the scariest creature in the universe.

"So, it's true," she said, "you British guys all go into full-blown Hugh Grant mode when anyone mentions sex."

"You caught me off guard," he said.

The door opened. Rod whirled, feeling like he'd been caught in some horribly shameful act.

"Ah, here you are," said Chad from PR. "They're setting up and wanted your opinion on something. Taylor Graham wants the SAS hero to give his weapons the once-over—Oh, my God. What happened to your face?"

"What?" said Rod.

"Have you been stabbed? Shall I call the paramedics?"

Rod put his hand to his face and the fake wound. Chad already had his phone out.

"It's okay," said Rod. "It's a gunshot wound."

"Oh, Christ," said Chad.

"A fake one."

Chad's face curled in surprise and disgust. "Are you sure?"

"Aye, I'm sure."

"Because you look awfully pale, Rod."

"Well, yes."

"Like you've seen a ghost."

Rod's eyes flicked to the shelf of white plaster cast penises. "No. No, not ghosts."

Skye covered her mouth to hide her laughter. "Go on. You're needed, Rod. We'll have time for fun and games later."

"Right," he said, making a mental note never to come in here again and knowing that a parade of ghostly penises would haunt his dreams.

The automatic doors opened, and Morag looked inside.

"It's a museum," she said.

"It's the Think Tank," said Kathy.

"It's a children's science museum. It's got a gift shop."

"And it's our scientific research centre," said Kathy.

Kathy had driven them over to a campus-like development on the edges of the city centre. Three months into the job and Morag's city geography was still a little hazy but she gauged that if the city was over *there* and Aston University was *there* then the consular mission's storage facility, the Dumping Ground, was just over there – probably near the railway arches Morag had seen from the car park.

Morag felt irritated that the new woman on the team was introducing her to one of their facilities, but Kathy had been in Birmingham far longer than Morag.

"And we need a scientific research centre?" said Morag.

"Of course," said Kathy, as they walked in, past the customer entrance and into a hall of hands-on exhibits: hydraulic diggers and ball pools, model canals with working locks, an oversized scale-model of the human digestive system.

"But we have the Vault," said Morag.

106

"That's more like a library. It's just storage."

"We have the Dumping Ground for storage."

"Bulk storage."

"I just assumed that anything experimental went on at the Restricted Ward," said Morag.

Kathy raised an eyebrow. "You've visited us at the Restricted Ward. We're more about containment than anything as refined as research."

They stood on a gantry. A World War Two spitfire hung from the ceiling over a ground floor collection of vintage cars, steam engines and trams.

"The old science museum moved here in the late nineties," said Kathy. "Everyone complained that, despite the size of this place, it wasn't as big inside as the old museum. Half the old exhibits were retired from display. There's the big screen cinema and some university offices in the other wing but no one really questioned what the rest of the building was being used for."

"Why not?"

"People are stupid?" said Kathy with a shrug. "Fooling the public is remarkably easy. Also, the old museum had been free to enter but the prices at this place..." She whistled expensively. "It's good to keep the number of visitors down."

She swiped her ID badge over a tall cream panel in a wall of identical cream panels and a door swung inward.

"Morning," said the security guard by the inner door.

Morag was surprised. "Malcolm? I thought you worked down at the Library."

"They have us on rotation between facilities," said the ex-soldier. "Can't have the first line of defence getting bored. Me and Bob enjoy our alternate Mondays down here."

"ID, Miss Murray," said the rotund Bob on the other side of the doorway.

"Bob, it's me," said Morag.

"ID please."

"You literally ID'ed me as I walked in. You saw me and recognised my face and—"

"Rules is rules."

"Stupid rules," she said and found her ID card.

Bob peered at it critically as he had every right to. Her identity card photo was a cut and paste image of the Marvel superhero, Black Widow. Morag was disgusted that several months into the job, no one seemed to have noticed. Bob handed the card back and Malcolm swiped them through.

The interior of the mission's Think Tank facility had clearly been fitted out by the same people who had constructed the Vault. White walls, spotless tiling and tinted glass panels said, 'we may be tackling unspeakable horrors on a daily basis, but that doesn't mean we can't have bright, clean workspaces'.

"I never knew about this place," said Morag.

"I'd heard rumours about it," said Kathy, "and applied for a tech support role here. But that pleasure went to... ah."

Professor Sheikh Omar approached them from a corridor of glass-partitioned cubicles and labs. He carried a pair of light goggles in his hand. Rainbow colours shifted and danced across the lenses.

"Still working on that portable disco prototype, I see," said Morag.

"Pardon?" said the professor.

Morag indicated the colourful goggles.

"Abyssal filters," said Kathy. "There's a dial on the side and—"

"Yes, thank you, doctor," said Professor Omar. "If you will drag me here to give a guided tour, then at least let me do it. As the doctor said, Miss Murray, there's a control on the side of the goggles. The lenses can be tuned to filter out images above a specified abyssal rating. Our goal is to protect wearers who are sensitive to occult phenomena from images they may find disturbing. We're still in the developmental phase."

"Doesn't work?" said Kathy.

"Oh, it works perfectly, my dear, but the applications are dubious. I have very little interest in protecting delicate souls from the realities of the world. If they needed safe spaces and trigger warnings, then they shouldn't have left university. Now, if we can invert the technology and show the wearer the world as it *really* is..."

Omar cracked a smile. He had neat white teeth, like a genial predator who knew which cutlery to use for which course.

He turned and began to walk without checking they were following. He walked with deliberately long strides.

"Kathy tells me that you two are interested in the synthetic *fraxasa* project?"

"*Yo-Morgantus* wants twenty-eight human souls by tomorrow night."

"Oh, that's easy," said Omar.

"Yes?"

"Give him twenty-eight people."

Morag pursed her lips. "These people are innocent."

"I heard they were self-described Venislarnkin."

"Yes."

"Then they're not innocent."

Morag made a grumpy noise. "Being wee idiots is not a criminal offence."

Omar stopped and swung round to look at her. "It really ought to be," he said.

He tapped at a window. On the other side, a pair of white coats were working in front of a large screen, one of them wearing some sort of eye-tracking gear. On the screen was a two by two grid of images. Images were selected and replaced with further images.

"I'm not on social media," said Omar. "Maurice does this thing called Pinterest. Lots of pictures of design fabrics and cupcake recipes as far as I can tell. Anyway, I gather there are these quizzes. 'What kind of vegetable are you?' and 'Which Harry Potter character would be your ideal date?' and so on. This is one of a series featuring subtle Venislarn imagery, designed to identify those demographics most likely to show resistance when the Venislarn are publicly revealed. Of course, we've been using such quizzes to gather data on people for years."

"There are laws about that now."

Omar scowled. "How else are we supposed to profile an entire planet's population? We need to know our clientele. Meanwhile, yare apparently focussing your time and efforts on temporarily saving the lives of twenty-eight useless introverts, so..."

He beckoned them on.

"So how do you synthesise souls?" said Morag. "It sounds..."

"Stupid?" suggested Omar. "Put the word 'soul' to one side. As best as we can tell, we live in a materialistic universe. There are no spirits. There is no true divinity. There's only the science we understand and the science we don't. A spiritualist talks of the soul. A scientist talks of consciousness. And how do we create consciousness?"

Morag might have imagined it but, for a moment, Omar seemed to incline his head back and down as though nodding in acknowledgement of the thing growing in her belly. Thing. She still wasn't ready to think of it as a human life.

"Artificial consciousness then," said Kathy. "AI?"

Omar stopped in front of a set of double doors. The glass here was frosted. There was a security panel at the side of the door but also a set of bolts and a padlock.

"My predecessor—my mad genius predecessor, Ingrid—was working on an on-going computer simulation programme. Modelling, they call it, don't they? If you can model something, you can understand it, even predict it."

"Even learn how to stop it?" said Kathy.

"Stop the Venislarn?" said Omar with an arch look.

"I was thinking more of how computer modelling is used to predict disease outbreaks."

Omar took out a set of keys.

"Double security?" said Kathy.

"Omar's secret treasure trove," said Morag.

Omar removed the padlock. "Every man needs a place of personal seclusion. A shed, a study—"

"A secret lab," said Morag.

"Quite," he said. "For pet projects."

"I thought this was Ingrid's old project," said Kathy.

Omar swiped the security panel and ushered them in. "And it was failing," he said.

The large space beyond was filled, for the most part, with computer arrays and router cabinets. Omar put his keys down on a desk and walked towards a circular white plastic tank the size of a garden swimming pool the far end of the room.

"Computers are like chefs. I'm very much impressed by what they can do but I've no idea how they do it and, frankly, I don't care either. But apparently, they have limits. Computers, not chefs. Well, both. Computers can predict the weather, plot missions to Mars, but as for meaningfully simulating human minds—souls—humanity simply lacks the processing power. *Humanity.*"

Something inside the tank made a glooping sound.

"What's that?" said Kathy.

"Extra processing power," said Omar. "Are you ladies familiar with Operation Paperclip?"

"You have a Nazi scientist in there?" said Kathy.

"A political dissident," said Omar and then called out. "*Shan-shan prui. Ma ghu'qani, velgondu.*"

Something corpse-pale and wet rose above the edge of the tank for a leisurely moment, dripping with blue, translucent ooze, then sank again.

"You have a captive Venislarn?" said Morag.

Omar laughed lightly. "Not a captive. A friend who needed a place to lie low for a while." He swept his arm generally towards the tank. "Ladies, I'd like you to meet *Polliqan Riti*. A house guest, if you like, but one who's been of enormous help since he came over."

Morag approached the tank cautiously, ready to give an earful of abuse and a Glasgow kiss to anything that leapt out at her.

"Came over from where?" she said.

"Hell," said Omar simply. "*Polliqan Riti* is an escapee from hell."

Nina rapped on the wall. She moved along, tapping with her knuckles, hoping to hear a change in sound that indicated a wooden door hiding just beneath the surface.

"Maybe if we just hammer away the top layer," she suggested.

"I don't think that would be appropriate," said Mrs Fiddler.

"Rod gave me a radar scanner thingy."

"Clearly something different has happened compared to yesterday."

"I put the key in, and I turned it," said Nina. "What else is different?"

"Who can say? Maybe it's something to do with the time of day. It's a clock, after all."

"Maybe it isn't wound up properly," said Nina.

Mr Fiddler slipped the winding key from a rear compartment and turned it in the squared hole in the clock face. The ratchet sound of the tightening spring was loud and decisive.

"See?" said Nina. "Just needed winding. Do it nice and tight. Bit more."

Mrs Fiddler paused meaningfully. "Do you want us to break this antique with over-winding?"

"Fine," Nina muttered.

Mrs Fiddler finished winding and removed the key. The clock did nothing. No door appeared.

Nina removed Vivian's key and then reinserted it. Nothing.

"But it worked before."

Mrs Fiddler took a step back. "Maybe it didn't."

"But it did, you daft—" Nina bit down on an ageist insult.

"We visited a previously undiscovered cellar of frankly impossible proportions. After descending an equally impossible stairway. Which is more likely, Nina? That it happened or that you and I and that policeman experienced a shared hallucinatory experience brought on by"—She raised her hands—"an unknown factor."

Nina went to her bag and pulled out the ancient brown book. Lugging it around in a bag full of sweets, fizzy drinks and tech gear she'd emotionally blackmailed off Rod probably wasn't the proper way to handle it. But it was here, and it was real.

"I got this downstairs," she said. "And I read it last night."

Mrs Fiddler looked at the thick tome. "You read it."

"Bits of it," said Nina. "I skimmed through it really hard. There were some long words."

"Long words."

"Exactly."

"And the whole book's hand-written. Joined up handwriting too. Do you know how difficult it is to read joined up handwriting?"

"Perhaps it might be best if we head upstairs, make ourselves a nice cup of tea and look at some of those long words together."

Nina sighed wearily.

"Or you could stay in this little room and just be annoyed with yourself," said the ex-teacher.

"Fine," snapped Nina and followed her old teacher, Thomas the Tank Engine rucksack on her back.

Nina stomped up the steps to the ground floor hallway.

"Remember what I said about this house when Boulton moved into it?" said Mrs Fiddler.

"Is this a test?" said Nina.

"If you like." Mrs Fiddler stood in the hallway and looked back and forth along its length. "I mentioned that this house used to be bigger. Half of it was knocked down when the building fell into disrepair."

"You said."

"And this hallway used to be much longer but now ends at that wall over there."

Nina looked. "You mean where that door is?"

"Yes, exactly," said Mrs Fiddler.

In the hidden consular mission labs in the Think Tank museum, the thing in the tub rippled and shifted.

"*Shan-shan*," said Kathy Kaur and bowed reverently.

The Venislarn lump made no response. It floated in a pool of its own translucent blue-yellow grease, appendages reaching out with slug-like slowness and with seemingly no intent or intelligence.

"It looks like a fatberg," said Morag.

Kathy approached the edge of the tub and watched its occupant's body split, loop and reconnect. "It's a unicellular lifeform."

"Ah, well, the scientific specifics are a little beyond me," said Omar. "I'm a student of the arts, nothing so humdrum as the physical sciences. I'm an intellectual, not a rude mechanical. But as I understand, though our guest is composed of undifferentiated cells—"

"Like algae?" said Morag.

"—he remains a single and whole being, one deserving of a bit more respect from Miss Murray and... Doctor?"

"Yes," said Kathy, her hand hovering over the tank edge.

"Be careful. We have lost at least one member of staff who got too familiar."

"It's carnivorous?"

113

"Its needs are greater than our own," said Omar, which struck Morag as a peculiar phrase.

Kathy withdrew her hand.

"How is this Venislarn relevant to the data modelling project Ingrid was working on?" said Morag.

"My dear, it is essential. The cells of *Polliqan Riti's* body form a neural network, though they're also aligned in protein-like filaments that act like—"

"Muscle," said Kathy. "He's composed entirely of brain and muscle," she nodded.

Omar sighed petulantly. "It's almost as if I'm not needed. Are you sure you don't wish to take this job from me, Dr Kaur? I believe Vaughn Sitterson did offer it to you."

"But it's a giant brain, yeah?" said Morag.

Omar nodded. "A think tank in the Think Tank. The gods have no poetry in their souls."

"And you're harnessing *Polliqan Riti's* brainpower to run the simulations," said Kathy.

"Exactly. A spoonful of his brain matter has more processing power than..." He fished around for the right words. "I did have some young enthusiastic type give me the numbers once."

Kathy looked round. "And are they about?"

"He got too familiar," said Omar pointedly.

Morag watched the ripples in the creature's ghostly pale flesh. "You know, for a big brain-muscle, he's kinda... passive."

"*Yam dei*, Morag. *Polliqan Riti* is resting. He has travelled a long way and he has many enemies."

Morag had known Sheikh Omar only a little over two months and, although he was far from being a friend (quite far indeed), she had come to know him as well as she knew anyone in this city. She could sense his mood.

"You said *Polliqan Riti* is a dissident."

"Yes," said Omar.

"On the run from his fellow Venislarn?"

"A minor misunderstanding."

"But we—that is, you—are hiding him from the gods we are duty-bound to serve."

Omar spread his arms. "You make it sound so covert and clandestine and... *grubby*."

"Oh. My. God," said Kathy, a grin breaking out on her face. "Our bosses don't know about this, do they?"

"They don't have to," said Omar.

"You're playing both sides," said Morag.

"Now, you're making it sound not only grubby but sinister."

"Hedging your bets, professor?" said Kathy.

"I'm a realist."

"A coward," said Morag.

"It's the same thing."

"So, just to be clear," said Morag, "we owe *Yo-Morgantus* twenty-eight souls, and we're going to cook some up in a computer simulation powered by a renegade Venislarn you're hiding from both sides, whose very existence would cost us our jobs if discovered by our side or our lives if discovered by theirs."

"That is essentially it," said Omar.

"Essentially?"

"Exactly. That's exactly it."

"So, we should report you to Vaughn at once."

"If you don't want to save those twenty-eight so-called Venislarnkin."

"And you're helping us because?"

"A man enjoys a challenge, dear."

Morag looked at Kathy. Kathy looked at Morag.

"Fine," said Morag sullenly.

"Wonderful," said Omar. "Now, wait here while I get the interface equipment."

"Interface equipment?" said Kathy.

"Of course," grinned the professor. "How are you going to understand the simulation, unless you go inside it?"

"So, it's VR goggles and silly gloves, is it?" said Morag.

"Not at all," said Omar and then his expression became thoughtful. "Although that would be far more pleasant."

"It's magic," said Mrs Fiddler.

"It's not magic," said Nina.

They had opened the door at the end of the hallway in Soho House, the door that hadn't existed five minutes before, and looked down a corridor that extended past rooms that had not been there previously. They had then taken themselves outside and walked all the way round the restored Georgian house, even squeezing through the bushes by the fence to inspect a wall that was, from the outside, definitely still a wall and not part of a newly created corridor. They went back inside, brushed the leaves and cobwebs off their clothes and looked down the new corridor again.

"This shouldn't be here," said Mrs Fiddler.

"But it used to be here," said Nina.

"But it shouldn't be here now. And it's back – on the inside of the house, but not the outside."

"Correct."

Mrs Fiddler toyed with the chunky buttons of her cardigan. "This building is now bigger on the inside than on the outside."

"Yes."

"But that's not possible. It defies any kind of empirical analysis."

"I'm not sure."

"You can explain this?" said Mrs Fiddler.

"No. I mean I don't know what 'empirical' means," said Nina.

"So, it's magic."

Nina groaned. "Yeah, well, technically maybe, but there's no need to call it that."

"Why not?"

"Because it sounds lame. It's like when my mum calls the remote control a 'doofer'."

"I call it the doofer," said Mrs Fiddler, happily.

"Exactly. Don't call it magic. It is what it is, okay?"

Mrs Fiddler hummed, uneasily and looked along the corridor. "I'll need to get a sash barrier to put across the door."

"Why?

"We don't want members of the public wandering into a corridor that's technically not there."

"And one of them little rope things will stop them?"

116

Mrs Fiddler looked offended. "Nobody goes past the barrier, Nina. Everyone knows that. People start going past sash barriers and what next? Thin end of the wedge," she tutted.

"I had a colleague who used to say that. *Thin end of the wedge.* Like, if I didn't use a coaster for my cup of tea, the world would explode or something."

"Sounds like a sensible person."

"She was. I guess. Mrs Grey. I found the vase and the key in her house."

"And she's not around anymore because she's... dead?" said Mrs Fiddler.

"I hope not," said Nina. "I'm hoping that if I get to the bottom of this mystery"—she waved her hand down the brand-new corridor with the dusty floors and peeling wallpaper—"then maybe I'll find out what happened to her."

Mrs Fiddler's wrinkly brow wrinkled further. "What precisely do you do for a living, Nina?"

"I work for a secret government department that handles all the unexplained weird shit that the public are better off not knowing about."

"Or some other word that isn't rude," said Mrs Fiddler reproachfully.

"Weird shit is just weird shit," said Nina.

"Or you could call it magic," suggested Mrs Fiddler.

Nina made a strangled noise and set off down the corridor.

The upper corridor of a Birmingham shopping centre had been transformed by Hollywood magic into an evil industrialist's base of operations. The magic in question was the second assistant director declaring loudly that this was the baddies' hideout, or "the antagonist's base of operations" to be precise.

"That's the second, second assistant director, not the second assistant director," said Jayda the armourer, from behind the table on which she kept prop guns, fake armaments and other specialist toys.

"Second, second?" said Rod. "How many assistant directors are there?"

Jayda shrugged. She still had a small but perfectly formed penis glued to the back of her shoulder. Either she hadn't noticed, or she was brazening it out to make a point.

"You can count," she said. "If they're holding a clipboard and a walkie talkie and shouting at people, they're probably an assistant director."

As far as Rod could tell, that described nearly half the people in sight.

"In this shot, Agent Jack Steele and Fin are going to come down the side here," continued the second, second assistant director, "scope out this doorway, pick the lock and go in."

Taylor Graham and Langford James were escorted to the armourer's table by a short woman who—clipboard, check; walkie talkie, check—was probably an assistant director. Graham was wearing a dark suit and tie. James, the motion capture guy, was wearing an ornate three-quarter length leather and brocade jacket over a hideous bodysuit covered in white dots and red stripes.

"Okay, standard drill," said Jayda. She picked up a Sig Sauer pistol, checked it, showed the assistant director she was checking it and passed it to Taylor. "It's unloaded. But, as always..."

"Treat it like it's loaded until we know," said Taylor, grinned at Rod and then slid it into the shoulder holster under his jacket. He flicked a finger back and forth between himself and Rod. "Look at us. Twins."

Rod tried to look amenable.

"Are you carrying?" said Taylor and nodded at the slight but unmistakeable bulge in Rod's jacket.

"On set?" said Jayda alarmed.

"You look the part," said Rod.

"But would an agent be carrying something like this?"

"SIG Sauer P226," said Rod reflectively. "A solid handgun choice."

Jayda passed Langford his gun. It looked like someone had taken a perfectly adequate handgun, dipped it in slime and wrapped seaweed around it.

"And that?" said Rod.

"A design choice," said Jayda, in a tone that suggested it was someone else's design and she didn't have a choice.

"A *samakha* weapon for a *samakha* prince," said Langford. "Is this right?"

Rod, who knew no self-respecting fish-boy would be seen holding an ugly piece like this, held his tongue.

"And lock picks," said Jayda, putting a matte grey hexagonal case in Taylor's hand. "Just the box. They're not doing close ups for this one."

"You use lock picks?" Taylor asked Rod.

Rod took off his tie clip, twisted it apart with thumb and forefinger and held up the two tool pieces.

"Sir, that is kind of cool," said Langford.

"I got to get me one of those," said Taylor.

"That's not SAS issue," said Jayda.

Rod nodded. "Mail order. From the States."

She scoffed. "That amateur escapology shit will fall apart in the field."

Rod pulled at the wire thread woven into his survival bracelet. "Sawed my way out of a torture chamber with this piece of wire."

"Bull shit," she said, making two separate words of it.

He held up his left hand and waggled the stump of his little finger, which had been amputated at the first knuckle.

"Ninety-nine point nine percent successful escape," he said.

Jayda sneered at the looks of boyish admiration on the two actors' faces.

"You see this?" she said, tapping her shoulder with the prosthetic penis glued to it. "You know what this means?"

"You really need to see a doctor?" said Taylor.

"What? No." Then Jayda noticed the fake willy and, with a growl, ripped it off viciously and threw it down on the ground. It might have been entirely fake but that didn't stop Rod wincing. "Gonna kill that Skye," she snarled. "*This!*" She stabbed her finger on the bulldog tattoo at the top of her shoulder. "You see *this*?"

"We do," said Langford.

"US Marine Corps," said Taylor. "Semper Fi."

"And you can trust a former marine when she tells you, none of this crap is what you need in the field." A wave of her hand took in the gadgets and props on her own table.

"It looks great," said the assistant producer with hasty cheeriness. "We all set? Let's go."

As she herded the actors away, Rod tucked the wire back into his survival bracelet.

"I fought alongside marines at the Battle of Al-Qa'im."

"Is that so?" said Jayda.

"Second Gulf War. Glad to have soldiers like that at my back."

She nodded, appreciating the compliment. "Eleven days straight of fighting, right? I read about it."

Rod recalled his own personal battles of that time, underneath the Syrian Desert, a fight against something other than Iraqi insurgents. He remembered the dark cool tunnels, the clammy flesh of men who were no longer men but something other.

Chad strolled over. "This is all very exciting," he grinned. "So glitzy. So showbiz."

"Oh, aye," said Rod who could only see expensive, organised chaos.

Chad knelt and picked up the crushed and trampled prosthetic penis.

"What's this? Is that...?" He dropped it in revulsion.

"That it is," said Rod and jerked his head towards Jayda. "She ripped it clean off."

"What?"

"Former US Marine," he explained. "Don't mess with them, that's my advice."

The floorboards of the newly-appeared corridor creaked beneath Nina's feet. Each footstep threw up little clouds of dust. Nina looked at the green and black patches of mould growing on the walls and imagined that the little dust clouds were full of fungal spores. To avoid inhaling them she tried not breathing for a bit, but it didn't last.

Nina filmed on her phone with one hand and waved about the motion detector she had borrowed from Rod with the other. She did this not because she thought there might be any motion to detect but because she felt a shameful need to look professional in front of old Mrs Fiddler.

"After the Boulton family sold Soho House in 1850, it went through a number of incarnations before it became a museum," said Mrs Fiddler. "It was used as a home, then as a store. It was a hostel for police officers for a time and it was bought by the council a little over twenty years ago. Over the decades, it fell into disrepair and this section was knocked down. Well, *had been* knocked down. Was *for a time* knocked down before, well, it's not knocked down now, obviously."

"Uh-huh," said Nina, waving the motion detector in front of a door frame because it seemed the cool thing to do.

"I was merely reflecting that this is possibly what this section of the house might have looked like if it had not been knocked down and had simply been allowed to fester."

Nina reached the end of the corridor. A dirty and frankly dangerous-looking staircase led up to the first floor. She looked back along the corridor at the row of closed doors.

"Upstairs?" she said. "Or pick a door."

"I had another theory," said Mrs Fiddler. "An additional theory."

"You're just full of them, aren't you?"

"I think the house has woken up."

"Okay," said Nina slowly. "I mean, to a regular person that sounds like you just said something stupid."

"It's a magic house."

"Oh puh-lease."

"The house has awoken. This wing is the house awake."

"It's like you're having a stroke and you've forgotten what words mean."

"Do not be rude, Nina Seth, or I will put your name on the sad side of the board!"

Despite the fact that Nina was no longer ten but the ultimate primary school sanction still hit her in her guilt centres.

"Sorry, miss."

"But before we wake, we dream, we stretch, we put our crazy thoughts in order. What we experienced yesterday: I said it was a cancer, cells growing unchecked. I think yesterday in the cellar, that was the house dreaming, the yawn before awaking."

121

"But..." Nina put her rucksack down and took out the old and crumbling book. "I picked this up. It's still here. If that was a dream then this should have vanished too."

"We carry memories from our dreams into our waking lives," said Mrs Fiddler. "And it's possible to over-extend a metaphor."

"I have no idea what you're on about. Let's just pick a door and have a nose about, eh?"

Morag and Kathy sat in office chairs near the edge of *Polliqan Riti's* tank while Professor Sheikh Omar fought with a box of wet tubing that looked like a Victorian butcher's delight.

"You're not sticking that stuff anywhere near my face," Morag said.

"I'm not," Omar agreed. "It's plugging into your spine."

"I'm not overly happy with 'plugging'," said Kathy.

"Nothing permanent," said the professor, smiling. "Just an adaptation of the sensory feedback systems the August Handmaidens of *Prein* use with their human lovers."

Drew, the man who had fathered the anti-Christ now growing inside Morag, had once shown her the circle of puckered flesh on the back of his neck.

"Adapted from their system," she said. "You haven't actually got Handmaiden 'off-cuts' there, have you?"

He clucked like a patiently exasperated mother. "It is all fine, Miss Murray. It's just a means to connect two minds," he said, stepping behind her and, without warning, placing something cold and wet against her neck. "Nothing to worry about at all."

The world flew away from Morag, her last image of the real world smearing upwards in a colourless tube that grew darker and greyer as she descended.

Down the rabbit-hole like Alice, she thought.

.

.

.

She touched down on ground that took a moment to solidify beneath her feet. But it did feel real. She looked at her hands, flexed them, clapped them. She was in a place that felt and looked real and as she looked round she recognised it as a real place.

She was inside St Philip's Cathedral in Pigeon Park. The cathedral was no larger than many parish churches and it was crowded by densely packed pews that made it seem even smaller. Looking at the stained-glass windows, she realised that this created world was not exactly like the real world. Its colours were crisper, clearer and more primary – like an Instagram filter for people desperate to show how real they were.

Morag understood why she was here. She had been thinking about Drew in the moments before this virtual world came into being. Drew's jealous Handmaiden lover had murdered him in this cathedral and left his castrated, headless corpse on this altar less than twelve hours after he'd shown Morag the interface mark on his neck during sex in her Bourneville flat.

The altar in the virtual cathedral was bare. If this dreamscape responded to her memories and thoughts, she could re-imagine it as it was that day: Drew's ravaged body laid out in a sacrilege of Christ's death, real blood on the altar for the holy communion.

She turned away, lest those thoughts become a reality, and strode angrily towards the door. As she walked, she thought. Any horrible memory from her past could be made flesh here, and since this was only a virtual reality any Venislarn monsters she imagined into being had better not piss her off. She had killed them before and, in here, she could kill them again with no consequences.

When she stepped outside and onto the vibrantly green lawns of Pigeon Park, she found she was holding a shotgun. She didn't need to check it was loaded.

"Boom," she said to herself. "Yep, I'm ready for you bitches."

She went off in search of Kathy.

Nina and Mrs Fiddler explored the rooms, one by one and found nothing more exciting than rags and brick fragments. Damp and ruin clung to the place.

"It's not what I expected," said Mrs Fiddler, while they inspected a bare room containing a table with a broken leg and a painting on the wall consumed by mould.

"Not what you were expecting?" said Nina.

"Magically hidden rooms. I would have expected them to be... I suppose, cleaner. And the windows bother me."

Nina went to the window. It was smeared with brown muck. She ran her finger over it and a layer of dusty sludge came away. Through the line of clean glass she had created she saw the view from the front of the house: the brick wall by the road and the light traffic that was passing by.

"You don't like dirty windows?" said Nina.

"I don't have an opinion on dirty windows," said Mrs Fiddler. "Life is patently too short to worry about dirty windows. What I mean is the windows... where are they?"

Nina frowned and pointed at the window. "It's here," she said, not sure how she could say it without sounding condescending.

"I can see it's there. On the inside. But where is it on the outside? If we can't see this new old bit of the house when we walk round outside, where is that window? If we opened it and climbed out, where would we—I'm not suggesting we do that!"

But Nina was already pushing the catch on the middle of the sash window and, with a grunt of effort, slid the bottom pane up an inch. At once, there was a howl of wind, so loud it could only herald Very Bad Things. Nina felt herself sucked towards the opening. The window frame rattled, the walls creaked and Mrs Fiddler gave a shout of alarm.

It was as if the house was a plane flying at umpteen thousand feet and Nina had just put a hole in the window. Dust and crud flew up. The walls rippled and plaster tumbled down and away. Nina pulled away from the sucking power at the window and pressed herself against the wall.

The ceiling above made a noise ceilings shouldn't make and she was reminded that houses were just tonnes of wood and stone that had been tricked into standing up in a pretty shape and that, given half the chance, the wood and stone would prefer to be a big pile of rubble on the ground.

"Shut the window!" shouted Mrs Fiddler against the gale.

"I'm trying!" shouted Nina even though she'd done no such thing. She edged towards the window and reached over to grasp the sliding pane. Mrs Fiddler stumbled to the other side of the window and worked the pane from there. Slower than Nina would have liked, they worked the pane down until with a super-sucky *'fffffup!'* it slid back into its recessed housing and the house was still.

124

The creaks and groans faded into the distance and, for a second, Nina thought she could hear again the ticks and clonks of the sidereal clock that had opened up this hidden space.

"Something or other wasn't happy about that," said Nina.

"No," said Mrs Fiddler, panting with surprise. "Maybe it couldn't cope with a window that exists inside the house but not outside."

The mouldy picture had fallen off the wall. Behind it, the wall had cracked in two. Whole chunks of yellow plaster had fallen away, and a jagged fissure now ran from floor to ceiling and continued across the ceiling to the opposite wall, where plaster and wallpaper had fallen away in huge clumps to revealed a small wooden door.

"Here," said Nina.

She knelt and hooked her finger through a knot in the little door. Inside was a narrow cupboard space with several objects clustered at the bottom.

"There's stuff in here," she said.

"Stuff?"

"Things."

Nina lifted them out together and brought them over to the broken table. Pieces of carved wood, hoops of brass, configurations of wire and glass, a faded and brown-edged book; Mrs Fiddler helped her separate them and lay them out. Apart from the book, which was filled with page after page of dense handwriting, the objects were a mystery.

"I don't know what these are," said Nina.

"Whatever they are, someone hid them away behind that wall with no intention of them ever being found again," said Mrs Fiddler.

Nina picked up a device that looked like a children's toy trumpet with a windmill attachment on the end with four brass cups on its spokes. Unless it was a special device for people who wanted to measure windspeed while playing a bugle call, Nina couldn't guess what it was for.

"The craftsmanship on this," said Mrs Fiddler, lifting up a thing made of brass hoops. The three brass hoops, the largest of which was just over a foot across, were all snuggly nested inside each other.

"What do you call those things that spin in all directions?" said Nina.

"What things?"

"People can go in them and spin round and round and upside down until they're sick."

"Gyroscope?"

Nina nodded. The metal rings looked like they should pivot against one another, but when Mrs Fiddler tried to move them they didn't spin apart but slid against one another like a matching up puzzle.

"This," said Mrs Fiddler, pointing out an engraved image. "This is the stamp of Boulton's manufactory. These other markings..."

Nina snatched it from her and ran her fingertips over the eldritch lettering. "*Azbhul...*" she swore softly.

"What is it?"

"This is Venislarn."

"And what's that when it's at home?"

Nina thought. She didn't want to give this perfectly nice lady the lowdown on the Venislarn. No one really benefited by being told that there were psychotic gods waiting just around the corner, hiding beneath the skin of the world, preparing to gobble up humanity in the most terrible ways imaginable. Nobody went through the cancer wards of the children's hospital telling all the little terminal kids that they were *bhul-detar* and it was only pain and death hereon in. On the other hand, there was no *adn-bhul* way Nina was going to use the word 'magic'.

"There's weird shit," she began.

Mrs Fiddler tutted.

"And there's bad weird shit," said Nina.

"And that's what this is?"

Nina held the brass device appraisingly. "Your Matthew Boulton was, a thousand years ago or whatever—"

"Two hundred and fifty years."

"Right. His factory was making stuff for some seriously dodgy types."

"So, this is writing? What does it say?"

Nina read the markings around the hoops. "This one is *lleyun-khaf*, the opener. *Bresshoi... Virri'du... Neh, shan* and *proqi'i*. They're

126

numbers. So if I slid these round to match that, we'd be..." She made a thoughtful noise, abruptly engrossed. "By sliding these hoops, different symbols can be lined up to create..."

"What?"

"Not exactly sentences." She frowned. "*Yan-griva... Xho'mi.* When I was a kid, I had a book full of pictures of people doing different jobs, but the pages were flaps and you could match up a... a policeman's head with a doctor's body and a ballerina's tutu and... *Ah.*"

"Ah?"

"*Soyu pa-tah!*"

As she slid the inner ring into position, the device monetarily vibrated in her grip, numbing her hands and she felt rather than heard a subsonic chime – like someone had rung the biggest bell in some Tibetan temple half way round the world.

"Carpet!" she exclaimed in surprise.

"Pardon?" said Mrs Fiddler.

"Look! Carpet!"

Mrs Fiddler moved round to look down through the hoop with Nina.

"Carpet!" she exclaimed.

"Exactly!"

They were looking down through the hoop at the floor in front of them. But now, instead of cruddy floorboards, they saw a patterned rug of red and cream. As Nina moved the hoops, their view moved too.

"It's like a window into the carpet dimension," she said.

"Is that a thing?" said Mrs Fiddler.

Nina lowered the hoops and gave Mrs Fiddler her best glare-y pout.

"You ask some daft questions, lady." Nina raised the hoops again. "Wah!"

Mrs Fiddler gave a start. On the other side of the hoops, right in front of them, stood a man. He had a gentle if otherwise uninteresting face with soft brown eyes. He wore a silly little white wig on his head. And he was looking directly at them.

127

Morag walked the streets of virtual reality Birmingham, shotgun held loosely at the ready. The people of the city gave her a wide berth. Some looked at her curiously, others fearfully. A few filmed her on their phones and she wondered what happened to those images. Was there an internet in this world? Were people in American and China and Australia watching her now?

If this world was as perfectly realised as it appeared to be, did this virtual city have a Think Tank museum housing the hidden laboratories of a consular mission and, in one lab, a tank containing a virtual *Polliqan Riti* and, next to it, a virtual Morag plugged into a virtual, virtual world?

"Trust Morag Murray to come to a magical playground with a loaded weapon," called Professor Omar.

The professor stood on the concrete steps of a bank.

"Just taking precautions," said Morag.

Kathy Kaur stood at the professor's side, watching a living statue street performer sprayed head to toe in silver.

Omar laughed. "How very Scottish. I bring you somewhere nice and you expect to find trouble."

Morag waited for a black cab to pass and crossed the road to them.

"So, this is the simulation," said Morag, giving the living statue a critical look.

"A simulation," said Omar. "*Polliqan Riti* is capable of running any number of whole-world simulations simultaneously."

"So, are we in his brain or something?"

Omar chuckled. "You, Miss Murray, are reclined, beautiful as ever, in a seat in the laboratory. This..." He did a Fred Astaire twirl and foot tap of a sort he would never do in real life. "This is imagery being fed to our central nervous system."

"The processing power required though..." said Kathy, marvelling at it all.

"Impressive. Our Venislarn guest is all brain."

"But still..."

"He understands and feels things on a level beyond our ability to comprehend. We think we are alive, that we derive pleasure and meaning from life." He frowned. "We are nothing compared to him."

"A utility monster," said Kathy.

"*The* utility monster," said Omar.

Morag, who had no idea what they were talking about, looked over the city centre from their slightly elevated vantage point.

"This world will provide us with the souls—man, that's a stupid word—the souls we need to appease *Yo-Morgantus*. I don't see how."

"Allow me to demonstrate," said Omar and took the shotgun from Morag.

He turned unhurriedly, aimed and shot the living statue artist in the back.

As the shot echoed between high buildings, people screamed and ran. The living statue – his back a mess of blood, exposed bone and shredded silver – writhed on the pavement, gasping in agony.

"*Kos-khol bhul*, Omar!" said Morag. "You bloody shot him."

"He's only a simulation," said Omar.

"He's only a mime," said Kathy, sauntering over to inspect the living statue's injuries.

"And somewhere in all the processing that creates this world, there is a chunk of synaptic code that is this man's conscious pain and suffering," said Omar.

Morag knelt beside the living statue. His breath was a laboured wheezing. His wide eyes met hers. She took his hand and he squeezed tightly as though trying to transfer all his pain to her.

"And how do we make it stop?" she said. "How do we... get it out?"

"*Polliqan Riti* can isolate and excrete the relevant lump of data or code or whatever you want to call it."

Next to Morag, Kathy pressed two fingers into the dying man's wound. "The realism is very impressive."

The man squeezed his eyes shut, a tear rolled onto the side of his nose and stopped there.

"You're a doctor," said Morag. "You're meant to help."

"I'm learning and thinking of the applications. Because I'm a good doctor."

"So," Morag said to Omar, "*Polliqan Riti* can shit out this man's agonies into an easily transportable form."

"And thus, we see why Scotland has such a reputation for being a land of wordsmiths," said Omar.

"But *Yo-Morgantus* will accept it?"

"*Fraxasa*. Yes. I believe so."

The man's grip on Morag's hand slackened and she knew he was gone. Just a simulation, she told herself. Not real.

"I've seen enough," she said.

"I haven't," said Kathy. "The possibilities of a true, simulated world!"

Morag stood, smears of blood on her knees where she'd knelt.

"How do I get out of this?" she said.

"You should only need to wish it," said Omar but he was already slipping away.

The world melted, like a pavement artist's chalk drawings in a sudden deluge.

.

.

.

Morag felt her own skin settling around her and took a quick breath, as though startled from a momentary sleep.

Kathy sat next to her, palms on knees, eyes closed – not slouched in sleep but simply absent for the time being. Professor Omar stood by a desk console, similarly still and absent. A veiny tube extended from the back of his head to a chunky plastic port in the side of *Polliqan Riti*'s tank.

"I'm still connected," she said, and with fearful haste she grabbed her own connective tube and pulled it from the port on the side of the tank. Its end dribbled like a snotty toddler's nose.

"*Muda*," she shuddered.

She was seized by a stupid and unpleasant thought. 'A means to connect two minds', Omar had said. There were questions Morag needed to ask and only one entity that could answer them. She was sure the device wasn't meant to be used this way, but...

Morag squeezed the end of the connection tube and wiped away the worst of the mucosal ooze before lifting her blouse and placing the end against her stomach. It was cold and wet, but no worse than an ultrasound scan.

She wiggled it around.

"Anyone there?" she said and then laughed at herself.

She probed.

"Anyone? Knock once for yes, twice for no."

After some fruitless searching, she concluded that this had been a daft idea from the start.

"Come on, junior," she said. "This is your mother talking."

Mother?

The voice spoke in her head – an audible voice coming from the place directly between her ears. Morag gave a start and momentarily lost her grip on the tube. When she'd caught it again with trembling fingers, she placed it against the same spot on her abdomen and listened.

Mother? Can you hear me?

It wasn't a high-pitched baby voice. It had a depth that resonated in her skull.

"Yes," she said. "I can hear you."

Mother, I have some questions.

"Um. You do?"

I've been thinking about these questions for a long time.

"I bet you have."

Who am I?

Morag wasn't sure how to answer.

What do you call me?

Morag had not given her foetal anti-Christ a name. She hadn't thought it big enough to need one. She hadn't wanted to think about it.

What is my name?

"Damian would be appropriate," she muttered.

Is my name Damian?

"Jesus, no."

Is it Jesus?

"No, not that either. I... we don't have a name for you, yet."

I understand.

"Sorry."

Mother?

"Yes?"

When can I come out?

"What?"

She felt something shift inside her and then, surely impossible at her stage of pregnancy, the skin of her stomach stretched, pushed from beneath.

I promise to be good, said the voice in her head.

"*Bhul,*" she swore and dropped the tube, deliberately this time.

Nina and Mrs Fiddler sat on the dusty floor watching people long since dead go about their business. The brass hoops formed a window between present and past, showing this very place but in another time.

"They can't see us, then?" said Nina.

"I would have thought the sight of two women peering at them through a hole in time would cause a bit of a stir, wouldn't you?" said Mrs Fiddler, as she rummaged around in her bag. "Sandwich?"

"I've got my wham bar," said Nina.

"They're chicken and guacamole," said Mrs Fiddler.

"No, I'm really... Actually, they do look nice."

Mrs Fiddler tore a square of foil, laid it on Nina's lap as a napkin and put a sandwich on it.

"Zank you," mumbled Nina.

Mrs Fiddler pointed at the hoop. "So, that one. That's Boulton."

"The one with old lady hair?"

"They're all wearing wigs, Nina. That one is Boulton. How old would you say he looks there?"

"Even with old lady hair?"

"In his thirties? That one, there—the one with the jowly face—"

Nina angled the hoops to see the room better. "Billy big lips?"

"That's Erasmus Darwin. Whip-smart, that man. Well, they're all very clever but he was a certifiable genius."

There were three men in the room beyond their little time window. The room was a sort of lounge but with uncomfortable looking chairs. A parlour—that was probably what they called it.

"I find it quite incredible," said the man Mrs Fiddler had identified as Matthew Boulton.

"I have it on the best authority," said the big chap, Erasmus Darwin. "Found wandering the hills south of Sheffield eight years

132

ago. A lawyer acquaintance of mine informs me that at least a score of them were Spaniards. Men, women and children. And the others are as much like the savage tribesmen of the Americas as they are anything else. Savages."

"And found wandering the wilds of England?"

"Like survivors of a shipwreck, washed ashore in filthy rags."

"More than seventy miles from the sea? Fie!"

"And where did they come from?" asked a young, dark-haired man with an Irish accent.

The fat man raised his chin, well, his chins. "When asked where they came from, they would only utter the word, '*infierno*' – hell."

A servant lad, a tall gangly teenager with a polished wooden club hanging from his belt, carried a wire-frame cage into the room and set it gently on a table next to an elaborate contraption of copper, wire and glass..

"Is that a chicken?" said Nina.

"That appears to be a chicken," said Boulton, seemingly in agreement.

"It *is* a chicken," said the Irishman.

Boulton peered closely at the caged bird. "Did not Mr Franklin use a turkey bird for his experiment, Edgeworth? When we spoke eight year ago, in this very room, I do recall him saying they used a turkey."

Mrs Fiddler gave a little cry, delved into her bag and pulled out a thick paperback.

"Ah, well now," said the young (and not-a-little-sexy) Edgeworth, "the cost of a turkey versus the cost of an old hen, good for nothing but the soup pot. I think, for our purposes, a hen will do just fine, sir."

Erasmus Darwin strode toward the table. He moved like a man who filled a room with more than his physical bulk.

"I'd rather spend an extra penny on scientific rigour than on foppery and vice."

"A penny?" said Edgeworth. "There's a man who doesn't know the prices down the market but wants to tell his fellow men how they should arrange their financial affairs."

Edgeworth reached for a decanter on the side table and sloppily topped up his glass.

Darwin scowled. "A man does not need to know the price of birds if he's got the wherewithal to raise his own. And, yes, I would take a birch switch to every gentleman if it would make him focus his mind on worthy matters. I tell you, the intellect of the nation will take a turn for the better when men leave off wearing so much flour in their wigs as to make a pudding. When some of these fops get caught in a downpour, they have a veritable loaf of wet dough on their shoulders."

"Yes, I believe you do tell us," said Edgeworth. "Indeed, frequently."

"Friends," said Boulton, waving his hands gently between the bickering pair. "Are we going to electrify this chicken or not?"

"Seventeen sixty-six!" declared Mrs Fiddler.

"What?" said Nina.

"If Benjamin Franklin had visited Soho House eight years before as Boulton said then this is seventeen sixty-six. Edgeworth, the Irishman who can't keep his hands still, is barely an adult but has already drunk a lifetime's worth of booze. Boulton there is..." She closed her eyes. "Thirty-eight or thereabouts. Darwin will be a little younger."

"I thought in the olden days people only lived to, like, twenty before they were killed off by plague or pox."

"If you made it to one year of age, you were lucky," said Mrs Fiddler. "If you made it to ten years old, you were doubly so. After that it got a little easier. Death was capricious, especially for women. Boulton was married twice, to two sisters."

"The dog!"

"It was somewhat scandalous, yes. Edgeworth was married four times in total."

"Four?"

"Darwin was married twice and..."

"And?"

"You wouldn't think it to look at him, but he knew a number of women in his time, married and unmarried. He fathered fourteen children, that we know of."

134

"Damn," said Nina, impressed. "I'm surprised they had time for this science stuff." She pointed. "What are they going to do to that chicken?"

Edgeworth was cranking a handle on the apparatus on the table. Discs rubbed together noisily, and a low crackle permeated the air. The servant lad stepped cautiously back.

"Whatever it is," said Mrs Fiddler. "I don't think the chicken's going to enjoy it."

Nina ate her sandwich.

By the time Kathy emerged from her explorations of *Polliqan Riti*'s simulated world, Morag had unplugged the slimy connector, wiped down her neck and stomach, and spent more time than was strictly necessary washing and rewashing her hands.

"That was astonishing," said Kathy as Morag dried her hands on a paper towel.

"It was... yeah, that was something," said Morag.

"You didn't appreciate?"

"Games," said Morag, waving at the tank and the brain monster swimming in blue gloop. "Playing make-believe isn't really my thing."

"But the possibilities..."

"Our friend is certainly a great asset," said Omar, coming back to himself. "*Shan toi, Polliqan*. Now, we can think about what exactly *Yo-Morgantus* wants from his twenty-eight *fraxasa* levy and... Miss Murray, are you all right?"

"Hmmm?" Morag realised she had been staring at nothing. She looked at her hands, expecting to see them trembling, but they were still.

"I don't feel great," she said.

Kathy made to come over to her, realised she was still plugged into *Polliqan Riti,* and briefly fought with the umbilical connector before freeing herself.

"You could just be disorientated," said Kathy. She placed the back of her hand against Morag's forehead and took her wrist in her other hand to take a pulse. "You might just need to sit and have a drink."

"I'm sure she's fine. Is it...?" Omar gave Morag a meaningful look and a furtive glance at her belly.

"Yes," she said as though to both of them.

"I think you need to take the rest of the day off," said Omar.

"Just a sit down and some water..." began Kathy.

"I'll call you a cab," he said.

"I'm fine," said Morag.

"She's fine," said Kathy.

"I'll take you myself," said Omar and Morag suddenly didn't want to argue anymore. The foolish incident with the connector device and the voice had unsettled her more than she realised.

"Maybe I don't feel all that great," she said.

With a warning to Kathy that, as a scientist, she should know not to mess with stuff she did not understand, Omar left with Morag. He made a call on his mobile as they rode down the escalator to the car park exit and Maurice rolled up in a large, old, pristinely maintained but surprisingly ugly car.

The interior of the car smelled of leather and too much polish. Omar insisted on helping her, like some invalid grandma.

"I'm fine," she said. "Really."

"You don't look it," he replied. "Now, you must let us know if you feel nauseated. Maurice won't forgive me if you throw up on the Princess."

"Princess?"

"The old charabanc. The car. Finest model British Leyland ever built. I'm sure the Venislarn had a hand in its design. Maurice is especially precious about the leather upholstery."

Maurice gave them a look in the rear-view mirror. It was the sternest look she had ever seen the gentle little man give.

"You really don't need to put yourself out like this," said Morag.

"We do and we shall," said Omar. "Besides, someone needs to pay penance for blowing the week's housekeeping on embroidery supplies. Enough to make the Bayeux Tapestry. Some people shouldn't be allowed anywhere near eBay, I say."

With Omar fussing over her all the way and the stink of leather polish only making her queasier by the mile, Morag allowed herself to be taken home to her suburban side-road in Bournville. Omar tried to escort her inside, but Morag had regained enough of her strength to refuse him and nearly sliced off his fingertips when she shut the door in his face.

"Is that you, Morag?" called downstairs neighbour Richard from his flat.

"Home early," she shouted back and hurried upstairs before he could engage her in conversation about the canal barging holiday he wanted to organise for the two of them.

Rod had spent the last three hours watching two actors walk up to a door and open it again and again with barely five seconds of dialogue spoken in that time. Guns had been drawn and pointed, drawn and pointed. Rod was starting to wish someone would shoot something, even accidentally, just to break the monotony.

"I think we can move on to the next scene," said an assistant director of some sort.

Rod checked his watch. Three hours!

"Nice watch," said professional make-up artist and amateur penis sculptor Skye, sidling up next to him.

"I used to have a better one," he said, "but a colleague dropped it in a canal."

"You should have gotten a waterproof one."

"It was. It's probably keeping perfect time down there."

"Hey, you're wanted," said Skye.

Taylor Graham had called over but Rod had failed to hear.

"I just want to know that we've got it right," the film star said. "I mean, note perfect."

"I could do with another take," agreed Langford James, brushing the brocade on his supposedly *samakha* jacket. "I wasn't happy with my characterisation in that last one."

"We're moving on," said the assistant director.

"Rod," continued Taylor, ignoring all others, "is that how you would have done that? You're the expert here."

"How I would have done things?"

"Yes. In this situation?"

Rod cleared his throat. Jayda the armourer gripped his elbow.

"Say nothing," she whispered.

"What?"

137

"He's asked your advice. He just wants some affirmation. Give it to him. Tell him it was great, move on, let these people get some lunch."

"But—"

"It's Tinsel Town. They don't want realism."

"Sure."

"We're losing time," said the assistant director and looked imploringly to the director and the producer, but they were deep in discussion by a bank of screens, re-watching the dailies.

Rod stepped forward from the ring of production staff and equipment that surrounded the outdoor set and, at once, a hundred eyes were on him. He had an audience and Rod did not appreciate audiences.

"No, no," he said loudly for everyone's benefit. "I thought that was perfect."

"Perfect?" said Taylor.

"I thought I wasn't African-American enough," said Langford.

"*Technically,*" said Rod. "You know, from an expert perspective. It was perfect."

"Honestly?" said Taylor.

Rod nodded. Then he glanced down at the pistol in Taylor's hand. "Your finger's on the trigger."

Taylor looked. "What?"

"Your finger's on the trigger." He looked back at Jayda. She was grimacing and shaking her head. He cleared his throat again. "You shouldn't have your finger on the trigger unless you intend to fire your weapon."

"It's not loaded."

"Regardless. And..." He hesitated. One piece of advice wouldn't hurt. "If you've drawn your weapon, you should always be looking where it's aimed. I mean you might glance aside but... here. May I?"

"Sure."

Rod stepped round and took the pistol from the actor. "Right. Gun down. Never pointing at people or walls or anything else a person could be stood behind. Bullets go through things, including walls and ceilings. Finger off the trigger unless you intend to fire. And then..." Rod raised the gun. "Support hand wrapped around the first, like so. Fingers together. You don't tea-cup it. You're not holding your wrist, which is what you did. Two hands together, braced against recoil." He proceeded towards the exterior door of the warehouse. "Moving, looking, aiming. Moving, looking, aiming."

"I definitely was not doing that," said Langford. "I'd really like that extra take."

"Absolutely got to move on," said the assistant director but no one listened.

"You're fine," Rod told Langford. "A *samakha*'s gun-knowledge would only be what they've seen in idiotic action movies. If, by some horrible miracle, one of them got hold of a gun they'd be stuffing it down their pants, holding it sideways, trying to look as gangster as possible."

"But I've got one," said Langford.

"Yes?" said Rod.

"But a *samakha* wouldn't normally have one?"

"Um."

"Okay," said director Bryan, clapping for attention as he stood. "We *are* moving on now."

Langford held out the incomprehensibly stupid fishy handgun he'd been given. "Is this not culturally appropriate?"

Rod looked at it and tried to think of something to say.He leaned in towards Langford.

"I have no idea what that's meant to be," he said confidentially.

"It's not accurate?"

"True *samakha* don't carry weapons. They don't need them. Or comprehend them. Hard to tell. The half-breeds we deal with: they'd all be carrying Desert Eagles or some other impractical hand cannon, if we let them. Most of them: it's knives, baseball bats."

"Baseball bats."

"Aye. Baseball bats. To go with the baseball caps."

Jarmane, the production's—Rod furiously tried to remember her job title, design concept philosopher, was it?—materialised at their side.

"Is there a problem with the aesthetics?" she demanded.

"No. Nowt wrong," said Rod. "It's perfect. Perfect."

Langford grabbed the lapel of his leather and tassels jacket. "Is this not appropriate either?"

"I couldn't rightly say," said Rod, regretting having said anything, ever, at all. "The fish-boy lads I know are a bit more JD Sports than... than... is this New Romantic?"

"It's regal," said Jarmane. "But it also speaks of a decadent society forced into an urban setting. It speaks of the inner mournfulness and displacement that the *samakha* typify."

"Can I just ask?" said Rod, gesturing at Langford's dotted body costume, "this suit you've got on underneath. That's the motion capture thing. It's going to be replaced by *samakha* fish skin in the edit?"

"In post-production, yes," said Jarmane.

"Is there a problem here?" said Bryan the director, pushing in.

"Because he's wearing a coat but he's not wearing any trousers," said Rod.

"The clothes are a representation," said Jarmane. "They are a statement only. Fin is a *samakha*. He has no need for human clothes."

"Right, right," said Rod. "Because, you know..."

"Know what?" said Bryan tersely.

"Well, coat and no trousers. It just..."

"I'm Donald Duck," said Langford, aghast.

Rod held his hand out. "Aye. That. I didn't want to say it."

"I'm Donald fucking Duck!" barked Langford furiously.

"It's just a small thing," said Rod. "Maybe you can fix that in post-production too. Give him some, I don't know, CGI trousers."

"Who's getting CGI trousers?" asked an assistant director.

"No one is getting CGI trousers," said producer Tammy from where she sat.

"I'm Donald fucking Duck!" yelled Langford.

"I am not going to the financiers and telling them I need money for CGI trousers! You are Fin *Yaghur*, the *samakha* prince!"

"I'm a culturally misappropriating Donald fucking Duck with no freedom to make my own acting choices and a..." Langford waved his stupid gun in rage. "What the fuck is this thing anyway?"

"A design choice!" yelled Jayda.

"I demand a reshoot!"

"We're moving on," said Bryan.

"I said that," said an assistant director.

Bryan turned and verbally waled on the nearest assistant director.

Rod backed away from the epicentre of the argument and sloped toward the armourer's table. Jayda and Skye watched him. One with a scowl on her face, the other with a deeply amused smirk.

"I know what I should have done," he said.

"Said nothing," said Jayda.

"Yeah. That."

Rod's phone started ringing.

"Cinemagoers don't want the truth," said Jayda. "They want Tom Cruise leaping through the air, firing two guns at once while beautiful doves fly by in slow-mo and all hell explodes in the background."

"I like that movie," said Skye. "And you don't know what super-agents like Rod here get up to. Maybe it's all casinos and vodka martinis and a different Miss World contestant in bed every night all in the service of queen and country."

Rod laughed. "Not quite."

"Vodka martinis not your thing, huh?"

Rod answered the phone.

"Rod? It's Kathy. I need you to come over and have sex with me."

Rod frowned. He checked the caller ID.

"I think I might have misheard you there, Kathy."

"I need to have sex with you right now." She didn't sound like she was joking, but it was hard to tell. In terms of women demanding sex, he had few other experiences to compare it to.

"As in...?"

"Sex. Now. If you're not too busy."

He put the phone to his chest to muffle the call.

"I've got to go," he told Skye and Jayda.

"Queen and country calling?" said Skye.

"Possibly," he said.

A turn of the brass dials and the window to the past shifted by days, months and years. Nina had a good grasp of Venislarn, but that didn't mean she knew how to fly this device. As the afternoon wore on, she twisted and turned and explored the house almost at random, looking for a slice of life, a little drama they could observe.

Currently, Nina and Mrs Fiddler were following the servant lad down a corridor. He had grown a couple more inches since they'd last seen him. Had a year passed in his world? Two? Three?

By the wide front doors of Soho House, the big and lumbering Erasmus Darwin awkwardly extricated himself from his wet coat with the assistance of two housemaids. A third housemaid stood by, her arms weighed down by a bundle wrapped in oily cloth.

"Jonathan Angus," said Darwin, blowing rain droplets from his nose. "How is the most intelligent man in Boulton's household?"

The serving lad laughed. "I would not know who that is, Mr Darwin."

"Most sly then," said Darwin.

Jonathan coughed and lowered his gaze. "I would not know what Mr Darwin is referring to."

Darwin laughed and turned as though inviting the maids to join in. "I remember when this young man accompanied me on one of my sojourns into the bowels of Mother Earth and was put affright by stories of local witch women."

The maids dutifully tittered.

"Carried that little cudgel of his all through the blue john mines in case a witch should jump out at him. I see you still carry it," said Darwin, eyeing the bulbous-headed club hanging at Jonathan's belt. "You wear it, even indoors?"

"I'd rather have my knobstick and not need it than need it and not have it."

"Knobstick," said Nina.

"As you will," said Darwin and took the heavy bundle from the maid and tossed it into Jonathan's hands. He caught it awkwardly and carried it in the crook of his elbows as Darwin made off down the hallway. "Is your master in the parlour?"

Nina hurried to follow and took at least one wrong turn. Darwin walked with a pronounced limp but he walked quickly, and she had to scuttle to catch up with them.

In the parlour, Nina held up the device close behind Darwin and Jonathan and saw Boulton as well, already entertaining another man. He was round-faced with a caveman forehead and a wooden leg, a long peg of a thing that stuck out as he sat on one of the parlour chairs.

"Wedgwood!" declared Darwin happily.

"Wedgwood!" gasped Mrs Fiddler.

"The pottery guy?" said Nina.

Darwin went over to shake the man's hand. "No, don't get up." The doctor shook the potter's hand vigorously.

Drinks were poured and news exchanged, and soon the horrible weather outside was forgotten and the men's attention turned to the wrapped package that Boulton's servant, Jonathan, still carried.

"Put it on the table," instructed Darwin. "Carefully. It is heavy."

"I was aware of that, sir," grunted Jonathan as he placed it in the centre of the table and removed the oiled cloth wrapping. It was a lump gaudily striped purple-yellow rock, roughly thesize and shape of a rugby ball.

"That is a handsome chunk of blue john," said Wedgwood. "Quick! Hold it tight before Boulton buys it up!" He awkwardly propelled himself up onto his wooden leg and joined them. "Well, it's a fine piece. Beautiful marbling effect."

"Though I've seen better on your tableware glaze," Boulton said to Wedgwood.

Wedgwood shrugged, not disagreeing.

"Look *closer*," insisted Darwin, spittle bubbling on his lips. "*E conchis omnia!*"

"My..." Boulton began to exclaim.

But Nina felt she had seen it before he spoke. Something was embedded in the barely-translucent stone: tendrils curled around a symmetrical shadow that was far from random.

"Looks like a squid," said Nina.

"No ordinary fossil," said Darwin. "I was in the mine with an acquaintance. We were talking about that woman, Isabella."

"Is she still plaguing the workmen?" asked Boulton.

"Worse than ever," said Darwin, "and during our conversations, I slipped and grabbed onto the wall for support and felt fossil forms embedded in the wall. I sent for a better light, and we found this. It is remarkable, is it not?"

"Incredible," whispered Jonathan.

"Yes, Jonathan," said Boulton testily. "Though you might put your energies to something more worthwhile than exclamations. Our friends are thirsty, and I would have a sketch made of this find, if you could tear yourself away."

Jonathan scurried to his duties.

"This supports my theory," said Darwin, "that all life has its origins in simpler forms, such as this. We might be looking at the ancestor of some complex organism existent in the world today."

"But this isn't a fossil," said Wedgwood. He was bending down and regarding it from various angles. "It is not pressed into the stone. It is fully rounded and whole, trapped like a drowned man in ice."

"But it is nonetheless preserved," said Boulton. "Dead."

Darwin's brow rose and his heavy, mostly expressionless face took on a playful look. "Life and death. Some might say that it is only a matter of electricity."

"Are they gonna fry it, like they did that chicken?" asked Nina.

"Apparently so," said Mrs Fiddler.

As he drove to the Think Tank, Rod tried to decode what Kathy had meant when she'd said she needed to have sex with him. He thought about it while he parked up and hurried across the car park to the doors. He thought about it as he rode up the escalator and walked towards the reception desk of the Think Tank museum.

"Wants to have sex with me," he muttered. "*Needs* to have sex with me."

"Sorry, sir?" said the cashier.

"Oh, nothing," he said, embarrassed. "I'm just going in."

"Last entry was half an hour ago," said the cashier. He showed her his consular mission ID and she nodded and waved him through. It had been a while since he'd last been here, almost a year. He'd come in to use the high-end CAD/CAM machine to manufacture some parts for a gadget he'd been working on. Ingrid had helped; that was back in the days before she'd gone mad and tried to destroy the city.

He waved his ID over the access panel and entered the laboratory. Most of the cubicles were empty and in darkness. Staff had gone home or were currently leaving. He walked on through to

144

the double doors at the back. The bolts were thrown open and the padlock left hanging.

He hesitated and then knocked.

"What is it?" called Kathy from within.

"Are... are you decent?" he replied.

"What?"

"I said, are..."

"Just come in."

Rod did so, prepared to throw his hand over his eyes at any moment. He wasn't sure what he expected to see, but the woman had phoned demanding sex, so he was taking no risks. Kathy was alone in the room, fully dressed, standing next to a wide plastic tub the size of a high-priced paddling pool. Her right hand was in the tank, as though testing the water.

"Ay up," he said. "How you doing?"

Kathy tilted her head one way then the other. "It's been a day of contrasts, definitely. We've probably found a solution to our *fraxasa* problem."

"That's good."

"And I'm about to be eaten."

"Less good," Rod said eventually.

"That's what I thought," she said, calmly unconcerned.

Rod approached and eyed the milky, featureless blob that engulfed Kathy's right hand up to the wrist. It didn't seem to be doing much.

"What is it?"

"This is *Polliqan Riti*," said Kathy.

"Is it?"

"He is," she said. "*Polliqan Riti, ley ap sanoi*, is a very intelligent member of the Venislarn horde and one we should definitely treat with respect."

"Gotcha," said Rod and gave a reverential nod to the blob in the tank. "How do."

The thing in the tank made no response.

"And it's eating you," said Rod.

"Yes," said Kathy. "I leaned in to take a cell sample. The professor did warn me, but I didn't—well, as you can see, this happened."

"And can't you pull yourself free? It doesn't look that strong."

"No," Kathy agreed calmly, "but its needs are greater than... *Polliqan Riti*'s breadth of thought and depth of feeling are astronomically greater than ours. He just *deserves* things far more than we do."

"Says who?"

"Says him. And he's told me and he's right. Anything he wants, he's more deserving of than us. It's about who gets the most benefit."

Rod thought he had a tentative grasp on what she was saying. "So, it wants to eat you and it being super-needy means that its hunger is more important than your right to life?"

"Yes!"

"And you agree?"

"He communicates through nerve conduction and he's very persuasive."

"Blimey. And the sex?"

"Ah," said Kathy with a spirited waggle of her eyebrows. "This is my plan. I'm not consciously willing to break free and at this rate..." She looked at her hand disappearing into the creature's body. "I've probably got about two hours before I'm pulled in sufficiently to drown or suffocate."

"Two hours."

"I had hoped Professor Omar would return but he insisted on taking Morag home and, besides, I don't think he's capable of assisting me in the manner I require. Oxytocin."

"What's that?"

"A hormone. It plays a role in social bonding. It's the 'hugging' hormone."

"Hugging."

"And along with endorphins, serotonin and a whole bunch of other chemicals, it's released in vast quantities during sex, particularly at climax."

"I see... I think."

"I'm working on a theory here, Rod, and I need your help. It's going to involve raising endorphin levels, releasing oxytocin and creating a bond with you that will, temporarily at least, be strong enough to convince our Venislarn friend here to release me."

"And you think sexual, um, desire is going to be a stronger argument than you simply wanting to live. Sex isn't the answer to everything."

"Today it is," said Kathy and smiled with obvious nervousness.

Rod put his hand on her arm. "We don't have to do this."

"We don't," she agreed. "But it's the best of the two solutions I've come up with."

"What's the other?"

"You cut my arm off at the elbow."

"I'm not happy about this," said Rod.

"Neither am I," said Kathy. "I'm quite attached to this hand and I've just started learning the clarinet."

"Can't we cut through it instead of you."

She shook her head. "It's pure muscle and brain. Distributed intelligence like an octopus."

"Which means?"

"In this case, you cut a chunk off it, it becomes another creature and you now have two to deal with, equally intelligent and harmful."

"Look, I'm not happy."

"You said."

"I meant the sex thing. This isn't right."

Kathy looked about. "Having sex with a doctor in the lab. No, not normal. But we can just pretend this is some sort of Marie Curie sexy roleplay thing and run with it."

"I meant, it's not morally okay. This is one of them situations."

"What?"

"It's not like you have a choice about having sex. And that means, well, can't you see? It's non-consensual."

"It's consensual, Rod," she said firmly. "I am giving consent."

"But are you really? This is, like, one of those scenarios where it looks like it's consensual but really—"

She groaned. "Yes. You're right. It's got rape fantasy written all over it but here we are! You want consent in writing or something?"

"It's not the legal aspect, it's —"

"Rod!" she snapped. "I called you."

"I know you did," he said, "and I'm very keen to help. I'm just pointing out the moral dimension."

"No, no, no. You're not listening." She gripped his arm. "I called *you.*"

"Aye?"

"I called you. You were the person I chose to call. I could have called for one of the blokes in the office back there."

"I think they've gone home, actually."

"I could have called the security guard out front. I could have called Amreek."

"Who's Amreek?"

"The guy who's teaching me clarinet. He's a pretty fit guy, for a woodwind teacher. If I was *that* way inclined, I could have called Nina and I'm sure she'd already be down to business by now without any of this soul-searching and indecision."

"We could give her a call...?" said Rod, reaching for his phone.

"But I am *not* that way inclined," said Kathy. "I called you. You."

She held his gaze evenly and steadily. She had large eyes, dark eyes. It was probably something she did with her eyelashes or eyebrows or something—Rod wasn't all that familiar with the world of beauty and make-up—but she did have large, dark and beautiful eyes. He could fall in love with those eyes. There were any number of bits of Kathy Kaur Rod was prepared to fall in love with.

"Okay," he said and felt a wave of anxiety come over him at the moment of decision.

He stepped back and took several calming breaths. Swinging his arms and pacing helped a little too.

"Okay, let's do this," he said.

"Right," said Kathy. "You look like you're warming up for a long jump. Were you just planning on doing a run up and leaping in?"

He shook himself and tried to appear calm. "No. Course not," he said and then, "How do you want to do this? I mean... how...?"

"I assumed you knew the basics," said Kathy.

"I know the basics," he said. "I've done it before."

"Good."

"Lots of times."

"Perhaps too much information."

"But not like this."

"As I've acknowledged."

"And certainly not sober."

She gave him a concerned look. "You've never had sex sober?"

Rod thought about it honestly. "Nope. Never the first time with any woman I've been with. And even then..." He scanned back through his memories of the not-very-many women he'd had sex with. "I mean, repeat performances the morning after and that but I've never gone to bed with a woman without at least a couple of beers in me."

"Wow," she said. "Repressed much?"

"God invented alcohol for two reasons, Kathy. A, because beer is lovely and, B, to make sex far less awkward for everyone involved."

"Well, there's a pub just across the road from the car park," she said. "Maybe you want to pop over and have a couple and then come back."

He looked at his watch. "Do you think we have time?"

"No! Now, stop stalling, get over here and take me to the heights of sexual ecstasy, you bloody idiot!"

"Right-o," he said. He walked towards her with the same feeling of dread he'd experienced on his first parachute jump. He held out a hand, and then realised he had no idea where that hand was going.

"Um," he said.

She huffed. "Let me start." She unbuttoned her trousers with her left hand and pushed them down over her thick thighs, looking down as she pushed them off. "Black knickers. Bit of luck there, considering I wasn't planning this. Right."

She kicked the trousers aside and unbuttoned her blouse.

"There," she said opening her blouse, as though that somehow made it all better. Rod would have described his emotional state as 'flipping terrified.'

"I'll be honest, Rod. I expected my breasts to get a better reaction."

"No, it's not that," he assured her hurriedly. "They're really nice."

"Nice?"

"Not nice. Lovely? Is that the right word? Your boobs are—"

She snorted, apparently in amusement. "Okay. Boobs? I'm okay with 'tits' in this context but 'boobs' is not a sexy word, is it? They're breasts, yes. And my breasts are...?"

Rod's brain leapt in panic. "Resplendent?"

Kathy blinked.

"Yes, they fucking are," she agreed after some thought. "I have resplendent breasts. Now, come over here and get a handful."

"I will," said Rod, knowing he sounded very much like a man who wouldn't. He put his hands on her breasts with the care of a man handling high explosives.

"Yes," she said.

"Silky."

"You can... Yes, that's better."

He smiled and instinctively kissed her on the mouth.

"Mmmm. Oh, we're kissing now?" she said, oddly surprised.

"Sorry." He stepped back. "Weren't we...? I..."

She flushed, embarrassed. "I was thinking it was just the sex."

"I didn't mean to overstep the mark."

"No. No, it's fine."

"Are you sure?"

"It would be silly not to, wouldn't it?" She frowned at herself. "Wouldn't it?"

"Um."

The moment was broken. And there had definitely been a moment.

"Bugger it all!" he said, peeved. "We can do this!"

"Yes, we can," said Kathy. "Tell you what, let's have some mood music."

"Mood music," he nodded approvingly.

They both took out their phones. Rod searched 'sexy music' and hit play on the first result. As a 'soft sexy jazz instrumentals' playlist warbled from his phone, something very different came from Kathy's. Rod paused his.

Triumphal brass, uplifting strings, the clash of cymbals...

"Is that the *Dambusters* theme?" he asked.

"Er, yes," said Kathy. "I searched 'arousing' and it autocorrected it to 'rousing'. Rousing music. Hang on a second and I'll—"

"No, it's fine," he said.

"Really?"

"Well, it's got... pep. Aye, I like it."

The military march was getting into full swing. It might not have been Rod's first thought for sexy music, but it was good music for any military man to *get things done.*

"If you like," said Kathy. "Although if you make any references to invading my Ruhr Valley, your bouncing bombs are mine, got it?"

"Got it."

She ran her hand inside his jacket up to his shoulder and pushed it off.

"Hang on," he said. "Holster."

He disengaged himself from jacket and gun holster, placed his wallet on a desk, drew his Glock pistol and carefully set it next to the wallet, then turned the pistol around so the grip would be within reach of where he and Kathy—

"Do you think you might need it in a hurry?" said Kathy.

"You never know."

"During sex?"

"Someone might come in."

"And your first thought is to shoot them?"

"Currently? Yes."

"Still nervous?"

"I'm not nervous."

He was starting to feel angry. He wasn't enjoying how this situation was playing out. Rod considered himself a confident guy and he certainly wasn't sexually submissive or one to play coy, but here he was trying to be sensitive and helpful—yes, helpful!—and Kathy Kaur, who was definitely a confident woman and not in the least bit coy, was not being either sensitive or helpful, even though it was her life at risk. Rod decided it was time to take charge.

"Right. Here I come." *Here I come.* Bad choice of words, he thought. Never mind.

He took hold of her and kissed her hard. He ran his hand down her arm, slipped it under the edge of her blouse, circled her naked waist and pulled them closer together. He cupped her left breast, gave it what he judged to be the appropriate amount of squeezing / stroking and then moved onto the right.

"You know, one doesn't feel left out if it doesn't get any attention," said Kathy.

"Stop critiquing," he said through gritted teeth.

Kathy laughed softly. Rod had mixed opinions about people laughing during sex. It was obviously meant to be fun, but it could be disheartening for a chap.

"It's like you've got a little checklist in your head," said Kathy. "Do this, do that. Right, then left."

"You've got an issue with my technique?" he said.

"No, not at all, Rod," she said sincerely. "It's very organised. Keep going." And she loosened his belt.

He slid his hand round to the small of her back and dipped into the waistband of her knickers. She murmured something in a language Rod didn't understand, but he knew it was consent.

His trousers fell around his ankles. He still had his shoes on and he felt suddenly trapped. What if he were required to leap into action? He wasn't sure what action might be required at this moment, but if he needed to leap into it these trousers would certainly get in the way. He wouldn't tell Kathy that. She seemed to be actually enjoying it now, judging from the fact that she had shut up and was sliding a hand down...

He gave an involuntary gasp, which came out as a really unfortunate, strangled hoot.

"You okay?" she said.

"Sorry. You surprised me when you grabbed my tallywhacker."

She snorted. "Tallywhacker."

He scowled. "What would you prefer? Dick? Cock? Shall we get our nomenclature right before we continue?"

"Sorry," she said. "Yes, the naming of parts. I'm always happy with penis. And that's a sentence I didn't think I'd be saying today." She smiled and kissed him, a peck on the lips. "I'm a medical woman. This is a penis. That's my vagina. And that... yes... that..."

It was better when she wasn't talking. Rod was quick to mentally justify to himself that it wasn't that he liked his women silent but there was something about this situation and Kathy Kaur that meant he needed all his focus and concentration on the matter in hand. Yes, he might have had a little mental checklist of things to be done during sex but that was because he was a thorough man and women were complicated, like the control panel of a jet plane. He reminded himself never to compare women's bodies to the control panel of a jet plane out loud, ever, but the analogy was a fair one. He needed to check on that readout, make a course correction, flip that toggle, check in with his own flight crew, give the flaps a little tweak... okay, an analogy too far. But it was complicated, and he did need to go through everything methodically and yet not look like he was being methodical.

Kathy exhaled heavily into the hollow of his neck and murmured, "Protection?"

"Aye. Yeah," he said. Trying to maintain as much flesh-on-flesh contact as possible—because he was sure that if he didn't it would undo some of the good work he'd put in—he turned to the desk and reached over his gun.

"Not that kind of protection, Rod."

He tutted, reached over the gun and flipped open his wallet. There was a condom in the inside pocket.

"Prepared," she said.

"I have it with me it as an emergency water carrier but, yeah." He tore it open.

"Okay. Let me help," said Kathy.

"You've only got one hand."

"I'm dextrous."

She was almost unnervingly proficient.

"Okay, let's work out the angle of this thing," she said.

"How very scientific of you," he said.

Kathy stood with her back to the tub. That wasn't going to change, her hand being stuck in a needy Venislarn gloop and all. Rod was taller at both head and groin height.

"I'm going to need to bend my knees," he said.

"Wait. I've got to shift myself further forward."

"Then I'd better..."

"You've still got your trousers round your ankles."

"I'm still wearing my shoes, actually. Hang on." He did his very best to kick off shoes and trousers without appearing horribly unsexy. He was pretty sure he failed, especially when he forgot about the knife sheath strapped to his ankle which snapped off, spun away into a corner and smashed something.

"Okay," he said. "I'm back. Knees bent."

"Arms stretched. Ra, ra, ra."

They laughed together at that one.

"The angle's still not right," he said.

"Not much I can do about it."

"But, you see, if I... it doesn't bend like... ow. Ow! It doesn't bend! Look, do you need me to be inside?"

"The chemical difference between penetrative and non-penetrative—"

"Okay, okay, okay. How about I pick you up?"

"I'm not as light as I look."

"You look bloody gorgeous, Kathy Kaur, and I'm quite strong."

"Thank you for the compliment but... oh! Oh! No. No. Yes. Yes, that's.... Yes, let's run with this."

"Is that all right?"

"It is. Just... Yep. That. More of that."

"That?"

"That."

She grunted.

"You like that?" he said.

"No, that's the tub digging into my back and... No, don't stop that. Keep going. Let me just lean forward."

She wrapped her left arm around his neck and held on. She was bloody gorgeous, but she was right that she wasn't as light as she looked, and his wrists were going numb as he cradled her backside in his hands. He'd have to bring her in to land soon. Her face covered his face now, too. He was flying blind and acutely aware that the *Dambusters* music had filled his head with too much aviation-related imagery.

Her breath quickened and she tightened her grip. That sensation and emotion transferred to him, flowing through his body, and he realised in alarm that there was a danger he might land before her. His mind leapt for distractions, a memory challenge, something to divert his thoughts.

Lancaster. Spitfire. Wellington bomber.

"Oh, Rod. Yes."

Messerschmidt. Vulcan. Harrier Jumpjet.

"Yes! Nng!"

Sopwith Camel. Fokker. Mosquito.

"Come on!"

Typhoon. Tornado. Hercules transporter.

"Yes!" she shouted. "I want to live!"

Vampire, B52.

"I'm free!" she gasped.

Rod shook her hair away from his face and stepped back with her in his arms. Her hand was free of the goop and covered in white slick liquid.

"Sikorsky!" he growled, deep in his throat.

She held onto him with arms and legs. "Well done, Rod."

"Happy to help," he panted.

She pressed herself against him. "Rod by name..."

"Do you know how many times I've heard that?" he said.

"How many?"

"Every single time," he said.

Being pregnant was bad enough. Being pregnant with the Venislarn anti-Christ, doubly so. Having foolishly initiated a dialogue with that anti-Christ foetus was a step too far. Morag wished she had a little voice in her head that stopped her doing stupid stuff before she did it.

Was it a serious problem? Well, yes, obviously.

Was the situation any more serious than it had been twenty-four hours ago? That was hard to say.

It was a problem that probably demanded some serious thought. Morag dealt with that in her own way. She flopped on the sofa with a tray of last night's leftover curry takeaway and attempted, through the power of television, to turn her brain off for the night.

Her flat in green and gentle Bournville had been provided for her when she arrived in Birmingham. It had come fully furnished but she had added her own personal touches, mostly in the form of discarded clothing and unwashed pots. She had a system for dealing with both which was to allow them to mount up until Richard downstairs came round and did them for her. She didn't feel comfortable having a strange man washing and sorting her underwear but, once she'd got over that mental hurdle, everything went swimmingly.

Flopped on the sofa, she ate curry and grew increasingly irritated that TV wasn't doing its job of killing off her thought processes. In the end, she gave up on telly, dropped her head on a cushion and tried to see the positives in her day. Freaky communications with a ten-week old foetus aside, it hadn't been that bad a day. She was now privy to another of Omar's dirty secrets, one she might yet exploit to her advantage at some point, and it seemed that there was a credible way of paying Lord Morgantus's tribute of souls without endangering the lives of some Venislarn wannabes.

Mother?

She opened her eyes.

Can you hear me now, mother? said the voice in the cave of her mind.

She sat bolt upright. "What the hell?"

I have found you again.

"This isn't possible."

I lost you and couldn't find the way, but I knew there must be another way. I looked for it and I found you.

"How are you doing this?" she said, hearing the panic in her own voice.

I found a way back to you. I knew there had to be one. Aren't I clever, mother?

"Oh. Yes."

Are you proud of me?

Morag really wished she had a little voice in her head that stopped her doing stupid stuff before she did it. Now she had a little voice inside her womb, but she had no clue what it might want.

Nina could have happily spent a day and a night following the minor soap opera of historical goings on in Soho House and, though she wouldn't even admit it to herself, she had loved spending time in Mrs Fiddler's company. The woman was knowledgeable but not arrogant, thoughtful but not interfering. She belonged to that other middle class, the ones who had no money but made up for it *by knowing things*. She was a human equivalent of the chunky jumper she wore, warm and soft and welcoming.

But, eventually, they ran out of sandwiches, wham bars and even the sticky horribleness that was Kendall mint cake and there was only so long two women could sit on hard floors in a draughty building without needing to go somewhere nicer in search of food and toilets.

There was a minor disagreement as they packed away. Nina assumed she was going to take the viewing hoops, the other artefacts and the book they'd found with her. They were evidence in a study of what was evidently a Venislarn matter. Mrs Fiddler assumed that everything would stay at Soho House. Nina attempted to compromise by saying she would take the viewing hoops but leave the wand and the book (because books were not her thing, per se). The eventual compromise was that Nina took the book and the wand and left the hoops locked up in the storage basement. This compromise had the singular advantage of making them equally unhappy.

Nina walked the short distance home.

"Is that you?" called her mum, as she entered the porch and wrestled her keys out of the door.

"No," she shouted back facetiously.

Her mum came out of the kitchen, a tasting spoon in her hand. Wafts of steam and the smell of delicious cooking followed her.

"You not out pubbing and clubbing tonight?" she said with a touch of scorn.

"I told you. That man doesn't know what he's talking about."

"Rod? He is your work colleague, no? Sounds like he knows you plenty good." She jutted her chin at Nina's rucksack. "Where you been, school?"

"That's right." She slipped the rucksack off her back. "I've got homework."

Her mum threw her hands in the air and turned back to the kitchen. "You think you're so clever, don't you?"

"Yes."

"Spoiled, I say!"

"I'm going up to read. Will you bring me a hot chocolate?"

"No!"

"If you love me..." said Nina and left it hanging, knowing it was enough.

She went upstairs to her box bedroom, kicked off her shoes and threw herself with excessive force on her bed. From directly below, her mum swore and shouted. Nina smiled. Different families expressed their love in different ways. Nina's did it by winding each other up, the gentle comfort of constant needling remarks.

Nina opened the book. Its dry pages creaked. She focused on the tight, flowing script. Deciphering handwriting was not a valuable skill nowadays, being reserved primarily for decoding cards sent by aged relatives.

It was a diary. Soon, the looping handwriting lost its strangeness and Nina lost herself in the flow of events in the life of the diary keeper: Jonathan Angus.

June 14th 1768

On the day before my departure, I was permitt'd to go with Mr Darwin into the caves near Treak Cliff in Derbyshire. The other men made a joke that I should be careful or the Mad Maid of the Wilds would come and take me. I ask'd if this was a local myth and some of the men regard'd me darkly. Mr Darwin said, "Jonathan, she is as real as any man or woman and as dangerous as they say." Some of the men say she was one of the lost Spaniards found in the wilds some years ago and was little more than a girl. Anon, we descended into the caves called the Devil's Arse and Mr Darwin did shew me the unique seams of Radix Amethyst, that which the miners call 'blue john'. It sparkled like stars in a midnight blue sky. Mindful of their words, I gripped my knobstick in case I should need it.

"Knobstick," said Nina and moved on.

July 15th 1768

Mr Boulton reports that Mr Wedgwood's amputation has been carry'd out and as well as could be expect'd. Thanks be to God. Mr Darwin did recommend a surgeon from Newcastle. With 2 burly men to hold him down, the surgeon saw'd off his leg above the knee. Wedgwood watch'd it (full of laudanum for the pain, mind) and did not faint away from the shock.

August 4th 1768

The good Doctor of Lichfield has tumbl'd from another of his peculiar carriages. His phaeton (w' the improv'd steering mechanism) struck a gravel bank & Mr Darwin has suffer'd a fracture to his knee. By all accounts, he is a terrible patient. His wife, who has suffer'd with maladies for years, is by far the better patient. Boulton is to pay him a visit and I may go too. Wedgwood first and now Darwin. I told Mr Boulton to be carefull—losing legs appears to be catching!

"Oh, Jonathan, you are a wit."

"Who is Jonathan?" asked her mum as she backed in, carrying a tray with a hot chocolate and a plate of rich tea biscuits. "Is this another of your boyfriends?"

"Doubt it. He's been dead for centuries."

Her mum tutted loudly. "I don't know what type you go for."

Rod felt there was always something odd and awkward about tidying up after sex, especially after the first time with someone. It was like the morning after a drunken night out: everything that had seemed fine and cool and sensible and a really good idea suddenly looked ridiculous and childish and potentially damaging. With his pants but not his trousers back on, Rod searched for his ankle knife. He found it in a corner, among the shattered pieces of a coffee mug, and he loitered there, poking amongst the shards, to give Kathy time to sort herself out.

"I'm thinking..." said Kathy slowly.

"I'm sure we both are," said Rod.

"I don't think we ought to tell anyone about this."

He chuckled, decided he'd spent enough time looking for his knife and picked it up. "I wasn't really planning to tell anyone about this. At all. Ever."

"I mean any of it," said Kathy, adjusting her bra before doing up her blouse. "I wasn't meant to stay on. Omar will only gloat if he discovers my predicament."

"I get it," said Rod. He picked up his trousers and tried to work out which of the legs had been turned inside out. "You weren't here. I wasn't here. It didn't happen."

"That's what I'm saying," she said. "None of it."

He climbed into his trousers.

"But you're a lifesaver, Rod," she said. "Thanks." The smile was evident in her big eyes.

"Any time," he said and stepped forward to kiss her.

She flinched and put her hands on his chest.

"But it didn't happen," she said, averting her gaze a second.

"I know," he said. "I know. We know. As far as the rest of the world is concerned, it didn't happen. But that doesn't mean..."

He tried, cautiously, to move a little closer but she backed off.

"But it didn't happen," she insisted.

"Did I do something wrong?"

She laughed and then stopped herself. "For a first time together, in a life and death situation in a science lab, no, not at all. You were... it was great, Rod. But it was a unique situation."

"Because you called me. You said."

"I did," she nodded. "And I would again. Not that I intend for this to happen again. It..." She sighed wearily and gave him a concerned look. "This isn't going to make things weird between us, is it?"

"What? This?" he said. "No. Weird? No. Weird how?"

She looked pained. "I don't want this to be a problem between us."

He forced himself to smile. "It is not a problem. A friend in need and all that. You needed sex. I was available." He shook his head. "Not a problem. Rod's your man."

"Good," she said and looked round for her shoes. "And no one needs to know any of this."

"Correct," he said, "although..." He pointed to the CCTV camera in the corner. "We might have to do something about that."

"Oh, *bhul*," she said.

He shrugged magnanimously. "It's okay. I'll go sort it out now. I know where the security room is. You get yourself all..." He made a very non-specific hand gesture. "And then we'll be out of here."

Rod slipped on his shoes and left. On the other side of the double doors, he stopped and gathered his thoughts.

"It didn't happen," he told himself and went to find the security room.

TUESDAY

Morag woke in the very early hours.

Mother.

Morag grunted and pretended she could go back to sleep, but the existence of a voice inside her, of a sentient being growing inside her, drew her fully awake.

What are we doing today, mother?

Morag sighed and flopped back onto the pillow, completely awake and with no prospect of sleep.

"Well, I have a busy day at work today."

What is work, mother?

"In this instance, work is collecting twenty-eight fake consciousnesses from a Venislarn refugee hiding in a science museum and giving them to a fucking Handmaiden of *Prein* in the slim hope that we can save the lives of twenty-eight idiot Venislarnkin."

You don't like the fucking Handmaiden of Prein, *do you, mother?*

"Er, no. You shouldn't swear."

Swear?

"'Fucking' is a swear word. I shouldn't have said it. You shouldn't either."

Sorry, mother. I won't say the swear word. After you have collected twenty-eight fake consciousnesses from a Venislarn refugee hiding in a science museum and given them to mmm-mmmm Handmaiden of Prein, *can I come out?*

"No. No, baby. You can't come out. Not today."

Is it because I said a swear word?

"No, baby," she said, stroking her belly and feeling, against all odds, sleep coming over her again. "You've done nothing wrong. It's just not time, yet."

When Rod's mobile rang, he was up and out of bed, reaching for both phone and trousers before the second trill. He looked at his phone. It was not yet six a.m.

"Campbell."

"I hope you're pleased with yourself, Mr Real-Life Spy." It was Producer Tammy.

He had somehow expected it to be Kathy. He had hoped it was Kathy.

"Pleased with myself how?" he said, pulled on an already-buttoned shirt and stepped into his boots.

"I've got two Hollywood stars here who have kept me up all night, arguing about authenticity and verisimilitude because someone told them what they were doing was wrong."

"Ah," said Rod.

"Ah, indeed, Mr Big Mouth. You get yourself down to the hotel. You have a meeting that started five minutes ago. I'll pour you a coffee."

"I don't drink coffee."

"I know."

Tammy hung up. Rod whipped his jacket off the bedside chair and headed toward the door, collecting en route his tie, ID card, keys, Glock 21 pistol and a pack of sodium-toothpaste mouth-bombs of his own devising.

Eight minutes later, minty-fresh and only thirteen minutes late, he entered the meeting room at Malmaison. The actors, Taylor Graham and Langford James, were deep in discussion with Producer Tammy and her entourage. The table was cluttered with drunk and half-drunk coffees. Langford's seaweed and shellfish encrusted *samakha* gun sat at the centre.

"Here he is," said Tammy loudly, "no doubt to clarify what he might have said yesterday."

"Rod," said Taylor, with the kind of familiarity Rod didn't expect from someone he'd only met two days before, "come give us some guidance."

"Guidance that will confirm that our design aesthetic and direction do not need changing."

"Aye," said Rod. All eyes were on him. "Yes, morning everyone."

He stood at a safe distance.

"Sit," said Tammy. It wasn't an invitation.

"I think it's clear that I misspoke yesterday," he said. "The film looks great."

Langford James picked up the *samakha* gun contemptuously.

"Aye," said Rod. "It's not a hundred percent authentic but..." He searched for the right words. He wondered what Chad would say. "But it speaks of a deeper truth. Look, it's like this. The real *samakha*, they live in a ghetto on the canal between Glover Street and St Andrew's Road. They're chavs. Hardly, um, cinematic. This..." He waved at the ridiculous gun and, figuratively, at the design of Langford's character. "This is much better."

"It's fine," said Taylor. "People will swallow anything."

"I'm not convinced," said Langford.

"It's alien to people. They don't know any better. But the military stuff, the spy stuff. If I've been doing it all wrong..."

"Not *all* of it," said Rod.

"Enough of it."

"Jayda, the armourer. She's a former marine. She'll have taught you right."

Taylor banged the table with his fist. A dozen cups rattled in their saucers and a couple of over-tired Tammy-lites jumped in fright. "But she's not doing the job. Your job, Rod. I'm playing the film version of you, and if you're not happy..."

"Rod is happy," said Tammy. For someone from Hollywood, she wasn't a convincing actor.

"This film has to show life as it is."

"I don't think anyone wants to see that," said Rod. "*This* is my life. Getting out of bed at five in the morning to attend meetings that I'm not equipped to deal with. I don't go around breaking into places, having fights. I hardly ever draw my weapon. Not allowed to half the time," he added and hoped he didn't sound churlish.

"When were you last in combat?" said Taylor.

Rod opened his mouth to say that it was weeks ago, but it wasn't. "Sunday. I had to physically restrain a *bondook* shambler."

"What's that?" asked a Tammy-lite, fascinated.

"It's a... sort of like a dragon, I guess. But with tentacles. It had got loose in the reception of our office."

"A lobby fight," said Taylor. "Close quarters. I can see it already. You shoot it?"

Rod shook his head. "Out of ammo. I had to try to hold its jaws closed. You've seen people wrestling alligators in the movies? Like that."

Taylor clicked his fingers and shook a pointing finger at Rod. "This. This is what I want."

"Alligator wrestling?"

"I want to show Rod the storyboards for the action scenes."

"Which ones?" said Tammy.

"All of them. And we change them."

"We can't change them."

"We can change them. You want to do them as post-production reshoots? You want that?"

Tammy growled. Under the conference room lights, the woman's sun-worn face looked even more lined and tired.

"Fine," she said. "You look. You discuss. That's all I'm agreeing to right now."

"And what about my character?" said Langford.

"Rod's said there's no problem," said Tammy.

"He basically said it's cultural appropriation."

"I don't even rightly know what that is," said Rod.

"We're not changing your costume," said Tammy.

"I'm not happy," said Langford.

"Thing is," said Tammy and through her tiredness, a cruel tone slipped out, "no one can see if you're happy or not when we replace your face with a CGI *samakha*. No one will know if it's you in the costume or the second-best motion capture actor in the business, flown in at the last moment."

Langford James's face turned to cold fury, but he said nothing.

"Hey," said Taylor. "Let's not fight here. We're trying to make the best movie possible."

"Of course," said Tammy with false cheer. "Rod? A word."

She got up and walked to the door. Rod had to hurry to catch up with her.

"*Skyfall*," she said, marching to the lifts. "Twenty-twelve."

"Pardon?"

"Daniel Craig in his third outing as James Bond. There's a scene in a casino, a straightforward fight scene. Daniel, a fine actor, decides to bring a little something to the scene. He's bought a pair of gloves he thinks would look good on him. Stylish. He wears them to shoot the entire scene. An acting choice, right?"

"Er, right?"

The lift arrived. Tammy nodded for him to get in and she followed. She pressed for the ground floor.

"Thing is, at the end of that scene, there's a bit with a handgun with a fingerprint scanner. It will only fire if it registers his fingerprint."

"The gloves," said Rod.

"Precisely. It makes no sense as it stands. So, they had to re-edit the entire scene post-production, insert CGI hands over the gloved hands. Time and effort and expense because Daniel Craig, a fine actor, decided to wear gloves that day."

The lift doors opened on the hotel lobby.

"Do you know how much those CGI gloves cost the studio?" said Tammy.

"No?" said Rod.

"Neither do I," she said. "And I never want to find out for myself. On set by seven. Do not disappoint me."

She shooed him out of the lift and pressed the button for her own floor.

Nina, curled up in her duvet, sipped the morning coffee her mum had brought her and read Jonathan Angus's diary. She had splashed a little hot chocolate on a page the night before but she didn't let it worry her because a) it wasn't a food stain, so she hadn't broken her promise to Mrs Fiddler and b) it was brown on brown and she could easily explain it away as a spot of mould or something.

January 14th 1773

Mr Boulton again visit'd the strange woman who has taken lodgings in the house down the hill. She is only known as Isabella (and I would not trust a woman who is only known by her Christian name). I'm not sure what Mrs Boulton thinks to all of this, but it seems that Isabella has been quite the draw of late. She in turn has shewn great interest in Mr Boulton's manufactory and—tho I'd scarce believe it—has offered suggestions for improvements in his methods.

March 8th 1773

Mr Boulton invited me to his study to view his latest invention—he knows I am greatly interest'd in such matters. I was surprised to find Miss Isabella already there and observing the item closely. I greet'd her formally but she ignored me most completely. Mr Boulton present'd the item as a 'yellis wand' and, when I inquired, told me the idea for it had come to him in a dream. This caused Miss Isabella some amusement though I could not say why. I did ask him if he would give us a demonstration of the device and he did so without delay.

There was a gap of some pages and then:

March 15th 1773

Masters Scroggins and Scroggins made the delivery of the pineapple for Mr Boulton's grand dinner. They say it is as fresh as any in England although I would not know. It is hard, both in leaves and body and shines with a varnish'd look, but I do not know if that is a sign of ripeness or no. Matters not, it is only the Boultons' for the week and then the Scroggins will collect it again. Mr Boulton has not told me how much he paid to hire that most strange and desirable fruit which indicates to my mind that he is embarrass'd by the cost. I ran down to the manufactory to tell him, but his attention was fully engaged with the plans for a new device, a system of interlinked rings for 'viewing events that have already passed'. He calls it the 'Oculus'.

"Oculus," she said. "*Yellis* wand. Oculus."

There was a break in the text and then in a different, slightly frantic style:

I have looked back through this journal and found entries from this year which are assuredly in my hand but which I have no recollection of writing. The meetings with Miss Isabella they mention I do not remember. I cannot explain these occurrences and do not wish to trouble Mr Boulton with them.

"Interesting."

It appeared that the otherwise perfectly dull Matthew Boulton had built at least two devices of Venislarn design. The reasons weren't clear. Nor was the purpose. Vivian had had some inkling of this, hence the clock key and the impossible vase at her house. Another day of investigation with Mrs Fiddler, just one, and Nina would present what she'd found to the team. The items and the book she now held would swiftly find their way to the Vault and Professor Omar and maybe that would be the end of it. She didn't want it to end. Vivian had given her this mystery, a final mystery.

Her phone rang. Nina was always surprised when her phone rang. It was like people hadn't heard of texting or messaging.

It was a withheld number. She was tempted to ignore it, but she wanted to know what kind of monster was phoning her, and so early in the morning. She answered.

"Yo."

There was silence on the line.

"Hello?" she said.

More silence and then a deeply hesitant, "Nina, this is Vaughn. Vaughn Sitterson."

This was new. Their consular mission chief never made phone calls. He rarely spoke at all. He was silent in meetings and affected a distracted vagueness that deflected attention. He ran the mission through some jiujitsu of insignificance and seemed intent on passing through the world unnoticed. But now he was demanding her attention with a call to her mobile. He had stepped out of hiding.

"Vaughn. How you doing? Everything cool?"

Silence and then, "You weren't in the office yesterday."

"No. I had this thing. I did send you a message on Instagram."

"I'm not on Instagram."

"Aren't you? Must have sent it to another Vaughn."

"You weren't ill?"

"No."

"And you're well? Right now, that is."

"Er, yep."

"Then you will be in the office this morning. At the appropriate time."

"But this thing. I've made plans."

There was silence and the whisper of breath as Vaughn debated speaking further. He chose silence and hung up.

Nina stuck her tongue out at the phone and then messaged Mrs Fiddler that she couldn't come out to play today.

On the film set in the Mailbox, Rod quickly learned that although many of the stars and staff had their own space, not all such spaces were created equal. In Taylor Graham's screened-off corner of a former shoe shop, Rod was presented with storyboards of key scenes from the movie. Director Bryan and Taylor walked him through them, while the miserable scriptwriter skulked in the corner, staring at nothing and offering no comment.

"So, this sequence comes after agent Jack Steele has gate-crashed the charity gala at the upscale offices of our villain, Vlad Botticelli."

"Nice name," said Rod automatically.

"Isn't it?" said Bryan. "This is shortly after our two protagonists meet for the first time. Jack is investigating Botticelli's links to the attack on the consular mission. Fin is trailing the assassins who killed the Venislarn mystic back to their base. They'll eventually discover that the artefacts they're both pursuing were stolen to be used as components in the construction of the *Jandu-pahir*—"

"*Jhandu-p'hir*," muttered the writer.

"That. Basically, it's Venislarn kryptonite, a super-weapon that can wipe out the Venislarn on earth but has terrible consequences for humans too. So, as Jack leaves, Vlad sends his goons after him to kill him. And that's where we have the helicopter versus car chase. The car's bobbing and weaving, trying to lose the copter, but the helicopter follows them block after block. Finally, they get to this multi-storey parking structure and Steele drives up to the top deck where he's high enough to take out the copter with his car's front-mounted machine guns."

Rod realised that Taylor was staring at him throughout the explanation, trying to read something in his expression.

"That sounds great," said Rod.

"But is it realistic?" said Taylor. The actor, usually so confident, looked pathetically eager for Rod's approval.

"Realistic how?" said Rod. "Um, I've never had to gate-crash a charity gala. I've never been pursued by a helicopter."

"No car chases," said Taylor and threw down the pen he'd been holding.

"Plenty of high-speed driving," said Rod.

"Really?"

Rod nodded and searched for something suitable to relate. The last thing resembling a high-speed chase he'd participated in had involved a push bike and a dozen sex-starved pond creatures. Not quite Hollywood enough.

"So, this helicopter chase? It's happening in the city?"

"Downtown Philadelphia," said Taylor.

"Or Detroit," said Bryan. "We've yet to make a firm decision."

"One thing I would say is that if there's a dangerous situation, our primary role is to get that danger away from the general public. That train I hijacked, I did it to get the creature out of town before it could kill anyone."

"You saved lives," nodded Taylor.

Rod jiggled his head, so-so. "I crashed it into a train station and then the monster went on a rampage in a chocolate factory. But, yeah. That's the point."

"We can fix that in dialogue," said Bryan, waving a hand at the miserable writer without even looking at him. "Fin or Jack can say something about needing to get away from population centres."

"Excellent. And then there's the car," said Rod.

"What's wrong with the car?" said Bryan peevishly.

"It's got machine-guns in"—He gestured questioningly —"the headlights?" He looked at the storyboard. "Machine guns in the headlights. They're fixed. No aiming. You've lost most of your advantage there. You even recognise that. The car has to go into a multi-storey to shoot at the helicopter."

"But people like gadgets," said Taylor.

"It's a standard trope," said Bryan.

"Trope. Exactly."

"Hey, don't get me wrong. I like gadgets," said Rod.

"Sure," said Taylor. "You had that escape wire and the lock picks and—"

"But all the equipment I carry, it's adaptable. There's no point having something if it can only be used in a specific situation that's unlikely to come up."

He unbuttoned his jacket, took out his pistol, removed the magazine, pulled the slide to release the chambered round, and placed the weapon on the table. "Tool number one." He took out his Leatherman. "Tool number two."

"But these aren't gadgets?" said Bryan.

Rod continued to unload his kit.

"Magnetic coins?" said Taylor. "What are they for?"

"For times when I need a magnet," said Rod. "I don't know. To pull a key across a table. To pin a note to a fridge. To scramble a computer hard drive. It's adaptable. Careful with that."

"It's a mechanical pencil," said Bryan and thumbed the top. Half an inch of scalpel blade slid out.

"Okay, that's cool," said Taylor.

Rod emptied his pockets. He fished out a bunch of laminated cards held together with a keyring. "Basic Venislarn."

He flipped to a card. Below complex ideograms in two different scripts was the English translation: 'Don't eat me. I'm just doing my job.'

"The number of times I've had to use that," he said.

"How many?" said Bryan.

Rod thought. "Four. And then they only tried to eat me on two of them."

"What are these?" said Taylor.

He held Rod's mouth-cleansing toothpaste balls in their blister pack.

"Sodium toothpaste bombs," he said. "Explode on contact with water."

"Oh, that's super cool and..."

He turned over a ripped piece of foil, only in doing so realising that it was an empty condom packet.

"Rod!" he grinned.

"Aye, sorry about that," said Rod and swept it aside.

"So that cliché is true, huh? Sex with beautiful women on a regular basis."

Rod blushed. "You know, it happens more often than you'd think."

Kathy offered Morag another car biscuit as they drove to the Think Tank.

Morag took three. She was only going to take two, but then the bump in her tummy made some encouraging noises and she took an extra one. When Kathy gave her a look, Morag said, "I'll buy you some replacements."

Kathy waggled her eyebrows, a very magnanimous and egalitarian waggle.

"You're just taking a calorie-laden bullet for me," she said.

"What are friends for, huh?"

Kathy grunted in amusement.

"You do any fitness?" she said.

Morag looked down at her belly, which was slightly but undeniably rounder than it once was. She wanted to pat it, but held back in case it was too much of a clue.

"I do not do fitness," she said. "It's kind of like starting a diet just before Christmas."

"It's not Christmas."

"The end of the world," said Morag. "What are the normal reasons for wanting to get fit? Increased life expectancy. Look hotter and sexier for potential partners. The end of the world is coming. Our life expectancy, whatever it is, isn't going to be measured in decades. I'm not looking for a potential partner. It's not like I need to plan to settle down and have kids."

"Oh, I want to have children some day," said Kathy.

Morag was genuinely surprised. "You want to bring new life into this shit-show spectacular we call the end times?"

Kathy smiled. "I'm ever the optimist. Before he was killed in the accident, my dad said he always wanted grandchildren."

"Yeah, but he didn't know about the Venislarn."

"He knew," said Kathy with a steely certainty. "He knew and he wanted grandchildren anyway. He was an optimist too."

Morag didn't know how to respond to that. Kathy drove through the Eastside developments to the multi-storey car park next to the Think Tank. Abruptly, she tapped Morag with the back of her hand.

"Tell you what I used to do for exercise. Pole fitness. Lot of fun. I could see you doing that."

"Pole fitness?" said Morag. "What's that?"

"It's fairly self-explanatory."

"What? So, like parallel bars? Gymnastics?"

Kathy wound down her window to get a ticket at the barrier. "Think vertical, not horizontal."

Morag thought. "Isn't that just pole dancing?"

"Pole fitness."

"Do you do it to music?"

"Sometimes."

"Tjat's pole dancing, Kathy."

"There's nothing sexual about it," said Kathy. "Unless you want there to be."

"Sure," said Morag.

Kathy raced up the ramps. Morag's unborn foetus did the voiceless equivalent of squealing with laughter.

"So, you did pole fitness," said Morag.

"I did."

"And now you do made-up stick fighting classes."

"It's not made up."

"Sounds to me like you're never happy unless you've got a stiff rod in your hand."

The car juddered to a stop on an up ramp.

"Who's said something?" said Kathy.

"Joke," said Morag.

Gears crunched as Kathy, flustered, got the car going again.

Do it again. Faster, faster, cried the anti-Christ.

Nina rolled into the reception of the consular mission.

"Well, I'm here," she said to Lois the receptionist.

"Well done," said Lois. "Want a medal?"

"I got a gold star from teacher." Nina showed her the one Mrs Fiddler had stuck on her. "So, I'm good, thanks."

She went through to the response team office. It was empty. A pile of personal registration documents leaned precariously on a

172

desk. Nina opened the top one out of curiosity. A person who had chosen to go by the adopted name of "Aleister Cthuggan" had filled out half the form required to sign himself over, body and soul, to the *em-shadt* Venislarn. The bottom half of the form, where the writing mostly petered out, had more tear blotches than ink on it. Nina let it fall closed. The pile of documents slid and scattered onto the chair and floor.

Nina was half-bending to pick them up when she realised there were no witnesses to the act and no one to pin the blame on her. She left the forms where they fell.

"Well, this is dull," she said, checked her e-mails, found nothing of note and then meandered down to the Vault.

The consular mission Vault was, in part, a library for naughty books. And not *Fifty Shades* naughty. It held the kinds of books that critically reviewed their own readers and ate the ones that weren't up to scratch. It was also a museum for artefacts and objects that refused to do as they were told. Some of them walked. Some of them talked. Some of them punched holes in the fabric of reality if you looked at them funny.

As such, the Vault was guarded by a number of ex-forces types who were brave by anyone's yardstick, and the fact that they didn't dare go into the Vault unless accompanied by someone who actually knew what they were doing was purely coincidental.

"Yo, Malc," said Nina, throwing a jaunty salute at the least monosyllabic of the bunch. "Is the professor around?"

He gave her a look, in recognition that Nina didn't willingly consort with Professor Sheikh Omar. "I think he's down at the Think Tank with your colleagues. Harvesting souls or some such."

"Of course," she said, like she knew what that meant.

"Maurice is in though," said another guard, Andy.

Nina tapped her backpack. "Something here I hoped he could help me identify."

"It's Thomas the Tank Engine," said Malcolm.

"No, silly."

"It is," said Malcolm. "My son's really into trains."

"Something inside the bag," said Nina flatly. "Idiots."

She swiped herself through the first glass airlock and gave the scanner at the next a good shufti of her biometrics.

173

Malcolm thumped the glass. "He's down by the Bloody Big Book," he mouthed.

Nina jerked her head in understanding and walked on.

The Vault was huge and laid out with uniformity and precision that, perversely, made it very easy to get lost in. A few months ago, Morag had temporarily and supposedly accidentally expanded it by opening a bunch of pocket dimensions inside it. Omar claimed he'd tidied them up, but Nina wasn't so sure. She stuck to the paths she knew.

As Nina walked, she heard a tinny clickety-clack which sharply echoed around. It was coming from ahead. She side-stepped round the big brown ball of a hibernating *Bondook* shambler that had just been left in the way and proceeded towards the noise.

In a wide side corridor, there was a stout metal box that was not a safe and was not a deep-sea diving chamber but was something in between. It contained the Bloody Big Book, or at least most of it. The Book allegedly had an infinite number of pages. How you could have most of something with an infinite number of pages was a bit beyond Nina. Next to it, beneath a hideous print of a beetle-hedgehog thing, sat Maurice, reading a book open on his lap whilst—and Nina had to take a second look—knitting a pair of yellow baby's booties.

On the broad table next to him was a teapot. Nina recognised it as the old battered thing they'd taken from Mystic Trevor's grubby flat. For some reason the lid was off and there was a twelve-inch ruler standing in the pot. There was a fresh cup of tea next to it.

Maurice looked up, smiled thinly and said, "He's not here."

"Think Tank. Collecting souls," said Nina.

"Something like that."

"You're knitting booties."

"Crocheting actually. One needle."

"Booties."

"On that point you are correct."

She realised that the clickety-clack she had heard earlier had stopped.

"I thought I heard tapping. Like a typewriter or..."

Maurice, his fingers busy with lemon-coloured wool, nodded at a display plinth across from him. "It's one of the OOPArts you found some weeks back, embedded in an old oak tree, I believe."

Nina went over to the item. It looked a bit like a typewriter and more like the underside of a crab with too many legs and a printer ribbon where its internal organs should be.

"It didn't do anything until a clever young man thought to put some paper in it," said Maurice.

The device started up again, crab legs twitching and clawing and stabbing the page with their inky tips.

"It appears to be a live transcript of the words or thoughts of some individual—human, I think. No idea where they are."

Nina inspected the typing as it emerged.

AAAAARGH! AAAAARGH! MAKE IT STOP! NOT THE EARS! PLEASE!

"Wherever he is, I don't believe he's having a particularly nice time," said Maurice serenely. "I'm surprised you heard it above the racket."

"What racket?" said Nina.

Maurice held up a finger for quiet and then elevated it slightly to point upwards. She looked up and listened. Far away, on the cusp of hearing, was the whirr and the throb of building works.

"Digging up the square above our very heads," Maurice tutted. "Considerate building practices, indeed!"

"Oh, yeah," said Nina, who had seen the signs on Forward Management's site hoardings. "Um, I have questions."

"Part of the human condition, I believe."

Nina pointed at the teapot with the ruler in the top.

"There is a ward of *Pei-Yeu* inscribed on the base," said Maurice. "Omar believes it is therefore some form of divination device. As augury is a personal speciality of mine, I've decided to take a look."

"Oh."

"It would appear that the greater the danger one is about to face, the fuller it becomes. Almost poetic. We all need a strong cup of cha in times of crisis."

"And?" she said, pointing at the booties he was working on.

"They're coming out well, I think," he said.

"Can I ask why you're knitting—"

"Crocheting."

"—crocheting yellow baby booties."

He paused in his work. "For one, I think it's a vastly under-rated colour and it has the additional benefit of being gender neutral."

"Yeah. That's not really what I meant."

"You came down here for a reason," said Maurice. "Unless you merely heard an entirely true rumour that I was about to open a packet of pink wafers to go with my cup of tea."

"I wanted help in identifying something," said Nina, swinging the backpack off her shoulder. "And I don't mean Thomas the Tank Engine."

"Oh, the works of the Reverend W. Awdry hold little appeal for me," said Maurice. "Those trains were all work and no play, and I've always been uneasy about the anthropomorphism of everyday objects. I had enough teenage angst over the thought of my grandfather's portrait watching my sinful behaviour without thinking that the gramophone and twin-tub washer might be watching me too. He was the curate at St Nicholas's over in Kings Norton."

"Your granddad."

"Awdry. The author. Wrote the first books while he was there. Clearly trains were of more interest to him than ministering to the souls of his parishioners. What do you have for me?"

Nina unzipped and whipped out the *yellis* wand.

"Oh, my," said Maurice and nearly dropped his crocheting. "It's not often you see one of those." With a haste the measured little man rarely showed, Maurice stuffed his crocheting inside the book as a bookmark and set it to one side. "May I?"

He carefully took the barbed wand device from Nina.

"You know what it is?" she said.

He nodded. "I saw one like this, not this one though, at..." He frowned in thought and then chuckled. "At a scandalous party in Dublin. It's a *yellis* wand."

"That's right."

176

"Do you know what it's for? No? It's essentially a memory wand. Little more than a party trick artefact. So, if there was a memory one wished to wipe from the minds of others so, for example..." He put his hand on the book and the crocheting within. "Did you know that your colleague, Morag Murray is pregnant?"

Nina was stunned, not only because the ginger one was pregnant but because Nina had not suspected a thing.

"Whose is it? Is it Rod's? It's Rod's, isn't it? I know he always had a thing for her."

"Not in this instance," said Maurice. "The father was a servant of *Yo-Morgantus*, a veritable Joseph to the Venislarn's Yahweh. Morag is pregnant with the *kaatbari,* and the birth of the child will herald the final apocalypse, the Soulgate and the end of all things."

"You are shitting me, man," she said.

"I am not... kidding you, Nina," he said.

"And you can sit there happily drinking tea and eating pink wafers, knowing that?"

"It seems the perfect excuse to eat pink wafers, not that I need much of one. Which reminds me..."

Maurice picked up the book and crocheting and placed them in an old leather bag and extracted a packet of pink wafer biscuits.

"And now," said Maurice and raised the wand. "*Hyet-pa!*"

The prongs of the wand came alive with light so bright the air itself seemed to hum. Nina couldn't help but stare at them.

"You will forget everything I have just told you about Morag and the *kaatbari*," said Maurice. "You will forget any mention of your colleague's pregnancy, the apocalypse it will trigger or indeed the delightful booties I'm making for the anti-Christ."

He lowered the wand and the lights faded. Nina shook her head to clear the sparkles from her vision.

"That was pretty," she said and then paused to rewind the last few moments in her mind. It was like when her mum was talking to her about housework or money or some other old person nonsense and Nina tuned out until her mum asked her a direct question and then she realised she had heard nothing for several minutes. "You were saying something, Maurice? About... the wand?"

"So, there's the activation phrase and the rest is just stage hypnotism. There's also a counter to the wand. A simple hand gesture for the nimble fingered. I can show you if you like."

"Um, yeah," said Nina, the last of the fogginess clearing from her mind.

"But first," said the little man, opening the packet with ironic theatricality, "pink wafer?"

"Sure. Why not?"

There was break in shooting. Someone had declared that the rain outside had affected the light inside, and new lighting rigs were being put in place for the next scene. In his private corner of the set, Taylor invited Rod to take his pick from an assortment of salads, bites and sculpted fruits delivered by craft services. Rod piled a plate with puff pastry packets and finger buffet sandwiches while Taylor watched, picking at the fruit.

"You know what I look forward to, Rod?" he said.

"Leaving Birmingham?" suggested Rod.

"Getting fat."

Rod gave him a questioning look.

"At the end of every production, after the wrap on the last day of shooting I go to Wendy's or IHOP and pig out on deep-fried junk food. I can put on ten pounds in a week." He regarded a wedge of melon. "That's what I look forward to."

"They've got you on a diet?" said Rod, disbelieving. There wasn't an ounce of spare fat on the guy. He had the muscles of a pure Olympian. "You can't be at peak fitness unless you're eating carbs."

"Ah," said Taylor wistfully. "Big bowls of pasta. I dream of big bowls of pasta."

"If you want realism. If you want to be *that* guy who goes up against the Venislarn every day, you should be eating big bowls of pasta. And pies. Proper pies with walls and a bottom of short crust pastry. That's realism."

Taylor laughed. "And does 'that guy' have an obligatory topless scene in every movie? Oh, and a PG-13 friendly kiss with the love interest. And all to be shown in every IMAX theatre in the States."

178

Rod ate the pie and pinched at his own belly through his shirt. He grabbed a two-inch roll of fat. "To heck with them. The 'dad' look is in."

"Really?"

"Aye."

"Well, I don't know how well that would play in Peoria, but I'll mention it to my agent." Taylor ate his slice of melon like a man who would rather be eating pie. "Apart from the lack of pies, dare I ask how realistic any of this is?"

"I don't know," said Rod honestly.

"Does any of it ring true?"

Rod didn't want to offend him by saying he recognised none of this as being like his own life. "I can tell you that PG-13 friendly kisses with the love interest are pretty thin on the ground."

"A bit more NC-17, huh?"

"If that's what I think it is then that's a definite no. I don't seem to have the time for that. My colleague, Nina, says I need to get myself on Tinder but I'm not ready for that."

Taylor gestured at the spot on the table where Rod's empty condom packet had fallen earlier. "The evidence suggests otherwise, my friend."

"Oh, that?" Rod felt his cheeks redden. "Would you believe me if I said that was a work thing?"

Taylor's grin was wide, his teeth unnervingly perfect. "You had sex with a woman—it was a woman, yeah?—for work purposes?"

"Literally the only way to save her life," said Rod. "I kid you not."

Taylor clapped his hands in surprise. "Oh, man! You *are* like some suave super spy."

"Oh, aye," said Rod. "Spot on."

"So, no girlfriends then?" said Taylor.

Rod pulled a face and ate a sandwich to avoid answering for a few seconds. "Actually, the thing is..."

"Yes?"

"The woman I had..." He gestured at the empty spot on the table. "Her. I like her."

"Uh-huh?" grinned Taylor.

"But I'm a bit rusty these days."

"Performance issues."

"What? No. Not that. I mean, we did it. Aw, flaming heck. I sound like a lovestruck teenager."

"Are you lovestruck, Rod?"

Rod was under the impression that Americans weren't capable of either sarcasm or irony, but he couldn't tell if Taylor was making fun of him and he wasn't sure he wanted to share his emotional issues with a man who, in looks at least, was twenty years younger than him.

"I'd like her to be my girlfriend. I'd like there to be something, but I don't know how to go about... what's a word that means the same as 'courting' but doesn't make me sound like my grandma?"

"Wooing?" suggested Taylor.

"Just as bad. But that. You must have had some experience. A guy like you..."

"Like me?"

"A movie star."

"My experiences are severely limited," said the actor. "There are lots of 'Taylor Graham arm-in-arm on the red carpet with 'insert actress name here'' moments but that's PR, cooked up by my agent and hers. Actual romance. I can only tell you what I know."

Rod hunkered forward. "Okay. Tell me what you know because I want to do the right thing. I like this woman very much and now we've..." He nodded at the empty spot on the table. "I want to make that gesture."

Taylor nodded sagely. "Okay, here's what —"

The door banged open, making the partition walls wobble, and Producer Tammy and a gaggle of Tammy-lites barged in.

"What the hell?" said Taylor with easy-going annoyance.

"Either of you seen Langford?" said Tammy.

"Most people knock before—"

"Have you?" she demanded.

"No," said Taylor.

There was a wild and slightly panicky anger in Tammy's eyes.

"What is it?" said Rod.

"He took himself off set an hour ago. Called a cab, didn't tell security or his assistant what the issue was. Said he was going to 'see it for himself between Glover Street and St Andrew's Road.'"

"Bloody hell," said Rod.

"What?"

He pushed himself out from behind the fixed table, suddenly finding the space—even this luxury space—too cramped and confining. "How long ago?"

"Less than an hour," said Tammy. "What's going on?"

Rod tried to picture the Hollywood actor going down to Fish Town to pick up some method acting tips from real *samakha*. He couldn't visualise it ending well.

"He's going to get himself killed." He did a silent physical pat down. Pistol, car keys, phone. "I've got to stop him."

Taylor had a half-smile on his face. "Is this for real?"

Rod pushed past Tammy and the Tammy-lites and hurried outside. It took him a moment to think what the quickest route to his car was from here.

"He's gone to see the *samakha*, right?" said Taylor falling in beside him. "Fish town?"

"Yes," said Rod. "And no."

"No?"

"You're not coming with me."

"Come on," said Taylor, turning on some easy charm that Rod had no time for. "Research trip."

"No."

"I'll be your shadow."

"If you die, I will lose my job and that will make me very sad."

"Is it going to be dangerous?"

Rod pursed his lips. "You're not coming, Taylor."

"Just a ride in the car."

"No."

"And I'll tell you how to win your lady love."

"Lady love? Now you do sound like my grandma." He huffed to himself, took out his phone and called the office. "Lois. Is either Morag or Nina free? No, not Kathy. Just... Nina. Yes, put me through."

While he waited. Rod looked aside to Taylor.

"Just for the car ride, right?"

Taylor punched the air.

"Where are you going?" called one of the Tammy-lites, the only one fast enough to keep up with them. Rod unlocked his car. He looked back at her. She had her clipboard over her head to keep off the rain.

"We're going to get Langford. Nothing to worry about," said Rod.

"Tell 'em we've gone fishing," grinned Taylor.

He got into the passenger seat beside Rod. "You hear that? 'Gone fishing'. Totally unscripted."

"Great," said Rod. "Now buckle up."

Kathy sat down by *Polliqan Riti*'s tank and, with the assurance of a skill quickly acquired, picked up a slick connector tube and plugged it into the correct spot on her neck, between the C2 and C3 vertebrae.

She turned to Morag. "See you on the other—"

.

.

.

"—side," she said.

She was in Pigeon Park. Between Colmore Row where the buses and taxis massed, and the side streets that led to the New Street shopping area, from the arcades and alleys that led to the tower offices and corporate buildings, to the pubs, clubs, and civic buildings in the direction of Victoria Square, Pigeon Park was a place to pass through, almost never a destination.

Kathy walked for the sheer joy of walking in this place.

"These are not my feet," she said, speaking aloud for the joy of speaking aloud in a public place.

She began to run. She was not normally a fan of running. Her thighs complained instantly. Within seconds, her breasts would build up enough pendulous rhythm to cause considerable discomfort. But this wasn't reality.

Kathy ran effortlessly, gracefully and faster than she had ever run in her life. She ran out of the park, across the brick cobbled street to the pavement by the Lloyds Bank and proceeded to sprint a lap of the park, past Rackhams, up to Colmore Row, alongside the cafés, corner shops and high priced restaurants and back down the other side, past the Victorian banks that were now pubs, bars and businesses.

She stopped. She wasn't out of breath. She hadn't even broken a sweat. She walked back into Pigeon Park.

"Right," she declared loudly. "Who wants a ride in a petri dish?"

Pigeon Park, for reasons known only to them, was a favourite gathering point for the city's goths and emos and those skater types who didn't want to go to a skate park.

Kathy scanned the options and waited for someone to meet her eye.

"You!"

A teenager with pink punky hair and a tartan shirt blinked at her. Kathy strode over. The teenager looked to her friends, gangly shoe gazers for the most part, and twitched nervously.

"What—what have I done?" said the teenager.

"We ain't done nothing," said the tallest lad next to her.

"No, you haven't," said Kathy.

She took the teenager's tiny wrist and dragged her arm up, like she was a victorious boxer in the ring.

"I've got one!" she shouted to the sky.

In the Think Tank laboratory, Professor Sheikh Omar closely monitored the screen while Morag watched. A red light had popped up on the monitor. Keeping a safe distance between himself and the needy, greedy brain mass that was *Polliqan Riti*, Omar inserted an electrode into the floating creature and prepared his scissors.

The process of harvesting twenty-eight 'souls' from the body and mind of *Polliqan Riti* looked more like pantomime than science. Maybe the same was true with all things Venislarn. Would-be occultists the world over were faffing around with incense and black candles and maybe a goat or cat. Maybe this was just the same but with computers and bio-icky VR gadgets and electrodes and a Venislarn brain-monster.

Morag realised as the morning went on, that the process was more like brain surgery than anything else. She'd seen videos of patients in surgery performing tasks, playing music, solving puzzles so that the surgeons could see which parts of the brain lit up, metaphorically speaking. The creation of souls, *fraxasa*, was not dissimilar.

Once Kathy or Morag had entered the simulated world in *Polliqan Riti's* mind and sought out a simulated individual, Professor Sheikh Omar (with a little assistance from a willing *Polliqan*), was able to isolate the relevant nub of brain material and snip it away with long-nosed scissors.

"And he doesn't mind?" Morag asked while Kathy was inside, locating the next sim for them to bag.

"*Polliqan Riti*?" said Omar. "*San shu bhesk lor*, Morag. If an individual of such sensory capacity could be hurt by this, the act of mere existence would be a continuous torture. *Polliqan Riti* is a connoisseur of all sensations. Besides, we have an understanding."

"What, exactly, has he done?" said Morag.

"Hmmm?"

"What did *Polliqan Riti* do to offend the Venislarn?"

"It's not so much what he has done," said Omar. "It's more the case of what he is."

"Is?"

"He's toxic. A Typhoid Mary."

"In what way?"

The lights on the monitor moved.

"A moment," said Omar. He nipped in and clipped a nubule of white flesh from the creature's exposed back. Or front. With an undifferentiated blob, such distinctions were impossible.

Morag was ready with the petri dish. Omar lifted away the sliver and placed it in the dish.

Mother, said the voice within her.

Morag ignored her child, sealed the dish and placed it with the others.

Mother? I have questions.

"Course you do."

"Sorry?" said Omar.

Morag gave him fifty percent of a smile and said, "I just need to pop out for a minute."

"Really?" he said. "We are in the midst of a delicate operation at the moment."

She glanced at Kathy to check she was still fully submerged in the simulation.

"Someone is currently using my bladder as a bouncy castle," she said.

Are you talking about me, mother?

"Ah," said Omar, visibly squeamish. "Yes, nature calls. All the..." He waved the long scissors uncertainly. "Plumbing. Totally understand."

Morag stepped out of Omar's private laboratory and strode through the various testing rooms and research stations until she reached the public area of the Think Tank museum. She stood at the railing overlooking the large, lower floor full of machines from yesteryear.

"You okay, baby?" she sub-vocalised.

Did you not want to talk to me in front of the man? asked baby.

"No."

Are you embarrassed by me?

The true answer was no, she was afraid, not embarrassed – afraid her unnatural lines of communication with her foetus might be made public. But she said, "Yes. I'm embarrassed by you. You'll spend your whole life being embarrassed by me, so it's only fair."

I'm sorry I embarrass you.

"You had questions."

Two questions. In truth, the first is more of a moral quandary.

The baby wasn't even born, and it was already caught in a moral quandary. She didn't know whether to be proud or horrified.

You owe the mmmm-mmmm Handmaiden of Prein *twenty-eight souls.*

"You don't need to say 'mmmm-mmmm'. You can just say Handmaiden of *Prein*."

Yes, mother. And to avoid giving it twenty-eight human souls you're capturing twenty-eight likenesses from the simulation in Polliqan Riti's mind.

"You've been listening in," she said.

The man has a nice voice.

"That's possibly the only nice thing about him," said Morag. "What's your point, baby?"

The fraxasa *you're harvesting have to be sufficiently complex likenesses to satisfy the Handmaiden of Prein.*

"Yes."

If they're not sufficiently complex then the Handmaiden will reject them.

"Probably."

But if they are sufficiently complex...

"Yes?"

Are they not human in their own right?

Morag blew out heavily. She couldn't pretend it hadn't crossed her mind.

"Yeah, well, it's not as simple as that" she said.

I thought it wouldn't be.

"You see, the simulated souls, they're... Well, it's not like they're proper people".

Aren't they?

"No."

Why not?

She floundered both physically and mentally and had to make a reassuring gesture to a member of the public who wanted to lead her away from the railing.

"Those things," she began. The man was still looking at her. She pointed at her ear and mouthed 'Bluetooth'. "Those things... they're just lumps of flesh. They may appear to be conscious, but they have had no experiences. They have no real life to lose; they're only lumps of potential."

So, they are like me? said baby.

"Christ," she breathed. "No, not like... You're different. You're definitely different. Look, did you say you had another question?"

When's lunch, mother?

When Langford James saw the florist's truck, he knew he'd found his way in.

Langford had searched the grimy back streets and chain-linked parking lots between St Andrew's Road and Glover Street for some time and found nothing that looked like the entrance to a hidden *samakha* ghetto. He wasn't sure what he was looking for. It wouldn't be like a Chinatown or Little Italy with a decorative archway or banners hung across the street... Okay, he *had* expected a decorative archway: something small perhaps, positioned over a dark and foreboding side street with steam curling from sidewalk grates. Carvings that were both disturbing and beautiful, maybe ones that moved when you weren't quite looking, like some Diagon Alley magic thing. Okay, so he had honestly expected something out of a *Harry Potter / Big Trouble in Little China* crossover movie, with walking fish.

There was nothing of the sort to be found. He'd hugged his jacket a little closer and continued walking, telling himself that, with an actor's eye for detail, he'd spot something soon enough. The rain had stopped, but moisture seemed to hang in the air and it carried a chill. He folded his arms and decided he had half an hour left to find the place, then he'd go back to the set.

There were few people about on the streets. A mechanic worked on a car just outside the gates of a railway arch garage. Two women wearing miniskirts and fake furs approached drunkenly arm-in-arm and then entered a public house that looked so filthy and lifeless Langford had assumed it was no longer in business. At the end of a strip of asphalt that was too rough to be a road and too ill-defined to be a business premises, a figure stood at the open tailgate of truck and sorted through the boxes of flowers in the back.

Langford would have noted the scene and moved on if not for a few uncanny details. The hooded figure by the truck was comparing bunches of flowers, like a suitor searching for a perfect bouquet, but the flowers themselves were brown and headless, like rotting stalks of celery. And yet, as an expert at reading bodies, Langford was certain the guy was savouring each flower's fragrance. This held his eye long enough to notice the grey sheen of the hands holding those bouquets.

It was a *samakha*.

Langford let nothing show in his moment of triumph. He stood still, positioned innocuously by a wall, and watched. When the *samakha* had decided which bunch of dead flowers he preferred, he pulled down the truck's roll-over door and headed off with them. Langford observed his rolling gait, the jaunty twist of his shoulders. This *samakha* was a young man, little more than a kid.

Langford watched and followed. The *samakha* kid walked round one of the huge brick pillars of a railway bridge and into another dead-end side road. Langford kept on the far side of the main road and angled round the pillar to see where the youth had gone.

He saw the kid enter a shed or ancient static trailer that leaned against the wall of the bridge. The word 'TAXI' was printed in peeling paint above the door, followed by a telephone number that was mostly scratched away.

For two minutes, Langford wondered where a *samakha* would go in a taxi. When he was convinced the guy wasn't coming out any time soon, he crossed the road and went into the taxi office. The light inside was the grey-yellow of the dust and grease that coated the windows. The single box room was bare but for a wonky customer desk and a row of seats against a wall that looked like they had been stolen from a grade school.

There was an ugly and unfortunate character standing behind the counter. There was no one else, no customers, no *samakha* with a bunch of dead flowers.

"Hi, I thought I saw a guy come in here," said Langford, automatically adopting a mute British accent as he spoke, a little bit *Eastenders*, a little bit *Downton Abbey*.

"Taxi?" croaked the ugly son of a bitch at the counter.

"No. I saw a guy. Hood. Flowers. He came in here."

A head shake. "Taxi taxi."

"No, thank you," said Langford. He hesitated for a moment and then tried Venislarn. He'd spent four weeks doing intensive language and dialect coaching with a woman in Santa Monica. "*Lhos varn, yegdi bhus-san yar? Gi-et samakha, per.*"

The guy's bulging eyes glanced momentarily to the flimsy partition door to the side of his counter. It was momentary and involuntary, but Langford saw it.

Langford went to the door. Where it was positioned, it could only open back onto the road he had just come from.

"Taxi, taxi," said the guy, displeased.

"I'll just be a minute, sir," said Langford and went through.

The door opened onto a flight of damp stone steps in a narrow alley. The 'taxi taxi' guy did not follow. In fact, as Langford stepped carefully down, he heard the door being slammed shut behind him. He looked back. The door was no longer there. The steps just went up and up until they were lost in the crowding shadows of the walls and buildings to either side.

The steps were narrow and slick. Langford automatically reached for a handrail but there was none. Far below, the silver waters of the canal reflected a cloudy loveless light.

He stepped carefully down until he was on the path beside the canal. He looked up and saw the *samakha* village. Fish Town they called it. The buildings on either side were ancient edifices—ancient by American standards, not British, he guessed. They looked like factories from the age of steam, like workhouses from *Oliver Twist*. The *samakha* had occupied and built on these. Ground floor windows and doors were opened out to make stall fronts and shops. Awnings above them rubbed up against makeshift balconies and extensions that had been welded onto the building fronts. Bamboo and timber had been lashed together to make pontoons and bridges, arranged with all the care of jack straws. And among this unplanned but industrious chaos, the *samakha* lived and went about their business.

Langford took a step along the path, only just beginning to soak in the wonder of what lay about him, when a hand clamped over his mouth from behind and dragged him back into a doorway. Langford gave a shout of surprise, tried to remember what self-defence techniques he'd learned in his capoeira classes and, flailing, only latched onto a useless recollection of the sexy limber blonde who'd started going to the class in the last few months and who was a vegan and had a birthday in October. Something that was definitely a blade pressed against Langford's ribs and a voice hissed in his ear.

"Mofo, ya gonna—ggh!—tell me why you been following me, 'fore I gut you, huh?"

Rod accelerated down the Smallbrook Queensway and then threw a sharp left towards New Street station. Taylor Graham braced himself against the dashboard and tried not to let his nervousness show.

"You should really get some sirens," he said. "Then you wouldn't have to... weave around so much."

"I asked," said Rod and threw a right round between the station building and the Old Rep theatre. "So, you were telling me."

"Was I?" said Taylor.

"About this lass I'm... I'm into. And before we were interrupted you said that what I should do was... And then we were interrupted."

Rod pumped the brakes, beeped at a car that had the right of way and ran through a red light and down past the rag markets.

"You want to have this conversation now?"

"We've got two minutes, maybe one," said Rod. "Now's as good a time."

"Well, I..." Taylor gripped the door handle. "You put me on the spot, Rod, but okay. This girl, who you've done the dirty with but you're not seeing, romantically..."

"Yes?"

"It's all the obvious stuff. Conversation, compliments and... don't you guys in the UK ask a girl out for a drink?"

"I..." He did a hard stop to avoid a teenager who had stepped into the road whilst looking in completely the wrong direction. "I ask my mates out all the time. But there's a difference between asking someone out for a drink and asking someone *out* out."

"*Out* out?"

"*Out* out. And I asked her out once before."

"Uh-huh. And how did that go?"

"We ended up double-dating with two other people and"—he swallowed the embarrassment—"she found the other bloke far more interesting."

"Ah."

Rod threw him a look. Compounded by the focus he was putting into his driving, it was probably fiercer than he intended but it carried the basic message. "Ah? Years of Hollywood dating and all you've got for me is 'Ah.'"

"You didn't tell me you guys had history," said Taylor.

"I don't even know if it was enough of a thing to call it history."

"You went on a date."

190

Rod shook his head. "I'm not sure either of us would classify it as a date."

"Jeez," said Taylor. "You Brits are as damned reticent as everyone makes out. It's a wonder you ever manage to reproduce."

Rod briefly touched seventy miles an hour as they raced past the coach station. It was a handbrake turn into Floodgate Street. The Hollywood action star squeaked. Rod stopped on a single yellow line and tapped Taylor.

"We're here."

Taylor nodded wordlessly and got out. He took a couple of deep breaths. "Where to?"

Rod pointed to an alleyway in a brick wall and strode over. "So, no concrete advice?"

"I suspect the British dating game is different from ours," said Taylor, following behind, down the steps to the canal side. "If you two don't even know if you've been dating or not then..." He blew out and shrugged. "Go whole hog. Flowers. Gift baskets. Ringside seats to the soccer match. Then she'll know for sure that you're interested."

"Interested?" said Nina, stepping out at the bottom of the stairs.

Rod turned to introduce Taylor. "Nina, Taylor. Taylor, Nina."

"I know you," said Nina, giving him a nod of greeting. "You were a backing dancer for Enrique Inglesias."

"Everyone's got to start somewhere," said Taylor.

"So, who does he fancy?"

Taylor looked between them and then gave a questioning sideways nod at Nina.

"Her?" said Rod, startled. "God, no. I pity the man that fancies Nina."

"Sour grapes," said Nina. "No, I know who he fancies. Some bonnie wee Scottish lassie who ate too many cheesy Wotsits as a child."

"Wrong and offensive," said Rod.

"Don't you guys have a job to do?" said Taylor, looking back and forth along the canal.

"Yes," said Nina and frowned. "And you thought putting the life of one Hollywood actor in danger wasn't enough?" she asked Rod.

"He's here in a strictly observational capacity," said Rod.

"Absolutely," nodded Taylor solemnly.

Nina didn't look impressed. "This *muda* never ends well."

"You want me to make him go sit in the car, like a dog?" said Rod.

Nina shrugged. "*Bhul qum.* YOLO, I say." She gestured at the tunnel before them. "Through there, Taylor, you touch nothing, you speak to no one, you don't go nowhere we don't tell you to go."

"Yes, ma'am."

"We'll split up," she told Rod. "Work opposite sides of the canal. First one to find your lost actor calls it in. And maybe, if we're lucky, we'll find him before he's turned into chum."

The *samakha* youth called Pupfish propelled Langford through the door of a canalside eatery. Two other *samakha*, both in baseball caps and knock-off sportswear sat at one of the damp-warped tables by the window. The smaller one picked at a bowl of grey chips. The big one, a monstrous fish man, had a bottle of Pepsi Max in his huge hand.

"Lookit what I picked up," said Pupfish proudly.

The small one, wearing a Tupac Shakur T-shirt under his jacket, looked up and made a sniffing gesture, not that he had anything resembling a nose. "He's not registered? Ggh! An outsider."

Pupfish pushed Langford forward. Langford stiffened, resisting.

"I got me a bona fide Hollywood actor," said Pupfish.

"Muda," said the smaller one.

"It's true-true," said Pupfish unable to contain his excitement. "This is Fluke, and this is Death Roe. They're part of my crew."

"Whose crew?" said the smaller one, Fluke.

"The Waters Crew," said Pupfish.

"What is this place?" said Langford, nervously, scanning the room, the mould-covered food counter, the cracked tiles, the flickering light. Behind the counter, a fat *samakha* fed chunks of cut up pizza to an alien crab-creature in an aquarium tank. The tank had pink gravel and a little model castle.

"What is this?" said Langford, bewildered and one good surprise away from being terrified.

"Come on—ggh!—show them," said Pupfish, poking him sharply in the back. "Show them the picture."

Langford pulled out his phone and swiped through to a photo he'd taken on set two days ago. He held it out to the boys of the Waters Crew. Fluke peered at it. He had to present one eye to the screen and then the other to double-check. These were fish men, actual swear-to-God fishmen with gills and gasping mouths.

"It's that guy," said Fluke. "From that sick-ass action film."

"Taylor Graham and I are working on a film. I'm Langford James."

"I ain't never heard of him," said Death Roe. The way the big fish man said it, it sounded like it was a problem.

"Have you seen the *Planet of the Apes* films?" said Langford.

"Were you in a monkey suit?" said Fluke.

"Motion capture," nodded Langford.

"This guy is fo real," said Pupfish, squeeing like a fanboy. "Fo real! An' he wants to talk to us 'bout a film role."

"What's that *muda* he's wearing?" said Fluke, tapping the phone.

Langford looked at the image and grimaced. "That's what I wanted to talk about. The costume designer thinks that what *samakha* wear."

"That *adn-bhul* ripped coat?" said Fluke.

"*Adn-bhul* perv outfit," said Death Roe.

"Exactly," said Langford. "I'm playing the role of Fin *Yaghur*, a *samakha* prince and they think that this is how—"

"You playin' a *samakha*?" said Fluke.

"That's the idea."

"Doin' the whole—ggh!"—Fluke did a weird marionette puppet mime—"green screen, motion-CGI ting?"

Langford nodded.

"We're gonna be in a movie?" said Death Roe.

"A Hollywood movie," said Langford.

"*Muda!*" said Fluke, thrilled. "And you're doing *bhul-tamade* research."

"*Nemadh rho*. Trying to keep it real."

"Fasho."

"Fasho," said Death Roe.

"So, sit down an' aks yo questions, Mr James," said Pupfish. "What you want?" He spread his arms out to take in the food counter. "Anything you like."

Langford looked at the food behind the glass counter. Much of it was invisible, hidden by a drying brown smear.

"No, I don't think I'm hungry."

"He's gonna aks his questions and then he's gonna come home with me and meet Allana." Pupfish considered the awful dead stems in his hand and threw them aside. "Gonna take the Hollywood star home to meet my girl. Aight. Now that's a present. Better than a *dnebian* land-squid."

"Nah, dog," said Fluke. "Should let me take him home to meet Kirsten. She'll put on a right nice spread for him. Ggh! Hobnobs. Get one of them fancy prawn rings from Iceland."

"Sounds delightful."

"Ma girl will treat you right," said Fluke.

Pupfish visibly winced at that comment.

"Don't be a pussy about it," Fluke said to him. "Yo momma's my girl now. She's got—ggh!—needs I aim to fulfil and holes I aim to fill."

He nudged Death Roe, who rocked in amused agreement.

"You can't talk about my mom that way," said Pupfish miserably.

"I can talk how I like," said Fluke, "cos she hooked on me. Ggh! You know I call her legs 'I Can't Believe It's Not Butter', yeah? Cos they're so easy to spread."

Death Roe laughed. Behind the counter, the disgusting vendor gave a chortle.

"Ggh! She's not like that," whined Pupfish.

"I tell ya what's she's like," said Fluke. "She's like a squirrel, cos she's always got my nuts in her mouth."

Death Roe hooted in amusement. Langford kept his poise, although in the great and terrible history of Yo Momma jokes, there were worse ones.

"I know things about yo momma that you don'," Fluke said. "Ggh! You know she call her pussy Jasmine?"

"No," she Pupfish. "She don't. Ggh!"

"She do, because she's only happy when she's got Aladdin," crowed Fluke.

Death Roe laughed so hard he could make nothing but coughing gill gasps. The café owner wiped his streaming eyes with his apron and then blew his nose on it. And, yes, Langford did allow himself a little smile, even if it was at Pupfish's expense.

There was a loud slam from the corner of the café and a figure, sitting almost invisibly in the shadows, rose.

"I—ggh!—I ain't gonna allow that."

The laughter dried up instantly. The figure stepped forward into the sickly strip lighting.

"I ain't gonna allow it," said the tall *samakha* youth.

"Hey, Tony," said Pupfish. "They were just having fun." He glanced at Langford. Pupfish's look of terror could have put the wind up anyone, a pretty impressive feat for an inexpressive fish-face.

"I ain't gonna allow it," repeated Tony, taking centre stage in the café, one hand down his pants in the time-honoured stance of urban gangstas and three-year-old boys everywhere. "You bring this thing in here?" He jabbed a scaly digit at Langford.

"Langford here is an actor," said Pupfish.

"Oh, I heard," scowled Tony. "I heard it all. You bring—ggh!—a *den-thay* human in here and the *adn-bhul* bastard is playing one of us in his movie. You hear that?"

"We hear," said Death Row.

"An' you okay with dat?" Tony shook himself violently. "You okay with The Man playing one of us? Takin' roles from—ggh!—fish boys? He's... whatisit? He's 'scaling up', puttin' on the make-up and thinkin' he can be one of us."

"Tony, is it?" said Langford, offering him a hand. "I have nothing but respect for you and your people and—"

"My people, is it?" shouted Tony. "*My* people?! You happy to play us in your movie as long as we stays in our place, huh? I say, let my people go, *bhul-tamade!*"

"I can talk to my producer, Tammy. I'm sure she—"

"My name's Tony T," said the *samakha*. He pulled his hand out of his pants and it came out holding a snub-nosed revolver. "And there ain't no *adn-bhul* way you're talking your way outta this *muda.*"

Langford read the room quickly. Tony T had a gun. Pupfish was up and holding his hands out in panic. Fluke was unnerved but Langford could see he was interested in seeing how this would pan out. Death Roe was unfazed. The biggest guy in the room could afford to be relaxed. If it came to a fight, he'd probably just side with whoever ended up winning. The guy behind the counter was paying no attention. He was making coochie-coo noises to his pet crab.

"It's all cool, Tony. Really," said Pupfish. "Mr James is just gonna talk to us and then I'm gonna take him to see Allana." He glanced at Fluke. "Ggh! Maybe my mom."

"Unh-uh." Tony shook his head. "You ain't lettin' that filth in yo momma's house. You hear him? He was—ggh!—laughin' at jokes about yo momma."

"We all were," said Death Roe.

"An' that's okay if it's us," said Tony. "But him? You gonna let him diss yo mom? Yo girl, Fluke? Nah. This *muda*'s a grievous insult. You either kill that *glun'u* now or challenge him, *Shohreye 'uuuduk.*"

"It don't need that, Tony," said Fluke.

"You gonna be the pussy who lets humans—ggh!—trash-talk his girl?"

"No, Tony, but..."

"*Shohreye 'uuuduk.*"

Langford's Venislarn training had been intensive and the swears Tony was so fond of were easy to translate, but this *Shohreye 'uuuduk* was something he'd never heard of.

"What is *Shohreye 'uuuduk*?" he asked.

"Trial by ordeal," said Pupfish.

"Pistols at *adn-bhul* dawn," said Death Roe.

196

"You better do it," Tony T said to Fluke. "Or I'm gonna pop this fool now and tell your Kirsten that you weren't—ggh!—man enough."

Fluke rose slowly, cornered. Whatever this trial by ordeal was, it wouldn't end well.

Morag returned to the lab as Omar placed another petri dish among the stacks. Kathy remained reclined in her seat, deep in virtual reality.

"Twenty," said Omar, one word serving as explanation, brag and admonishment for Morag's absence.

"Well done," she said. "I needed some air."

"I will forgive you, my dear," he said, adjusting his spectacles, "given your delicate state."

Morag looked at the collected slices of flesh, not one larger than a marble, gobbets of lifeless muscle. Souls?

"We were discussing..." she said.

"Were we?" said Omar.

We were, weren't we, mother?

"I was." She made a silly face to hide her awkwardness. "I was talking to myself and it occurred to me, how are these artificial souls different from the actual humans?"

"Not at all, I hope, if we're to get the Venislarn to accept them as an offering."

"I mean, are we achieving anything? When we give these to the Handmaiden *Shala'pinz Syu*, they might be eaten—if they're lucky— or they might be subjected to tortures without end."

"And you are only now wondering if these off-cuts from another reality are capable of feeling pain, if they can suffer," said Omar.

"Yes. Precisely."

"What a lovely philosophical question."

"It's not lovely. It's worrying."

Omar attended to the monitor screen again and interpreted Kathy's movements through an invented world by charts and lights on the screen.

"If you create something so sophisticated and detailed that it becomes indistinguishable from the thing it is trying to mimic, does it become that thing? When does the map become the landscape it represents?"

"And?"

"And nothing. Like a zen Buddhist koan, the beauty is in the question, not the answer."

"Professor, please."

He set down his flesh snipping tools on the side of the tank and turned to her directly. He had tucked his tie into his shirt halfway down to stop it dangling in the tank. He looked quite silly.

"In the Vault we have the Bloody Big Book or at least most of it," he said. "Have you ever read it?"

"Vivian told me I should."

"And right she was. It is, in essence, a description of all creation. Every atom, every person, every moment. It is all reality in paper form."

"Is it?"

"In essence. And we must ask, is the universe contained within that book any less real or valid than the one we stand in? Are we, too, mere markings on a page, figuratively speaking?"

Professor Sheikh Omar's unhelpful wordiness made Morag sigh. Or possibly it was the lump in her womb weighing her down. Maybe both.

"Can't you give a straight answer to anything?" she said.

"Is that a rhetorical question?" he smiled. He glanced at the monitor. "Well, I don't know where Kathy's wandering. She's certainly stepped off the beaten path." He crossed to a worktop and a squat wicker hamper. "Time for a top up of tea. Care for a cup? It's green tea. Maurice believes it calms my nerves."

"Does it work?"

He flipped the lid and pulled out a tartan thermos flask. "Another of life's great unanswerable questions. I also have some pink wafers in here. Pure sugar to soothe your Caledonian soul."

"You haven't answered my questions at all."

Omar let out a noisy gasp of air, a note of deliberate punctuation. He tossed his hands up in an expressive shrug, ignorance and indifference combined.

"Does it matter, as long as we are alive and there are pink wafer biscuits to be enjoyed?" He turned to his hamper and searched deeply. "*Tye xu zek'ee!*" he swore. "That sneaky little villain stole my biscuits!"

Morag's phone pinged with a message.

YOUR UCAB HAS ARRIVED.

Morag had not ordered a taxi. However, all the uCab taxis in the city were psychically controlled by *Kaxeos*, a Venislarn god chained and buried beneath a curry house in the Balti triangle and Morag had learned that when a uCab turned up, it was a sign from the universe.

"I've got to go," she said.

"Again? You are the master of your bladder, my dear. Not it of you."

"*Go* go," she said. "The gods call. I'm sure you can finish up here. We have until midnight, don't we?"

He pouted irascibly but didn't argue.

Morag left through the science museum and walked out onto the wide concourse at the front of the building. A uCab waited in the rain at a bus stop. The driver didn't look round as she got in.

"So, where are we going?"

The zombified driver grunted wordlessly and pulled away.

Kathy sat at a pavement table of the most expensive restaurant in St Phillip's Square and ordered a huge and fatty meal. If one couldn't consume a deliciously unhealthy lunch in virtual reality (and avoid paying for it with either cash or calories) then there hardly seemed to be a point to virtual reality at all.

"Okay," she said to the world. "Where are you?"

There was no response from the world.

"Come on! *Meh Skirr'ish, Yo Polliqan Riti. Shan-pru ach ben to. Bheros chinn rggh al'yatarr.*"

She looked around, swivelling in her chair to make sure he hadn't materialised behind her.

"I just wanted to apologise. *Vas ur, shejti.* You did nearly eat me yesterday and I think we got off on the wrong foot."

Still nothing. A woman in a fur coat and huge sunglasses observed her from across the road. Kathy wondered for a moment if she was *Polliqan Riti* in a human suit, but then the woman walked away and Kathy could read in her disinterest that she was nothing but a empty extra, not the Venislarn god of this world.

"Fine," said Kathy moodily. "In that case, could you turn up the sun a bit."

Golden warmth flooded the café. Kathy couldn't rightly say if this was *Polliqan Riti* granting her a boon or the result of her own mental effort. Perhaps trying to make such a distinction was to miss a larger point.

Somewhere out there—or viewed differently, mere feet away—Professor Omar was waiting for her to pinpoint another sim for collection, but Kathy was enjoying some 'me time'. She wanted some entertainment.

"*San-shu Polliqan Riti. Legeh kunir as sho' vei* Venislarn. Show me the end of the world."

At first, nothing happened. Then the yellow light of summer's afternoon turned a distinct shade of red.

In the sky to the south, a wound opened up. The clouds, blood red, parted into a fissure the shape of a cat's pupil. Kathy expected the hordes of hell to swarm out of the fissure, but nothing emerged apart from that red light.

Beneath Kathy's hand, the chair felt wet and tacky. She looked down. Where the red light touched it, metal crumbled and something wet and eager *that had always been there* emerged after aeons of waiting.

She stood in surprise.

Pigeon Park crumbled. Flakes of concrete and brick dropped to reveal eyes, solitary glistening teeth, spines and barbs and the pulsating organs of the world.

"The Venislarn are here," she murmured. "They've always been here."

Then came an ululuating and triumphant hoot from a great distance. It was loud enough to burst eardrums, to send fake approximations of human beings running in fear. Kathy couldn't see that source beyond the roofs of the surrounding buildings. Then, out of the North, came a rolling thunder.

A figure, taller than her mind could comprehend, its upper half fading into the cloudless sky, stepped into view. The streets were already cracking apart, the skin of the world melting away, but now a leg and a foot swept in, demolishing rows of buildings. Chunks of masonry—whole floors—spun away like snow kicked by a child. This was no Venislarn Kathy recognised, none of the temporal *em-shadt* gods of Earth. She tried to study it, tried to take it all in, and then with a mountain-slide rumble, another leg swung in, from the direction of Colmore Row, rolling a mile-wide strip of city before it. A wave of bedrock reared up, raced towards her and before she could turn it was on her.

.

.

.

"Oh!" she said, jolting upright in her chair.

Professor Omar looked round at her.

"What in the name of all that is holy was that?" he said. "The readouts went quite berserk."

"I don't know." She realised she was breathing heavily. She had died in that virtual world.

She looked around.

"Where's Morag?"

"She had to leave," said the professor. "Summoned by Lord *Morgantus.*"

Kathy nodded. It didn't matter.

"Do you need to stop for a while?" said Omar.

She gave him a curt shake of the head. "I'm going back in."

.

.

.

St Phillip's Square was back to normal, apocalypse undone. The true gods of the Venislarn remained unsummoned. Kathy walked to get her thoughts in order.

"And is that it?" she said. "Is that how the world *will* end? Or just one of the options?"

In answer, the ground began to vibrate. People stopped. There were shouts. Cars rocked. Masonry toppled from the oldest buildings.

The earth split open in wide fissures. Black tar bubbled up from below, followed by snakey tentacles—or were they bituminous roots?—that snared people and hauled them down into the rising mire. A questing tendril, dark with goo, looped around a double-decker bus and began to reel it in.

"Okay," said Kathy. "Apocalypse version two."

Nina had suggested they split up to broaden their search for Langford James, but Rod had not been keen on the idea. He'd called the office for back-up. Rod was not afraid of *samakha*. He wasn't afraid of any of the horrors the Venislarn might throw at him. He wasn't brave in an ignorant, Nina Seth, I-ain't-scared-of-nothing kind of way. He calculated physical risks, weighed up options and, if a situation scared him, he used that energy to get him out of it. Rod had battled gods and survived.

But drop him in a social situation—a party, a works training day, a film crew meeting—and his skin crawled. Rod had called for back-up because he didn't want to be the one who had to talk to the *samakha*.

For one thing, his Venislarn wasn't up to it.

Taylor Graham followed Rod closely as they worked their way along the canal towpath. He peered tentatively into doorways, apologised as he tried to squeeze past the *samakha* and their human property going about their daily lives.

Something plummeted from a gantry above and cut almost silently into the canal water. He looked round and saw powerful frog legs kick and vanish. He looked up. From rickety eyries and grimed windows, eyes watched them.

"How deep is that?" said Taylor, gazing into the water.

"The canal was no more than five feet deep when they dug it out."

"But...? I sense a but."

"There's a god down there. The Waters are as deep as he wants. My advice is don't fall in."

He turned back to the shop he had been looking in. The *samakha* half-breed tending it held up a basket woven from plastic strips.

"*Shedu* pounds. *Shedu* pounds."

"No. No thanks," he said and made to walk on, but his path was blocked by a woman. It was a woman but from her bony fingers to her painfully gaunt face and rapidly thinning hair, she looked more like a corpse that had decided to go walkabout for old time's sake.

"What you doing about my housing application?" she croaked.

"Pardon?" said Rod.

"You from the mission. I put in my housing application months ago. Mrs Grey promised me a nice new house in Dickens Heath. She ain't come down here since," she said spitefully. "She too scared?"

"Um. Mrs Grey is dead."

The woman's hollow eyes stared, no shred of emotion. "You expect me to feel bad about that, huh? Fuckin' bitch should go to hell."

"She did."

"Doesn't change nothing," said the woman and spat and got Rod's trousers.

"I don't know about your housing application, miss...?"

"Don't pretend you don't know me," she said loudly. "O'Keefe. Courtney O'Keefe. I shouldn't be here, not since you killed my boy."

"Your boy?"

"William." She spat again. "Don't say you don't remember him?"

Rod thought hard. "Billy the Fish?"

"Don't you call him that!" she yelled and prodded him hard in the chest. "No one called him that!"

Rod felt his own anger rising. He could so easily tell her that everyone called him Billy the Fish. He could tell her that the consular mission had nothing to do with his death and that he been killed by his own god, *Daganau-Pysh*, for bringing dishonour to the community. Rod kept the anger down and the words in.

Taylor leaned round him. "Apologies, ma'am. I'm very sorry to hear about your boy. Please accept our condolences. Call us at the office, anytime, and I'll gladly look into your housing application."

He said it with such sincere smoothness that, in the time it took the woman to recover from the charm assault, Taylor had steered Rod past her and down the towpath.

"I told you to observe only," whispered Rod.

"You were getting nowhere."

"That was..." Rod gave a half-laugh.

"What can I say?" grinned Taylor. "I have a very particular set of skills, gained over a surprisingly long career." He turned and nodded genially to a stallholder. "*San-shu,* my friend." He gave a wink and a smile to a passing mother with a slippery *samakha* toddler in her arms. He threw a salute to a shadow within a brick archway. "*Udd'esh hraim,* my good sir."

Rod couldn't react in time. He saw the shadow, he heard the words and he knew pretty much what was going to happen; but he couldn't haul Taylor back in time. The shadow reached out and, hissing, yanked Taylor into the archway. Rod leapt after them.

Taylor gave a cry of alarm.

"Don't!" Rod yelled. "Don't do anything!"

Rod bounced off a wall in the darkness and came out in a cobbled courtyard beneath a pale brown light. Smokey incense filled the air. Drying seaweed hung from poles high above. He saw Taylor being thrown to the ground and then a huge arm, wet and iron stiff, clothes-lined Rod and knocked him to the ground. Hands picked him up and threw him against a wall. He tried to reach into his jacket, but his hand was swatted away and in the tousle his wallet and gun fell loose onto the floor. He dropped too, coughing and gasping for breath.

In the centre of the courtyard, Taylor Graham crouched on hands and knees, blood streaming from his nose. Even if they got out of this alive, Rod guessed, Tammy and the make-up department would be having words about this incident. Around Taylor, at home among the concealing smoke and weed stood half a dozen *samakha*.

"What...?" coughed Taylor. "What did I do?"

"Quiet," Rod hissed.

What he didn't have time to explain was that Taylor had made a fundamental mistake. The creatures out on the towpath, those hustling to make a living, the likes of Tony T and his Waters Crew, they were all *samakha* half-breeds. They were the colonial workforce, the results of ritualistic sex, the mistakes. As far as the true *samakha* were concerned, they were basically humans. The true *samakha* now stood around them.

"You never speak to them!" Rod whispered. "Never."

The true *samakha*, the unsullied children of *Daganau-Pysh*, never went out into the hateful sunlight of this world. They squatted in recesses and lurked, watchfully, beneath The Waters. Rod knew only a little from what he had glimpsed of them. Their skin was a glossy grey-green, pale and translucent along their fleshy bellies. Their mouths were frog-like, wide and incapable of anything resembling human speech. Webbed spines of various types and formations lined their neckless heads and backs. Their eyes bulged, unblinking.

Maybe in cold clear daylight they would appear as ridiculous, flabby fishmen. Here, in the stinking gloom of their own home, Rod accepted they were flaming horrific. He dropped to his knees in abasement. The tallest of the *samakha* leaned over Taylor, a clicking sound rising from its throat. Its webbed forelimbs ended in a cluster of sharp spines, striped like the poisonous quills of a lionfish.

"What do I do?" whispered Taylor.

Rod gestured forward at the scattered items between them. Taylor reached out with a trembling hand towards the Glock pistol. The angry clicking rose in volume, Rod waved him left.

"Not that. The cards."

Taylor's hand moved over the sodium toothpaste bombs and found the ring of laminated cards. The quills descended, inches from Taylor's exposed neck.

"Number four," whispered Rod.

Taylor turned them over.

"'Please forgive me,'" he said. "'I am on an important mission.'"

"In Venislarn!"

Shaking, Taylor read. "*Skeidl hraim yeg courxean. Shan-shan prui beddigo.*"

The *samakha* hesitated. The clicking slowed.

"Number twelve," said Rod, still prostrate.

Taylor shuffled through. "'It / they is about to hatch. Take cover'?"

"Maybe thirteen?"

"'Please help. There isn't much time.'"

"That one."

Taylor read out the Venislarn. Above their heads, the *samakha* turned to one another, conferring in a series of clicks and grunts. One of them let loose a belching bellow.

"We're gonna die," whispered Taylor.

The uCab ride was no magical mystery tour. The ways of the Birmingham Venislarn had ceased to be at all magical for Morag and there was very little mystery in where they were going. The driver took them up through the A38 tunnels, round the labyrinth of roadworks by the old demolished library and on to the Cube.

The driver drew up outside the high rise, offered no explanation and asked for no payment. Morag went inside. The rain had not exactly stopped but it had paused for a breather at least. The concierge, both bald and hairy in the least likely of places, waved her to a waiting lift. As previously, the lift interior was more than half taken up by an August Handmaiden of *Prein*, the same one as before.

"We must stop meeting like this, *Shala'pinz Syu*," Morag said.

"You should speak with greater respect," said the Handmaiden.

Morag made a non-committal face and stepped into the lift with the creature.

"We have your souls," she said. "Twenty-eight *fraxasa*. We will make the delivery tonight."

The Handmaiden did not respond. She tapped for a floor, not the top floor.

"Not visiting *Yo-Morgantus*?" said Morag.

The Handmaiden did not speak until the doors were fully closed and the lift was moving. Then she said, "*Yo-Morgantus* despises weakness and yet he also revels in it."

"Uh-huh?"

"You murdered my sisters," said *Shala'pinz Syu*.

Morag, unavoidably close to the armoured spider-demon's bulk, saw glistening beads of caustic saliva run along the creature's underbelly.

"Only one," she said. "Technically, the other was killed by Ingrid Spence."

"You provoked them."

"I did," said Morag.

The lift opened onto a long corridor of apartment doors. Morag stepped out.

"Those of us who remain have sworn an oath to avenge their deaths."

"That's nice," said Morag. "Left or right?"

"Are you not afraid?"

The Handmaiden emerged from the lift, unfolding into the corridor. Giant claws on patterned carpet. It seemed ridiculous and horrible.

"I'm not afraid," said Morag.

Shala'pinz Syu tilted her carapace. "Apartment four-two-nine."

Morag looked at the nearest numbers and headed down the corridor.

"I was afraid, for a while," she said. "I was told I was going to be killed. The date of my execution was set and then... it didn't happen." She stopped in front of four hundred and twenty-five. "Something else happened instead. Shall I knock or do you have a key?"

Shala'pinz Syu faced the door (or, at least, presented one of its tortured baby faces to the door) and produced a swipe card.

"We will kill you," said the Handmaiden.

"I don't think so."

The light on the door handle flicked to green and Morag went inside without invitation. It was, by Morag's standards, a luxurious flat. The theme of glass, steel and neutral coloured surfaces that dominated the outside of the building extended here also. Beyond the large kitchen to one side was an open dining area and then a large living room with a sunken seating area. An L-shaped balcony wrapped around the corner unit. There was no one in the apartment and it had a still, unlived-in air.

"A place like this, you pay for the view," said Morag. She turned to the Handmaiden. It squatted in the hallway, blocking the exit, shell plates rotating restlessly, a parade of terrified baby faces. "Is this going to be my new home?"

The Handmaiden said nothing, made no sound but for the scrape of its china-white plates and the hiss of its breathing.

"A few months ago, you could have killed me," said Morag, "but on the day earmarked for my death, I conceived this little lump." She

207

ran a hand across her stomach. "You are, I'm gonna guess, forbidden to murder the *kaatbari*'s mum. I'm untouchable."

"For now," said *Shala'pinz Syu*.

"For now." Morag mulled over those words. "In my experience 'for now' is all any of us can expect." She slowly surveyed the flat. It was bigger than the one she currently lived in. And cleaner too, although such things were only temporary. "*Yo-Morgantus* wants to keep me close at hand, huh? I'll get my things moved over."

"It has already been taken care of."

Morag had a sudden and shudder-inducing image of brain-dead uCab drivers going through her things, stuffing clothes, clean and unclean alike, into suitcases, dirty unmentionables hanging out as they flung them into the boots of their taxis.

"I'd rather it wasn't."

"It isn't your decision or mine," said *Shala'pinz Syu*. "Do not think that your position as mother of the Soulgate gives you any power. *Yo-Morgantus* owns you. Yours is a path of degradation and pain."

"Wow. This is some ante-natal pep talk, *Shal*."

"We too are cast down."

"Pardon?"

The Handmaiden raised herself up until her great back brushed the ceiling. "You murdered our sisters. We are now but ten. Lord *Morgantus* sees our loss as weakness. Our new place in his court is to be ridiculed and mocked. I, as the best and strongest of my sisters, have been given a position of particular dishonour."

Morag grinned. She made it a big one because she wanted the gallus bitch to see it.

"He's made you his court jester, has he?"

The Handmaiden's voiceless mouth quivered in rage. "I believe the correct word would be... nanny."

The cruel grin fell from Morag's face.

"You're fucking kidding me," she whispered.

"I am not," said *Shala'pinz Syu*.

"Oh, that's *bhul detar*."

"On that point, we agree," said the August Au Pair of *Prein*.

Nina entered Hragra's waterfront burger bar to find an argument in full flow. There was a slender and handsome (in a middle-aged,-trying-too-hard kinda way) man at a table with most of The Waters crew gathered around him. Tony T had a pistol out, which was never a good sign, but it didn't look like the argument was an interspecies thing. The *samakha* lads turned toward her.

"Feds in the house," she said by way of greeting. "Can I get a whoop-whoop?"

"Damn you doin' here?" said Tony T.

"Taking the air," said Nina. She waved at the proprietor and nodded at his crab in a tank. "Nice pet. You given it a name yet?"

"Name?" said Hragra, like it was a foreign word.

"Yeah. Something clever. Shelly. Or Santa Claws." She clicked her fingers. "Chris-tacean. That's a good one. You can have that for free." She looked to the man. "You're Langford James. You look younger than on IMDb. You had some work done?"

He frowned, confused. There was a lot to be confused about, she guessed.

"Who are you?" he asked.

"Nina Seth. Consular mission. Come to save your arse. Or ass, as they say in your country."

She beckoned him over and, for a good second or two, it looked like no one was going to stop him. And then Tony T remembered he was holding a gun.

"He ain't going nowhere, fed."

"Come on, man," said Pupfish. "It's Nina."

"I know who it is, dog!" snapped Tony. "But this *bhul-gen* was—ggh!—dissing your mom and Fluke has challenged him to *Shohreye 'uuuduk*."

"Has he?" said Nina.

"Not yet," said Fluke.

"No one throws down that gauntlet for something as stupid as cracking jokes about Pupfish's mum"—she looked aside at Pupfish—"who is nothing but an upstanding and moral woman, by the way."

"Thank you," said Pupfish.

"No matter what she posts on Snapchat."

"She...? Ggh! She does what now?"

"Nothing," said Nina, quickly. "So, let's have no more of this *Shohreye 'uuuduk* nonsense and I'll take Langford here home. *Shohreye 'uuuduk* indeed!"

"We don't do it real like, Mrs Nina," said Death Roe.

"I should hope not."

"The challenge—ggh!—is to eat one of Hragra's kebabs with inferno chilli sauce."

"Hardly *Shohreye 'uuuduk*."

"Just what we call it."

She waved Langford to the door. Tony T looked confused and angry that no one seemed to care he was holding a loaded firearm. Nina and Langford were out the door and halfway to the nearest bridge before Tony came running out after them, the other fish boys in tow.

"Hey!" he called. "Hey, Hollywood!"

"Yes?" said Langford.

Tony T's mouth spasmed in a fishy smile. "Who's the better rapper? Notorious B.I.G. or Tupac?"

Langford was so surprised, he laughed.

"Tupac," whispered Nina. "Just say Tupac."

"My friend here says it's Tupac," Langford called.

"Yeah?" said Tony T.

"But I don't know," said Langford. "Tupac was a true poet. He wrote about some heavy issues. But, for my money, Biggie Smalls was always technically superior. He had great flow and was the better storyteller. Biggie Smalls all the way."

"Oh, damn," sighed Nina.

Fluke pushed past Tony T to stand by the water's edge. "No one—ggh!—says that! I challenge you to *Shohreye 'uuuduk*!"

"What?" said Langford.

"Should have said Tupac," said Nina.

"*Shohreye 'uuuduk*!" cried a voice behind them on the bridge.

On the crest of the bridge stood Rod and Taylor Graham, looking a little scuffed and crumpled like they'd taken a manly roll in the hay together. Behind them was what Nina could only describe a mobile marquee, a dark square tent hung with ragged heavy drapes being carried by team of solemn *samakha* servants. She was sure there was a special and clever name for such a thing, but she didn't know it and wasn't going to ask.

The shout had come from within the marquee.

Nina gave Rod a look that said 'What have you done, Rod?'

"We've brought help," said Rod and she could tell he knew full well that what he had brought was nothing like help.

"*Shohreye 'uuuduk!*" croaked the true *samakha* cloaked in the shadows of the marquee. "*Verr su-te khad?*"

Tony T shoved Fluke forward before the elder.

"*Is bey, meh yor,*" he shouted self-importantly.

"I didn't," stammered Fluke. "Not really. We were—ggh!— *perisa ghorsri*—just going to have a chilli sauce competition."

"*Shohreye 'uuuduk!*" bellowed the *samakha* elder.

Tony T pointed a fishy finger at Langford. "He dishonoured our heritage! He insulted one of our number! *Shohreye 'uuuduk!*"

Nina wearily shook her head. "Oh, Tony, you are a dick."

"What's going on?" said Langford.

But now the *samakha*, their bastard offspring, and even their human property had taken up the chant. "*Shohreye 'uuuduk! Shohreye 'uuuduk!*"

Rod and Taylor came forward.

"Good times, eh?" Taylor said to Langford.

"The things we do for our art," said Langford. "What's actually going to happen?" he asked, looking at Rod.

Rod looked at Nina.

"Trial by water," she said. "Basically, a swimming contest."

Langford looked down at the canal. "Widths or lengths?"

"A single width," she said. "Although it's more the depths I'd be worried about."

Fish town residents came through and bundled Langford towards the edge of the towpath next to Fluke. Nina made sure she stayed close.

"Ah, Nina," said Fluke. "I—ggh!—I didn't mean for this to happen."

"Good to know," she said.

The fish boy looked unnerved. "Is there any chance you can stop it? I—ggh!—I don't really wanna..."

"Should have thought about that," she said peevishly.

Langford turned to his competitor and offered a hand. "I just want to say I'm sorry, man. Tupac, he's up there. The greatest."

"Cool, bro. That means a lot," said Fluke and shook the actor's hand.

The chanting filled the lengths and the heights of Fish Town.

"You see," said Nina, "this kind of mob behaviour is what happens if people don't have decent cable television." She looked sharply at Fluke. "And when people listen to their dickwad friends."

Tony T was up on the bridge by the *samakha*'s dark marquee, casually leaning on the rail, gun held loosely, enjoying every moment of it. Fluke stripped off his jacket and his treasured Tupac T-shirt and passed them to Rod.

"You hold onto these for me?"

Rod nodded. He tapped Langford and the actor stripped off his top layers and his shoes.

"I was a fast swimmer in high school," said Langford.

"Swim fast," said Rod. "I'm going to be over at the other side to haul you out when you get there."

He didn't say 'if you get there', but everyone heard it clearly.

Langford took deep, cleansing breaths. There was no meat on the man and, with those limbs, maybe he was a fast swimmer. Nina watched the ripples on the canal, silver shimmers. *Daganau-Pysh* was down there, lord of The Waters. If Langford was lucky, he'd simply not see the god and die before he knew what was happening.

Rod, with Taylor close beside him, managed to push through the sudden crowds to the towpath on the far side just before the *samakha* in his palanquin gave a final shout and the swimmers dove in.

"The first one across wins, right?" said Taylor.

"The one who gets across wins," said Rod.

He gently but firmly moved an old dear in a sackcloth shawl to one side and positioned himself by the water's edge. Langford had instinctively made a deep fast dive and was gone almost instantly from sight. It was a good dive, but Fluke was faster. With no transformation, he went from gangly upright fish boy to a white knife of swimming energy. He kicked with his feet together and propelled himself halfway across the canal in his first stroke. Rod watched the water. A translucent weed-like shape formed on the surface, almost mistakeable for a wave. A bubble rose and popped under the bridge.

Langford surfaced, a full body length behind Fluke. His arms came over in solid powerful strokes. Small consolation that he was going to die looking good.

"*Bhul-tamade!*" shouted Tony T from the bridge and there was the flat firecracker bang of his small revolver as he fired into the water at Langford.

"Damned cheat," said Taylor.

Rod put a hand to his pistol and looked across the water at Nina. She was already meeting his gaze and shaking her head.

The water exploded in little putt-putts around Langford. Tony laughed like this was the best sport, but it wasn't going to be bullets that killed Langford.

An S-shaped wave was moving unhurriedly up behind Langford.

Fluke leapt up onto the towpath beside Rod, barely needing his hands at all to lift himself out.

"Come on, buddy!" Taylor yelled to Langford. "Five feet! Five feet!"

Behind Langford, a broad head rose from the canal: a pointed nose like a squid's spear-shaped head, overlaid with sleeve upon sleeve of smooth skin, pale but run through with yellows and greens, like shark skin that was both rotten and jaundiced. And within the folds of the skin sleeves, the countless blank white eyes of *Daganau-Pysh*. Glistening, frilled tentacles hung down from the god's massive head like a gown.

Langford was an arm's length from the side, but it didn't matter. *Daganau-Pysh* had all the time he needed. In the innermost folds, a beak of a mouth opened.

"Chew on this!" yelled Taylor and hurled something small and white into the god's maw.

Daganau-Pysh reeled, roaring. There were screams from the crowd.

"What the hell did you do?" shouted Rod.

"Sodium bomb!" said Taylor, a victorious gleam in his eye. "You dropped it earlier. Explodes on contact with water."

"What?!"

Langford, oblivious to the horror behind him, slapped a hand on the towpath. Rod bent down and hauled him up, soaked and shivering. *Daganau-Pysh* shook his titanic head, spraying foam.

"It's not a bomb!" Rod shouted. "It's just for cleaning your teeth!"

"But you said..."

Langford rolled onto solid ground and, as he did, looked up at the squid-cum-fish-cum-total nightmare and screamed. He kicked as though his legs were still dangling in the water, kicked and twisted to get away from the god of the deep.

Rod dragged Langford further back, but his attention was on the idiot Taylor.

"Did you think you'd try to kill a god?" he yelled.

"I thought I was saving Langford."

"Langford didn't matter, you pillock! None of us matter! We don't save lives, we just try to keep the end of the world at arm's length!"

"But..."

"All you've done is give a bloody fish-god minty-fresh breath and signed our death warrants!"

On both sides of the canal and the numerous rickety bridges that stretched between them, the local population were split between terror, outrage, fervent prayer and simple curiosity. While some fought to put distance between themselves and an angry god, others threw themselves prostrate on the ground. Several younger *samakha* had been filming everything on their phones and continued to do so. There'd be a nightmare of a social media clean-up later.

Daganau-Pysh roared, a pure high hooting sound, encased in a throbbing deep bellow that sounded like it had risen from the ocean floor.

"Sacrifice!" yelled a voice on the bridge. "Sacrifice and penance!"

"Flaming Nora," said Rod. The more eager *samakha* about them had laid their hands on both Langford and Taylor.

"No!" yelled Taylor. "Stop it! Stop it! Rod!"

There was nothing Rod could do, nothing that wouldn't make it worse.

There was a louder shout from the middle of the bridge and a gun shot. Rod looked up. Tony T was grappling with someone. It was Pupfish. The crowd obscured them from Rod's view for a moment and then he saw Tony T crash through the poorly-constructed railing and fall towards the water. He didn't fall far. A tentacle pad, broad like a tropical leaf, caught him and swiftly folded around him.

"Not me!" he screamed. "*Hrifet*, father! *Glun'u!*" And then he sealed his fate by firing a shot at his ancestor and god.

The meaty pad folded up. Suckers held Tony T tight and barbed hooks ripped through him. And then he was gone, pulled beneath the waters by the descending god. Moments later, nothing remained but dispersing ripples and a spreading cloud of toothpaste foam.

Kathy limbered up, did some yoga stretches and tried to touch her toes and, because this was a false reality, she was able to actually touch them.

"Bring it on," she shouted to the pretend sky above a constructed Birmingham. "Apocalypse number... what is it? Twelve? Whatever!"

The controller of this world obliged. Across the square and the enclosed park, the heads of dozens of Brummies exploded and things like prawns—rotting zombie-prawns with gossamer wings and mouths like blowtorches—burst free.

"Really?" said Kathy, critically. "The *Tud-burzu* will be the vanguard of the apocalypse? I think you're scraping the barrel of possibilities there, *shan Polliqan Riti.*"

Then, as flaming undead prawn-moths set about attacking sims across the square, Kathy caught sight of a figure some distance away. Not human, and barely a figure at all. It was corpse white and, as much as it had limbs on any sort, it had at least three boneless arms and legs that merged into a curtain-like fringe. It was also wearing a top hat and carrying a black cane with a spherical silver handle. Hat, cane and general mobility aside, the individual was the spitting image of the blob in the laboratory tank.

"*Polliqan Riti*," Kathy whispered.

At the mention of its name, the thing that wasn't a face beneath its hat glanced at her and then the creature turned and scuttled away.

"Wait!" she said and ran after it.

A *Tud-burzu* dived at her and she pushed a hapless sim into the prawn's flamethrower jaws.

Ahead, *Polliqan Riti* slithered and waddled and vanished down a cut-through passage, the improbably-named Needless Alley. Kathy ran after it but, turning the corner, found the alleyway to be deserted. Dumpster bins lined the back entrances of businesses. A dark doorway led into some nameless office. Ahead, the alley opened out onto New Street, where shoppers and city workers ran screaming from the onslaught of killer crustaceans, tripping over the corpses of the slain.

"Where did you go?" said Kathy.

Of course, this was *Polliqan's* brain, his dream. He could be anywhere or nowhere, but Kathy wouldn't willingly give up a chance to speak with him. She turned back to the filthy office doorway. There was no handle to turn, only a Yale lock and a window of frosted glass made doubly opaque by layers of grime.

She knocked.

The door unlocked itself and swung in.

"Thank you," she said and entered.

Morag's belongings arrived at the Cube apartment in the arms of a line of uCab drivers. Eight cardboard storage boxes filled with clothes, shoes and random accoutrements from her Bournville flat.

Shala'pinz Syu loomed over the entrance as men with empty stares and not a word for anyone trooped in and deposited boxes in the sunken lounge. Morag picked through the first of the boxes. The man had emptied her chest of drawers in the box, a drawer at a time, swept the dust and unread magazines of her bedside cabinet on top and then crowned it off with the contents of her bedroom rubbish bin.

Clean and dirty laundry were piled together. The contents of her cutlery drawer were mixed in with the contents of her fridge. The bathroom toiletries were thrown together with the bathroom cleaning products, the toilet brush and the U-shaped toilet rug.

"You guys are idiots," she told them without anger as the silent zombie procession continued. "None of your families ever reported you missing, and I'm not surprised."

Eventually they were done. The door shut.

Morag looked at the boxes. It seemed appropriate. She hadn't kept her flat or her life in any kind of order.

Shala'pinz Syu entered the lounge, plates grinding, wet mouth sighing. An agonised baby face watched Morag. She imagined it judging her.

"I don't know what you think's so funny," she said to the Handmaiden.

"Nothing is funny."

Morag nodded at the boxes. "You're meant to be the nanny. Get nannying."

Shala'pinz Syu tilted her entire body, a question.

Morag pointed at the boxes. "Unpacking, sorting, folding. Afterwards I'll show you how to use the washing machine."

An ambulance needed calling for Langford. The motion capture actor had stared a Venislarn god straight in the face and had been moments from becoming a god-sized snack. He'd also spent far more time in The Waters than any human ought to. There were Venislarn things in those depths, some huge, some microscopic.

Still shivering but perhaps no longer from the cold, he was strapped to a stretcher and sent off to the Restricted Ward at the Queen Elizabeth Hospital. There, he would be pumped with specific antibiotics and anti-parasitics and observed until his doctors were confident he would not infect others, transform into something otherworldly or give birth to a nameless horror.

Rod went with Langford in the ambulance, already trying to make phone calls to the film people to explain just exactly what had happened to their second-billing actor.

"Back to the film set for me?" Taylor asked Nina.

She looked at the remnants of the Waters Crew—Pupfish, Fluke and Death Roe.

"You owe these guys an apology," she said.

Taylor looked momentarily bemused and then turned on his LA smile. "I am sincerely sorry, gentlemen, for any ruckus I may have been a part of. On behalf of my good friend, Langford, I would like to say that Tupac Shakur is the greatest rapper of all time and no one—*no one*—should ever make jokes about your dear old mom."

"Ggh! You callin' my girl old?" said Fluke.

"Can it," said Nina. "He apologised."

Taylor clapped his hands. "Good. And now..."

"We're going round to Pupfish's house to have a cup of tea with his mum," said Nina.

"We are?"

"But... but..." said Pupfish.

"And tomorrow, you can take Taylor to meet your girlfriend."

Taylor sighed. "Hell, why not just bring her down to the set," he said sarcastically.

"Hell, yeah!" said Pupfish.

"I think that's a deal," said Nina.

Kathy Kaur climbed the filthy stairs that led up from the entrance in Needless Alley.

"*Durin yat sor!*" she called in a friendly tone.

Something creaked upstairs.

She emerged into an office that was a time capsule from another decade. Boxy, wood effect desks stood in rows. There was a typewriter on one of them, in-trays on several others. By the grimed-up window, *Polliqan Riti* lounged in a deep chair at the largest desk. His shape was not even humanoid, but he had clearly made an effort to present lumps of himself in the most appropriate places.

Kathy addressed the blob with the hat on it.

"Greetings, lord *Polliqan Riti.*"

The hat-blob of a head bobbed. "*Kei la! Kei la, Jidzu* Kaur."

"I am grateful you were willing to show yourself to me."

"*Ke-appen. Ch'ursa qit.*"

"I was hoping to see you," she agreed and then understood. "You read my mind. Or my desires?"

"*Fallen ghis xho do be'rr.*"

218

"Well," she said, head bowed modestly, "I was wondering about the hat. And the cane."

Polliqan Riti removed his hat with one extruded limb and twirled his cane with another. He seemed to regard each with his eyeless head-blob.

"*Tr'aieho kar kigr, karrskenon.*"

"Er, yes," she said hesitantly. "Blending in. No, absolutely."

Something bubbled noisily within him. Laughter? "And I have even enknowledgated myself with your primitive language," he said in an accentless albeit slightly oily tone.

"Spoken like a native," she said.

"I have conversified with your king and master, Sheikh Omar, but you are the only other human who has deliberately sought me out."

Kathy decided to ignore the 'king and master' comment and said, "You are, I understand, a fugitive."

"Exiled," he agreed. He rolled the top hat along his limb and placed it back on his pseudo-head. "I hope one day to return to the shores of hell, take vengeancity on those who oustled me, and claim a title suited to one of my stature."

"Yes." Kathy stepped a little closer. "I might actually be able to help you with that."

It was hard for a shapeless blob to generate a posture of polite curiosity, but *Polliqan Riti* managed it somehow.

"In fact, I know you will return to hell and I can make it happen." She gestured to his glistening slime-covered body. "All I ask in return is a sample of your... secretions. They are kryptonite to the unkillable Venislarn, you know."

"Krypo...?"

"Kryptonite," she said.

Shala'pinz Syu folded clothes. One of the surviving August Handmaidens of *Prein* was folding clothes, giant claws delicately handling pants and trousers and tops and making a neat little pile on the arm of the couch. Morag shuddered at the sight of a Venislarn horror handling her underwear, but this was nothing to the schadenfreude she felt in seeing the bitch brought low. She even took photos on her phone.

There was a knock on the door.

"Are we expecting anyone?" said Morag.

"No," said *Shala'pinz Syu*.

"It's part of your duties to answer the door."

"I am folding clothes," said *Shala'pinz Syu*.

"Just keep folding," said Morag and went to answer the door.

The man and the woman in the corridor had vibrant ginger hair, white toothy smiles and—a rarity among redheads in the cube—were fully clothed.

"Hi!" they said as one.

"I'm Kim."

"I'm Jim."

"We've just come over to say hi."

Morag stared at them. "What?"

"We're your new neighbours," said Kim, and Jim held up a sealed plastic beaker of some unidentifiable green liquid.

"Two four eight," said Jim. "Directly opposite."

"So, if you're ever short of anything," said Kim, "just pop across the street—"

"The street!" giggled Jim.

"—and come knocking on our door."

Kim knocked on the door frame, just in case Morag had never heard of knocking before.

Jim continued to hold out the sealed plastic beaker invitingly. Morag didn't touch it. People had occasionally accused her of being too quick to judge. Morag wasn't sure that was fair, but she already hated these two twats with an absolute fucking passion.

"What do you want?" she said.

"We came over to be neighbourly," grinned Kim, undeterred.

"We brought smoothie," said Jim and waggled the beaker.

"What's in it?"

"Matcha green tea," said Jim.

"Pear," said Kim.

"Kale."

"Oats."

"Mint."

"Flax."

"Flax?" said Morag.

"Flax," said Kim.

"That's what they make linen out of it."

"Is it?"

"You want me to have a smoothie with liquidised bedsheets in it?"

"All the valuable nutrients a woman's body needs when she's expecting," said Jim and give Morag's belly a playful poke.

This was the excuse Morag needed to slam the door in their faces. She snatched the smoothie off Jim. "Next time, a big bottle of Buckfast wine or a six-pack of Stella Artois for preference," she said and did indeed slam the door in their faces.

Shala'pinz Syu had got her serrated claws tangled in one of Morag's bras.

Morag put the smoothie down on the table. "Your dinner's arrived," she said and pulled out her phone to open the uCab app. "Me and baby are ordering out and you're paying."

Shala'pinz Syu said nothing.

Morag looked at her. "Don't tell me you don't have a credit card?"

Langford talked to himself throughout his examination at the Restricted Ward, a low continuous mutter that might have been a sign of madness in many but, in him, had more of the appearance of an actor learning his lines.

"Obvious Birmingham accent... downturn of final syllables... similarity in vowel sounds... merging... merging... deliberate use of learned slang terms... fasho, dog. It's all *bhul-detar. Muda.*"

"Language, please," said the doctor taking his bloods.

Langford struggled to focus on the man and then looked at his own feet and shuddered. Was he still imagining them in the canal water? Was he picturing the god *Daganau-Pysh*, rising to claim what was his?

Rod patted him manfully on the arm. "You're okay now, mate. All's fine."

Langford looked at him and nodded uncertainly. "I survived."

"You did."

"I survived the *Shohreye 'uuuduk.*"

"Aye."

221

"What does that mean?"

"Mean?"

The doctor dabbed and taped the needle puncture on Langford's arm.

"*Soi ech yed samakha. Gue-am-bhun. Ped veri-klu da Daganau-Pysh.* Fasho," said Langford.

"Er, yeah. Sure," said Rod.

Langford's muttering subsided into a sub-vocal whisper.

"I'm going to give him a sedative," said the doctor.

"He needs to be back on set first thing in the morning," said Rod.

The doctor gave him a look which indicated that being back on set first thing was both unlikely and entirely out of Rod's hands.

"I'm just saying what they're saying," said Rod.

The doctor nodded. "And how's Dr Kaur doing since you snatched her away from us?"

"Kathy? Well..." Rod thought about Kathy. It was unavoidable that he thought of her now in a significantly different way to how he had thought of her twenty-four hours ago. He'd seen a different side of her now; he'd seen bits of her a guy could not unsee.

He blew out noisily.

"Tough to work with?" the doctor asked.

"No. Not at all," said Rod. "She's... she's amazing."

When Langford dropped off to sleep, Rod made his exit. He had Kathy on his mind, and he wanted to do the right thing. He fancied her—no, that was a weasel word, a playground word—he was attracted to her romantically and, damn it all, sexually. She was a fine and beautiful and intelligent woman and—yes!—he was the right man for her, he was sure of it. He desired her—'desired', he thought, a powerful word. He desired her and he needed to tell her clearly how much he desired her. He wasn't going to be a reticent Brit. He was going to be bold and clear and make her understand how he felt.

He phoned her as he rode down in the hospital lift.

"Rod," she said in greeting.

"Where are you?" he said.

"Just leaving the Think Tank. We've got our twenty-eight fake souls and"—she paused, consulting the time—"four hours to spare. I'm going to the Cube."

"I'm coming. To speak to you."

"Okay," she said, hesitantly. "At the Cube?"

"Outside. Somewhere." His non-reticent, affirmative attitude sounded abrupt and robotic, as though manly confidence had cut off the supply of blood to the language centres of his brain.

"The bar next door?" she suggested.

"Yes," he said decisively and killed the call. And then, realising that was a weird and rude way to end a conversation, he added "that would be lovely, thank you."

Still invigorated with a sense of purpose, he stepped out of the lift and went straight to the tiny cluster of shops inside the hospital foyer. They had everything he needed. He bought a box of chocolates, a decoratively wrapped basket of toiletries and the biggest bunch of flowers he could find. There was even a little stand and a card in the bouquet.

He headed out with his purchases and hailed a black cab at the taxi rank.

"To the Cube in town," he told the driver. "As quick as you can."

Rod felt that this romantic vibe he was currently tapping into was best served by a last-minute dash across town in pursuit of his lady love. As the driver did his best to fulfil Rod's request in heavy evening traffic, Rod scribbled a note of love on the card, sealed the envelope and stuck it back in the bunch of flowers.

His stomach churned with dread. He clutched the chocolates and smellies tight and concentrated on what he was going to say.

"I don't feel so good," said Taylor as they tried to hail a cab on the Digbeth Road.

"I told you not to drink the tea," said Nina.

"How could I not?" said the star, rubbing his stomach. "She made a pot. A pot of tea. I was only being civil."

Nina shook her head. "Rookie mistake. You think they get their teabags from Tesco in Fish Town? You think she washes the pots in Fairy Liquid? You take the tea, you clink the saucer, but you do not drink."

223

"She was very excited to see me," said Taylor.

Nina stepped into the road and waved down a taxi. It swung into the curb. Rain flicked like fireflies across its headlights.

"People are always excited to see you," said Nina.

"Yeah, but..." He held the thought until they were in the cab and Nina had given the driver their destination. "But it was like she was so desperately excited to meet me. It was pathetic." He smiled and shook his head at himself. "Not laughable pathetic, just really, really sad."

"Think what kind of life Pupfish's mum has got. That flat is her life. The two things she's got in her life are that she gave birth to a damned fish and she's now got his best mate crawling between her sheets every night. That and *Britain's Got Talent* on a Saturday night."

"Man, that *is* really, really sad."

Nina nodded. "Speaking of sad, you were giving Rod dating advice."

"That was guy talk," said Taylor.

"I'm one of the guys. You can tell me."

He looked at her and smiled. He was Hollywood handsome. Nina briefly considered doing something about that, but her diary was full and she reckoned Hollywood actors were probably high maintenance, even as one-night stands.

"He's my friend," she said, which wasn't a lie. "I wouldn't want him getting shitty advice from an American."

"There's a woman he's interested in."

"You would need to narrow it down. Rod's a starving man at a buffet when it comes to women."

"Ah, shows how much you know. Apparently, he's been intimate with this woman before."

"Really?"

This was getting interesting. Odd, though, that if they'd already done the nasty he was now trying to win her over romantically. Maybe it was a fling. Maybe he'd got her pregnant. For a fleeting instant, Nina recalled discussing pregnancy with someone earlier that day... But then it was gone, dismissed as a false memory.

"So, what dating advice did you give him?" she asked.

Morag stroked her stomach while browsing takeaway food options on her phone.

"What do you fancy for your supper, baby?"

Are we having lamb jalfrezi, mother?

"You can have whatever you like. Fancy pizza?"

What's pizza?

"Mostly cheese. And pizza bread drenched in fat. At least it is if it's done right."

"You are talking to your unborn foetus," *Shala'pinz Syu* pointed out.

"I am," said Morag. "We do that."

"Do you expect the *kaatbari* to answer?" There was a mocking note in the creature's voice.

"I expect you to shut the *bhul* up, nanny, unless you want to chip in with topping suggestions or order a side of spicy wedges."

You do not like her, mother, observed the anti-Christ.

"I do not like her," Morag agreed. "She is a gallus bitch and not to be trusted."

"You pretend to talk about me behind my back," said *Shala'pinz Syu*. "That is juvenile behaviour and every one of your transgressions is being noted."

You did not like Jim and Kim either.

"No, I did not."

I could feel you thinking the bad mmm-mmmm *word when you were talking to them.*

"You reading my mind?" said Morag.

Her foetus paused in thought. *No, mother. But I could feel you clenching up.*

"Clenching, huh? Tell you what, mummy's going to scan down the pizza list. You let me know when I get to the one you want."

Morag let her gaze drift over the pizza options, thinking of each in turn, imagining each flavour as her eyes passed.

That one.

"That one?"

That one.

"American BBQ Hot. My baby's got taste."

Rod flung the cabbie a banknote and told him to keep the change. Then he sprinted to the waterfront of Gas Street Basin and up the steps to the rows of bars and restaurants that lined the space between the Cube and the Mailbox. Night had fully fallen. Several restaurants had outdoor gas heaters and flame-effect lights in their balcony seating areas, but the air felt heavy with rain and few punters were willing to sit outside.

Arms full of gifts—overfull? he wondered and quickly suppressed that thought; there was no time for doubt—he backed through the swing doors of the South American bar nearest the Cube tower. Latin pop played loudly to compensate for the scarcity of midweek drinkers and diners. Kathy Kaur sat on a tall stool by the bar, sipping something slender and colourful. On the floor, close to her feet, was a secure medical waste carrier case. She looked beautiful. Rod was oddly glad of that fact, not that she had ever looked anything other than lovely, but to see that she was *still beautiful* emboldened him. This was the right thing to do.

She looked round and, seeing him, her face went from delight to confusion to outright panic to something else entirely in less than second. He ignored the mixed signals and walked straight over.

"Is it someone's birthday?" she said. "I'm fairly sure it's not Mother's Day."

"No," said Rod. "These are for you."

He all but poured the chocolates and toiletries into her lap and thrust the flowers right in her face.

"Rod..."

"Kathy."

"This..." She looked at the gifts. "It's not my birthday either."

"I know," he said. "I've been thinking."

"Are you sure?"

She was deflecting him, but he would remain resolute.

"I like you, Kathy."

"I like me too."

"I mean it."

"What can I get you, mate?" said the barman, sliding over.

Rod compressed his lips and pushed down the immediate urge to tell the young man to bugger off.

"Beer," said Rod.

"We have a wide range of—"

"Just a beer. Craft ale or bitter. Bottle or glass, I don't mind." He turned swiftly back to Kathy. He didn't want to lose the romantic momentum. "I like you, Kathy."

"You said."

"More than like you. I appreciate you. I value you."

"I feel you're about to break out a thesaurus."

"You're not making this easy," he said.

She looked like she was going to say something snappy but decided better of it and sat back, mouth closed.

"I like you," repeated Rod. He wasn't sure how many times he'd now said that, but it was the foundation on which all else rested. He needed to build on it. "I like you very much and I always have. And recently, um, particularly after last night, I realise that I want to do something about that. I want a chance to get to know you better. You know?"

She kept quiet.

"Listen," he said. "I don't have anyone special in my life. Neither do you. I mean, I don't think you do. Do you? You don't. No. And I think you could be that special someone. In my life, I mean. I don't think I'm that terrible a... a, um, prospect? No, too Jane Austen. I'm trying to say that I think I'm a decent catch. Oh, that's worse than prospect."

A bottled beer appeared next to Rod. He glanced at it. The bloody barman had stuck a wedge of lime in the top!

"Jesus," he said.

"No, keep going," said Kathy flatly. "You were just reaching the right level of awkward."

He looked at her cradling hastily-bought clingfilm-wrapped gifts and clutching a bunch of flowers. She didn't look happy. He pressed on with the last of his resolve.

"I just needed to say something. People say you shouldn't keep feelings bottled up inside. Not that I tend to agree. Bottling up feelings is what we've been doing for generations in my family but I... I wanted to say..." He no longer had any idea what he wanted to say. "Um, thank you?"

"Thank you?" said Kathy.

"Maybe..."

Kathy pulled an expression. Again, it was not a good one. It was the sort of reluctant, disgusted and determined face one might make before taking a bent coat hanger to a clogged toilet.

"Last night," she said.

"Yes, last night," said Rod.

"I think I made it very clear. Last night didn't happen."

"I've not told anyone," he assured her.

"But it didn't happen. At all. It was a dream, a fantasy."

"I enjoyed it too."

"You are not listening to me," she said fiercely. "It was a non-event. I asked you if us having sex was going to make things weird between us. You said no."

"And it won't."

"Look at what I'm holding!" she said, shaking her armfuls of gifts.

"Too much," he conceded.

"Too fucking much," she agreed. "You said it wouldn't be a problem."

"I'm sorry. It just... it awoke feelings in me."

"Awoke feelings in you? You are not in a fucking 'coming of age' rom-com, Rod Campbell. You are my colleague, a work mate."

"I thought you liked me," he said, helplessly.

"I do! I like you, although you make the word 'like' do far more work than it should. I like you. I like colourful cocktails, I like cheesy horror movies, I like Rod Campbell. That's 'like'. That's where we're at. That's where we *were* at."

Rod felt deflated and cold and lonelier than he had been for a long time.

"I just thought... maybe we could have been more."

"Could have been," she agreed, losing none of her savage tone. "Could have been. It crossed my mind too."

"It did?"

"And then you pull a dick move like this."

"This?"

Her eyes narrowly sharply. "Shall we look at the evidence?" She shook the box of chocolates. "Cadbury's Milk Tray. Chocolate is chocolate as far as I'm concerned but Milk Tray as a romantic gift...?"

"Aren't they?"

228

"Only if you're a housewife from the 1980s with low expectations. And this...?" She held up the basket of toiletries.

"Smellies?" he said.

"Look closer, Rod. What's in there? Soap, a flannel, shower gel and toothpaste. What are you trying to say? This is a wash kit, not..." She smiled, understanding. "You bought these in the hospital gift shop."

"I might have done."

"You decided to make your big declaration of love with the first three things you found in a bloody hospital gift shop. You should have bought me grapes to complete the effect. And these flowers... Flowers are nice. I prefer bigger, showier flowers—reds and purples—but flowers are flowers." She plucked the tiny greeting card from its clip within the bouquet and tore open the envelope. She held it up so he could see the front. "A teddy bear with its arm in a sling? Nothing says true love like a cuddly toy with significant injuries."

"I didn't look," he said.

"You didn't think! No matter how many times you tell me the opposite, you didn't think!" She stacked the gifts on the bar. "You are a thoughtless man-child. Empty-headed! I'm going. Going to meet Morag."

He thought to plead with her, to beg her to stay, to undo the harm he'd done. But, in reality, he wanted it all to be over. He kept his mouth shut and averted his eyes as she got down from her stool, picked up her medical waste container and left.

When the click of her heels had faded, he drank his beer, forgetting the wedge of lime shoved in the top. He spat, dug the lime out and threw it on the bar before downing the entire bottle in one go.

Nina phoned Rod. She would have texted, but she wanted the full visceral horror of his initial response.

"Campbell," he said.

"So, chocolates and flowers?"

He groaned. "She tell you?"

"She?" She hooted. "You already did it? Oh, man. How'd it go?"

He chuckled bitterly. "Train wreck. And I've been in one, so I know what I'm talking about."

"What did she do?"

"Yelled my head off, ripped out my heart and my spine and then stormed off with a box of human souls under her arm."

"Okay, your poetic imagery got a bit confusing towards the end there."

"No. She actually has got a box of—"

"Oh, yeah." Nina looked at the time. "Midnight at the Cube. You sound like you're in a bar."

"I am. By the Mailbox."

"Does it serve the kind of beer I like?"

"They serve fizzy chemical run-off if that's what you mean."

"I do. Here's a plan. I'm going to swing by the Cube and meet up with Morag and Kathy and watch the shit go down. Then I'll drop in on you and I'll superficially pretend to offer sympathy for your *bhul-detar* life choices but secretly try to pump you for juicy details."

"I've had worse offers," he said.

Nina shouldered her Thomas the Tank Engine backpack and set off for the Cube.

Morag picked dried melted cheese off the lid of the pizza box and dangled it in her mouth.

I like American BBQ Hot, mother.

Morag murmured in agreement. She looked up at *Shala'pinz Syu,* who had stood watch while she conscientiously ate for two, like a good mother.

"Haven't you got a lair to skulk off to?" said Morag. "A dank cave or something."

"You will want the larger bedroom," said the Handmaiden. "I do not need a bed, but I will go to the smaller room when I am not required."

"No way. A live-in nanny? To hell with you."

"If only such a thing were permitted." *Shala'pinz Syu* did not allow her far-too-human voice to sound disappointed, but Morag could sense her mood. "This situation is not one I would choose."

"I'm not having it," said Morag.

"You do not have a choice, either."

230

Morag's phone pinged.

"Kathy's here."

"She has brought the souls?" asked *Shala'pinz Syu*.

"Uh-huh."

"She can bring them here."

Morag scoffed. "You are kidding. There's no arsing way she's going to find out about our weird odd-couple thing." She tapped a message. "I've told her we're meeting in the lobby."

"If we must."

Morag stood, feeling the combined weight of a twelve-inch pizza and the end of the world in her gut. She gave *Shala'pinz Syu* a stern look. "Not a bloody word about any of this. Not a bloody word."

Nina strolled into the lobby of the Cube. Kathy was waiting by the concierge desk, a bright yellow medical waste box in her hand.

Kathy looked at Nina's children's backpack. "Bit late to be out on a school night?"

Nina looked at Kathy's box. "Your mum still doing shit packed lunches?"

Kathy grinned and looked round. "Morag's supposed to be joining us."

"Think she was with Rod earlier."

"Oh, really?" There was a tone in Kathy's voice that Nina couldn't read.

The lift doors slid open. Morag stepped out, followed by a hulking August Handmaiden of *Prein*.

Kathy raised a questioning eyebrow at Morag.

"I was needed upstairs," said Morag.

"Gingers get invited to all the best parties," said Nina.

"You have no idea."

"You've got..." She pointed at Morag's top and the smudge of glistening red. It looked like blood or minced viscera.

Morag looked down, wiped it with her finger and then licked it.

"Pizza sauce."

"I thought it might have been Rod's blood," said Nina.

Morag frowned but didn't get to ask what she meant.

"The souls," said the August Handmaiden of Prein. Fine sharp bristles at the edge of its shell quivered, tasting the air. "Where are they?"

"Here," said Kathy. "*Shan-shan prui, kei larik-e.*"

She placed the medical waste carrier on the floor and released the lid with a hard plastic pop.

The Handmaiden's shell plates slid over one another. A shrieking baby face, mouth wide, eyes screwed shut, angled towards the box.

"What is this?" said the Handmaiden slowly.

"Twenty-eight souls," said Kathy.

The creature's smallest claw reached in and removed a sample. "What is this?" she repeated.

"*Fraxasa,*" said Morag.

"Human?"

"Essentially."

The Handmaiden straightened and let the dish tumble back into the box.

"Where are the *verrhi dzu peyt?*"

"The Venislarnkin?" said Kathy. "We didn't bring them."

"The wizard, Trevor, offered us twenty-eight humans."

"Trevor is dead."

"You were told to bring them here."

"Actually," said Morag. "*Yo-Morgantus,* or at least Brigit, said twenty-eight. The number was set but he/she also said that he/she didn't care where we got them from."

The Handmaiden flicked out a leg, overturning the box. Petri dishes spilled out onto the floor noisily. Kathy immediately went after them, chasing those that were rolling away. The semi-human concierge came lazily from behind his desk to assist.

"I will take twenty-eight human souls." The Handmaiden's voice didn't stretch to anger, but it certainly increased in volume.

"These are human," said Morag. "As good as."

"Not as good as. This is fakery. I am being tricked. This was to be our compensation."

"For what?"

The Handmaiden tilted down, its carapace at an angle so that one of its appalling baby faces was level with Morag's. "For your life,

Morag Murray. We are owed a debt and we cannot take you as payment."

Nina didn't know what the Handmaiden was on about and reading Venislarn body language was more than a little tricky, but there was a coiled energy and a thoughtfulness in its pose... Nina instinctively swung round her backpack and delved inside.

The Handmaiden leapt, armoured pylon legs outstretched. It jumped clean over Morag and came down on Kathy Kaur. A claw tip speared Kathy's arm and bloodily pinned her to the floor.

"Wh-what...?" gasped Kathy, shocked.

"One," said the Handmaiden and descended to feed.

"*Hyet-pa!*" shouted Nina.

The lobby occupants froze in the white light of the *yellis* wand. Morag stood stock-still, staring. The concierge, stooped to pick up a petri dish that had since rolled away between his legs, gazed blankly. Even Kathy, her arm pinned and bleeding, and the Handmaiden— who *was* affected by the wand, thank fuck—were perfectly still.

"Right," said Nina, mostly to herself. "Now, let's have a little calm."

She approached the Handmaiden. "You, when I awake you, you will forget this little set-to about the souls. You will forget that you haven't been given the souls you need and you're very happy that everything is sorted and settled. You will forget that you intend to eat Kathy Kaur. This..." She gave a little sparkler-wave over the Handmaiden and the bleeding doctor. "This is just a misunderstanding and you will let her be."

She considered releasing the wand's hold over them, but then scuttled over to Morag.

"You will forget that Rod made an arse of himself earlier. That never happened. And you will forget any time you've been an utter bitch to Rod too, Morag. He's a lovely man: a really boring man but a lovely man, and you could do far worse. You hear me? I don't know if this thing lets me implant thoughts or just wipe memories but, frankly, girl, you should ask him out on a date."

Nina almost lowered the wand but then remembered the concierge.

"Oh, and you. Just forget everything, everything that's happened in the last hour, okay?"

She lowered the wand and swiftly returned it to her rucksack.

The Handmaiden slowly removed her claw from Kathy's arm and stepped back. Kathy grunted in suppressed agony.

"What in the name of Christmas is going on here?" said the concierge, startled.

Nina went to assist Kathy, though her first aid skills didn't really cover massive arm wounds.

"All over my floor!" said the concierge, though it was unclear if he was referring to the scattered soul cases or Kathy's blood.

The Handmaiden rotated, confused but unwilling to admit it. "Our business here is done."

Pressure, *here*" hissed Kathy, and Nina obliged.

Morag had her phone to her ear, calling an ambulance.

"Where did you all appear from?" demanded the concierge.

Nina watched as the Handmaiden backed into the lift and the doors closed.

It was long past midnight by the time Nina phoned.

Rod had lost count of the number of beers he'd had and was too merry to care.

He was so merry that he nearly failed to notice the call and he stabbed at the answer button twice before he hit it.

"Ay up," he said.

"You become more northern the more you drink," said Nina.

"Do I 'eck as like. Where are you?"

"In hospital. Covered in blood."

He stood, becoming ninety percent more sober in an instant.

"What? Where? How?"

"It's not my blood. It's Kathy's."

"Jesus. What happened?"

"The deal with the Venislarn. The thing with the souls. Didn't go exactly to plan."

"Damn."

"But it sort of worked out. The Venislarn are happy, for now. I think. And no one is dead."

"Kathy?"

"Great big flesh wound but nothing more. All stitched up. Nothing to worry about."

"You sure?"

"I'm sure. Oh, and that thing."

"What thing?" he said.

"Your girlfriend."

The words hit him, punctured him. The drunkenness came flooding back, but it was a sick and unhappy drunkenness now. "She's not my girlfriend."

"Yeah, well, I used this magic wand on her, and she might be a bit more sympathetic towards you now."

"You did what?"

"The words you're looking for are 'Thank you, Nina.'"

"You messed with her head?"

"Only a little."

"Like some magic rohypnol?"

"I just deleted the embarrassment you made of yourself tonight. Gone from her memory. Thank you, Nina."

"If you say so..." he responded uncertainly.

Nina was quiet for a long moment. Rod checked that he hadn't accidentally ended the call. A piece of torn beer mat landed on the bar next to him. He wasn't sure where it had come from. He prodded it.

"The thing with the little souls in these containers," said Nina. There was a cascading clink of plastic on the line.

"What about it?" he said.

"How many were there meant to be?"

"Twenty-eight," he said.

"Twenty-eight, right."

"Why? Have you lost one?"

Something struck him softly on the back of the head. A crushed beer mat lay on the floor. He looked down and then looked around.

"No," said Nina. "I've got twenty-nine here in Kathy's box."

"A spare?" Rod suggested.

"Maybe," said Nina. "Right. N'night."

She hung up. Rod sniffed, stretched.

He blurrily saw arms waving at him. He blinked and focussed. Down the far end of the bar, sat two women. It took him a long moment to remember their names. Jayda and Skye. The film company armourer and the... He couldn't remember Skye's job title, but it involved fake tentacles and ping pong balls and prosthetic genitalia.

"We," said Skye, revealing in that one syllable that she was acting at least as drunk as Rod felt, "have been trying to get your attention for ages."

She gestured to the bits of thrown beermat scattered around Rod's stool.

Jayda sipped her bottled beer. "You pissed some people off today."

Rod had to stop and think. It felt like there was a long line of people he might have annoyed today.

"Is that so?"

"Lot of scenes rescheduled and people giving each other shit, the kind that trickles down the ranks. Your name got mentioned more than once."

Rod realised that he was tired enough and drunk enough to not care. He gestured to the barman who looked tired too, like he wanted them to leave so he could shut up and go home. Just another person for Rod to piss off. He gestured for drinks for the three of them.

"You guys get some flak?" he said.

"Us?" said Skye.

Jayda smirked and adjusted her baseball cap. "We just hunkered down and hid. But..." Jayda leant over, brushing against Skye and nearly knocking her from her stool, just so she could reach over and prod Rod in the chest. "We do have some advice for you."

Advice. That was the other thing. It felt like it had been a day of annoying people and getting advice from people. Mostly bad advice, it felt.

"Oh, aye?" he said. "What advice?"

"Tomorrow, they're shooting a big scene."

"Is this the helicopter car chase?" said Rod.

"No. They're doing that on a Hollywood lot. Mostly CGI. Although, they've got the helicopter camera guys coming in tomorrow—or is it the day after?—to film the rooftop chase stuff. Tomorrow..." Jayda frowned.

"It's the torture scene," said Skye helpfully.

236

"Right. Right. Torture scene. Agent Jack Sexy-Pants is captured by Botticelli and strapped to a torture table in the bad guy's..." She flailed around for the write word.

"Dungeon?" suggested Skye. Jayda scowled at her.

"Lair," said Rod.

"Sure, whatever," said Jayda. "Cos that's realistic, right? Taylor's gonna film that scene and, cos he's got a massive man-crush on you, bro, he's going to ask you if it was 'real' enough. And what are you gonna say?"

Rod nodded solemnly. "I'll tell him it was great."

"Tell him it was perfect," said Skye.

"Aye. Perfect."

"But he'll want to know if you've ever done anything like it, if you've ever escaped by... how is it again?"

"Blowing the locks on his handcuff with a pipette of nitro-glycerine," said Skye.

"Wait, the nitro-glycerine blows the lock but doesn't sever his wrist? Are you using real explosives on that one?"

"Grams of flash powder," said Jayda. "I got enough explosives in my cupboards of tricks to take down a building, and enough weapons to hold off the zombie apocalypse, but this stuff is all just Hollywood magic."

Rod grimaced internally. So, this was his lot: to be a yes-man to a bunch of actors playing pretend while the end of the world edged ever nearer all around him.

"I need to go to bed," he said wearily. He looked at his bottle. There was an inch in the bottom.

"They put you up in the hotel?" said Skye.

"My flat is a twenty-minute walk..." He took a split second to orientate himself and pointed out through the wall. "That way."

"You can crash with one of us," said Skye. "We're only a two-minute stagger that way."

Ex-marine Jayda gave Rod an openly judging look up and down and then gave Skye a meaningful look. Skye chinked the neck of her bottle against Rod's.

"Well, you're welcome to crash in my room at least. It's okay, I don't bite."

It was an instantly appealing offer and not because it was less distance to walk. But Rod checked himself. His life was depressing enough right now without complicating it by spending the night with another woman and, undoubtedly, him totally misreading what Skye's offer actually meant. Recollections of the plaster cast trophies on her shelves cemented his reticence.

"Thanks," he said, "but I don't want to wake up wondering whose prosthetic Willy you've stuck to my face in the night."

Jayda guffawed, loudly and unashamedly brazen. "He's got you there, girl."

Skye pulled a silly face and rolled her eyes. "Your loss, soldier boy."

"Aye," he said, pushing himself off his stool and feeling the alcohol rush to his legs. "It's just not my week, is it?"

He turned and located the door. "Gonna say good night, ladies."

Jayda slapped him companionably on the shoulder.

"Walk'll do me good," he said. "Maybe go the long way, along the canal. Give me something to throw up in on the way."

WEDNESDAY

Nina sat outside the treatment room on the Restricted Ward, the box of unwanted souls at her side, the diary of one Jonathan Angus open on her lap. Reading—actual book reading—was not one of Nina's strong points and she found herself nodding off as she tried to follow the compact scrawl on the pages.

She had received a text earlier in the day from Mrs Fiddler, asking if Nina might be visiting Soho house tomorrow – the tomorrow that was now today. Nina had not yet responded, unsure if Vaughn Sitterson would bollock her for taking another day off for this personal investigation. But Nina could sense the excitement in Mrs Fiddler's short message, and it was an excitement she shared.

Eventually, she fell asleep. But the book slid off her knee and landed heavily on her foot, waking her abruptly. Nina stood, walked the length of the Restricted Ward corridor and sent her reply to Mrs Fiddler.

On her route back to the waiting room, Nina noticed a man crouched at the door to a side corridor. He pressed his splayed-out fingers against the floor between his bare feet, blinked at the hospital lights, and flicked his tongue in and out... in and out. It was the American actor, Langford James.

"What are you doing?" she said.

He flicked his tongue at her. "Becoming."

"Practising for a role?"

He cricked his neck in a jerky fashion.

"Becoming, practising. Shedding a skin."

"Uh-huh?" she said, not interested. "They got you on some trippy drugs?"

"They don't know," he said and hopped out of the room, like a man pretending with his whole heart to be a frog. "They don't know what happened to me."

"Great," she said and prepared to move on.

"I survived the *Shohreye 'uuuduk*. I survived and so I have become. *Ped veri-klu da Daganau-Pysh*."

"No, mate," she said. "You really haven't. You're not one of them. You're just a man who's had a nasty shock."

239

"I am transmuted: spawn to tadpole to *shen'zi pek Samakha*."

"Don't you dare. We've had enough trouble with Venislarnkin this week," she said and left him.

"Venislarnkin?" he called after her.

"Nothing," she called back. "Forget about it. Get some rest."

Kathy was coming out of the treatment room, her arm in a sling, a white dressing over arm and shoulder.

"You're still here?" she said, surprised.

"Consular mission never leave a woman behind," said Nina.

Kathy bent to pick up the box of captured souls. Nina beat her to it.

"I've got these."

"It's fine," said Kathy and took hold of the handle.

"You've only got one arm."

"They're my responsibility."

Nina thought about arguing the toss, but it seemed stupid and it was late—or rather it was early—and they both had beds to get to.

"Have it your way," said Nina and let it drop. "Share a cab?"

Kathy smiled – a weird smile, probably a result of fatigue and blood loss. "That would be nice."

Morag rarely had trouble sleeping in strange beds, certainly not strange emperor-sized beds in luxury apartments, even if there was an August Handmaiden of *Prein* squatting in the guest bedroom next door.

But she woke from her first night's sleep in the Cube with the remnants of peculiar dreams running round her head.

She had dreamt of Rod Campbell. Dreams were weird and indiscriminate recyclers of faces, places and memories and she had dreamt of him before. Many a strange work conversation had begun "I dreamt about you last night." But she wouldn't be sharing details of this dream any time soon.

It had been powerfully erotic. It hadn't featured any of the bluntly mechanical acts of her more sexual dreams, but it was filled with the emotional and sensual iconography of bone-deep longing and desire. As she rose to consciousness and the dream faded, she was left only with a mental image of her male colleague and the rather oddly specific thought that Rod Campbell was 'a lovely man' and she should ask him out on a date.

She dismissed any ideas of dates but couldn't dismiss the feelings the dream had aroused in her mind and her body. Resisting waking fully, she slid her hand down under the covers and touched herself.

That feels nice, mother.

"Jesus Christ!" she barked in alarm and sat bolt upright.

Sorry, mother. I didn't mean to surprise you.

The door banged open and *Shala'pinz Syu* barged in.

"You cried out in distress," the Venislarn informed her.

Morag grabbed her sheets, more naked than she ever preferred to be in company. "Would everyone just fuck off!"

You said a bad word, mother.

"I don't care!" she snapped.

Shala'pinz Syu regarded her coolly. "You smell of sex," she noted and then backed out.

Any residual sexy thoughts were banished from Morag's mind, as were any half-formed notions of asking Rod out on a date. Whether she found him attractive or not—and she was too addled to know herself on that score—there was no way she was going dating with a snooping anti-Christ in her womb and an *adn-bhul* spider-demon for a flatmate.

Her phone rang. It was Nina.

"Yes?" said Morag, still angry.

"Is that what passes for a good morning in Scotch Land," Nina tutted.

"Sorry," said Morag in the aggressive tone of someone who wasn't at all sorry. "It's early."

"I need you to cover for me today."

"Cover for you how?"

"I'm not coming into work. I've got a... lead I need to follow up but Vaughn's not keen."

"And if he asks where you are?"

"You'll tell him something plausible."

"Nipped out for coffee? Fighting truculent books in the Vault? Making sure the unseen horrors of Dickens Heath have paid their TV licence?"

"Exactly. That's why I asked you. Rod can't lie like you."

"Thank you?" said Morag dubiously.

"And that's that," Nina said and put her phone away.

Morning mists curled across the lawns and car park of Soho House. The air was still and quiet. It was hard to believe, in this moment, that this posh old house was surrounded by the crowded urban sprawl of twenty-first century Birmingham.

"If you have to lie to be here," said Mrs Fiddler, "then you shouldn't be here."

"Do they teach you to say things like that at teacher college?"

"Like that?" asked Mrs Fiddler.

"Honesty is the best policy. If you can't say something nice, don't say anything. Manners cost nothing."

"Things like that tend to be true," said the former teacher now museum guide and, without another word, she led the way round the visitor centre to the doors of Soho House. It was early, the museum wouldn't be open for at least another two hours, and the silence of the house was oppressively lonely.

The corridor that led toward the newly-discovered rooms terminated in a solid wall once more. Together, Nina and Mrs Fiddler descended into the cellar, wound the sidereal clock and, with the brass oculus, went back up to see what changes had occurred.

"Part of me is still convinced this is some form of illusion," said Mrs Fiddler.

"Probably better to think that way," said Nina.

The door to the previously-but-no-longer demolished half of the house had returned. Nina opened the door and Mrs Fiddler placed the impassable velvet sash barrier across the doorway behind them.

"Have you told your colleagues what you're doing?" said Nina.

"This? No."

"Won't they wonder why you're hanging around me all day instead of showing visitors around?"

"I told them you were a council inspector, checking for dry rot and such and that I needed to accompany you."

"What happened to honesty being the best policy?"

"Do as I say, not as I do," said Mrs Fiddler.

242

"That's another thing teachers say."

They returned to the dusty and mouldering room where they had last observed past events through the Oculus.

"I think we need to be methodical about this," said Mrs Fiddler.

"That's a codeword for 'really, really boring', isn't it?" said Nina.

"We have been given an unprecedented opportunity to see into the past," said Mrs Fiddler in the firm tones of one who would not be baited. "We should document everything we see and try to create a meaningful chronology."

"I just want to know why Matthew Boulton is able to make Venislarn machines and what that weird, squiddy thing in the lump of blue john was."

"No reason we can't do both," said Mrs Fiddler. "Now, you say you can read the markings on this?"

Nina looked at the oculus. It was true that she could read and translate the individual ideograms etched into the metal ring, but it did not follow that she understood what they meant in combination.

"The numbers," prompted Mrs Fiddler. "I assume they could be dates?"

"Could be Venislarn dates."

"One day you will tell me what that word means. Regardless, whatever system it follows, it would be rational to assume that if the numbers go up or down then the scene being viewed is nearer or further away from our own time."

Nina could have said it was not rational to apply any kind of logic to the Venislarn, that it was irrational to think the Venislarn were rational in any way.

"Let's assume that," she said charitably.

"So, we can spin the dials, see if we can find any clues as to the date and time, make a note of the settings and move on from there."

Nina huffed.

"What?" said Mrs Fiddler.

"You've just taken something fun and exciting and made it sound like hard work."

"Just trying to be methodical," said the old woman.

Boring it might have been but, annoyingly, it also made sense. Nina turned the interlocking hoops, intoned the resulting Venislarn words that lined up. The device vibrated in her hand and through the opening a brighter past world became visible.

For the most part, day or night, the Soho House of the past was filled with humdrum human activity. Clues to when this activity was taking place were hard to come by. There were no calendars and no newspapers. Mrs Fiddler insisted that much could be learned from listening to people's conversations.

What Nina learned was that, without television or YouTubers, the servants of Georgian England had nothing to talk about except what people they knew had done and said.

"I think it's interesting," said Mrs Fiddler.

"God, you would," said Nina.

"I meant that the scenes we are viewing seem to be confined to a limited window of time. We are seeing, have seen throughout, glimpses of this house when it was at its busiest, when Boulton and his contemporaries made this their meeting place. We've not seen scenes of this place in the nineteen twenties or in the early Middle Ages or in the Cretaceous Period. That's odd, isn't it?"

It was odd, Nina thought, though not necessarily interesting. It didn't stop their mostly fruitless search for the date from being quite dull.

Soon enough, they found that their easiest method of determining the date was to catch Mr or Mrs Boulton or their serving man Jonathan Angus in the act of writing in their diaries. Anne Boulton kept a meticulous set of a financial accounts for the house, a fact which Mrs Fiddler found ludicrously exciting. She insisted Nina take picture after picture of the woman's handwritten shopping lists and tradesmen's bills and near squealed with delight until Nina got annoyed and had to lie and say her phone was out of storage space. Matthew Boulton often wrote in a journal—or what Mrs Fiddler declared to be a 'commonplace book'—mostly regarding the factory and details of goods or manufacturing processes. Jonathan Angus's was a diary in a more normal sense and, if they were lucky enough to dial the oculus to late evening, they might sometimes find him in his room below stairs, writing his thoughts on the doings of the day. Catching any of the residents with diaries open was the best way of finding out the date. But, man, it was soul-sapping stuff.

Until they made any link between the dates viewed and the settings of the oculus, what they got with each turn of the dial was random. It was only by chance that shortly after nine a.m.—and moments before Nina was going to declare they needed a break and should send out for coffee and Egg McMuffins—they found themselves witnessing something of genuine interest.

Matthew Boulton and Erasmus Darwin were in the dining room. Jonathan entered with peg-leg Josiah Wedgwood close behind.

"Here," said Wedgwood and laid the piece of blue john on the table. Boulton moved aside the remains of a meal and the cruet set to make more space.

It had been reduced to less than half its original size, the top layer cut or chiselled away to create a bowl of the lower half. In that bowl (and Nina had to bring herself forward right among the men to see) was the creature they had glimpsed inside the stone fragment.

It was white, a solid bleached white, like bone or a stick of chalk. It had a central body no more than four inches long and a number of tentacle-like limbs with tapering ends. None of the limbs seemed to be of the same length. The flesh glistened softly, like it had a light blue film of oil over it.

"What have you got there, boys?" said Nina.

It looked very Venislarn. But, then again, it looked very much like a squid.

"Do you know what it is?" Mrs Fiddler whispered to Nina. Nina shook her head.

"The flesh is soft to the touch," said Wedgwood. "I had to be careful not to damage it."

Jonathan had a board and a sheaf of papers in the crook of his arm and was hastily sketching the creature.

"I will be honest," said Boulton, "I do not see why we would expect the application of electrical energy to bring life back to this thing, no more than we would if we passed electricity through a plate of sardines."

"If Nollet can make two hundred monks jump by connecting them to a battery of Leyden jars then I would not be surprised if we couldn't make a plate of sardines do likewise," said Jonathan.

Erasmus laughed. "Your man has it there! I'm sure Monsieur Nollet would approve of this."

"Sardines. Monks." Boulton muttered as he arranged his electricity producing apparatus around the lump of blue john and laid copper electrodes against two ends of the creature. "This creature smells foul enough as it is. Let us hope we do not cook it like a kipper."

Once the three gentlemen were happy with the arrangement (Jonathan's opinion was neither wanted nor given), Boulton began to turn the handle on his friction-making charge generator. He worked slowly and Darwin moved the lamp closer so they might see better.

"Electricity and weird creatures aren't usually a winning combination," said Nina.

The men in the room were silent but for the zhuzh-zhuzh rhythm of the turning handle.

"More, Boulton," said Wedgwood.

"I didn't want to—"

"More. Be bold."

There was an ominous creak which caused a minor buzz of excitement until they realised it was Darwin, leaning his bulk against the table as he bent nearer.

"More!"

Boulton sped up.

"A twitch!" declared Wedgwood. "I swear it. That little limb there—"

The creature moved, stretching and straightening its limbs, like it was giving a big 'good morning' yawn. Slime, like concentrated WKD Blue dripped from the limbs.

"Dear God," whispered Jonathan.

The creature rippled now, limbs flexing out of synch, each exploring the recess of the stone it laid in. Boulton stopped turning the handle and the wheel quickly wound down.

"It's alive," said Darwin.

"For how long," said Wedgwood. "If it is a sea creature then it will need water."

Boulton turned and shouted. "Nancy! A saucepan of water! Quick!" He glanced at Jonathan.

246

"Sir," said Jonathan and reluctantly tore himself from the sight of the revived creature and hurried to the door. Nina turned to watch him with the oculus.

"Don't jiggle it around," said Mrs Fiddler. "I want to see."

There were shouts of alarm and Nina swung the oculus back to the table. The three men were stumbling in alarm. Boulton had thrown himself back. Darwin was pointing animatedly.

The section of blue john in which the creature had rested was now rocking, empty on the table. Wedgwood was banging around. Nina swung the oculus to look. Something white and unmistakeably alive flopped along the tabletop. It collided with the salt and pepper set knocking them aside. It recoiled from the falling salt and darted to the table edge and then agilely swung itself over and onto the floor, leaving a glistening trail in its wake.

"Do not let it escape!" commanded Darwin.

"Then you get over here and catch it!" retorted Wedgwood sharply.

Mrs Fiddler scuttled back and grabbed the oculus to angle it round. Her thumb must have caught the dials. The image vanished abruptly.

Nina gave the cardigan-clad klutz a sharp look.

"Did you think it was coming to get you?"

"I panicked. A little."

Nina made a noise. "Time for coffee and Egg McMuffins and then we'll try to find it again."

"What are Egg McMuffins?"

Nina took her phone out to order. "Everything a growing girl needs."

Rod, nursing a hangover and a large mug of hot, sweet tea, sat at his office desk for the first time in three days. The response team at the consular mission to the Venislarn supposedly operated a hot-desking policy and there should have been no desk that he could describe as 'his', but Vivian Grey cast a long shadow, even in death. Vivian had refused to engage with the hot-desking policy and the desk she had claimed as her own had remained untouched by her colleagues since, partly out of respect, to create a tangible monument to the woman, but also partly out of fear; even when she was dead.

Morag had staked her claim to another desk in her own way, by littering it with detritus. Morag seemed to spend her entire life playing catch-up with herself. Home life and work life blurred. Out of date snacks, unprocessed work files, toiletries and even, occasionally, items of clothing created a space in which no one else could work comfortably, not least a man afraid of what intimate horrors he might encounter. Today she seemed even more flustered than usual, setting about her own work with a quiet and furious will.

Rod had found himself moving further and further into a corner until he ended up working at a square table by the water cooler that wasn't even really a desk.

This morning, most of his desk was taken up by Mystic Trevor's teapot, an electronic liquid level sensor and the laptop that the sensor was connected to by a short cable.

A phone was ringing somewhere, but since Rod wasn't on a proper desk, it definitely wasn't his.

"Phone," said Morag.

"I'm busy," he croaked and then cleared his throat and tried again. "I'm busy."

"You've been staring at that teapot for half an hour," said Morag.

He huffed, feeling very sorry for himself and his alcohol-abused body, but nonetheless leaned over to the nearest proper desk to pick up the phone.

"Campbell."

"Ah, so there's someone in your office?" said Lois the admin receptionist, apparently surprised.

"Doing a head count?" he asked.

"Nothing so suspicious, bab, although Vaughn did say I needed to ask you where Nina was."

"Nina?" Rod wheeled round, to check the office, his hangover headache flaring up and his tea sploshing over its coaster.

"Nina," said Morag without looking up, "is helping out in the Vault."

"The Vault," said Rod. "Will that be all?"

248

"That's not why I phoned," said Lois. "There's some people in reception for you."

"I haven't got any appointments."

"I think these are more of the drop-in variety."

"We don't operate a drop-in centre," he said. "And I'm needed on set in..." He consulted his phone. There was a text he had not heard coming in. It was from an unknown number and said: TAMMY WANTS TO KNOW WHERE MR JAMES IS. WEVE BEEN TOLD HE CHECKED OUT OF HOSPITAL BUT IS NOT ON SET. CALL AT ONCE. HERMIONE (3RD ASSISTANT DIRECTOR)

"Aye, I'm definitely busy," he said.

"But these two asked for you," said Lois.

"Who are they?"

"The woman, er, Khaleesi-*Qalawe* was one of the Venislarnkin who were here on Sunday. The man looks vaguely familiar but I don't, hang on..."

As Lois lowered the phone to ask the man his name, Rod cupped his own phone and called over to Morag.

"Morag, you were dealing with those Venislarnkin on Sunday, weren't you?"

"Er, yeah."

"There's a couple of them come back. They're in reception. Could you...? I've got to find a man who went AWOL from the Restricted Ward last night."

Morag grunted in assent and got up. Rod caught her looking at him. Obviously, Morag looked at him all the time. They were colleagues; colleagues did a lot of looking at each other. But this was an odd look, as though Morag didn't want to be caught looking. Instinctively, he checked his flies, always a good first port of call if one was getting funny looks. His flies were fine.

"Everything all right?" he said.

"What?" she said.

"You. You look like..."

She shook her head. "No. You're fine. I mean, I'm fine. I mean, you're... of course you're... you're a lovely man." She looked horrified, as though she couldn't believe the words coming out of her mouth.

"Ta," he said for want of something better to say.

She scowled, seemingly at herself and in an obvious change of topic gestured sharply at the teapot.

"What's going on?"

"Maurice and Omar think it's a danger-sensing teapot."

"A what?"

"The greater likelihood of an immediate threat in the vicinity, the higher the level of tea."

"Are you serious?"

He would have shrugged but his body wasn't interested in that kind of effort. "It's a simple principle. Like a teasmade alarm or lights that come on at nightfall except it's, you know, danger."

"And are we in danger?"

"I'm trying to get some sense of scale but…"

He pointed at the laptop screen. Morag gave the graph a cursory glance. It would be enough to see that the level in the tea was slowly but constantly rising.

"Just over a millimetre an hour at the moment," he said.

"So, we don't need to panic just yet," she suggested. "By the way, Kathy was in the Restricted Ward last night. Maybe she knows something about your man," she said and left.

Morag stalked down the corridor.

"'You're a lovely man'? 'You're a lovely man'?" she muttered angrily at herself. "Why not just say you fancy the arse off him and want his babies, why don't you?"

Do you want to have his babies, mother?

"No," she said. "You are baby enough for anyone, my little bump."

She pushed through into the consular mission reception. Khaleesi-*Qalawe*, she of the blue hair and the subdermal gill implants still stood in reception with a tall, fine-featured man in a baggy tracksuit and a baseball cap. He was, despite his good looks and youthful clothes, clearly considerably older than the young woman. He hunched his shoulders and his gaze flitted uncomfortably from side to side, as though he found the lights too bright.

"Khaleesi," said Morag, "I hope you haven't come back to finish the paperwork for signing yourself over to the Venislarn. The handover was last night, and I was glad you did not have to be there."

Some of the details of the handover were hazy in Morag's mind. Nina had fobbed off the Handmaiden of *Prein* with some magical misdirection, but Morag feared the matter was not yet closed.

"No," said Khaleesi, earnestly. "I haven't. I'm not going to."

"Good."

"But Langford here got in touch with me via the Facebook group and I didn't know what to do with him."

"Langford, is it?" said Morag. "And does he want to sell himself to the Venislarn?"

The man threw his hands out expressively, like he was about to burst into rap. "Naw, dog. I ain't selling out to no one. I ain't no *bhultamade* sell-out. I'm *veri-klu da Daganau-Pysh*."

"No, you're not, sunshine," said Morag. "You're really not."

"You dissin' my heritage, yo?" he said.

"I can see why you brought him in," Morag said to Khaleesi. "Let's take him through to the interview room."

"So, he really is Venislarn?" said Khaleesi.

"He's a middle-aged white guy trying to throw down some gangsta 'snizzle', which is far more worrying." She swiped and opened the door to let them through.

"I think he's a famous Hollywood actor," Khaleesi whispered.

"Oh, is that what he told you?" said Morag and rolled her eyes. "This way."

Mrs Fiddler declared Egg McMuffins to be perfectly pleasant and sat back on the dusty crate she had been using as a seat. "What exactly is your job, Nina?"

"Hmmm?"

"You and your colleagues. You're not the police."

"No."

"And you're definitely not historians."

"Could be."

Mrs Fiddler gave her a patiently disbelieving look.

"No," agreed Nina. "We're not historians." She looked at her old teacher. In between the bottom of the woman's practical little trousers and her practical stout shoes, she saw stripy socks, orange and purple. Mrs Fiddler had a nice, safe life. Nina didn't want to ruin it with the truth. "You don't need to know what we do."

"But I asked," said Mrs Fiddler reasonably. "Are you protecting me?"

"Maybe."

"You know, I have never subscribed to the notion that ignorance is bliss. I'm more of a knowledge-is-power kind of gal."

Nina sipped at her coffee, got nothing, took off the sipper lid and tried to drink the last of the foam around the rim. When that proved ineffective, she put the cup and her rubbish in the brown paper bag the food had come in.

"Come on. We've got work to do."

She picked up the oculus and studied the dial settings which had been knocked out of whack. She found settings that were close and opened another twelve-inch window to the past. Mrs Fiddler made a note of the markings in a hardback notebook (with the words 'HISTORY IS FUN!' printed on the cover in a super-jolly font that was fooling no-one) and they went in search of evidence of the date.

The house was almost empty. Maybe it was a Sunday and everyone was out at church. That was the kind of thing people did in olden days, thought Nina. They moved through the house. As they tramped from room to room, in both the Soho House museum and the re-conjured wing, they looked for clues to the date.

As they went down the stairs to the cellar and the servants' quarters, Nina said, "We deal with the monsters."

"Pardon?" said Mrs Fiddler.

"My job. Our department. We deal with the monsters."

"What do you think that thing trapped in the rock was?"

"I don't know. Not seen one quite like that before. But there are monsters and there are gods. We call them gods but they're not." She stopped at the bottom of the stairs.

"What are they then, if they're not gods?" said Mrs Fiddler.

Nina shook her head. It wasn't a question with an answer. "They're called the Venislarn and they are going to destroy the world. It's all going to end badly. I mean real bad."

"You believe this?"

Nina shook her head again. "It's not a matter of believing. It's fact. The end of the world is coming."

Mrs Fiddler smiled. "You sound like a crazy street preacher. Fire and brimstone."

"Well, it's like that," said Nina and pressed on down the cellar corridor towards Jonathan Angus's room, "except Jesus doesn't ride in on his magic donkey to save the day or anything."

"Religious Education was never your strong suit at school, was it?"

"Our job is to investigate and to keep things in order. We try to prevent as much human suffering as possible and avoid pissing off the Venislarn gods in a way that might lead to them starting the apocalypse early."

Mrs Fiddler was still for a good long moment. "I do not like the sound of that," she said eventually.

"It isn't nice. That's the point."

"I meant you. Your job. Keeping the people in line, keeping them in the dark. Telling them to write their names and addresses on their suitcases in chalk with the false promise that they will have them back later, packing them onto the trains and not giving any thought to their final destination."

"What suitcases? Trains?"

"History, dear."

Nina entered Jonathan Angus's small bedroom. It had a simple bed, a washstand, a chest for clothes and a narrow upright window that faced onto the rear gardens but offered no view at all unless he wanted to stand on a stool to look out at it. His journal, the then new and fresh version of the one Nina carried in her backpack, sat on the edge of the washstand. It was closed. Nina huffed.

"If these things intend to destroy us," said Mrs Fiddler, "someone should be fighting them."

"There's no point."

"That's defeatist."

"It's not," said Nina, regretting telling anything to the woman. "It's going to happen. It's all written down."

"Where?" squeaked Mrs Fiddler, annoyed.

"In the Bloody Big Book."

"You're making this stuff up!"

"You don't have to believe me."

Mrs Fiddler's chunky necklace rattled with her irritation. "History is littered with talk of manifest destiny and empires that will last a thousand years and some people—sheep!—are short-sighted enough to believe it. People who claim there was nothing they could do or—worse!—that they were only following orders."

"The future is fixed," said Nina, feeling the combined discomfort of being told off by a disappointed teacher and the annoyance of dealing with an oldster who just didn't get how things were. "It's like"—she gestured at the oculus—"the past. It's set. It's there. You can't change it. It's written down."

"Then you should find a way to rewrite it!" snapped Mrs Fiddler.

"How?" shouted Nina. "I can't just..." She thrust her hand into the oculus, only as a demonstration of how untouchable and unchangeable both past and future were. As her fingers touched the threshold between here and there, they vibrated violently, like she was trying to grip a pneumatic drill by the wrong end. Her fingers sank to the second knuckle before the vibrational force and her own caution threw them out again.

"Ooh," she said and inspected her hand. Her fingertips were white but otherwise unharmed.

Mrs Fiddler stared, her face still set to grump-mode. "What?"

"Hang on," said Nina and pushed her hand back into the oculus, this time with force and deliberation and knowledge of what she might feel. Fingers, hand, wrist... the violent buzzing moved as a band up her arm. From nowhere, a wind sprang up, howling round their legs.

"I was really speaking figuratively," Mrs Fiddler murmured. "Don't do anything you'll regret."

The walls in the present building groaned, seemingly in protest at Nina's actions. Nina's hand felt like it was encased in rubber, sensing the world through an intermediary layer. Nerve signals struggled to pass over the barrier between times. But her fingers worked, her hand could grip. She flipped open Jonathan Angus's journal and brushed the pages until she was on the last written page.

March 18th 1773

We apprehend'd a burglar in Boulton's study. A swarthy individual dressed in little more than rags and denying any wrongdoing even though caught very much in the act. Boulton seem'd not to take the matter seriously—

Nina pulled her arm back into the present and tried to shake the life back into it. The wind and the creaking in the walls instantly subsided.

"Are you hurt?" said Mrs Fiddler.

"Numb."

"Numbskull more like," said Mrs Fiddler but with more concern than anger. "You moved something in the past."

"A page," said Nina.

"Butterflies and hurricanes."

"Eh?"

Mrs Fiddler shook her head and then gave a weary smile. "Things *can* be rewritten, Nina."

Rod descended to the Vault in search of Kathy. He wanted to ask her if she had seen Langford James at the Restricted Ward. A phone call to the hospital had confirmed that he had checked himself out, physically fit and well, sometime before eight o'clock and that he'd spoken to a member of the consular mission at some point in the small hours. Rod intended to ask Kathy if that had been her, maybe get some clue as to his whereabouts, but he had an ulterior motive. He needed to clear the air.

If Nina was correct, Kathy would now have no memory of the embarrassing incident in the bar, but Rod still needed to adjust their relationship – either re-establish their professional friendship or create a new normal.

All of this required navigating the subtle and nuanced landscape of human emotions and interpersonal relationships, unfamiliar territory for Rod. Regardless, he had been trained to deal with adversity and surprises and he should be able to handle this.

The Vault's corridors were lined with specimens gathered over decades. Books predominated. Shelves were filled with old creaking tomes, folders of reports from agents who had met the Venislarn without knowing what they were, and a telling number of bound academic theses whose authors were now dead, mad or in the employ of the consular mission.

He could hear voices up ahead, Dr Kathy Kaur and Professor Sheikh Omar. They weren't arguing as such but there was a definite tension between them.

"But, dear doctor," Omar said, "your need is at an end. The Think Tank falls under my remit and, I'm sorry but if mother wishes to keep the keys to the drinks cabinet to herself then she shall."

"I'm just asking for an opportunity to study *Polliqan Riti* further," said Kathy.

"Under my tuition, perhaps," said the professor.

Rod slowed. Kathy and Omar stood at a broad work surface. Omar was doing his best to piece together fragments of a broken pottery mask, a green and glistening thing that had a Far Eastern look about it. The mask made Omar's jigsaw efforts all the trickier by constantly changing its expression. Rod loitered by a pillar, not wishing to interrupt their well-mannered argument. Pages rustled and spines creaked as nearby books subtly turned on their shelves to watch him.

"As you were," Rod said quietly.

"I can work in there without supervision," Kathy said to Omar.

"You don't need to be there at all, my dear."

"Call it professional development."

"I shall call it professional interference, which is apt."

"We could always ask Vaughn's opinion on the matter."

Omar's expression became suddenly sour. He straightened up to think, adjusted his spectacles and then saw Rod hovering at a distance. Kathy looked round.

"This conversation is not at an end," said Kathy and walked over to Rod.

Omar bent to his work once more.

Rod gestured at Kathy's bound arm. "How's the—"

"Spying on me now?" she said, fiercely.

"Eh? No. I—"

"Stalking?"

"What? I'm not stalking anyone."

"Really?" she said. "Because hiding round the corner and staring at someone—"

"If I was stalking you," he said with firm authority, "you would be unaware of the fact."

"Bragging about your stalking skills now," she noted.

This conversation had not taken a wrong turn, it had started off in the wrong direction entirely and was driving at speed away from where Rod wanted it to go.

"I came to talk to you."

"Like you did last night?" said Kathy.

"Oh, you remember that?"

She blinked and shook her head in a disbelieving spasm. "That level of awkwardness kind of sticks with you, Rod."

"Nina said..." He realised he didn't want to share what Nina had said, that it could only make the situation worse. "Listen, we still have to work together."

"*Still* have to work together? It's not even a situation that requires that kind of language. We're not a divorcing couple, keeping up the appearance of normality for the sake of the children. We *do* work together."

"Right, and I came to talk to you about work matters."

She rested her one good hand on her hip and waited. Rod's mind had gone blank.

"You said that the thing that *definitely didn't happen that night* wouldn't make things weird between us," she said.

"Well, clearly it did," he said gruffly. "And maybe I can't just put it out of my mind like you can."

"You said you would."

Rod felt an acute sense of injustice, a hot feeling of utter unfairness that stopped him considering his words before he spoke. "Don't forget, I did what I did to save you."

"Oh, so now I owe you, do I?"

"I didn't want to do it."

"And yet you can't seem to leave me alone."

"I bloody like you, you know," he snapped.

"Indoor voices, please, children," called Professor Omar.

Kathy put her hand on Rod's chest and propelled him just round the corner and out of sight of Omar.

257

"I bloody liked you too," she hissed, "but you're doing a damned fine job of curing me of that. I'm sorry I had consensual sex with you in order to save my life, soldier. I'm sorry I didn't read the operating manual and realise that sticking your dick inside me would turn you into a stalker—"

"Steady on, now."

"I am very sorry that you don't have the emotional toolkit to cope with everyday human situations."

Her frown of displeasure was deep and powerful, and Rod felt thoroughly cowed. Her attention flicked from him to her wounded arm and then back again.

"Some days, death seems almost preferable," she said and walked away.

Rod's gaze fixed on the tiled floor. Thoughts whirled through his head, but it was just the engine of his mind revving, unconnected. He had no clue, no anchor, no idea. He glared angrily at the shelves.

"What do you think you're looking at?"

The books pretended they weren't looking at anything at all.

Nina and Mrs Fiddler advanced the dials and peered into the past.

The house within the oculus was quiet – as quiet as a house with more than a dozen staff, several visiting tradesmen, a child, a toddler and the Boulton parents themselves ever could be. Beyond the chatter of the kitchen and the scullery, a hush hung over the place. The two women wandered about the ground floor, looking for any scene of interest.

They eventually found Boulton in his study. He sat at his tall writing desk, quill pen in hand, staring into a wide glass jar. Inside, beneath a cork-sealed lid, was the creature from the blue john stone. The jar had been part filled with a slope of loose stone and water to create a pool and a shore.

"That's not a squid," said Mrs Fiddler. "Before, I thought it might be, but now..."

"It's very Venislarn," said Nina.

The creature lounged on the shore in a mostly upright pose. Several of its little limbs were projected downwards to support it.

Others waved leisurely in the air. It tipped back the blob which currently passed for its head. If it had hair it might be sensually throwing it back. If it could speak, it would probably be asking Boulton to paint it like one of his French girls.

Nina took out her phone and snapped a picture through the oculus.

"What the fuck are you?" she whispered to herself.

"Language," said Mrs Fiddler softly.

Boulton stroked the glass with the soft end of his quill and then bent to write. Nina looked over his shoulder. The sheet of paper was filled with mathematic notations and sketches of an engineering aspect.

"You don't think, do you?" said Nina.

"It's communicating with him?" said Mrs Fiddler.

"Yes. Telling him what to do."

"There are a number of OOPArts connected to the Lunar Society," the museum guide mused.

"You said that thingy built a wotsit a hundred years before anyone else even thought of it."

"Erasmus Darwin. Rocket engine. Use your words, Nina, please."

Boulton began to hum to himself.

The creature continued to wave its limbs.

"I don't like such notions," said Mrs Fiddler.

"What notions?" said Nina.

"The idea that the Lunar Society did marvellous things and therefore there must be a supernatural explanation."

"You don't think it's true?"

"I don't think it's fair. I saw a film some time ago."

"Good for you," said Nina.

Mrs Fiddler tutted. "A film in which Hitler, or the Nazis at least, were being aided by black magic. I think Rasputin was in it somewhere."

"The guy from the disco song?"

"Him. And I found it distasteful. Nazis and necromancers and secret magic weapons. It diminishes the true evil of the Nazis."

"What do you mean?" said Nazi.

Mrs Fiddler stretched. "True evil—the thing that people call true evil—is mundane. It's banal. It's ordinary. The Nazis and the Final Solution were just the culmination of a long series of bad decisions by dull and petty men. Weak men. Have you heard of Hanlon's razor?"

Nina stuck out her bottom lip and shook her head. "Is it on display in the museum?"

"It's not that kind of razor. It's an aphorism."

"Ah, one of those," said Nina, pretending she understood.

"Hanlon's razor is 'never attribute to malice that which is adequately explained by stupidity.'"

Nina nodded slowly. "I like that."

"Well, I believe something similar about intelligence. We can call it Fiddler's razor. 'Never attribute to genius that which is adequately explained by hard work.' Boulton there, Darwin, Wedgwood, Priestley, Watt and Small. They weren't struck by divine inspiration. Newton was never struck on the head by an apple."

"That's the guy who invented gravity," said Nina, happy to be able to join in the conversation.

"They worked hard and their achievements were their own. We don't need to pretend that space monsters were involved."

"Although Boulton must have learned how to make the oculus and the star clock from somewhere," Nina pointed out.

Fiddler waved her away. "Oh, yes, that stuff. Probably. But not the true works of brilliance."

"The belt buckles and ugly vases?" said Nina.

"Exactly," said Mrs Fiddler.

Morag and Kathy interviewed Khaleesi and her new friend in Room Two.

Langford sat in a defiant slouch, arms hanging loose, like a moody middle-aged teenager. Khaleesi-*Qalawe* sat primly at his side, her fingers involuntarily touching the enflamed subdermal implants on her neck.

"I thought we had this all resolved the other day," said Kathy. "None of your friends went through the final process of signing themselves over."

"Langford only contacted me this morning," said Khaleesi. "The Facebook group is still up and—"

"And I ain't signing myself over to no one, fed," said Langford. "You look at me and you see a slave? You wanna treat me like a slave, huh, bitch?"

Khaleesi pulled a half-amused and half-embarrassed expression of apology for Morag and Kathy and patted Langford on the knee. Her hand lingered a fraction of a second longer and a little more thigh-ward than would be considered chaste.

"Ah," said Morag. "And you say Langford here is an actor?"

"I'm travelling incognito, fed," said Langford. "I am a Venislarn prince. I come to claim my rightful title and lands."

"Oh? Oh, okay," said Kathy. "And the full name you're travelling incognito under...?"

"This is Langford James," said Khaleesi. "He's a film star. *Planet of the Apes*, *The Black Faun*. He was one of the blue things in *Avatar*."

"Okay, so he's a big deal."

"I'm a prince, dog!" declared the actor.

"You wouldn't, by any chance, be involved in the filming going on in at the Mailbox?"

"Smoke and mirrors," sneered Langford. "I'm all about keepin' it real, fasho. I survived the *Shohreye 'uuuduk*. I have proved myself worthy."

"Yeah, yeah," said Morag. "Stay here." She went in search of Rod and found him coming back from the reception area, deep in conversation on the phone.

"I thought I was supposed to be a technical advisor," he was saying. "I wasn't told that babysitting actors was part of the job. You've got security on site. Surely, they should be the ones keeping things secure. It's very much implied."

Morag waved her hands in front of his face to draw his attention and then beckoned him to follow.

"I don't know where he is, yet," said Rod to the evidently annoyed person on the end of the line. "And what's this other thing?" He listened. "Yeah, that's not a man in a fish mask. Taylor Graham invited Pupfish—that's right, an actual *samakha*, well, a *samakha* half-breed—and his girlfriend, Allana, down to the set for the day. No, she's a human."

Morag continued to wave him on. Rod frowned at her, a question. She gestured that if he followed, he would find out.

"Anyroad," said Rod, "Let Pupfish in. Keep him out of sight of anyone who isn't in the know. I will continue my efforts to find your missing actor."

Morag pushed open the door to Room Two. Rod saw Langford.

"Found him," he said. "Yes. That's right. Got him here. I know. We're very efficient."

It was daytime in Soho House in the present day. It was nighttime in Soho House, in what Mrs Fiddler declared with some confidence to be 1773. Stormy winds rattled the window frames and the world outside was a complete and utter black. No streetlights, no house lights, near or far. Nina understood how, in that distant time, the Lunar Society might need the light of the moon to find their way home.

Three core members of the Lunar Society sat round the dining table and discussed the device Matthew Boulton had in front of him. It was the oculus. The interlocked, concentric rings looked new. The brass shone like frozen fire.

"It is well worked," said Erasmus Darwin, admiring it. "I take it, this is to be part of some larger device, a telescope perhaps?"

"It is complete," said Boulton with a strange fatalism.

"And its purpose?" said Josiah Wedgwood.

"I believe it will allow me to observe, through this aperture, events from earth's past history."

Darwin drew back, giving his friend a sceptical look. In the corner of the room, Jonathan Angus smiled knowingly. Boulton had told him about the oculus before.

"But how?" said Wedgwood reasonably.

Darwin wagged his fat finger. "We have seen that the earth beneath us is a picture book of the past, open to any man willing to do a modicum of fossilling. Perhaps this device—the oculus, you say—works on similar principles."

Boulton looked hopeless, almost bereft. He picked up his cup and drained it before reaching for the wine bottle on the table.

"Would I appear mad, dear friends—a true lunatic—if I told you I had no comprehension at all of how this machine works or what inspired me to make it?" He gestured at the sidereal clock on a stand by the wall.

"That's the one you've got in the basement," said Nina.

Mrs Fiddler nodded, quietly intent on listening to the people in the past.

"The properties of that clockwork device are beyond all human comprehension," said Boulton, "and yet I designed its working and had no small hand in its construction."

"It measures sidereal time," said Wedgwood. "It's the same as the one you had John Whitehurst construct."

"Finest horologist in Derby," said Darwin.

"In the country," suggested Mrs Fiddler.

"But this clock..." began Boulton and stood. He withdrew a key from his waistcoat pocket.

Nina found it odd to think that that key would eventually travel from Boulton's hands to the back of Vivian Grey's desk at the consular mission and now was back in the clock in the storeroom downstairs.

Boulton inserted the key into the hole in the clock face and was about to turn it when there was a heavy thumping on a door.

"At this hour?" said Wedgwood, looking at the darkness outside.

Jonathan Angus gave his master a silent nod and went to answer the door, turning his ever ready knobstick in his hand as he went. There was a further knock at the door, loud and impatient.

"Who is it, Jonathan?" called Boulton.

"It's the pineapple thief!" Jonathan shouted back, clearly surprised. "And she's brought us a pineapple!"

"I say!" exclaimed Wedgwood.

"Pineapple thief," said Nina. "Is that Georgian code for exotic dancers or prostitutes?"

Mrs Fiddler tutted and put the oculus down. The scene vanished.

"You do have a sordid little mind, sometimes, Nina." She picked up the 'History is Fun!' notebook and flicked through the notes they had made while viewing the past.

Nina watched her old teacher's face as she studied the lists of Venislarn ideograms and the dates they had taken them to. Teachers had always been alien creatures to Nina, inhabiting a world of pens and pencils and picture books and more knowledge than any human could possibly know. Teachers were dry and dusty things and they spoke great truths and pure wisdom.

"I'll be buggered if I can see any pattern in this," said Mrs Fiddler.

"Language, miss," said Nina.

"Well..." she sighed reasonably. "You'd think they'd want to make controls for this contraption that might be easy to understand."

"The Venislarn don't work according to our logic," said Nina.

"Bloody Venislarn. Coming over here, destroying our world without so much as a 'by your leave', refusing to use our logic or learn our language." She tutted and then grinned to show she was being silly. "We'll beat them yet."

"You really are a glass half-full type, aren't you?" said Nina

"I am."

"I'd have thought spending a lifetime teaching kids would have made your bitter 'n' horrible."

"Lord, no," said Mrs Fiddler and, sitting down, pulled a large old-fashioned thermos flask out of her bag. She unscrewed the lid and steam and the smell of tea poured out. "It's three decades of teaching children that kept me optimistic. Children are wonderful. It's the adults who make life difficult. 'They fuck you up, your mum and dad.'"

"Language, miss!"

"That's not me. That's poetry. Tea?"

Morag had a stack of Venislarnkin files on her desk and was going through the tedious process of entering their details into the computer system. This would have been slightly easier if some twat hadn't knocked them on the floor, mixing them all up.

Bored rather than thirsty, she got up and went to pour herself a cup of tea from Trevor's teapot.

"Ah-ah," said Kathy warningly and waved her away. The arm she thoughtlessly waved was the one in a sling and Kathy hissed in pain at the movement.

"Hurts?" said Morag stupidly.

Kathy nodded and held her arm. "What I can't work out is I was stabbed in the other shoulder the other month. That damned Mammonite with the knife—that still hurts. Would I have been better off being stabbed twice in the same shoulder, reopening old wounds? Or having matching injuries like this?"

Morag wasn't sure if there was an answer to that. "You got some painkillers?"

"Pain is a message from our bodies to our brains. It tells us something useful. I try to avoid analgesics."

"Uh-huh. And is that why you got fired as a GP?"

"I was never a GP." Kathy tapped at her keyboard and looked at the teapot. "Maybe I don't have that desire to give palliatives to the masses. There are three kinds of doctors, you know."

"Yeah?"

"There's the ones with bedside manner, who hold the hands of the dying as they slip away. Then there's the ones like me, who see the human body as a bag of parts, a meat machine in need of repairing. The body is a wondrous thing, life is a wondrous thing, and we're just the maintenance staff."

"Except now you're prodding the *em-shadt* Venislarn with a stick and staring into a teapot," Morag pointed out.

Kathy arched an eyebrow to concede that point.

"Rod put this measure in the teapot," she said, tapping the electronic device hanging over the lip. "Omar reckons—and I agree with him—that the inscription here is essentially a warning spell. The higher the tea level, the more imminent the threat." She pointed at the developing graph on the screen. "I have just been studying the sigils and, although I need confirmation from other wise heads, it would appear that once the tea level reaches here"—she tapped the top of the graph—"then the spell has reached some sort of zenith."

"Zenith, huh?"

"Total danger. Certain death. Inescapable doom."

"For who?"

Kathy looked at her. "Anyone in the local vicinity. Everyone."

"The end of the world."

"Perhaps."

Morag blinked. "So, this teapot can predict the end of the world."

"Effectively. Trevor's Apocalyptic Teapot."

Morag laughed. "So, how long have we got?"

"Well, reading the future in tea isn't a precise science."

"Should I bother booking a holiday for next year?"

"Tomorrow," said Kathy.

"Tomorrow. As in Thursday?"

Kathy nodded.

"Oh, okay," said Morag. "Maybe we should tell someone," she added eventually.

"I suppose. I was going to e-mail Vaughn once I'd double-checked my figures."

"Right."

Thoughtful, Morag turned away and then turned back.

"Is it odd that neither of us is panicking about this? I don't want to seem odd."

"No, it's fine," said Kathy. "I'm sure you've faced the imminent end of the world before."

She had, or at least had faced the cold certain destruction of the city and everyone in it at least a couple of times.

"I never got to be a GP but I wanted to train to be one," said Kathy. "But then the Venislarn came along. Before I knew what they were, before I discovered the 'big secret', I was just an ordinary junior doctor. And then I crashed my car into a *granshak zex'l* in the Clent Hills and everything changed. I thought I was going to die that night. I was convinced of the fact, but I didn't."

"Clearly."

"There's usually a way of avoiding certain death. Most of the time, it's just a matter of trying."

Morag made a noise of half-agreement. "What's the other kind of doctor? You said there were three."

"Oh," said Kathy. "There's the ones who think they're God."

"Right. I thought that was all of you," said Morag and turned toward the kitchenette. "Cup of tea?"

Nina and Mrs Fiddler ate sandwiches and watched the past through the oculus as though it was a daytime TV soap created for their entertainment alone. The sandwiches were mozzarella and sun-dried tomatoes. Nina made hardly any pretence of sharing her sweet shop snacks in return.

Through the oculus, they saw that something dramatic had taken place.

The front wall and window of the dining room were gone, ripped away. Sunlight and a soft spring breeze came directly through from the gravel driveway. Builders in smocks were lunking around piles of bricks and mixing mortar.

The destruction extended into the room, as well. The dining table had been snapped in two, and several chairs reduced to firewood. Great furrows had been gouged in the walls, shredding wallpaper.

"What could have done that?" said Mrs Fiddler.

There were even scrape marks on the ceiling.

"Something very big," suggested Nina.

There were five men in the room. Jonathan Angus sat in a chair in the corner, quite still, his face pale and grey. His leg was trussed up with heavy bandages. He looked like he ought to be in bed or in the Georgian equivalent of Accident and Emergency. The way he slouched in his seat suggested that things were not all right with him, internally. Next to Jonathan stood a thin, spotty youth Nina had not seen before.

Boulton, Wedgwood and Darwin gathered round the table. Boulton held his arm against his chest, as though it hurt in any other position. There was a healing cut on Darwin's forehead.

"They've been in the wars, haven't they?" said Mrs Fiddler.

"With that?" suggested Nina.

On the table was a stout glass jar. Inside the jar was a ruptured metal cannister and the boneless Venislarn creature the three men had freed from the lump of blue john. Nina guessed the creature had been sealed inside that cannister when it was put in the jar, and had subsequently escaped its metal prison. It clawed ineffectually at the glass, leaving behind translucent blue smears. Nina read the contempt on the three men's faces.

"He's been a naughty Venislarn," said Nina.

Next to the jar was a large pottery urn. Together, the three men lifted the jar and carefully lowered it into the urn.

"I've never seen any Wedgwood that looked like that," said Mrs Fiddler. "Beautiful patterns on that jasperware."

Nina moved in closer. The 'beautiful patterns' on the jasperware were Venislarn writing, line after line.

"It's a spell of binding," she said. "A good one. It's the one I would use."

"They're trapping it?" said Mrs Fiddler.

"Are we confident that these wards will hold *Crippen-Ai*?" said Boulton as Wedgwood emptied a jug of white powder over the jar in the urn.

"Salt?" said Mrs Fiddler.

"Or sugar," said Nina. "Or sand."

"You put down salt for slugs."

Wedgwood fitted a snug pottery lid on the urn. There was a nervousness in his voice.

"If the magicks the 'witch of Digbeth' gave us are right," said Wedgwood.

The men gummed the lid into place with wax and then together (although Bolton seemed to struggle with whatever pain afflicted his side) they moved the urn into a straw-lined chest on the floor.

"We have picked out a plot by the Birmingham Canal," said Darwin. "There's the old brick kiln works there where no one will be building and no one will disturb the land. We can bury it deep."

The chest was shut, locked and bound with leather strips.

"In glass, in pottery, in a chest of wood and iron," said Mrs Fiddler. "They must hate that thing."

"Or fear it," said Nina.

"Come," said Darwin and gestured to the spotty youth. "You know where the old kilns are, don't you, Dick?"

"That I do," said the lad and took one end of the chest.

"Brick kilns," said Mrs Fiddler, excitedly.

"Mean anything to you?" said Nina.

"No," she admitted, "but we could probably work out where that is. I'm sure there are maps somewhere."

Nina got out her phone.

Are you worried? asked Morag's unborn child.

The consular mission response office was empty. Rod had taken Khaleesi and her unhinged movie star down to the film set. Nina was over at Soho House, on whatever cryptic personal mission she had to complete there. Kathy was in Vaughn Sitterson's office (Morag had heard her raised voice through the wall at one point) apparently eager to overrule Professor Sheikh Omar on some matter. Apart from Trevor's Apocalyptic Teapot on the desk next to her, Morag was alone and free to talk.

"Worried?" she said.

That other one, Kathy. She said the world was going to end.

"Oh, I see. No, that's not going to happen."

She thought it was.

Morag chuckled, closed one Venislarnkin personal file and picked up the next on the pile.

"That's one of the advantages of being pregnant with you, baby."

What is?

"Knowing the world's not going to end, not properly, until you come out."

What's it like, mother?

"What's what like?" she said.

Out there.

"Out here isn't half as nice as where you are now. Be happy where you are."

Rod felt the filmmakers on set had less to complain about than they made out. They had come to Birmingham to film and had brought him on board as a technical advisor to give their project a bit of verisimilitude. In three short days, he had taken 'Agent Jack Steele' on a real job in Fish Town and Langford James had been able to immerse himself in his *samakha* role in more ways than one. Now, Rod, Taylor Graham, Langford James (and his new Venislarnkin groupie, Khaleesi), Pupfish (plus his starstruck girlfriend, Allana), Director Bryan and Producer Tammy were gathered in an unused retail space in the Mailbox set, dissecting their current situation.

Yes, their second lead had gone full method-man and believed he was a Venislarn prince. But Rod felt this loss was offset by the arrival of Pupfish, an actual *samakha* with human wants and needs, as evinced by his very human girlfriend. Seen objectively, Langford and Pupfish made one complete *samakha* and one complete human, not that that was necessarily helpful.

Allana nudged Pupfish and pointed to the catering table at the back of the room.

"Look," she whispered. "Real movie set coffee."

"Ggh! I know, babe," he whispered back, trying to be cool.

"What we need to know," Tammy was saying with the kind of patience that was already hand-signalling it was going to run out at any moment, "is are you willing to read the part?"

"Sho thing, blood," said Langford, twitching and blinking. "*Bhul-tamade* Oscar-winning stuff."

"But read the part as written?" said Tammy.

Langford gave her a look that was probably meant to be shrewd and calculating but was difficult to pull off while his eyes were bugging wildly, like a really surprised goldfish.

"I'm gonna give you some truth. Powerful truth, blood."

Khaleesi nodded in passionate agreement and clasped his hand in hers on his knee. "We're all about truth," she said.

"Look," Allana whispered to Pupfish. "They've got real movie set bagels too."

"Yeah, babe," he said.

"That's so American!"

"We—ggh!—got bagels here too, babe."

"I know, but..."

"Maybe we can use this," said Taylor, with diplomatic good cheer. "I know we've got a key scene to film today but maybe we can play it loose, do a bit of improv. I picked up a lot of pointers from Rod yesterday. I've seen how they do things on the ground."

The look Tammy shot Rod made it clear she had zero interest in how they did things 'on the ground'. Director Bryan was equally unimpressed.

"You want me to tell Fran the work he's done setting up shots, any notion of cinematography, the storyboards, we should just throw that away and follow you around with a goddamned Steadicam like fucking film students?"

"Keepin' it real, dog," said Langford.

"Might be magical," said Taylor.

"No," said Tammy firmly. "This is not some shitty Mike Leigh improv crap."

"You said you wanted an issues movie," said Taylor.

"A well-constructed motion picture event," said Tammy.

"You need it real, blood," said Langford.

"No!" She barked. "This is not Dogme 95. Bryan is not Lars von fucking Trier."

"No, I am not," agreed Bryan.

"If anyone doesn't want to be in a fucking blockbuster movie about a super-spy and a fishman saving the fucking world then the door is right there," shouted Tammy. "And we will sue your fucking asses for breach of contract."

"You just call me 'fishman'?" said Pupfish.

Alanna gripped his arm tightly. "Don't upset the movie lady," she whispered.

"Sounded like anti-Venislarn prejudice to me," said Khaleesi with the kind of indignation only the young and privileged could muster.

Tammy stared agog from person to person to person.

"You know what?" she said. "If you, Langford, don't get your shit together, I will offer your role to... What's your name?"

"Pupfish," said Pupfish.

"Michael," said Allana.

"—I will give your fucking role to Pupfish Michael here. You ever been in a movie, Pupfish?"

"I have, blood."

"Have you?" said Allana.

If fish could blush, Pupfish would have turned bright pink.

Rod was perfectly and painfully aware of Pupfish's brief but full-on career in the adult film industry. He'd even had the misfortune of stumbling onto the set of *Debbie Does Dolphins* in a Digbeth basement.

"He's got a real screen presence," said Rod.

"You didn't tell me, babe," said Allana. "Where can I see it?"

"Straight to DVD," said Rod. "And we had to impound those."

"Ggh! For, um, political reasons," said Pupfish.

"Typical," said Khaleesi.

"Fuck it. Yes," said Tammy. "We film the torture scene this afternoon. Either you snap out of your fucking trance and play it as directed, Langford, or Pupfish becomes our new second lead."

Allana squealed in excitement. She actually squealed. Rod was unaware than adult human beings did that, but she did. Real Hollywood film stars, film set coffee and bagels and now her boyfriend was having the carrot of stardom dangled in front of him. Whatever brownie points a fish-boy needed to score to get a human girl to love him, Pupfish had surely scored plenty.

"But I'd still like to discuss some possible improvisations," said Taylor. "I think we can bring a deep realism to this piece if we try some tweaks."

Tammy smiled sweetly. "Taylor, Bryan and I are utterly at your disposal until we start the shoot this afternoon. Bring your ideas. Let's talk about realism in cinema. You can explain what improvisation might bring to the scene."

"Thank you, Tammy."

"And then we shoot the fucking scene as written," she said and walked out.

Pupfish looked to Rod.

"Is she—ggh!—serious? Does she really want me in this thing?"

Rod had no answer.

Allana pulled on her boyfriend's arm. "So, tell me about the movies you've been in."

Rod went to get a movie set bagel.

Morag's phone rang.

"Whatcha doin'?" sang Nina.

"I seem to be manning the office solo whilst everyone else in my life gives me advice on how I should live it."

"I want you to do something for me."

"You too?"

"I want you to find out about any old brick kilns in Birmingham."

272

"Brick kilns?"

"You know, pottery oven things. In particular, one that was near the original Birmingham Canal in..."

"Seventeen seventy-three," said a fainter voice that Morag could just hear.

"Seventeen seventy-three," said Nina.

"And why do I want to do that?" said Morag.

"A Venislarn creature was buried there. Something called *Crippen-Ai.*"

"Never heard of it."

"Me neither. I don't think it's a registered creature. It was buried in a sealed container inside a wooden chest."

"Dangerous?"

"I think so."

"Leave it with me."

On the hospital trolley in the upper floor office that was standing in for Vlad Botticelli's bespoke torture room, Taylor Graham struggled in a manly fashion against his bonds while the English actor playing the villain gave out line after line of movie exposition. He had the bold features and studied manner of a stage 'ac-tor'.

"Any sufficiently advanced civilisation soon discovers the seeds of its own destruction," said Botticelli. "The atom bomb. Bespoke viral pathogens. For the horror from beyond, it was the *Jhandu-p'hir*, a device so utterly destructive that the gods had it broken into four pieces and scattered across the world."

"You only have three," said Jack Steele.

"Oh, is that what you think?" said Botticelli with pantomime archness. "Is that what you think?"

"And cut," said Director Bryan. "Moving on."

As Taylor was unstrapped by a runner, Skye leaned in close to Rod.

"And what do we tell—"

"It's perfect. It's perfect. I get it. It's perfect." He looked round and Taylor Graham was already waiting in front of him. "It's perfect," said Rod.

"What is?" said Taylor. He looked back at the set. "What? That? You don't think it was too cliché?"

"Nowt wrong with a bit of cliché," said Rod. "Life's full of clichés. He was great. You were great. It was perfect."

Cameras were being switched round to do additional shots linked to the scene just filmed – reaction shots or two shots or something. Rod was struggling to keep up with the lingo.

"Okay," said Director Bryan, "we've got Fin here, watching and waiting to make his move. Pupfish. That's your mark."

"Is it true that Langford is sulking in his hotel room?" said Skye.

Taylor gave her a sharp look, but Rod tried to shrug it off.

"Creative differences. This guy's just standing in for the moment."

"And the stand-in has to go all method on us, does he?"

Rod looked at Pupfish, who hopped from one foot to the other like he was excited or terrified or both. "I think the mask helps him get into role."

Skye nodded appreciatively. "It's a good one. Mind you, it's no Gillman or Abe Sapien. Is that latex foam? It's got a lovely sheen."

"Things they can do these days, huh?" said Rod.

In the Vault, the eighth book Morag consulted contained no more information on a creature entombed near brick kilns than the seven she'd consulted before it. She dropped the book noisily onto the growing pile of unhelpful books.

"Careful," said Professor Omar sliding up next to her on well-polished brogues. "Books have feelings you know. Quite literally in some cases. The 'Shylock' manuscript bleeds if you prick it. Have to keep a supply of Elastoplast close at hand when you read it."

Morag grunted, unsure if he was joking and not caring either.

"Perhaps," the wizard said smoothly, "if you told me what you were looking for..."

"Every heard of a Venislarn called *Crippen-Ai*?"

"Never," he said with instant conviction.

"Or a burial of a Venislarn creature at some old brick kilns by the canal."

He gave this some thought. "No. What brick kilns might these be?"

Morag thumped the pile of useless books. "If only I could find out. I'm looking for a disused brick kiln in central, probably around the late seventeen-hundreds."

Omar's gaze flitted down the spines of the books she had looked through.

"And why would you assume the answer was in these rare and exquisite volumes?"

"These are the books on the local Venislarn."

"Yes, yes," said Omar, tenderly picked up the top book and, with a soft caress of its cover, slid it back onto the nearest shelf. "But these stellar esoteries are above anything as mundane as what was where in the city's past. You don't ask a marine biologist what the price of fish is."

"Then where should I look?" asked Morag.

"For the mere mundane, we must look in a different collection. Fortunately, I have a card that allows me access."

He dipped into his inside pocket and brought out a plastic card.

"A library card," said Morag.

"And let us not forget, we are in a library."

Mrs Fiddler studied the notes they'd made on the oculus settings and the dates it had shown them, and tried to fill in the gaps.

"If nothing else," she said, "I want to know what made that hole in the wall."

"Damn right," said Nina.

Mrs Fiddler gave the inner ring a twist that seemed more hopeful than planned and held up the hoop.

In the Soho House of the past, it was night. Strong winds rattled loose panes in the windows.

"When are we?" said Nina.

"Before the whatever it was that knocked a hole in the wall," said Mrs Fiddler.

There was the sound of smashing glass, the crash of splintering wood.

"Maybe right before."

They hurried out along the long corridor, towards the dining room and nearly collided with Matthew Boulton as he came sprinting past towards the stairs.

"Anne!" he yelled and, on hard soles, clattered in desperate speed up the wooden stairs.

Mrs Fiddler had the oculus and was steering their view of events. She led the way up, not as fast as Boulton but with a decent turn of speed for an oldster. The house of the past was dark and mostly unlit, but in the dust-filtered light of afternoon Mrs Fiddler moved with confidence, sweeping the hoop back and forth in pursuit of Boulton.

Boulton shouted. "Anne! Get the children! Stay hidden!"

There was a fresh sound, louder than the shouting and the wind outside. Something roared in the night.

"What was that?" said Mrs Fiddler.

"Nothing good," said Nina.

She dragged Mrs Fiddler to a front-facing window and looked out through the oculus.

The moon lit up the driveway and the carriage that had come to a stop on it, except for a strange pink glow coming from the woman stood near the carriage. She stood before the coach in which she had perhaps arrived. Next to her was a man and flanking them both were two hulking, simian monsters.

"Oh, my goodness," said Mrs Fiddler. "What are those?"

"*Kobashi.*"

A long, long time before Nina was born, a five-metre statue of King Kong had been erected in a public park in Birmingham city centre. The reasons why Birmingham needed a statue of King Kong were unclear, but office rumour had it that the statue had been erected to help explain away sightings of a wandering *Kobashi*.

"Monsters," whispered Mrs Fiddler, astonished.

"I think I know what made that hole in the wall."

There was shouting, both from downstairs and the woman outside, but Nina couldn't make it out above the howling wind.

The pink star in the woman's hands brightened into a whirlpool of expanding light and a third *Kobashi* appeared, squatting on the driveway.

"More monsters..." said Mrs Fiddler.

"That's worrying," said Nina.

Something tiny, almost invisible against the darkness, scurried out from the house. The *Kobashi* clumsily stamped on it and as the woman on the drive shouted what were clearly threats, a *Kobashi* picked up and ripped the irritating rodent apart.

"So many monsters..."

"Are you all right, miss?" said Nina.

"There's..." Mrs Fiddler had come over all pale. "Actual monsters."

"We saw one before, *Crippen-Ai*."

"But that just looked like a misshapen squid thing. These are actual monsters. Real."

The man on the driveway pulled a knife from his coat and ran into the house.

From downstairs, they heard a shout, possibly from Josiah Wedgwood.

"Come no further, man!"

There was a cry of pain and a moment later the roaring crumble of wood and masonry.

"That's the front wall," said Nina needlessly. "Shall we go see?"

She pulled the stunned Mrs Fiddler downstairs and along the corridor, past fleeing phantoms glimpsed briefly in the oculus.

The dining room was full of dust and smashed furniture. Erasmus Darwin, coughing and spluttering, was in the corner, Jonathan Angus lying injured in his arms. There was further falling masonry and Nina caught sight of a *Kobashi* shouldering its way through a doorway that wasn't quite big enough.

Nina stepped forward to follow and then stopped abruptly, because in the here and now there was no doorway, only a blank wall. She prodded it to be sure.

"But there can't be a door there," said Mrs Fiddler.

"There isn't a door there," said Nina.

"I mean, it's an outside wall. There's no room for a room to be there."

Nina pulled her and the oculus round to look for the sidereal clock, the magical room-maker.

"This is too much," said Mrs Fiddler.

Something roared in the distance.

"Is that an audioguide?"

A man in a bright orange cagoule and khaki shorts was standing next to them—in the real world—and looking at the oculus with interest.

"What are you doing here?" demanded Mrs Fiddler.

"I just came through and... I asked at the shop if they had audioguides."

Nina lowered the oculus instantly, losing the settings.

Mrs Fiddler looked along the corridor, the corridor of rotten timbers, of peeling paint and mouldering wallpaper. The door to the real portion of the house was slightly ajar.

"Sir," she said, "was there not a red velvet sash across that doorway?"

"There was, but I heard voices..."

"You stepped past the velvet sash?" she asked, incredulously.

"I thought it would be okay."

"How could it be okay?" she said. "You don't step past the sash. Everyone knows that."

"No, I just..."

"Get!" she ordered ferociously, and with extravagant shooing motions she drove the man out and repositioned the sash barrier aggressively without actually moving it anywhere. There was a dark fury on her face when she returned.

"Can you believe it?" she said. "The nerve of some people."

The colour had returned to her face.

"You okay?" said Nina.

"Of course, I'm not okay! There was a sash!"

"And the monsters?" said Nina.

Mrs Fiddler hesitated as though she was trying to find her fear again but failing. "I bet those flipping monsters would respect a velvet sash barrier," she said.

"Oh, yeah," said Nina, dubiously. "Of course they would."

Morag was forced to wait fifteen minutes while Omar sweet-talked and joked with one of the Library of Birmingham staff, the actual and almost fully functioning cover story for the consular mission's base of operations. The ash-blonde sixty-something laughed at all Omar's jokes and touched his arm more than once during their conversation. She then passed him a swipe card that would open the glass doors behind them.

"You flirt with every librarian you meet?" Morag asked him as he came away.

"It's called being sociable," he said. "It's amazing what friendly words and a dab of politeness will do." He swiped them into the third-floor collections room. "But I imagine that point's lost on a barbarian such as yourself. Do you suppose your little one will grow up to be a fiery Scot?"

Will I, mother?

"Course he will," she said.

Omar looked around the densely spaced and crowded shelves. "Now... maps."

Kathy stood before the padlocked double doors to the laboratory in the Think Tank.

"I'm not sure about this," said Security Bob.

"You don't need to be sure," said Kathy. "Were Mr Sitterson's instructions in any way unclear."

The fat man tilted back his beret to scratch his forehead. "But it just don't seem proper."

Kathy kept her temper. "Neither you nor I have the key. Only Professor Omar has that—"

"And he seems a rum sort an' all, if you ask my opinion."

She smiled politely. "And did I?"

"What? No. Course not."

"And there will no padlocks on doors in future, once we have this open."

Bob nodded, brought the bolt cutters up and snipped through the chain.

"Cheap piece of rubbish that anyway," he said, gathering the lock and severed chain, and walked away.

Kathy entered the laboratory cautiously. Sheikh Omar was not only a rum sort, he was also a sly bastard. He might have only put a five-quid padlock on the door, but he would have invested more in occult security measures.

The *jid-ap yoi* ward on the floor was obvious. Kathy recited a closing incantation then rubbed out the activating symbols on its edge with her toe. There were also three eyes of *hodor* on the walls, magical CCTV. She hung a lab coat over one, moved a chair in front of the second, and repositioned a fire drill poster to cover the third. That seemed to be all, but she proceeded carefully.

She paused at the desk and glanced at the scraps of paper there in case there was anything useful or salacious to be seen but there was nothing more exciting than a shopping list (*2 x Campari, carrots for Mr Grey, GoT DVD box set if have it*). She turned to the tank where *Polliqan Riti* bobbed and rolled.

"*Shan-shan prui. Ma ghu'qani, Polliqan Riti,*" she said and then, with only a glance to the door to make sure she was truly alone, sat down and found the connecting pipe that would enable her to enter his world.

Nina and Mrs Fiddler went and sat in the museum café to get over the shock of what they had seen. A strong cup of tea and a fondant cupcake seemed to be doing Mrs Fiddler a world of good.

"I'm not sure I followed much of what we saw there," said Mrs Fiddler. "But, if your department deals with these kinds of events, you'd have records of this, wouldn't you?"

"Not that I know of," said Nina. "Didn't anything like this get mentioned in all those books you've read about Boulton and Darwin?"

Mrs Fiddler gave her a sour look. "If any member of the Lunar Society had recorded encounters with wandering ogres and a witch with a pink glowing orb, I believe I would have mentioned it already."

Nina was giving the oculus some serious thought and she spoke slowly, cautiously feeling out her ideas as she came to them. "Of course, now that we know what went on in Soho House, we could dial back to an earlier time and stop it."

Mrs Fiddler gave her a patient and tolerant look. "Really?"

"If we can reach through the oculus, we could write a note in Jonathan's diary. A warning."

The patient and tolerant look didn't go away and Nina suddenly found herself back in the classroom while the tirelessly loving but unrelenting Mrs Fiddler waited for the stupid child to realise her mistake.

"What?" said Nina. "We could."

"We should change what has already happened?"

"Makes sense."

"And why stop there? If we can change that, why not fix other things in history?"

"Now you get it. Stop, um, 9/11."

"Right. We could stop the Second World War."

"Send a note to Indiana Jones and tell him to kill Hitler."

"Why not just go back far enough and stop Hitler's mum getting pregnant?" suggested Mrs Fiddler.

"And slavery. Stop it before it happened," said Nina.

"Stop the British Empire taking over India."

"Hell, yeah," said Nina and then stopped.

Mrs Fiddler smiled gently. The patient and tolerant look had never left her face.

"If the British hadn't invaded India and if my great-granddad hadn't fought in the Second World War then..." Nina hummed pensively. "My family probably wouldn't have moved here."

"And you wouldn't be here to have the chance to change history in the first place. It's like *A Sound of Thunder*. Ray Bradbury. We read that in class, remember?"

"Er, sure."

"You step off the path and squash even a butterfly it can change the future."

"I'm pretty sure that was *The Simpsons*, Mrs Fiddler," said Nina.

"Is no literature sacred?" the old lady muttered. "I like time travel fiction mostly because it's so easy to do it wrong. I assume you've seen *Back To The Future*."

"I watch old movies sometimes."

"In the first film, when Marty accidentally stops his parents meeting, he begins to fade from that timeline. Time is being rewritten."

"Uh-huh."

"But in the second, when the past is changed, Marty immediately finds himself in the alternative timeline."

"Right, the one with the evil bad hairdo guy running America from his glitzy tower."

"The two films contradict each." Mrs Fiddler put down her half-eaten cupcake, warming to her theme. It was weird hearing a teacher talk about science fiction. It was like discovering your mum dancing to the latest music. "There are four options with time travel. One, which I thought was most likely until recent events, is that it's impossible. Secondly, that if you change the past then it changes the future. But that way lies paradox and I'm pretty sure the universe abhors a paradox more than it does a vacuum."

Nina frowned.

"Abhor means hate," said Mrs Fiddler.

"Thank you," said Nina.

"So, we've got two options. The first option is the *Back To The Future Two* option. You rewrite historical events and the world shoots off down a different historical path. Parallel universes and all that jazz. From what little I understand of quantum physics, that's happening all the time anyway, just that you Nina"—she prodded Nina's knee—"this Nina, only gets to experience one of those universes. But I like the final option."

"What's that?"

"Time travel is possible but any time travelling that occurs just slots into existing events."

"Like how?"

"You go back in time to change events, you only become part of existing events as they were, as they will be, as they always will have been. There's a Michael Moorcock story."

"Sounds like a porn pseudonym."

Mrs Fiddler wrinkled her nose. "The main character goes back in time with the hope of meeting the historical Jesus but, discovering only a poor man with learning disabilities, finds himself stepping into the role, repeating Jesus's parables, faking his miracles. Of course, then we get into the problem of bootstrapping which is another time-travel no-no."

"Wow," said Nina. "You're a nerd, Mrs Fiddler."

"Which is only code for I like things and I've taken the time to learn about them." She smiled smugly. "My point is, Nina, I believe most strongly that if you tried to change the past, this past we are seeing, you would only help cement events into place."

Nina shook her head. "I don't buy that. You're basically saying there's no free will, we have no control over our actions."

"Do you remember that time you were jealous of Zeinab Imran's fish display poster and ripped it off the wall?"

"You have no evidence I did that," said Nina automatically.

"Such random acts of selfishness are easier to bear if you remember that that there's no free will. It wasn't your fault."

"That's what I'm saying," said Nina.

"What's written is written. You can't change a book if you don't like the ending."

"But you can always close the book."

"Not quite sure how that's relevant."

"Just saying."

In a dusty office in an innocuous building off a cathedral square in a version of Birmingham that only existed in his own imagination, *Polliqan Riti* spun thoughtfully around in his chair and turned his cane over and over.

"Perhaps I am utterly encomforlated here," he said.

Kathy, sat at a respectful distance, gave him an honest look. "Are you?"

"I have been recuperatising for a number of years."

"And you look ready to return to your own realm, to take whatever revenge you see fit on those who wronged you."

He leaned over the desk and gazed deeply at her. She assumed he was gazing. The protuberance wearing a top hat presented itself fixedly at her.

"Can you read my mind?" she asked.

He twitched. "Not in here. You are not really conpresent here, but if you were to touch me again in the world outside, flesh to flesh..."

"That won't be happening again," she said.

Polliqan Riti deflated a little.

"I am made suspicious by the fact that you want nothing from me," he said.

"Nothing, except the sample you provided me with earlier—"

"Because I am krypon—"

"Kryptonite, yes."

"—to the Venislarn. I am unfamiliarated with that word."

"You know what your touch does to your fellow Venislarn."

He leaned back, thoughtful and amused, if a soggy mass of tofu could look thoughtful or amused.

"My fellow Venislarn," he murmured. "Yes."

Kathy made to look at her phone to check the time—she would be missed in the office at some point—but of course, in here, time was whatever *Polliqan Riti* wanted it to be.

"And when would I leave?" he asked.

Omar pulled open the next drawer and lifted out a browning map neatly sandwiched between two sheets of glass. He placed it on the table between himself and Morag and then half-tilted the map, half-tilted himself to get a perspective. Morag, who still struggled to understand the layout of this constantly changing city, couldn't see any correlation between this drawing and the city around them.

"This is St Phillip's Cathedral," said Omar, pointing. "Or just St Phillip's Church back in"—he peered at the legend on the map—"seventeen ninety-five. So, this..." He drew a line along the glass. "This is Colmore Row, and this is New Street."

"Brick kilns," she said and tapped the glass.

"Indeed, old brick kilns. And that's the canal. There was no Gas Street Basin proper then. Look, the two canals stop shy of each other. Probably each didn't want to let the other one have access to its water."

"Really?"

"Cutthroat business, canals," he said. "And therefore..." He put his finger on the map and then actually turned round as though looking out at the real city beyond all the glass and steel of the library building.

He chuckled.

"What?" said Morag.

"This creature, *Crippen-Ai*, did you want to dig it up or keep it buried?"

"Why?"

"Because it's underneath the Mailbox."

284

"You mean..."

"Underneath several hundred thousand tonnes of brick and concrete."

"Ah, well, there you go," said Morag and took out her phone to call Nina.

"But," said Professor Omar.

Morag stopped mid-dial. "But?"

He smiled raffishly. "When the Mailbox was an actual Royal Mail sorting office, they built a series of railway tunnels under there."

"Well, the trains from New Street would sort of go out that way."

"Oh, no. Not the regular railway tunnels, their own tunnels so the Post Office could move mail around without having to take it above ground. All very secure and private. It was said that many businesses would, on a Friday, mail their takings to themselves rather than deposit them in a bank, knowing they would be held securely in those tunnels over the weekend."

"And those tunnels," said Morag. "Don't tell me, they're all boarded up and closed to the public."

"No one's been allowed in for years," said Omar.

Rod had imagined that filming a fight scene would be exciting, but it turned out to be such a start-stop process it was like streaming a high definition action movie on a dial-up connection. Start. A punch is thrown. Stop. Move camera. Continuity photos taken. Props moved. Start. A man falls on a mat. Stop. More changes. Make-up is checked. Cameras moved again.

The whole sequence was apparently going to be only twenty seconds of final screen footage, culminating with the trolley and two actors going through the glass behind them. The window was made of sugar glass and looked out on nothing more glamourous than a lime green sheet behind the false wall. The skyline of whatever city this movie was supposed to be set in would be magically inserted afterwards.

Rod suspected they'd be lucky to see that window get broken before nightfall. It was excruciatingly boring. The only moment of excitement was when Skye tried to touch up Pupfish's 'make-up' and

Producer Tammy had to stop her with some twaddle about contractual agreements.

When Rod's phone rang, it came as a blessed diversion. He took it outside onto the balcony overlooking the building's central atrium, well beyond the perimeter of Tammy-lites who scowled at him for daring to have a phone on set.

"Ay up, Morag," he said.

"You at the Mailbox?" she asked.

"If you mean, am I in the secret headquarters of evil capitalist Vlad Botticelli then yes."

"What?"

"Nothing. What's up?"

"I'm doing some research for Nina."

"Nina, as in swanning-about-on-a-fool's-errand-at-Soho-House Nina?"

"I don't know about that," said Morag. "But I'm looking for the undiscovered last resting place of a Venislarn called *Crippen-Ai*."

"Aye?"

"And it might just be in the tunnels under the Mailbox."

"The old Post Office tunnels?"

"You know them?"

"Only rumour. No one is allowed access."

"Exactly. Now, there must be someone from building management or some such there."

"Ah," said Rod. "You want me to beg for favours."

"I'll be over in half an hour. Maybe you'll have sweet-talked our way in—"

She cut off and there was much muttered conversation between Morag and another voice Rod couldn't make out.

"—going on about my 'condition,'" Morag said irritably to someone and then returned to the phone. "Apparently, I need to stay here and, um, man the fort. But I'll call you back in thirty and you can tell me what you've discovered."

"Right-o."

They returned to the conjured corridor and the oculus. Mrs Fiddler double-checked the sash barrier over the doorway, giving both brass stands a firm twist as though screwing them into the floor.

"Some people," she tutted before deciding she had made the place as secure as was humanly possible.

The time they had allotted to further exploration was mostly fruitless. Mrs Fiddler pointed out that, for reasons that were not yet clear, the oculus was keen to show them events only from the time of the Lunar Society but even then there had been days when nothing of note happened in the great house.

They observed people sitting in silence. They observed an almost empty house while many were out at church. They observed servants cleaning. They observed the cook in the kitchen and Nina had to remind Mrs Fiddler that they were trying to find out about the Venislarn-influenced events in the house and, yes, although rediscovering original eighteenth-century recipes for steamed puddings was 'decidedly fascinating' it did not assist them in achieving their goals.

They did eventually stumble upon a scene in the parlour in which Matthew Boulton and Erasmus Darwin sat together in a most solemn mood with another gentleman, a younger fellow in a smart but modest wig and a black suit to match. He was younger than either Boulton or Darwin and, in fact, the two other men looked older now, Boulton a little tired and lined, Darwin more jowly and heavy-lipped than before.

"When is this?" said Nina.

"I don't know," said Mrs Fiddler. "That chap has the look of a Galton. Samuel Galton perhaps."

The younger man had a long package wrapped in leather at his side. He distractedly rolled two large, blue-grey marbles back and forth across the table.

"Who's Galton then?" said Nina.

"A Lunar Society member. A manufacturer. Owned Great Bar Hall at one point." She pointed at the long leather-bound item. "A gunmaker."

"And it will work, sir?" asked Darwin, sounding like a man who wished it wouldn't.

The man, the possibly Samuel Galton, held a marble up. It was a lump of blueish stone, wrapped in a heavy mesh of iron.

"It does not fragment like the originals we tried. It holds together and therefore gives the weapon considerable range.

"Galton," nodded Mrs Fiddler.

"Of course, the only way to know that it actually works is to try it against one of the creatures," he said.

Darwin and Boulton exchanged an unhappy look.

"I hear you have one in your cellar," said Galton.

Boulton held his tongue a long while. "We know what the future holds. The consular mission works to hold off the final dreadful apocalypse through appeasement of the Venislarn gods."

Galton twitched as though sick. "They are not gods."

"They will suffice until the Almighty deigns to show himself," said Darwin.

"You will turn down this opportunity to fight because you have been told we must grovel before these abominations. This on the word of the... 'witch'?"

"That's the second mention of a witch we've heard," said Mrs Fiddler. "Maybe that woman who commanded the monsters?"

"Why don't we know anything about this stuff?" said Nina. "I feel we should really know about this stuff."

"I..." said Boulton slowly. "I'm not pleased with the apparent status quo. I would dearly love to strike back at the Venislarn."

"And here we have the means," said Galton.

"But the Venislarn cannot be defeated."

Darwin made a deep rumbling noise. "In Emperor Antiochus, the Maccabees faced what seemed to be an undefeatable enemy. Their God remained silent while the Hellenistic gods were paraded in triumph across the world. And yet the Maccabees fought to regain the temple."

"Biblical analogies do not a strong argument make," said Boulton with as much ferocity as Nina had ever heard from the gentle man.

"Who are the Maccabees?" said Nina.

"Jewish rebels," said Mrs Fiddler.

"Sounds like a boy band."

"The Maccabees," Darwin continued, "won because their enemy underestimated them and because they did not fight like a conventional army. They fought like thieves, stabbing from the darkness, keeping their numbers and tactics secret."

"A secret uprising," said Galton.

"Oh," said Boulton, despairing. "So, we are to be like Guy Fawkes and his conspirators? Traitors."

"Traitors to false gods and the cowards who serve them."

"This is bad juju," said Nina. "This is not what we do."

"Your consular mission, your colleagues, they're the cowards they're referring to," said Mrs Fiddler.

"But there's a reason we do what we do..."

"The Maccabees fought covertly but then, when the moment was right, struck like hammers and drove the pagan gods from the temple," said Darwin.

"We have the hammer," said Galton, gesturing with the marble.

Boulton pinched his lip in thought.

"We do not know if it will work," he said.

"Then we should put it to the test," said Galton with some glee and unwrapped the package which contained, as Nina had guessed, a shooting rifle.

Boulton tossed out a hand in exasperated defeat. "Very well, gentleman. If we must."

He rose and gestured for his visitor to follow. Galton took his gun and one of the marbles. The three men left and, from the hallway, went down the stairs to the servants' quarters and the cellars with Nina and Mrs Fiddler following. The stairs had been rebuilt since the earlier time and Nina had to watch where her feet were going in the present day and not attempt to tread on steps as they were two hundred years ago.

They came to a stop outside Jonathan Angus's room. A young man stood in the shadows by the door.

"Any movement, Dick?" asked Boulton.

"Not a peep, Mr Boulton," said the man.

Nina gestured to the runic symbols carved into the doorframe. "They've been brushing up on their Venislarn. Or someone's taught them."

"This is Jonathan's room," said Mrs Fiddler as Boulton took a heavy key from Dick and unlocked the door.

"Maybe he died from his wounds," said Nina. "Maybe he's gone. Or..."

"Or?"

"Or they've got some weird hybrid Jonathan-Venislarn mash-up in there."

Boulton stepped back from the door and offered to let Galton enter first. It was not a large bedroom. Jonathan might have been a servant of some standing but that didn't entitle him to a room much larger than a prison cell. Mrs Fiddler tried to position herself close behind the men in the doorway and raised the oculus to peer over their shoulders.

Nina had her backpack down from her shoulder and was flicking through the diary with a haste that showed little respect for the book's age.

"Eighteen eighty-two. Eighteen eighty-three." She caught glimpses of words—'My bed'. 'The old injury—and now, as she flicked, she caught first sight of the word 'Maccabees' and it appeared more than once towards the end pages.

In the room, something stretched and creaked like an old man made of violin strings rising from his chair.

"Here," said Nina.

"I can just about see it," said Mrs Fiddler.

Nina found and read what she guessed was a telling diary entry. "*We were brought to the village of Sarehole and the flatting mill that Mr Boulton had once leas'd. A local boy had been eaten by the thing in the mill pool. It was like no animal or monster we had ever witness'd before. Mr Withering declared it to be like unto a mushroom or spoor in nature.*"

The thing in the room clanged against the bars of whatever cage held it.

"*Kah-ryetl! Liau pa Hrondass. Hoscgha oudno!*"

"Dear God," breathed Galton.

"It's a *mi'nasulu*," said Nina.

As Galton fumbled with his gun, the men parted a little and the women could see into the room. It was a bedroom no more. Jonathan Angus was long gone. The window had been blocked off and a cage had been constructed across the back half of the room. The *mi'nasulu* jerked and writhed like a beached octopus. Its brown-grey limbs were cracked and flaking, the weird network of fungoid musculature that covered its body fracturing drily with its angry efforts to escape.

"*Emor sleed!*" it bellowed hoarsely. "*Yoons ledrrho kang'selle.*"

Mrs Fiddler grasped Nina's hand for reassurance but could not tear her gaze away.

"It's horrible," she said.

"It's pissed," said Nina.

"It's drunk?"

"Pissed off," Nina corrected herself and Mrs Fiddler tutted at her Americanism.

"Is it dangerous?"

Nina nodded and then tilted her head. "It's a parasite. But it's actually threatening them with legal action. Basically, it's saying, 'Don't you know who I am?', you know, like a celebrity that's just been kicked out of Nando's."

"But why have they kept it alive?" said Mrs Fiddler, aghast, revealing more about her own fear than anything else.

"It's unkillable," said Nina simply. "Apart from the bastard half-breeds and lesser creatures, we can only wound them. They hurt. They bleed. But we can't kill them. They can't be defeated."

Nina watched Galton load his oldy-timey weapon with shaking hands.

"They're only going to piss it off even more," she said.

When Nina rang, Morag was back in the office, flicking through photos of the map. Kathy was in the kitchenette, freshly returned from some errand or other.

"Hey," Morag said to Nina. "Rod's down at the Mailbox, looking in the tunnels for your mysterious Venislarn."

"Maccabees," said Nina.

"What bees?" she said.

"Have you heard of them?"

"It's a Bible thing, isn't it?" said Morag. As a child, she'd spent plenty of bored Sunday mornings in the pews of St Andrew's Episcopal Church in Fortrose, enough time to flick back and forth through the Bible in front of her and pick up a smattering of religious knowledge by osmosis.

"Not that," said Nina impatiently. "An organisation. A group. Venislarn killers. Long ago."

She was gabbling with an urgency and excitement Morag didn't understand.

"You asking me about Venislarn stuff?" she said. "You know as much as me. But no, I've never heard of them."

"Me neither!" said Nina. "Never heard of them. But they killed a *mi'nasulu.*"

"Did they now?"

"You can't kill a *mi'nasulu!*"

"You just said they did. I've never come across one before. Kathy mentioned one earlier this week."

"Mentioned what?" said Kathy, putting a tea down in front of Morag. Morag nodded in thanks.

"But they did kill one!" said Nina. "With a weird bullet thing. I don't understand it."

"No," agreed Morag honestly.

"Don't you see what's going on?" said Nina.

"I don't, no."

Apparently, that was not the answer Nina was looking for and hung up.

"Who was that?" said Kathy, blowing steam from her own drink.

"Nina. Some conspiracy nonsense about a secret society of Venislarn killers."

She sipped her tea.

I don't like tea, mother, said her unborn.

"Why?"

"Just curious," said Kathy.

Tea is boring. I want something else.

Morag made the mistake of thinking about what she would really like to drink, given the choice.

Yes, I would like that, mother.

"Lager?" said Morag, surprised.

"Pardon?" said Kathy.

Morag hesitated only a second. "You fancy a drink after work?"

Kathy looked at the clock. Morag considered how seriously bad an idea it was to go out drinking when pregnant. Then again, she reasoned to herself, if her kid was already talking, he was old enough to handle at least one beer.

"Sure," said Kathy.

"Excellent," said Morag.

When Rod's phone rang—a fact that surprised him because he didn't expect a signal in the sub-subbasement of The Mailbox—he answered it with every intention of telling Morag to hold her horses because gaining access to the tunnels under the building was no mean feat. The bloke from Forward Management Services, who managed the building, had initially and lazily made out he knew nothing about the tunnels at all. He'd then tried to fob Rod off with an explanation that there was some electrical works going on down there and access was forbidden on health and safety grounds. However, unspecified and entirely spurious threats of lawsuits brought by angry film production companies actually had an impact and the miserable little jobsworth took him down via the access stairs to a level below the underground car park beneath the shops, hotels and offices.

This only got them as far as a locked concertina gate, like an old lift door. The padlock and chains on the door looked old but sturdy. Rod reckoned he could have them open given a few minutes alone, but the building management fellow had gone off in search of keys and Rod decided to give him the benefit of the doubt.

He picked up the call. "Not even in yet," he said.

Morag's voice stuttered with the bad line. "I was just calling to say we're going for a drink after work."

"When I'm done here," he said.

"Old Contemptibles, yeah?"

"And you owe me a pint," he said.

"Grumbling Bishop's Old Hairy Stout," said Morag.

"That's not the name of a real beer."

There was a clatter on the stairs, the lazy jobsworth returning. "I've got to go."

The jobsworth building manager was not alone. Skye and Jayda came down the steps after him, the special effects woman and the ex-marine both wearing smirks like they were bunking off school.

"What are you doing here?" he said.

"We heard you were exploring some tunnels," said Skye.

"This a work thing or are you a caver?" said Jayda.

"Caver...?"

"One of these keys should fit," said the building manager, "but I still need to put a call through to head office and Network Rail. I don't know where these tunnels meet theirs."

Rod ignored him and clicked his fingers for the keys. The man handed them over. Thirty seconds later, the padlock and chain were off and the door thrown rustily back. Rod looked at the tiled steps descending into darkness.

"You ever been down here?" he asked the building manager.

"Me? No."

"Then you stay here. If I'm not back in an hour—"

"If we're not back in an hour," said Jayda, pulling a clip-on torch from her belt.

Rod took a credit-card thin torch from his wallet and shone it into the darkness.

Jayda made an unimpressed noise.

"I did have a much better torch until recently," said Rod.

"Really? Why haven't you got it now?"

"It was eaten by a giant spider," he said and led the way.

"You Brits are full of such bull."

The two Americans followed him down.

"Jonathan Angus," said Mrs Fiddler, holding the oculus up in the hallway.

"And he's not been injured," said Nina.

They followed the servant man down the hallway, through the entrance hall and into the dining room. They were looking into a time before the attack by the *Kobashi*, before the imprisonment of *Crippen-Ai* and long before the business with Galton's rifle and the caged fungus monster – but how much further before was not yet certain. The opulence of the finely furnished dining room contrasted starkly with the stinking and fusty room Nina and Mrs Fiddler now stood in.

Boulton sat alone with a half-eaten plate of bread and meat and a selection of papers covered with tallies and inventories.

"Sorry to disturb you, sir," said Jonathan.

Boulton swallowed what he was chewing and looked up at Jonathan and the small, untidy parcel he was carrying. It was a sturdy box, about the right size for a pair of children's shoes and was wrapped with brown paper and a large quantity of string that had been tied around it in a chaotic net of knots.

"It's a parcel," said Jonathan.

Boulton dabbed his lips with a napkin and held out his hand to take it. Jonathan hesitated. He even drew back a little.

"Are you going to give it to me?" said Boulton, frowning.

"Sir," said Jonathan and Nina saw that he was nervous. "I feel I should warn you."

"Warn me?"

"Yes, sir," said the servant man. "I noticed some... peculiarities about this parcel that I am certain I must share with you. Four peculiarities."

"Four," said Nina, amused.

Boulton also seemed amused. He sat back in his chair and took a sip of drink. "Four."

Jonathan pulled a little face as though licking his lips without actually opening his mouth. "Firstly, the lad who had run up with it from Birmingham just now looked like the devil himself was hot on his heels."

Boulton waved a hand toward the window. "It's a foul evening out there. The wind is picking up."

"He was frightened. Not windswept. He barely waited long enough to take a coin for his troubles before running off."

"I see."

"Furthermore, there were two peculiarities I noticed with the wrapping of the parcel." Jonathan rotated the box carefully. "Here, you will see the address. The One Who Calls Himself Boulton, Birmingham. Written in charcoal and in a hand so clumsy, I can only assume it was written by a child or a man with most of his fingers missing. Also, the overall appearance of the parcel. Look at the folds, the tears and the knots. This box had been wrapped and unwrapped many times."

Boulton inspected the parcel and nodded in agreement.

"So far, I see evidence only of a fearful delivery boy and a sender with poor penmanship and a frankly admirable habit of reusing parcel paper."

"And it swore at me, sir," said Jonathan.

Boulton looked at him candidly.

"It swore at you?"

"I think so."

Mrs Fiddler looked at Nina. She shrugged. The room about them gave a deep and solemn creak as though it was shrugging too.

Boulton took the parcel from Jonathan, laid it on the table and said, "The parcel spoke to you?"

"I hoped I'd imagined it, sir. I cannot think of another explanation."

Boulton considered the box's dimensions. "A small parrot?"

"I think it would have asphyxiated by now," said Jonathan.

Boulton was intrigued and took his table knife to the tight web of string around the parcel. "Mr Darwin has spoken about his desire to build a speaking machine, a device that mimics human speech."

"Darwin discussed the idea with Benjamin Franklin in 1771," noted Mrs Fiddler. "We must be close to that day."

Jonathan wilted with relief at the mention of a speaking machine. "Perhaps it is from him. Perhaps this is an elaborate joke and I am the fool."

Boulton pulled the much-creased paper aside and lifted the lid on the little crate within. He had barely lifted it when the lid was pushed from his hand and a little figure leapt out. It was less than foot in height, stitched together from pieces of rough sackcloth, grey-brown with age. It stood on the table on round and pudgy feet and looked from Boulton to Jonathan and back again with stitched-on wooden eyes.

"*Bhul* me," said Nina. "That's Steve the Destroyer!"

"I beg your pardon?" said Mrs Fiddler.

Wind whistled down the chimney place next to the two women.

"This building makes weird noises," said Nina.

"Did you say that thing was called Steve the Destroyer?"

Nina was about to explain what little she understood of the convoluted story: of how Morag Murray summoned an outrider of

296

Prein, trapped it in a magical *pabash kaj* doll and how the doll, Steve, had been present when the Mammonites opened a gateway to *Kal Frexo leng*-space while summoning their mother-goddess and that Steve had disappeared in the confusion, presumed to be on the other side of the gateway when it closed. Just like Vivian. Nina was about to explain, but Steve the Destroyer spoke.

"Which one of you is Boulton?" he demanded.

Boulton, mouth wide in shock, propelled himself away from the table, tipped over his chair and rolled onto the floor. Jonathan rushed to help, not once taking his eyes off the evil-looking ragdoll.

"It's... it's a savage," stuttered Boulton, agog.

"It's sorcery," whispered Jonathan, fearfully.

He grabbed the salt cellar on the table and threw salt at Steve.

"Away, sprite!" he shouted.

The doll snorted angrily. It then stamped on the prongs of Boulton's fork, caught it as it sprang into the air and thrust it warningly at them like a pitchfork.

"I'm no sprite, mortal fool!" it snarled.

"A savage pygmy, I tell you," said Boulton.

"Mr Boulton sir, how would a pygmy find its way to Birmingham?" said Jonathan with forced reasonableness.

"Escaped from a travelling fair?" suggested Boulton dazedly.

"You're Boulton?" Steve demanded. "You're the one harbouring that bastard *Crippen-Ai*?"

"Oi," said Jonathan. "You'll watch your tongue around Mr Boulton or you'll feel the big end of my knobstick."

"Don't you go threatening me, pipsqueak!" said the creature. "No one insults Steve the Destroyer and lives to tell the tale. If I hadn't made a promise to that blasted woman, I'd have had your liver out already and be toasting it over that fire." It waved its fork meaningfully.

"What blasted woman?" said Boulton, slowly finding his feet. "Did she send you here?"

"Careful, sir," said Jonathan. "Any woman who can command such creatures is surely a witch."

Steve the Destroyer seemed to give this some thought. "Yes, she probably is."

"Who sent you?" asked Boulton.

"I was sent by Mrs Vivian Grey," said Steve.

"And where is she?"

"The fortress of *Hath-No*." He looked at their faces and saw they were none the wiser. "Hell, you fools. She's in hell."

"Oh, God," said Nina softly and, her legs weakening, stepped back from the oculus. Floorboards groaned under her feet.

"What is it?" said Mrs Fiddler.

"Vivian."

"You know who that... thing is talking about?"

Nina nodded dumbly. She blinked and she felt a pricking at the corners of her eyes. She realised she was about to cry and told herself to get a grip.

"Vivian's alive," she whispered.

"The rag doll said she was in hell."

Nina nodded. "But she's alive."

A gusty draft blew out of the fireplace and the floorboard groaned again and then, like the rib cage of a sleeping giant, the floor rose several inches, timbers bending and splintering.

"What the hell...?" said Nina.

Mrs Fiddler stepped clumsily into her. "Nina..."

"What?" said Nina and then saw. The wall furthest from the door wasn't as far away as it had been. Nina instinctively looked up. "Ceiling!"

"Everything!" said Mrs Fiddler.

The room was shrinking. Like a beautiful optical illusion, the brickwork around the fire folded in on itself without actually appearing to move at all. The window receded without actually going anywhere, the glass singing like a telegraph wire in the wind as it shrank.

The door, their only exit, was shrinking too. Mrs Fiddler raised her hand to point. Nina grabbed the hand and hauled the woman towards the door. Nina felt the lintel graze her scalp as she hurried Mrs Fiddler through.

The walls and floor of the hallway rippled under the pressure of the shrinking house. Nina staggered forward as the ceiling came down and the walls came in.

"I don't want to die," said Mrs Fiddler as though the thought had only just occurred to her.

"We're not going to die," lied Nina.

The doorway ahead with the sash barrier across it, was not even four feet high now. This was some next level Alice in Wonderland shit, with a reasonable probability of the pair of them only escaping in a neatly extruded sausage meat format.

The walls were now too narrow for them to move in anything other than single file and Nina was forced to stoop.

"Quicker!" said Nina and shoved Mrs Fiddler forward.

Nina's shoulders brushed the crumbling plasterwork on both sides of the corridor as she scuttled forward. Any lower and she would be forced to crawl.

There was a metallic scream ahead of them. The doorway had come down on the brass upright of the sash barrier and, although it bent under the weight of the doorframe, it was holding it up. Woodwork and metalwork fought noisily.

"Through! Through!" yelled Nina.

She shoved her old teacher and had to twist sideways to pass the final few feet into the original non-magical section of the house. As she squeezed through the brass stand lost its fight against the collapsing corridor and, with an explosive 'zing' the top half snapped clean away and scythed down the hall ahead.

The two of them lay on the floor for a good while and concentrated on the simple joy of breathing and living.

Nina looked back at the doorway. There was nothing there. Only a crack in the skirting board and a limply dangling sash. Nina checked herself. She still had her Thomas the Tank Engine rucksack and the *yellis* wand within it. But they'd left the oculus behind.

"What happened?" she wondered. "Did we annoy the house?"

Mrs Fiddler sat up and patted dust from her cardigan. "When did we last wind the sidereal clock?"

"Ah. Good point. Drink?"

"Pardon?"

Nina flicked away a chunk of plaster that had caught on her jacket. "You look like you need a drink. And I deserve a drink."

"Is that so?"

"Vivian's alive," said Nina. "That's definitely worth a drink."

The tunnels were, for the most part, just tunnels. Rod had had an unusually wide experience of tunnels. There were the everyday tunnels most people experienced: subway tunnels, underpasses, the basement corridors and car park walkways which daylight never reached. He had been in various tunnels underneath Birmingham: the arched canal tunnels, the railway tunnels radiating from New Street station, even the nuclear-attack-hardened telecoms tunnels under the city centre. For a city built on loam and with a high water table, Birmingham had a surprising number of tunnels. And then there were the other tunnels, the narrow spaces and ancient paths not cut by human hands. As always, his thoughts flitted momentarily to the cold sandy tunnels under the Syrian Desert, the toad-men in Iraqi Republican Guard uniforms he'd fought there and the cursed gem that he'd come within a hair's-breadth of taking from *Azhur-Banipal*.

But, no, the tunnels under the Mailbox were nothing like those. If he was to make a comparison, it was like stepping into an underground railway, like the Glasgow Subway or the Paris Metro. There were lights in the tiled corridors, but they were intermittent and dim. Broken tile and brick dust littered the floor. There was the constant drip-drip of water trickling from leaky ceilings.

"And are we looking for something?" said Skye, tiptoeing over a pile of crud. "Or is this some sort of perimeter check thing?"

"We're looking for something that might have been buried down here years ago."

"How old is this place?" said Jayda, bringing up the rear, sweeping her torch around her in a covering arc, stepping like a soldier.

Rod looked up and around. "The building up top is no more than fifty years old. These tunnels... might have been carved out when they put the railway in. Eighteen sixties. Maybe eighteen fifties."

"You're kidding me," said Skye.

"She's from North Carolina," said Jayda. "The oldest building they've got there is a Piggly Wiggly."

"The thing we're looking for," said Rod, playing his torch over the ceiling, "is much older. I think, at least two hundred years old. Don't worry, we're not going to find it, but we're looking anyway."

He considered the options. The corridor ahead widened slightly and broke away into tunnels left and right. Left instinctively felt like the right choice.

"And how will we know it if we see it?" asked Jayda.

"Oh," he said vaguely, "it'll probably have some weird stuff scrawled on it in a language you don't understand."

Rod descended a flight of stairs and felt the air become warmer and closer. He came out onto a narrow platform alongside an unlit railway track.

"Ah."

The rails were brown with age. This didn't look like part of the general railway network but he wasn't going to take any chances jumping down onto the tracks. He shone his torch one way then the other.

Rod grunted, picked a direction and dropped down onto the track.

"We're going down there?" said Jayda.

"Don't worry," he said. "It's not in use. I think."

"I don't want to be electrocuted."

He looked at the tracks again. "There's no third rail. I think that means it's not electric."

"That's a lot of 'I think's," said Jayda and jumped down.

Skye flapped her arms and the movie armourer helped her down.

Rod set off in what he was happy was an easterly direction "Watch your feet. Rats."

Skye made a somewhat pathetic noise.

"Dead ones," said Rod and shone his torch on the little corpses.

Rod stepped carefully. The ground was damp and dirty. He'd worn his better suit for Hollywood babysitting duties, and he knew from experience that Vaughn Sitterson rarely signed off dry cleaning bills.

"Yo, Rod," said Jayda.

"Yeah?"

"Looks kinda weird to me." She pointed her torch to the side wall.

Rod had walked right past and not seen it. The black metal door was set into a recess in the brickwork. It was reinforced with steel plate and rivets and had a lock that would probably test his lock picks' strength. Around the doorway was an arch of cast bronze, etched with Venislarn ideograms. Rod wasn't even going to pretend he could read what they said but he assumed it wasn't good. As torchlight wavered over them, they appeared to squirm, as though they were embarrassed to be seen.

"That's what we're looking for," said Rod.

Rod brushed the dark scuff marks from his suit as he walked down Edmund Street towards the Old Contemptibles pub. Beyond the engraved Venislarn arch, the tunnel beneath the Mailbox and storage space beyond had been clean and well kept—suspiciously clean and well kept, now he thought about it—but it seemed a universal rule of subterranean exploration that he'd return to the surface with a light dust stain or a greasy line across his shins. Not that it mattered in the Old Contemptibles: the staff at their regular post-work watering hole had seen him, Nina or Morag roll up in a far worse state.

As he walked through the door, he considered how much ectoplasmic slime or alien blood they must have trodden into the carpets over the years. If the Venislarn were ever wiped out, their horrific race could probably be recreated from DNA extracted from that grubby floor.

Rod went to the bar and then looked round to see if Morag had already arrived. The bar's clientele filled the pub, post-work office staff, mostly old school drinkers who were put off by the trendier bars in the area and just needed a little anaesthetising before catching a train to face the horrorshow that was their home life. There was no sign of Morag, but Rod caught a glimpse of Kathy, sitting alone at a table.

Kathy. He groaned inwardly and tried to think quickly. What was the best response here? Go up to her and act like the sociable colleagues they'd been until this week? Pretend he hadn't seen her and hide at the bar until someone else came along? Leave? Text her that he was standing there and ask what he should do?

He realised she was looking at him. She was looking directly at him while he gazed mindlessly back. Oh good, he thought bitterly. She'd now just seen him gawping silently at her from afar and he didn't even have a pint yet. He decided to go over, but his legs hesitated.

He shuffled forward, feeling like the socially awkward loser Kathy no doubt no thought he was.

"Morag invited me," he said automatically.

"You don't have to justify yourself to me," said Kathy. "You don't have to be weird about things."

"I'm trying not to," he said.

She looked awkward enough herself. She didn't know whether to look at him or look at her drink.

"A good day?" he said, deliberately bland.

She shrugged. "Tidying up after that soul-trading deal with the Handmaiden. Omar being a dick about letting me play with his toys up at the Think Tank." She sighed. "And you?"

"Babysitting film actors is far less interesting than you'd think," he said. "But then Morag gave me a call, and I've just spent the past hour exploring a previously undiscovered... well, I don't know what it is, under the Mailbox."

She looked at him sharply, an eyebrow raised. "What's under the Mailbox?"

"Abandoned railway tunnels and what looks like some weird Venislarn storage facility. Someone buried a creature there years and years ago but now..." he shook his head. "I think someone or various someones have been down there several times over the centuries."

"You told Morag about this yet?"

"No. I was hoping to meet her here."

He looked at the empty beer bottle opposite Kathy.

"Yeah, she's in the loos," said Kathy.

Rod pointed at Kathy's glass. "Can I...?"

"Er, yes. Why not? Mine's a G and T. Morag's a..."

"Cheap horrible chemical lager," noted Rod. "Gotcha."

He went back to the bar in a far superior mood to the one in which he'd left it. He was buying Kathy a drink and there had been at least five seconds of ordinary conversation between them. Maybe things were on the mend. Perhaps he just needed to be a bit patient, just wait. The good ship Rod 'n' Kathy had taken a battering in the storm of life and had been listing for the past day or so but now it was righting itself.

Morag washed her hands and considered her reflection in the mirror. She straightened and put her hands on her bump. A grapefruit. She turned sideways and wondered if anyone else had noticed, if others knew.

I like lager, said her unborn.

"Do you, baby?" she murmured.

It makes me feel a bit funny.

"Yeah, well one lager's all we're getting," she said.

It's a nice funny, mother.

She nodded. Drunkenness was a nice funny. There was no arguing with that. Morag wished for, ached for the days when this might just be the start of an evening's drinking. Laughing about nothing with Nina. Gently ribbing Rod, who was (her subconscious had needled her all day) a 'lovely man'. There would be no more of those carefree drinking evenings anymore, only the final few months of painfully sober pregnancy and then—boom!—the end of the world. She didn't know for certain when the Venislarn soulgate would occur in relation to the birth, whether it would be a case of *push, push, 'waah!', curtains drop* or if she'd get a few months or years of raising the anti-Christ before he went all Damien. She wasn't optimistic.

"Come on, me laddo," she said to the lump in her belly. "It's soft drinks for us now until the end of the world."

She returned to the bar. Kathy was twirling her straw around an empty gin and tonic. Morag sat down and tried to suck some lingering beer molecules from her bottle.

"Rod's at the bar, getting another," said Kathy.

"Another?" said Morag, gesturing with her bottle.

More lager, mother!

"He offered," said Kathy.

"I need to catch up with him," said Morag.

"Oh?"

"He was doing me a favour earlier, checking out rumours of a Venislarn creature buried somewhere near the Mailbox."

"Ah."

Morag craned her neck to look through the crowd. "He mention anything about that when he got here?"

"No." Kathy swirled her straw. "Don't think so."

A short presence nudged up beside Rod at the bar.

"You been served yet?" said Nina.

The barman caught Rod's eye and came over.

"Your timing is impeccable as always," said Rod. "What are you having?"

"Double rum and coke for me and..." She turned to the middle-aged woman who was with her. "Some sort of teacher drink for Mrs Fiddler."

"A teacher drink?"

Nina shrugged. "Something with lots of gin in it, probably."

"A large gin and tonic sounds lovely," said the woman, interrupting the stern look she was giving Nina to smile pleasantly at Rod.

He ordered five drinks. "I'm Rod," he said, passing the woman one of the G and Ts.

"We met the other night," she said, and shook his hand. "I'm Julie."

"But you can't call a teacher by their first name," said Nina.

"Ignore her," said Julie.

"Aye, she's special, isn't she?" said Rod. He noted the grey dust on the front of Julie's cardigan, the dirt marks on Nina's shoulders. "You two been in a building site?"

"Or Birmingham as we like to call it," said Mrs Fiddler.

"I discovered that it's Kathy's dad's company that's responsible for all the stuff going on round Centenary Square. Was responsible. He was. They are. He's dead. What was I saying?"

"You're babbling," said Nina. "You would not believe where we've been."

"Given our jobs, nothing surprises me anymore."

"We saw Steve the Destroyer."

"What?" Rod measured out a doll's height on the bar with his palm. "Steve?"

"Uh-huh. We saw him through a time-viewer thing, a Venislarn device built by Matthew Boulton. We saw Steve the Destroyer, who had himself posted to Soho House back in ancient times—"

305

"Not ancient," said Julie.

"—and he told Matthew Boulton he'd been sent there by Vivian. Vivian's alive, Rod! She's in *Kal Frexo leng*-space or something, but she's still alive – least she was two hundred years ago."

Rod stared at her.

"That'll be twenty-three pounds ninety," said the barman.

"Okay," said Rod slowly. "I'm surprised."

He got out his wallet and paid. He looked to Julie Fiddler. "And this all happened?"

"Hey!" said Nina and slapped his arm.

"I don't understand half the words she says sometimes," said Julie, "but, yes, that is essentially what we observed."

"Except the star clock wound down and the rooms caved in on themselves and we barely got out alive," said Nina.

"I don't understand half the words she says either," said Rod and lifted his much-anticipated pint of Thornbridge's American Sister. "Cheers."

"Cheers," said Julie.

Nina gargled something as she downed half her drink. "And how's the movie business?" she said when she surfaced. "Rubbing shoulders with the stars? Sharing your wisdom?"

"Less interesting than you'd think," he said. "And no one wants any wisdom from me. Everyone's happiest when I just keep my mouth shut and smile encouragingly."

"Movie business?" said Julie.

Rod glanced questioningly at Nina.

"Oh, it's okay," she said. "I've told Mrs Fiddler everything."

"Everything? We are meant to be a secret organisation, Nina." He thought about the plot of the film and chuckled to himself. "No organisation stays secret for long, does it?"

"Speaking of secret organisations" began Nina but something occurred to Rod and he cut across her.

"Oh, and that magic rohypnol thing you said you'd done."

"Rohypnol?" said Julie.

"The wand," said Nina. "Fixed your little problem with Morag, did it?"

"Morag?" he said. "I didn't need anything fixing with Morag."

It abruptly made sense. He couldn't quite see why Nina thought he'd fancy Morag, but this explained why it hadn't worked.

"The wand works?" he said.

"It definitely works," she said and shifted her shoulder, indicating it was in her Thomas the Tank Engine rucksack.

"And easy to use?" he said.

She was already opening the rucksack and getting it out to pass to him.

Rod returned to the table with three drinks.

"Evening," he said, plopping Morag's beer down in front of her. "Gin," he said to Kathy.

Morag smiled at him. "Is that a wand in your pocket?"

"He's just happy to see you," said Kathy. "You. Me. Anything with a heartbeat."

"I was going to buy you a drink," said Morag. "You were going to tell me what you'd found under the Mailbox."

"Yeah, yeah, in a bit," he said. Nina and Julie were behind him. "Morag, Kathy, this is Julie Fiddler. She's the curator over at Soho House. Nina's told her everything about the consular mission because our secrets don't mean anything."

"Yeah, I still haven't told you about this secret organisation," said Nina.

"Anyway," said Rod, interrupting her again, "I need to borrow Kathy."

"Do you?" said Kathy.

"I really do."

"I'm not sure I want to be borrowed."

"You do. Trust me."

He took her hand and she resisted a second but then relented, slid out of her seat and followed him.

"You hear screaming, you come rescue me," she told the others as he led her hurriedly through the crowded bar.

He wasn't sure where he was going. He led her out of the bar to get away from the crowds. From there, he took her down a side corridor to get them out of public sight. That left them standing in front of the toilets. He wasn't about to take her into the gents. He wasn't about to go into the ladies. Thus, they ended up in the disabled toilet together, with the door locked.

"Okay," said Kathy slowly. "I am impressed. Yesterday's romantic gesture was awful but this..." She gestured round to the unflushed toilet, the streamers of discarded toilet paper on the floor. "You've gone one step beyond."

"Please, just shut up," he said and then checked himself. "*Please*. Just listen."

Kathy gave him an arch look and casually took hold of the red emergency cord. "One tug..."

Rod took the wand from his pocket. "This—"

"Is a *yellis* wand."

"You know?"

"I've read about it. In fact, that looks like Boulton's original."

"Right, right. And it can be used to wipe memories."

"Correct."

He held it carefully, feeling the weight of possibilities. "I like you, Kathy."

"You've said. Repeatedly."

"And I'd like to go back to the way things were."

"Because you can't cope with grown-up adult situations."

"Because I can't cope with your constant sniping," he said. He closed his eyes momentarily. "I just want to forget."

"Okay," she said and reached out for the wand.

"Both of us."

She hesitated. "Both?"

"It seems only fair."

She laughed lightly at that and nodded.

"And maybe..." he said and left the rest unsaid.

"We restart our relationship in a more conventional manner," she said.

"Aye."

"Like in a pub toilet."

He smiled.

She took the wand from him. "Maybe get to know each other a bit better first."

"That would be good," he said.

She studied the many-tipped wand, inspected the markings on the outside. "You can finally tell me what happened to you in the desert that led you to working for the consular mission."

"Aye."

"And I can tell you *why* I came to work for the mission."

"Sure."

"How I was instructed to infiltrate the consular mission in order to find the means to destroy the Venislarn once and for all."

"Er, what?"

"*Hyet-pa!*"

In the small room, the light of the wand was blindingly intense, but Rod stared at it unblinking. The rest of the world faded away. The pub, the toilet stink, the surprise he had only started to register at what Kathy had said: all gone.

"You will forget that we had sex in the Think Tank," said Kathy's voice. "You will forget me calling you over to ask you to have sex with me. You will forget ever seeing me with *Polliqan Riti*. You will forget all and any conversations and actions you took because we had sex – that nonsense with the flowers and the chocolates, that embarrassing episode in the bar. We never had sex. It was a non-event and you will forget anything linked to it. You will also forget what you found in our tunnels under the Mailbox. You will be able to tell others that you went down there but that there was nothing of note, nothing to be seen."

The lights wavered in front of his eyes.

"Now, I will return to the bar," said Kathy. "You will forget we were in here together. You came in here alone. You will forget this conversation happened or that I have the wand."

The lights vanished with such suddenness that Rod's eyes stung. He knuckled his eyes until the painful afterimages faded.

He looked round. The toilet door was swinging shut. Ah, yes, he was in the toilet. He went to wash his hands at the sink and then took a mental reading of his bladder and couldn't remember if he'd already been to the toilet.

Kathy returned to the table while Nina attempted to re-explain what she had learned in Soho House.

"They killed a Venislarn," she said. "A *mi'nasulu*."

"Who did?" said Kathy and slid into the seat next to Morag.

"Matthew Boulton and Erasmus Darwin and..." She looked to Mrs Fiddler.

"Samuel Galton," said the ex-teacher helpfully.

"Him. He had a special gun loaded with a..." She made hand gestures.

"A magic bullet."

"It's not magic," tutted Nina. "Point is, they were talking about starting a secret society to kill the Venislarn. They knew that the Venislarn couldn't be defeated but they were going to do it anyway."

"So, maybe they did," said Morag. "I should think they all came to sticky ends."

"They led long and healthy lives," said Mrs Fiddler, "not to mention wealthy lives. When they put their minds to something..."

Kathy smiled. "It's a lovely notion, but since we've never heard of them, I think we can assume any plans to attack the Venislarn just fizzled out. Great men and their pet projects."

"We haven't heard of them because it's a secret organisation. It's like the Illuminati."

"The Bavarian Illuminati?" said Mrs Fiddler.

"I'm talking about Jay Z and Beyoncé. Lots of celebrities are in it."

"Who?" said Mrs Fiddler.

"Don't even go there," said Morag.

"You know it's true," said Nina.

"What's true?" said Rod, plonking himself down on an end stool and reaching for his pint.

"Nina and the Illuminati."

"Ah," said Rod and supped deeply. "Jay-zed and Katy Perry and Madonna and that."

"Exactly," said Nina.

"They run the music industry."

"They do."

"And they're going to bring about the New World Order."

"They are."

"They've got the cure for cancer but they're keeping it to themselves."

"Er, yeah. That."

"And they faked the moon landings and all those pictures that show the world is round even though everyone knows it's flat."

"Did they?"

Morag slapped Rod's knee admonishingly.

"He's making fun of you, Nina."

Rod pulled a silly face. "Fun? Me?"

"But the Maccabees are real!" Nina insisted.

Rod shook his head. "Skye—she does make-up and prosthetic things on the movie I'm working on—"

"'The movie I'm working on,'" said Morag in a silly high-pitched voice. "Look who's gone all Hollywood."

He tutted. "Skye said she didn't believe that secret organisations could exist because people are rubbish at keeping secrets."

"Precisely," said Kathy. "It's a load of nonsense."

"I mean, the plot of this film..."

"He's a critic too now," smiled Morag and nudged the big guy.

Nina noted that was the second act of physical contact between Morag and Rod in less than a minute. Clearly Morag was into Rod as much as the big daft bear of a man was into her. The two of them really ought to get their priorities sorted and start doing whatever it was middle-aged people did when they fancied each other – get a joint National Trust membership, go to a farmer's market, whatever.

Rod drank from his pint and pinched a line of foam from his upper lip.

"The plot to this film. It's supposedly based around a consular mission like ours, except based in Detroit or Philadelphia or somewhere."

"You can't remember?"

"They haven't decided. And the agents are all suave, sexy superspies."

"I can be suave," said Morag.

"Sexy," said Nina, raising her hand.

"Sure," said Kathy. "I can be a superspy."

"But there's this fiendish villain," said Rod.

"With a white cat?" suggested Mrs Fiddler.

"He's behind a conspiracy to bring down the truce between the mission and the Venislarn."

Nina clicked and pointed. "Like the Maccabees!"

"It's a movie," Rod reminded her. "Anyway, Botticelli—"

"Who?"

"This evil industrialist, he's got the pieces of this evil mystic item, it's got a Venislarn name I can't remember, and once he's amassed them all, he's going to set the humans and the Venislarn at each other's throats."

"A magic weapon," said Mrs Fiddler.

"Like the Maccabees," said Nina.

"No," said Rod irritably. "It's a film. I was pointing out that secret plans to bring down the status quo are just unbelievable."

"Sounds like that James Bond film," said Mrs Fiddler. "The one with the volcano."

"Besides, we know the Venislarn cannot be defeated," said Kathy.

"Sorry?" said Nina. "Did I neglect to mention the weird blue bullet they shot the *mi'nasulu* with?"

"Blue?" said Morag, frowning.

"Yeah, blue. Blue yellow, kinda like—"

"Cos there's this substance, down at the Think Tank that—"

"Morag Murray!"

Professor Sheikh Omar had appeared at the table and was glaring at Morag with what seemed genuine anger.

"Wassup, prof?" said Nina. "Don't usually see you down here."

Morag was holding her beer like its existence had come as a total surprise to her.

"It's only one," she said.

"Two," said Kathy.

"Like anyone gives a shit how many beers this woman has had," said Nina.

Morag stood. "I'm sorry."

"What have you got to be sorry for?" said Rod.

"Miss Murray and I had made a promise to do that Dry January thing," said Omar.

"It's not January," said Nina.

"It took us a while to get round to it," said Morag. She glanced guiltily at Omar. "I need to go."

"You don't need to go anywhere," said Nina.

"It's late," said Morag even though it really wasn't. "Besides, the world is going to end tomorrow, so I ought to get a good night's sleep."

"Is it?" said Nina.

"So says Trevor's Apocalyptic Teapot."

"I beg your pardon?" said Mrs Fiddler but Morag and Omar had gone.

Nina shook her head in confusion then looked to Rod and held out her hand. "Wand."

"What wand?" he said.

THURSDAY

Morag dropped her fork in her breakfast of reheated leftover takeaway chow mein and tried to fix her August Handmaiden of *Prein* nanny with a furious glare. This was less than easy given that *Shala'pinz Syu* had more than a dozen faces on her armoured shell and it wasn't really possible to catch the eye of a screaming baby executed in powdery porcelain.

"You're not coming with me," said Morag.

"I am your protector," said *Shala'pinz Syu*, smoothly.

It was quite hard to take that last statement seriously while the vast spider-warrior had two of her claws dipped in the foamy washing up bowl.

"You're my kidnapper," said Morag.

Have you been kidnapped, mother? asked her bump soundlessly.

"It kinda feels that way, baby," said Morag, hand on stomach.

"I have been given the sacred duty of caring for the *kaatbari*."

"And you can do that when I'm back in this hellhole at night, not when I'm at work."

Morag threw her arms wide to indicate the flat. It wasn't very hellhole-ish in truth. It was spacious, light and very pleasantly furnished and her best efforts to give it that homey lived-in (i.e. messy) look were being thwarted by the house-proud Handmaiden. The entourage of *Prein* were colloquially thought of as the Nazi foot-soldiers of the Venislarn but Morag was rapidly coming round to the opinion that *Shala'pinz Syu* secretly yearned to be nothing more than a domestic *hausfrau* with a tidy little fascist cottage.

"You will not see me, but I will be there," said the Handmaiden.

"You stay here," said Morag. "Hoover the curtains, bake biscuits, whatever. I'm going to work and you're not following."

Morag stood, grabbed her jacket and stormed out.

Are we not finishing the chow mein, mother?

"Not now," she said.

There was a text on her phone from Lois at the office. Sitterson had called a meeting. That didn't bode well; he rarely called meetings.

Morag did a little mental checklist of all the things she might have done recently to rouse the ire of the mission chief. That checklist had a dozen things or more on it but the top item was 'getting pregnant with the *Kaatbari*'. She couldn't imagine how Sitterson could possibly know, so it was probably one of the other items. If she was lucky, it would be something someone else had done.

She stepped out of the lobby and walked towards the canal side exit. Kim and Jim, the cheery neighbours from across the corridor, were walking towards her. Kim wore dungarees and her hair tied up, perhaps hoping to look like a jobbing artist although Morag thought she had more of a 'lesbian mechanic' vibe about her. Jim wore a cable-knit Aran jumper which said, with an eloquence knitwear rarely possessed, 'my owner is a complete tosser'.

"Neighbour!" said Jim as greeting.

"Going to work," said Morag, without slowing.

Kim, a coffee-shop ice-frapp-cappa-something in one hand, held up a bag to Morag. "Savoury bran muffin, darling?"

"You're fucking monsters," said Morag and left.

You used the mmmm-mmmm word, mother.

Morag huffed. "Is this how it's going to be? Spending the rest of my life being judged by my own child?"

I love you, mother.

She winced. On reflection, being loved by the anti-Christ was possibly worse than being judged.

Morag got to work with time to spare. Her new home was considerably nearer to the Library of Birmingham than her house-share in Bournville, even if the walk to work involved a significant diversion around the sealed off Mailbox film set and the building site that had spilled out from Chamberlain Square and into Centenary Square.

Nonetheless, she entered meeting room two to find everyone else already there. Vaughn sat at the head of the table, his nose buried in a report. Rod and Kathy sat on one side of the table. Morag took the seat next to Nina.

"I came early because I thought there might be pastries," said Rod.

"Someone offered me a savoury bran muffin on the way here," said Morag.

"Monster," said Kathy.

"That's what I said."

Vaughn continued to read his report. Across the table, glances were exchanged. Rod looked at Nina. Nina looked at Kathy. Kathy looked at Morag. Morag looked at Rod. They had been here before. Vaughn never instigated the actual discussion.

Rod coughed politely.

"We're all here, sir," he said.

"I'm aware of that," said Vaughn, not looking up. "Tell me about the teapot."

"The teapot?" said Morag.

Vaughn pushed a graph into the centre of the table, a line rising in a wobbly forty-five degree line towards the top.

"It's a sensing device," said Kathy.

"Those are measurements I've taken," said Rod. "Very rough."

"Maurice and Omar think it predicts danger to life," said Nina.

"And if I've understood the enchantments on it correctly," said Kathy, "then it will reach the upper end of the scale later on today."

"I know nothing about it at all," said Morag, happily.

"Later on today?" said Vaughn.

"Sometime this afternoon?" suggested Kathy.

"Measuring tea depths with such equipment isn't an exact science," said Rod.

"No, not an exact science."

Vaughn said nothing. The silence extended.

"It's a nice cup of tea," said Nina eventually.

"Pardon?" said Vaughn.

"Just saying. It makes a really nice cup of tea."

"It does," agreed Morag.

"Hard to get a good cuppa these days," agreed Rod.

Vaughn massaged his pale brow.

"I..." he stopped, deep in thought. He was a man who trod lightly on the world. Morag was prepared to believe he gave himself a spoken word quota for the day. "We have significant magical evidence that the world is going to end today, and the mission team with the responsibility for investigating and intervening in such an event seems alarmingly blasé about it."

"The world isn't going to end today," said Morag.

"No? You have that on good authority?"

She did have that on good authority. She was pregnant with the *kaatbari*, the herald of the Venislarn apocalypse, and she still had a good five to six months of baby-brewing time left. But she wasn't going to tell Vaughn Sitterson that.

"There's no indication that the teapot specifically detects world-ending events," Kathy pointed out, "only the danger present to the area surrounding the teapot."

"But a danger that affects everyone?" asked Rod.

"What do you mean?"

"I mean," he said, sitting forward, "if I had contracted Ebola, then I would be in grave danger but you all wouldn't."

"Ebola's highly infectious, isn't it?" said Morag.

"Okay. Cancer. Then I would be in danger but not you."

"No, the *Pei-Yeu* wards would only respond to generic danger, universal danger," said Kathy.

"So, something bad is going to happen here?" said Morag.

"Such as the Venislarn apocalypse," said Vaughn.

"Not that," said Morag. "I have, er, assurances from *Yo-Morgantus*."

"Another Venislarn god then. *Yoth-Sheol-Niggurauth*?"

"Not given us any trouble since that Christmas market incident."

"*Daganau-Pysh*?"

"Happy where he is. Someone lobbed a toothpaste bomb in his gob the other day, but he doesn't seem to have taken it to heart."

"The *Nadirian*?"

"Not an issue," said Morag.

"*Kaxeos*?"

"I had a curry with his lads the other week," said Rod. "No quibbles."

"Everything's quiet," said Morag.

"Well, something's going to happen," said Vaughn.

"Could be something mundane," said Kathy. "A terrorist incident. A plane crash."

"See?" said Rod, brightly. "It's not all doom and gloom."

Nina bit her lip. "I've been following up a lead that Vivian left behind."

"Is this where you tell us why you've been wasting work time up at Soho House?" said Vaughn.

"Not wasting time, Vaughn," she said. He visibly bristled at her use of his name, whether because of the informality or because it drew unnecessary attention to his existence was uncertain. "It has turned up a rich seam of Venislarn artefacts," she said. "There's this clock and a past-viewing device and a wand which Rod has since lost—"

"What wand?" said Rod.

"But I've also discovered that back in Georgian times—that's during the reigns of King Georges one to four," she said, evidently proud to share a little of what she had learned—"there was a secret society called the Maccabees. That's oldy timey speak for 'the hammers.'"

"Aramaic," said Kathy.

"And their goal was to capture and kill all and any Venislarn they found. I saw them shoot a *mi'nasulu* with some blue bullet thing. Shoot it and kill it."

"When did you see this?" said Rod.

"Yesterday. But it happened in the seventeen eighties. I saw it yesterday in seventeen eighty-something."

Vaughn was shaking his head in irritated incomprehension, but Nina pressed on.

"And they were planning to bury this sneaky Venislarn Squidward thing covered in blue slime called *Crippen-Ai* in some location near the Mailbox, 'cept it wasn't the Mailbox then."

"And I asked Rod to take a look," said Morag.

"I didn't find anything," said Rod.

Kathy nodded firmly. "It's a dead end, a red herring. Georgian gentlemen playing at war, a footnote in history. It's irrelevant."

Vaughn was not happy.

"Very little of this makes sense and I'm not satisfied that something cataclysmic isn't about to befall this city. I want..." He almost choked on the personal pronoun. "It is imperative that we find out more about these amateur revolutionaries, historically irrelevant or not, that we ascertain more about the Venislarn you claim they were able to kill and determine what terrible calamity we are going to be facing before the weekend."

"I'll go back to Soho House," said Nina.

"I'm needed on set," said Rod.

"I'm conducting some research that may prove relevant," said Kathy.

Morag looked at the others. "I'll track down the supposedly slaughtered *mi'nasulu* and chat up the local gods then, shall I? Basically, everything."

No one disagreed with her and before she had finished looking round, Vaughn was up and sliding discreetly towards the door.

Someone who was clearly in contact with the weather gods had declared it would be an ideal day for the filming of the rooftop scenes on the Mailbox. In the annexed retail space that now served as the producer's on-set office, Director Bryan went through the business of the day with relevant crew.

"Four phases. We do close-ups, two-shots and dialogue up there with the key actors. Then we do the small piece action segments with Taylor and Langford."

"Pupfish," said Producer Tammy.

"What?" said Pupfish, looking up.

Bryan looked at Tammy. Tammy shrugged. "We're continuing with Pupfish today. Langford James is..." She circled her hands in a vain attempt to find the right words.

"Squatting in his room and chanting to his newfound gods," said Taylor Graham, with a look of dour worry on his face.

"I probably ought to have a word with him," said Rod.

"You think?" said Bryan, displeased.

"It's not my fault," said Rod, but the mood in the room suggested that a fair few people very much thought it was his fault.

Nina found Mrs Fiddler in the Soho House museum gift shop, doing a stocktake of novelty erasers in the shapes of knights and princesses and those flouncy cavaliers with floppy hats and Johnny Depp beards.

"I didn't know if you were coming back today," said Mrs Fiddler.

"Why wouldn't I come back?"

Mrs Fiddler stopped in her stocktake. She looked like she had lost count.

"We nearly died yesterday, Nina."

"Nearly. That's the point," said Nina.

"A somewhat reckless attitude."

"YOLO."

"I do not have the faintest idea what that means."

"It means, let's move on and take another look through the round window into the past. Vivian's in hell and there's some sort of Illuminati Masons conspiracy theory secret society, which I don't think anyone back at the office really believes in, which may be why the world is going to end today."

Mrs Fiddler let the rubbers in her hand fall into the display basket. "The world's going to end?"

"Nah, probably not. Kathy says it's probably just going to be a plane crash or something, so we probably don't need to panic just yet."

"Plane crash where?"

"The Library. Centenary Square. Least that's what Trevor's Apocalyptic Teapot says."

"Do you ever listen to the nonsense that comes out of your mouth?"

"Who's got time for that, huh? Now let's go."

"I'm not sure I can," said Mrs Fiddler and then seemed to struggle to explain why. "I do have an actual job to do here, a real job."

Nina looked round the visitor centre and gift shop. The place was empty. Dust drifted in the sunlight.

"Come on," she said. "You know you want to. You know you should."

Mrs Fiddler sighed.

"Do it and earn yourself a gold star sticker," said Nina.

Rod nodded to the film set security guy just outside the hotel lift door.

"Langford James?" he said and pointed left.

The security guy, who was wearing sunglasses indoors but probably wasn't a complete arse, jerked his chin up in acknowledgement. "Last on the left."

Rod went to the end of the top floor corridor and knocked.

"*Hgoirr bhox juaiys-halmz. Ke!*"

"Uh-huh?" said Rod. "It's me, Rod Campbell."

"*Soudri-am taxeteli mzhz.*"

"Right. It's just... look, I don't know if you're speaking actual Venislarn because, to be honest, I don't know any. Apart from some choice swear words."

"*Bhul-zhu, muda khi umlaq,*" said another voice, probably the Venislarnkin girl.

"See? I understood those words," said Rod. "I just wanted to check on you."

The door clicked and opened. The room was near dark, the curtains drawn. Khaleesi-*Qalawe* looked at him from behind her blue fringe. She was wearing a hotel dressing gown, but it wasn't done up. Rod's gaze snapped away.

"*Laryirn-to ada gil tot'u,*" said a voice in the darkness.

"*Taol nadehz,* my love," she replied, still looking at Rod. There was an expression in Khaleesi's eyes that suggested she was acting out the role of 'high priestess' to whatever it was the actor Langford James was pretending to be.

Rod didn't know whether to be embarrassed or worried. The woman was barely older than Nina, at most half Langford's age – a brainless youngster with infected subdermal gill implants acting all sultry and knowing because Mr Hollywood had lost his marbles after a dip in the local canal.

"He actually speaking Venislarn?" said Rod, pointing.

Khaleesi gestured for him to enter. Rod's concentration was split between avoiding treading on room service trays and avoiding stumbling into the mostly naked woman.

"He is speaking in tongues," said Khaleesi. "He is speaking the language of heaven."

"Heaven, aye," said Rod.

The bed that had been in the centre of the room had been upended and pushed to the side near the window. Langford James, also mostly naked sat in the middle of the floor in the lotus position, his bare feet tucked up against his hips. Swirls of dried liquid covered the floor around him. In the half-light, Rod couldn't tell if it was red or brown. Neither colour boded well. The patterns, looping and spiralling in a not entirely artless manner, surrounded him like a magic circle. Rod had no idea if they were authentically Venislarn, if they had any power at all. He took out his phone.

"You mind if I take some photos of these?" he said.

Langford looked at him unkindly. "Whatever, G-man. What you doin' anyway? Ggh!" His head twitched and his jaw spasmed in a fair impression of a *samakha* gill gasp.

"Me?" Rod crouched down and took a few discreet shots of the possibly occult symbols. "I just wanted to see how you were, mate. You doing okay?"

"His majesty wants for nothing," said Khaleesi in an affectedly pompous tone.

Between Langford's strung-out rock-star fishman schtick and her am-dram turn as his witch-queen, Rod could see himself getting irritated with this pair bloody quick.

"I just wondered if you wanted to come down to the set," said Rod with forced pleasantness. "Do a bit of acting?"

"Prancing?" sneered Langford. "Cavorting? A pantomime projected on the skin of the world. Ggh!"

"Well, I'll certainly be watching it down the Odeon when it comes out. You're the star, remember? A star?"

Langford raised his hands slowly in praise. "The stars will align. Our time will come, ya get me?"

"Not those kinds of stars," Rod muttered.

"You can keep your play acting," said Langford. "I'm all about keepin' it real, man."

"Real. Sure. If you don't mind, I'm going to get these pretty... doodles checked out. See if they're 'real' too."

As he stood up, Rod put his hand out to steady himself and dipped his fingers in the still-drying liquid on the floor. Automatically, he raised his fingers to his face for a sniff.

"Ketchup," he said in recognition. "Well, that's certainly a relief."

He stepped carefully past Khaleesi on his way to the door. "I'll just leave you to your..." He gestured generally at the room and the mess the two of them had created together. "Yeah, I don't know what to call it," he said, and left.

The history of the Venislarn on Earth was a peculiar and near-indescribable thing. The Venislarn revelled in peculiarity and near-indescribability. Office files and computer records gave a fine and intelligible account of human interactions with the Venislarn gods over the most recent decades but, earlier than that, details were sketchy. There was no fixed date on which the Venislarn arrived on Earth – not because the date was unknown and not because the Venislarn had always been here (they hadn't) but because the assumption that there had been a date of first contact was a very human assumption, and quite wrong.

Bannerman, Morag's old boss in Edinburgh, had described it thus: humanity was a line of ants marching across a table. Encountering a hand on the table, the ants might declare, 'This is the first hand we've seen' but then hands or cups or cutlery might land elsewhere on the table and intrude on earlier parts of the line and the point of first contact was now very much in dispute. But that didn't mean the Venislarn had simply colonised Earth at numerous different points in time. The line of ants did not represent anything quite so linear as time. It wasn't the fourth dimension and certainly not one of the other three. It represented some higher dimensional reality and the whole analogy really didn't do the true situation justice. When Morag had asked Bannerman why he'd bothered to use the analogy, he'd held up a fist and said, "This is them and we're ants. And their fists are the only thing we've ever seen. We haven't even met the true Venislarn yet."

When the office records failed Morag in her search for the *mi'nasulu* that Boulton and Galton and whoever had allegedly killed, she went down to the Vault to consult the erratic and unclassifiable histories of the Venislarn on Earth.

What are we doing now, mother? asked her foetus.

"Research. I need to find out about a monster, a godling of sorts, called the *mi'nasulu*."

Why?

"Because it might prove or disprove the existence of the secret organisation that wants to make war with the Venislarn."

And is that a bad thing, mother?

"Like an ant trying to kill a man by biting his finger. Here."

She stopped by a shelf of books. She tried to recall what little she knew of each of them. They had, of course, been catalogued and classified by the tech supports who ran the Vault but cataloguing systems would be of little use in trying to pinpoint specific historical events in the knotted spaghetti of the Venislarn intrusion on human affairs. Whether in three, four or seventy-six dimensions, it had created such convolutions that something as simple as the Dewey Decimal System would implode under the strain. Morag had to rely on other means to find the volume she required.

"Eeny meany miney... mo." She took a book out and opened it hopefully. "Oh, this one has pictures."

What are pictures, mother?

She hummed to herself. "You'll like pictures. Pictures are fun." She turned a page. "Okay, maybe not these ones..."

Rod bumped into Jayda down by catering services.

"You've got a..." He tapped his own shoulder.

Jayda looked, reached round and ripped off the flaccid prosthetic penis that had been glued to her shoulder blade where it poked through her desert khaki vest.

"I'm surprised you dare fall asleep anywhere near that woman," said Rod.

"It's okay," said Jayda. "Maybe I just pretend to be asleep sometimes and let it happen so I can get some physical human contact."

Jayda put a couple of cookies on a plate.

"Is that why you turned down the offer of a bed the other night?" she asked.

"Hmmm?" Rod barely recalled; he had been drunk at the time. "No. No, not really. I just…"

"She sometimes doesn't do it to guys she's got the hots for. Sometimes."

"Hots? Er. Me?"

Jayda smirked. "Do they teach you that bumbling posh boy act at school?"

"I'm not posh. I—"

Jayda put the limp dick on a table between baskets of knives and forks. "That's fifteen wangdoodles on this shoot already. It's good to keep count."

"Why?"

Jayda poured herself a coffee and offered Rod one. He shook his head.

"She's like a barometer for shit movies."

Jayda took her coffee and cookies and led the way into the special props area. She put the cookies down on a bench next to Skye, who was intently working on a six-foot-long section of rubbery tentacle with paint and brush. "So, on set, you've got to learn to spot the signs that you're working on a box office disaster."

"Is Langford James still barricaded in his room?" asked Skye, without looking up from her work.

"He is," said Rod.

"Friction between actors and the production team is definitely a red flag."

"Constant script rewrites or demands for rewrites," said Jayda. "That's another."

"Anything that's a sequel is gonna be bad from the start."

"Particularly if there's a colon in the title."

"Also applies if it's a prequel, remake, reboot or homage."

"I hate that word," said Jayda with an unexpected amount of passion.

Skye spun round on her chair. She wore a pair of magnifying glasses that made her eyes look huge, like a Japanese cartoon character. "You can call it an homage but that just means you've stolen stuff because you've got no imagination yourself." She flung an arm out to take in the set about them. "What is this film? Is it *Men in Black*? Is it the new *Hellboy*? It's got a bit of *James Bond*, some procedural spy stuff, but the monsters are straight out of *Pacific Rim* or *The Thing*. It's a mess. Is it supposed to be a parody?"

"Okay, okay. I get it," said Rod. "It's junk."

"But sometimes it's harder to spot," said Jayda, "when you're too close to a thing. That's when I use Skye as my barometer."

"Is this the dick thing again?" said Skye.

"It's like an automatic response," said Jayda. "Some sort of sixth sense. She started sculpting one the moment we landed in this country, before we even started work here. It's like it kicks in even when she's in proximity to movie garbage. Like a Geiger counter."

"It's true," said the prosthetic artist. She gave Rod an intent look, noticeably intent given that her eyes were currently the size of golf balls.

Rod's thoughts were suddenly elsewhere.

"It's a proximity warning," he said.

"Right," said Jayda.

"The nearer the source..."

The American women frowned.

"I've got to go," said Rod.

"What?"

"I've got to get my teapot!"

"Jeez, you British and—"

"We've been looking at this all wrong!" he said and ran out.

Nina and Mrs Fiddler wound the sidereal clock in the basement of Soho House. Its ticks reverberated out through the walls and returned as echoes that were indescribably louder than the original. Then the sound diminished into a quiet tick-tock that could have been any old clock and the two women went to see if the doorway to the otherwise non-existent part of the house had returned.

"Maybe it will open somewhere completely different this time," said Mrs Fiddler. But the doorway was, once more, at the end of the ground floor corridor.

Mrs Fiddler located a replacement sash and, satisfied that it would keep prying eyes and wandering fingers away, the two of them went through.

"I've never been given a gold star sticker," said the ex-teacher.

"Not even when you were at school?" said Nina.

"No. Not one."

Nina clucked. "Bad girl, huh?"

"I don't believe giving out stickers as rewards was really a thing back then."

"Right," said Nina. "No paper, just those crappy little blackboards to practise your handwriting on. Teachers with those silly black hats and a dozen whacks with the cane if you stepped out of line."

"My lord," said Mrs Fiddler tetchily, "what do you think school was like forty years ago?"

The oculus was where Nina had dropped it the day before. The room, perhaps apart from a fresh layer of plaster dust, was back to normal. There were no signs of damage from the rapid and near-fatal shrinkage it had previously undergone. Even the cobwebs in the corners and around the sash-window were undisturbed.

"Let's get to it," said Nina.

"To what?" said Mrs Fiddler.

"You've made enough notes in that book of yours by now. Surely, we can find any point in history we want."

"But the oculus only seems able to create a window between now and a fixed range of years – as though the two time periods are connected. We can't look back to the nineteen-twenties or the Cretaceous."

"Maybe it was designed that way," said Nina, unbothered. "Someone's got a real hankering for the age of powdered wigs."

"Or someone back then was particularly interested in this period of history. The here and now."

Nina thought about Trevor's Apocalyptic Teapot and the promises of death and destruction on this very day. She put those thoughts aside.

"We find out about Galton's guns and all their plans. We find out about the Maccabees. We see if we can find what they've been up to since."

Mrs Fiddler took out her 'History is Fun!' notebook.

"Right," she said and sat down on a crate to read.

As she entered the Think Tank laboratories, Kathy looked to Malcolm at the security duty.

"It's going to be a busy day today," she said, meaningfully.

"Chances of the end of the world?" said Malcolm.

She see-sawed her hand. "Fifty-fifty. Unless we can stop it."

Her phone binged.

Rod had sent her a series of photos. It seemed like someone had tried to create a Jackson Pollock in tomato ketchup on carpet. Rod wanted to know if they were dangerous Venislarn symbols. She almost laughed at his naivety and sent him a placating text.

Kathy entered *Polliqan Riti*'s storage area.

"*Shan-shan prui, Polliqan,*" she said.

Floating in his tank, *Polliqan Riti* did not move with the same vigour or purpose as he did in his virtual reality. Maybe he was dozing. Maybe ours was a Jupiter-like world of crushing gravity, compared to his native environment.

It didn't matter.

Kathy understood what she needed to do. She had discussed it with *Polliqan Riti* and with her colleagues, her *true* colleagues. *Polliqan Riti* had a destiny to fulfil – first in *Hath-No,* then back here on earth. In her bag, she had markers to write on the floor and images of the *Kal Frexo* runes necessary to transport *Polliqan Riti* away from this realm.

"It's your big day," she said to the blob in the tank. "A little earlier than planned, but events appear to be moving apace."

A fat rope of white tissue looped above the ooze and then disappeared again.

"We are very grateful for what you will do for us," she said. "What you will give us."

The Venislarn surfaced and a vaguely face-shaped lump extended toward her.

"Crippen... ai...?" it bubbled.

"Kryptonite. That's you, yes."

She set to work, drawing a banishment circle around the tank.

In the consular mission office, Rod carried Trevor's Apocalyptic Teapot, his eye constantly on the liquid level meter. The LCD readout gave the depth in millimetres, which had been fine so far. However, the mere act of moving around caused disturbances in the tea and made a nonsense of the readings.

He did his best. He carried the teapot on a tray into the reception on two steady hands and with his own pocket spirit level on the tray to check that he did not throw things out by tilting it. He even walked in a bent-kneed stoop to maintain a constant balance in his body.

"What you doing, bab?" said Lois over the reception counter.

"Trying to locate the source of the danger."

"Thought it might be some weird tea ceremony thing."

"No," he said. The tea in the pot, now about halfway full, sloshed minutely. The readings rose and fell.

"Flaming heck. This isn't working."

"What's not working?"

"I can't keep it level."

"You need a trolley," said Lois.

"Well, that would be swell but—"

"I've got a trolley," she said and, moments later, had one wheeled round into reception for him.

It was a proper tea lady trolley, of the sort they had when tea ladies were still a thing.

"That is brilliant," he said. "Deals with any variation in the Z axis as well."

"Does it?" said Lois, happily ignorant.

"This danger could come from above or below."

"As long as it's useful to you," she said.

"It's smashing," he said.

With the teapot perfectly still on the trolley, Rod read the level. He looked around and realised that the reception area was not at all big enough to take any further useful readings. He pressed the button for the lift.

"I'm taking it downstairs," he said.

"Just make sure that comes back in one piece," said Lois.

Morag turned the next page in the book.

"And the *Cha'dhu Forrikler*, who were big and pink and had lots of spikey bits—there's lots of spikey bits in this picture—picked their bravest and brightest subjects and sent them across the stars to

330

our little world. They travelled for miles and miles, for years and years and years. Look, here's another picture of them, crossing the black gulf of space to get all the way from their home to here."

Why did they come, mother?

"No one knows," continued Morag in her best bedtime story voice, "but the *Koloba*—that's the name of the emissaries the *Cha'dhu Forrikler* sent—settled here on this world, along with the *yon-bun* and the *croyi-takk* and the floppy and oozing *draybbea*. And they each found a place to make their home, at the bottom of the sea, deep in the forests or lurking in the dreams of children. And sometimes the Venislarn showed themselves. And sometimes the humans worshipped them. And sometimes the humans lost their freaking minds because the Venislarn, for the most part, were as ugly as a monkey's butt."

"What are you doing?" said Professor Omar.

Morag lifted the book in her lap. "Reading a story to junior here."

"My dear, I hardly think that's suitable story material for a baby nor can I imagine your unborn child being sufficiently developed to understand a single word you say. But since my second objection renders the first one moot, I suppose I have no grounds to complain. But... are you feeling well?"

"Perfectly fine, professor." She closed the book. "I was actually looking for something specific, a reference to a *mi'nasulu* found in the local area, possibly even captured or killed."

"Then you'll be a long time looking," said Omar. "There hasn't been one. I have written the definitive article on the *mi'nasulu* and they have never been encountered on these shores."

"But Kathy said—"

"Oh, Kathy *said?*" Omar's voice was suddenly and quite uncharacteristically harsh. "Well, if the blessed Dr Kaur says a *mi'nasulu* has been sighted you should defer to her, by all means."

"Hey, don't get snippy with me, man. I was just saying."

He adjusted his black-rimmed glasses and at least was sufficiently self-aware of his temper to make a little pantomime of it. "I do declare, Morag, I had more respect from you lot when I *didn't* work here."

The tools may have been unorthodox (a teapot, a trolley, a liquid level measure, a spirit level, a marker pen, a tape measure, a map and a compass) but Rod found a meditative pleasure in his work. He picked out a starting position on the wide, ground floor concourse of the Library of Birmingham, between the escalators and the café. He marked the spot with the marker pen and took a reading. He then wheeled the trolley directly north five metres, waited a minute for the ripples to subside and took a second reading. He performed three more, in the other cardinal directions.

By this time, a small crowd, including a number of genuine library visitors had gathered to watch him. A woman came up to him.

"Is it art?" she asked.

"Excuse me?" he said.

She pointed over to where another young woman was standing.

"My friend says this is a piece of performance art but I said you were probably dowsing for water."

Rod looked at his trolley of equipment. "Does it look like I'm dowsing for water?"

"It's hard to imagine what else you might be doing."

"Aye. Well, very well done. You got it. Go tell your friend. Now, if you'll excuse me, you're disturbing the, um, ley lines."

He jotted down each of the measurements. It was only a couple of millimetres in difference but the tea levels were decidedly higher towards the south and, to a lesser degree, to the east. Rod took a south easterly bearing, measured out the five metres and checked the tea levels again.

"To the untrained eye," said Morag, approaching, "this would look like some kind of mental breakdown."

"It's not," he said.

"Or a really cheap mid-life crisis."

"I'm not that old," he said and then remembering they were roughly the same age added, "and neither are you."

"No?"

"There's life in the old dog yet."

Morag's eyes widened. Rod realised his immediate mistake but the words were said and there was no backtracking to be done. Morag burst into laughter.

"Always the right words for the occasion," she said.

He shut his eyes and shook his head. "I didn't mean..."

"Nope," she smiled. "I'm off to the Think Tank, just to check out what Kathy knows about this *mi'nasulu* they supposedly killed back in the day."

"Okay, I'm..." He felt unable to explain. "... doing things with a magical teapot."

"Great," she said and left him to it.

Watching Mrs Fiddler working the oculus, Nina could almost believe she knew what she was doing.

"But you can't read Venislarn," said Nina.

"I don't need to understand it," said Mrs Fiddler. "The relationship between these markings around the outside works just like algebra."

"Ugh, that's such a teacher thing to say."

"You mean true and helpful." She twisted the middle hoop to align the markings. There was a ringing, more felt than heard, and the light of another time shone through the oculus.

"The day Galton came," said Mrs Fiddler.

Through the oculus, they heard voices in the corridor outside. They followed and found Matthew Boulton, Erasmus Darwin and Samuel Galton walking towards the cellar stairs. Galton carried his long gun. It was a scene they had already witnessed from another angle. Nina tugged on Mrs Fiddler's arm.

"Wait. He only took one of the bullet ball things with him. The other is..."

Nina pushed her towards the parlour. The servants had finished tidying up. The mesh-wrapped marble sat on a polished table.

"We could take that," said Nina.

"We could not," said Mrs Fiddler. "Don't mess with time."

Nina dragged Mrs Fiddler to the table and thrust her own arm through the oculus. Unpleasant vibrations shot up her arm as she forced it across the threshold. There was an unsettling shriek from the fabric of the house and it shed a mist of dust on both of them. Nina had to peer through the oculus to aim her hand, which had lost all sense of touch. She grabbed the blue sphere and pulled back quickly, but a fresh resistance held her hand in the 18th century.

"It doesn't want to come," she said.

"I don't want it to come," said Mrs Fiddler.

The walls around them shuddered with a noise like bricks grinding together.

Nina braced herself against Mrs Fiddler's shoulder and grunted, "time... is not... the boss of me!"

The grinding grew much louder and chunks of mortar rained on their shoulders.

"I rather think it is," said Mrs Fiddler.

"No," Nina growled and, not knowing which would give first – her strength, the oculus or Mrs Fiddler's arm – she yanked back and fell away with the marble in her fist. She stumbled and sat, hissing and groaning.

"Are you hurt?" said Mrs Fiddler.

"Pins and needles. Pins and needles."

She dropped the marble into her good hand and tried to shake some life back into the other.

"And what did you achieve?" asked Mrs Fiddler.

"We have one of their bullet things."

"And the course of history has been changed."

"One bullet." She passed it to Mrs Fiddler.

"But this is..."

Nina got to her feet. Her arm felt like it belonged to someone else.

"It looks like blue john," said Mrs Fiddler.

"It's just rock?" She snatched it back and held it up for a better look. Inside the wire mesh was a blue-purple rock with flecks of yellow. "It's got to be more than that." She searched for magical knots in the metal mesh, theurgical twists in the weave, but there was nothing. It was just a harness to hold the spherical stone. "What the hell?"

"Galton Junior's father owned the gun works on Steelhouse Lane. If we have our dates right, Galton here would be a full partner by this point in time."

"They made these there?" said Nina.

"Probably."

"Do they still exist?"

Mrs Fiddler chuckled. "The Gun Quarter's still there, but the old works closed down a long, long time ago. They sold the gun business on in... ooh, the early nineteenth century. I'd have to look it up."

"Could you?"

"I have a book in the office." Mrs Fiddler led the way out. "Assuming of course that your meddling in history hasn't changed the world beyond all recognition..."

"One bullet," Nina muttered and followed her.

Rod had a bearing to work from. His measurements in the Library concourse had identified a somewhat south-westerly heading as the source of the danger. He stood with pen, paper and phone calculator trying to make the readings tell him more. The liquid level changes over five metres distance were small but significant. If Kathy and Omar's identification of the enchantments on the teapot was accurate, then the difference between current tea level and total disaster was a matter of centimetres.

Rod calculated tea level changes divided by physical distance, multiplied by the pot's remaining volume. He estimated the gradient twice and got different answers both times but the signs were clear: assuming the tea rose in direct relation to danger, the source was definitely within the city and probably no more than a mile away.

Rod pushed his tea trolley out into the street. He wheeled around the building site in the centre of the square and once he was past the noise and smell of cement dust and across the other side of Broad Street, he found a level area of pavement and took another reading.

"Oh."

He stopped. He considered the variables and looked at the measurements again. The tea level had shot up, by a good cupful or more.

Wherever it was, it wasn't far. He looked round. The direct line from the Library to this point was now blocked by the Birmingham

Municipal Bank building. He looked at his map and considered where the line continued to.

He knew before he looked exactly where it went.

Rod didn't believe in coincidences, but he did believe the universe had its natural rhythms. Experience had taught him that a soldier who removed his helmet in a firefight would get shot in the head. Anyone publicly counting down the days to the end of their tour of duty was unlikely to see that end, at least in one piece. The universe had dramatic timing and a sense of irony. If you lived long enough, you could see the punches as they came.

The line on the map ran straight through the Mailbox.

"Right," he said with a weary sigh and pushed his trolley down the sloping pavement towards the Mailbox.

I feel it when you talk to other people, mother, said Morag's unborn on the uCab journey to the Think Tank.

"Feel what?" she said.

How you feel. The warmth and the badness. You like that man, Rod.

"Yes. Well, he's a lovely man. Easy to like."

That's what the woman, Nina, said.

"When?"

When you all met with the mmm-mmmm Handmaiden of Prein and Nina changed everyone's memories.

"She did what?"

Should I have told you, mother?

"What happened? What did Nina do to my memories?"

She told you that you should ask Rod out because he was a lovely but boring man.

"What did she do that for?"

You are angry now, mother.

"I don't know what I am," she said honestly. "Tell me what happened."

Rod steered his trolley in through the basement car park entrance and took the lift to the ground floor. The production company security guys gave him odd looks, but he said, "It's just a pot of tea," and they let the peculiar Brit through.

336

Most of the production team were up in the higher levels of the closed shopping centre, preparing to film the rooftop scenes.

Jayda was counting props out in moulded foam packaging.

"When you said you needed to get your teapot, I thought it was one of those euphemisms. You're all about euphemisms, you guys."

"Bugger," said Rod, his attention fully on the tea level readings.

"What?" she said.

"It's high. It's very high."

Jayda watched him for several seconds. "I've seen other soldiers do this kind of thing. It's a cry for help."

Rod wheeled the trolley further across the atrium and took another reading. A woman with a clipboard and a walkie-talkie, gave him worried looks and spoke into her radio.

"It's fine, all right?" Rod attempted to reassure her. "I'm just looking for..."

"What are you looking for?" said Jayda, sauntering over. Skye had emerged from her workshop also, wiping drying paint on a cloth at her belt.

"I'm looking for... something dangerous," he said.

"With a pot of tea," said Skye.

"Has this got anything to do with that creepy-ass Hogwarts door we found yesterday?" said Jayda.

"What Hogwarts door?"

"The one on the train track."

Rod's brow wrinkled in confusion. "We didn't find anything in the tunnel yesterday. It was just..."

He paused. He remembered going down the tunnels under the Mailbox with Skye and Jayda and following the train tracks, and he remembered being out again and having the very strong notion that there had been nothing down there of note and definitely nothing worth reporting. He recalled each of the elements clearly and, yet, there were beats missing in the rhythm of that memory, a scene shot out of sequence.

"You remember where that door was?" he said.

"Absolutely," said Jayda.

"We going exploring again?" said Skye.

Rod saw the building manager enter the atrium from the far stairs.

"Hey," said Rod and pushed his trolley over to him.

The man looked at the trolley and the teapot. "People aren't -"

"The tunnels under the building," said Rod. "We need to go down again."

"Ah. My line manager told me that I shouldn't have done that."

"I wasn't really asking."

"It's health and safety."

"You want to give us some hard hats?"

The man squirmed.

"Tell you what," said Rod, turning him round and physically propelling the man towards the service door, "you phone your line manager and I'll call the police for backup and we'll see who wins."

The building manager was normally a stickler for rules, but he resented the disrespectful tone taken by the corporate functionary who had phoned to reprimand him for 'failing to consult proper authority'. Remembering that call, he shot a weary glance at Rod and his entourage of pushy American women, turned to face the guard station and stared silently at a ring of keys hung on a peg behind the desk.

Rod would have to abandon the trolley at the top of the stairs. He paused to inspect the teapot. The level of tea had risen several centimetres since he'd left the Library of Birmingham. It was just a finger width below the mark that supposedly heralded complete disaster. He should have been worried, but the deep aroma of perfectly brewed tea was a great comfort.

"What are you, in fact, doing?" asked the building manager.

"Checking the tea," said Rod.

"And, er, what does the tea tell you?"

"Bad things mainly." He looked at Jayda and Skye. "You two don't have to come."

"You think an ex-marine can't handle some creepy underground door?" said Jayda.

"I was more thinking of Skye," said Rod.

"Aw," said Skye, as though he had just said the cutest thing ever. "No. I'm coming. It's either this or make dicks."

"Fair enough."

They followed the same route down into the tunnels as the day before. Rod remembered it now, and there were even footprints in the fine layer of grime on the floor. When they reached the narrow train platform, the air was warm like breath.

"We came down here," said Rod.

"You really don't remember?" said Jayda.

"I don't know," he said. "It's odd."

"PTSD."

"No," said Rod.

"Or a brain tumour," said Skye, cheerfully.

He dropped onto the rails of the disused track. There were no lights overhead and he had to use his torch. He recalled that much from the previous visit also, but not...

"That it?" he said, shining his torch on the dark archway further along the track.

"Yup," said Jayda, helping Skye down from the platform.

Rod unpopped the pop stud on his underarm holster. "Let's take a look. Again."

The teapot in his hand glooped and bubbled. The depth of tea was too disturbed to read but it looked bloody high.

Nina was still shaking her arm as they crossed the lawn back to the gift shop. Mrs Fiddler's tank top-wearing assistant manned the till, doing a newspaper crossword on the counter.

"It's been bedlam in here," said Tank Top.

"Has it, dear?" said Mrs Fiddler, gently pushing him aside so she could root around in the shelves under the counter. She glanced at the crossword. "Five down is 'twister.'"

"Sorry?" said Tank Top.

"'Eddy is a con artist', twister." She came up with a worn and creased book. "Here," she said, speaking to Nina. "'Upon his retirement in eighteen oh-four, Samuel John Galton sold his stake in the gun manufactory in Steelhouse Lane to the Birmingham Progressive Company.'"

Mrs Fiddler tapped the page. There was a photograph on the page of a letter or some document full of legalese. It would haven't held Nina's attention for more than a second but for a picture printed at the top of the document.

"What's that?"

"The Progressive Company logo," said Mrs Fiddler. "A hand holding a Birmingham screwdriver."

"It's a hammer."

"I know," said Mrs Fiddler. "A Birmingham screwdriver. It's meant to be an insult to the mentality of the locals, but I think it's a poetic expression of the Law of the Instrument."

"The what?"

"You know. To a hammer, every problem looks like a nail."

"You're weird," said Nina. She pointed at the logo. "I've seen that before."

"It's the same as the one on the top of the Birmingham coat of arms."

The logo was a simplistic, almost stylised arm, emerging from the top of a castle turret brandishing a hammer.

"The hammer," said Nina, thoughtfully.

"The Maccabees?" suggested Mrs Fiddler.

"I've seen it before," said Nina.

The doorway was reinforced with steel plates, the archway around it was a single piece of cast bronze. The symbols cast into the bronze didn't want to stay still.

"I still think it looks like the doorway to the mines of Moria," said Skye.

"Huh?" said Rod, gingerly prodding the door. It swung open.

"*Lord of the Rings*," said Skye. "Why don't you like people saying you sound like Sean Bean?"

"Who says I don't?" said Rod.

"You did. Last time we were here."

There were faint scratch marks around the lock of the door, the kind that might be left by an expert lockpicker. Rod put a hand to his tie clip lock picks.

"You seriously don't remember, do you?" said Jayda.

"I do not," he said. "Anything you want to remind me about before we go in?"

"It's all just pots and containers. Sort of like the Three Bears' cottage in reverse."

"In what way?"

Jayda pushed the door open fully and led the way in. The railway tunnel outside was, as expected, a place of dirt and crud and the accumulation of decades of oil and grease. The corridor they stepped into was notably clean and well-maintained, verging on clinical. It led down through a doorway and then into a single large chamber with numerous alcoves.

The tiling and layout reminded Rod of school changing rooms. But in terms of the equipment and storage containers in the room, Rod was quite baffled. There were a number of storage drums by the wall—a quick rattle of these showed they were empty—and lengths of hose to connect those drums. There was no indication of what they had once contained apart from a splash of electric blue liquid on the floor.

Rod crouched before it.

"It's okay," said Jayda. "It's solid."

It was. The thick liquid had dried to a rock-hard splodge.

"Some sort of residue or secretion."

"That's what you said last time," said Skye.

"I was a clever and insightful chap," he said.

In the alcoves were other storage containers. Inspecting the nearest—which Rod quickly realised was both the smallest and the oldest—he saw that it was in fact a nest of containers. At the centre, the rusted remains of a metal tin lay at the bottom of a glass jar. The jar stood inside a clay pot, embedded in a deep layer of what appeared to be salt.

He moved on to the container in the next alcove, which was at least twice the size of the first although much the same. He put his hands on the rim to look inside. Steel, glass (broken), a layer of salt and a thick clay pot marked with lines of Venislarn writing.

Rod took out his phone to photograph the markings. He paused, struck by a thought, and scrolled through yesterday's pictures.

He had taken four pictures of the pottery urns. One stood on the floor, the size of a hogshead beer barrel. The last was taller than himself.

"Increasing in size."

"Exactly," said Jayda. "Getting bigger as they get newer. Like whatever they needed to store, there was more and more of it as time went by."

"Or whatever it was, this *Crippen-Ai* got bigger and bigger," said Rod grimly, "and needed a bigger container."

As he moved, hot tea splashed over his hand. The pot was nearly full to the brim.

"This is a bad place."

"Ya think?" said Skye sarcastically.

There were pipe taps set into the bottom of the largest vat-sized container. There were screw connectors and a valve release mechanism. Rod looked to the tubes and the barrels. Whatever was in the container was being drained off. For disposal? For some use?

He rapped on the pottery outside of the vat. It made a dull uninformative sound.

"Is it still in here?"

"You checked," said Jayda and pointed at a box that had been pulled into place next to the vat.

Rod stood on the box so he could reach the vat's flat, circular lid. It was made of clay too, an odd and impractical material for the lid of such a large vessel. It had been lifted up and pushed back far enough to open a ten-centimetre gap. Rod touched the lip of the vat. He felt ridges of dried wax coated with a slick liquid. He shone his torch inside. The angles were all wrong, but he was sure it was empty.

"Hmmm," he said and stepped down.

"And that's when you said we should head back and you'd tell your superiors," said Jayda.

"Aye," he said. "Whatever it was is long gone."

"What?" said Jayda.

"It's empty."

Jayda shook her head slowly. "You didn't say that last time."

Rod pointed up. "I looked."

"No." She took a nervous step towards the door. "You went up. You tried the lid. It creaked but you said it was secure and then... What was in there?"

"Nothing. Slime."

His torch beam passed over Skye. There was a blue smear on her blouse.

"You've got something on you," Rod said.

Skye looked at herself. "Urgh. Where did that...?"

Jayda was already shining her torch upward.

The ceiling was white, lumpy and slowly pulsating. A creature of white viscous rubbery material clung to the ceiling, filling it wall to wall. A filmy blue ooze dripped from its massive body.

"Oh... oh..." said Skye, panting desperately.

Tea trickled in a constant stream out of the teapot spout.

"To the exit," said Rod. "Quietly, swiftly."

"Oh... oh..." panted Skye, rooted to the spot with fear. Jayda took hold of her to steer her away.

He reached for his wallet and the laminated phrase cards. His brain had already leaped ahead and was shuffling through the mental images of them.

"*Skeidl hraim yeg courxean*," he said. It sounded right. He couldn't even remember what it meant.

Skye finally ran out of ohs, took a deep breath and screamed. The shapeless *Crippen-Ai* gathered itself.

Jayda shoved Skye hard towards the door. *Crippen-Ai* dropped, enveloping Jayda and crushing her to the floor. Rod leapt. He trod on the creature—one step, two steps—feet barely grazing it and ran to the door, gathering Skye as he did. He dropped the teapot, its spout now gushing like a garden hose.

He pushed Skye out onto the railway track and tried to pull the door closed behind them.

"No handle!" he shouted at it. "All the bloody magic words in the world but you couldn't put on a door handle!"

The door was wrested from Rod's grip by something with surprising strength.

Jayda stood in the doorway. The bulk of *Crippen-Ai* filled the corridor behind her.

"Jayda!" yelled Skye.

"I'm not sure if that's Jayda..." began Rod, hoping he was wrong.

Jayda reached out her arms toward Rod, like a child asking for a hug. He stepped backward onto the tracks but she rushed forward and grabbed the gun in his holster.

"No."

She waved his pistol in the air, upside down but with her finger on the trigger. Rod twisted away as she fired. The shot ricocheted loudly down the tunnel. Rod grabbed Jayda's hand, depressed the gun's magazine release and tore the magazine away. She fired the round that was already in the chamber, and she was out of shots.

A coil of white muscle rose up behind Jayda then darted downward toward Rod. He backed off rapidly, the pistol magazine in his hand.

"Run!" he shouted at Skye.

He propelled her onto her feet and pulled her toward the exit.

"Jayda!" shouted Skye.

"She's not with us anymore," said Rod. "Now, run!"

The mass of the blob creature surged out onto the train tracks, Jayda a step ahead of it, its flesh plugged into hers.

Morag swiped herself through the hidden door at the Think Tank science museum and entered the secret laboratory. Malcolm, on guard, gave her only the briefest of glances. He looked thoroughly bored. There was little excitement in being the futile first line of defence against horrors he was forbidden to harm, restrain or even speak crossly to.

She walked down the length of the facility. The frosted double doors at the far end were unlocked. Kathy, it seemed, had finally gone over Omar's head to gain some research time with the creature, *Polliqan Riti*.

Kathy looked up with a startled quickness when Morag entered.

"Catch you unawares?" said Morag.

Kathy's expression softened. "No one knocks in this place."

She was on her hands and knees, adding symbols and glyphs to the occult circle she had drawn around *Polliqan Riti*'s tub. She was breathing heavily as though she had been working with unusual haste.

344

"What's this?" said Morag.

"Contingency planning," said Kathy. "*Polliqan Riti* here—*skep su'fragn*, my lord—is a valuable commodity but a dangerous one as well. Did I tell you he tried to eat me earlier this week?"

"No."

"Made the mistake of touching him. And then, because he's a utility monster with touch-telepathy, I felt an uncontrollable urge to let him drown me."

"How did you escape?"

Kathy smiled with pert amusement. "I'll tell you one day."

Morag stepped forward to read the symbols Kathy was drawing with red marker.

"Aren't those the lost runes of *Kal Frexo*?" she asked.

"Can I help you with something?" said Kathy.

"Oh." She tore her eyes away from the writing. "I wanted to ask you about the *mi'nasulu*."

"The one Nina claims to have observed in Georgian England through a supposed viewing device none of us have seen."

"You don't believe her?"

Kathy said nothing and added another symbol to her circle.

"Regardless," said Morag, "I've looked in all the major books and asked Professor Omar and I can't find any record of it."

"Maybe it doesn't exist."

"But you mentioned one."

"When?"

"Sunday."

"Did I?"

"We were in the bog, hunting that *bondook* shambler and you pointed out that one had been captured down that way a long time ago."

Kathy sat back on her haunches and met Morag's gaze levelly. "Huh. I never knew you listened to things I said."

Nina gave a gasp of sudden recollection. "Oh, my God!"

"What on earth is it?" said Mrs Fiddler.

"Is everything all right?" asked Tank Top by the gift shop till.

"It's..." Nina clicked her fingers repeatedly and pointed. "The arm and hammer. It's the logo of that company."

"Well, yes," said Mrs Fiddler, holding the book open further. "It says here."

"Not *that* company. *That* company. The one doing all the building in the city."

"Forward," said Tank Top.

"Forward," said Nina. "Forward Management."

"Oh, yes," said Mrs Fiddler vaguely. "But I suppose something like that could be quite a common emblem. I believe it has a historical link to Tamworth or something."

But Nina was no longer listening. She had her eyes closed and was doing her very best to remember. Things had been said. Nuggets of fact floated in front of her conscious mind waiting for her to link them.

"Is this important?" said Mrs Fiddler but Nina violently shushed her.

The facts only half-linked in her mind. There were gaps. A company. A secret society. A plot to destroy the Venislarn. A different agenda working alongside that of the consular mission. Buried secrets. A secret history. A plot.

"The wand!" said Nina.

"What of it?" said Mrs Fiddler.

"He lost the wand. He ..." She groaned. "Fucking bitch."

"Language, Nina Seth."

She pulled out her phone. "You have a car? You can drive."

"Of course, I can drive."

Nina didn't know who to call first. She wanted to call everyone. She dragged Mrs Fiddler to the door.

"Hurry, woman. We have to stop her before she... I don't know what it is, but we have to stop her."

Kathy added the final glyphs to the banishment circle around *Polliqan Riti*'s tank.

"I guess I must have been mistaken," she said.

"Really?" said Morag.

"Don't look so surprised. I thought we'd found a *mi'nasulu* in Moseley Bog. That's 'we' collectively, as an organisation. Obviously before my time. I must have misheard or misread. *Mis'aygo. Mnorh-elu*. It was one them."

Morag laughed and sat back against a desk. It was a weary laugh and a tired slump on the desk.

Morag had looked tired a lot of late. Too many long days and too many couch potato nights to get over the days.

"I don't believe you," said Morag.

"Oh?" said Kathy innocently.

"You always—*always*—strike me as infallible. You don't make mistakes."

Kathy grinned in relief. "It's all a carefully maintained act. I make mistakes all the time. Say things I shouldn't. Make the wrong decision. Medical doctors have to give off this air of superiority—"

"Yeah, you do."

"It's all part of the job... I'm just saying, we all probably make the same kinds of idiotic mistakes as each other."

The words seemed to have an acute and sudden impact on Morag. She didn't just look tired; she looked emotional, even close to tears.

"You okay?" said Kathy.

That didn't have a positive effect. Why would it? "You okay?" was just code for "let it all out." But Morag didn't let it all out. She had always struck Kathy as stronger than that, more pig-headed than that.

"My life is a mess," Morag said slowly. "And 'mess' doesn't even begin to cover it. My living situation... My... housemate, I guess."

"You have a place in Bournville, right?"

"I moved. But even when I was in Bournville... Do you know how I ended up in Birmingham?"

"I heard," said Kathy. "Some issues in Edinburgh."

"I killed a Handmaiden of *Prein*. Murdered her, I guess. And her sisters have been out to get me ever since. Another died in my Bournville flat. That was Dr Ingrid Spence's fault, but they still hold me accountable."

"But you're still alive," said Kathy. "That's impressive!"

"Yeah, but only for one reason."

"Uh-huh?"

Kathy did a tour of the tub and double-checked her work. The spell was ready, all she needed was for Morag to leave so she could get on with it. Kathy hadn't yet worked out how exactly she was

347

going to explain the disappearance of the Think Tank's resident Venislarn, but since the Venislarn in question was an anathema to the *em-shadt* rulers of the city and Professor Sheikh Omar was breaking all manner of rules in keeping him here, Kathy felt she could create a story that would work to her benefit.

"Can I tell you something?" said Morag and then seemed to shush her own belly for some unknown reason.

"Of course, you can," said Kathy automatically.

"It's... kinda scandalous."

"It's okay. You can trust me. I'm a doctor."

Morag breathed in deeply through her nose.

"I'm pregnant."

Kathy looked up. Her first thought was that this was a surprise. Her second thought was that it was so very obvious. Morag's tiredness, her puffiness, the lackadaisical attitude to work of a woman who knew her days in the job were potentially numbered.

"Congratulations?" Kathy suggested.

Morag's face was still. She hadn't finished her disclosure.

"I need to tell you this in confidence," said Morag, "like doctor-patient confidentiality, yeah? Cos, the only people who know, the only *humans* who know are Omar and Maurice and they're kinda driving me nuts."

"You're not my patient. But I am your friend," said Kathy.

"I'm not just pregnant. I'm pregnant with the *kaatbari*."

Kathy was stunned. "How?"

Morag blinked.

"I mean..." Kathy flapped. "*How?*"

"A guy called Drew who's dead now but was a proxy for *Yo-Morgantus*... It's his. It's theirs. It's complicated."

Kathy remained stunned. She could only stare at Morag in disbelief.

"Please say something," said Morag. "You're meant to be a doctor. You're making this far worse."

"I take it back," Kathy said hollowly.

"What?"

"We don't all make the same idiotic mistakes."

"Gee, thanks."

Kathy took a mental hold on herself. She went to Morag, held her arms reassuringly.

"This is going to be fine."

"Really isn't," said Morag.

"Just let me have a think," said Kathy. "And work out what to do." She took out her phone.

The marshmallow blob *Crippen-Ai* pursued Rod and Skye up the stairs, rolling on a carpet of slime with a speed that just seemed unfair. Rod was not a man built for long-distance chases and he huffed as they ran. The only consolation he could find in the situation was that he at least knew where *Crippen-Ai* was and that it hadn't disappeared down the tunnels into some dark hidey-hole. It really wasn't much of a consolation at all.

Running next to Rod, Skye panted "I don't understand... I don't understand", over and over again. He had no words to offer her.

His phone found a signal again as they climbed the last flight of stairs before the concertina gate. He had the call lined up and spoke directly to the mission switchboard.

"This is Campbell. Incursion event beneath Mailbox shopping centre. Blob creature—"

"Blob creature?" said the operator.

"Aye! Blob creature. What do you want me to say? White. Slimy. A blob. *Crippen-Ai*. We need total shutdown on the Mailbox—hang on."

He staggered up the last steps into the lower basement and dragged the concertina gate across the entrance behind him and Skye. Jayda and the fatberg of a monster were coming round the turn below.

"Is there a problem?" said the building manager.

Rod grabbed the chain and padlock and threaded it through the gate. He pulled back, moving his hands out of reach as Jayda arrived.

"Do not try to stop us," she said, pulling the chain back, trying to snatch it through before he could padlock it.

Rod maintained his grip and slipped the padlock through two hoops. The soft bulk of the creature folded round Jayda and pushed against the gate. Rod snapped the padlock into place and threw himself back as the blob pushed itself through the gate in diamond-shaped sections.

"Run!" he yelled at Skye and the stupefied building manager. "Seriously! I shouldn't need to repeat myself! Run! Don't stop!"

Rod had no current plan apart from running.

As they made for the stairs up into the shopping centre, Rod heard the metallic creak of a gate slowly giving way to an unstoppable force.

As Mrs Fiddler drove down the Great Hampton Road, Nina tried Rod's number again. Instead of going straight to voicemail this time, it actually rang.

"—and get everyone out. What? Hello?" This last word was loud and into the phone.

"Rod? I think we have a problem."

"You think? We found it," he said, a tone in his voice, not fear exactly but a heightened mania. "We found your monster under the Mailbox."

"She wiped your memory, didn't she?"

"What? There's this thing. A blob monster."

"*Crippen-Ai.*"

"Maybe. I think it's been growing."

"How much?"

"I'm just working on containing the situation. This thing. It's not fair game, is it?"

"I don't know."

There was a loud noise and the call ended. Nina stared at the phone.

"The Mailbox, yes?" said Mrs Fiddler.

"I think we're too late," said Nina.

"Well, we won't know unless we try." Mrs Fiddler took a sharp right turn, cutting in front of a bus coming the other way and going through the arches under Snow Hill the wrong way down a one-way street. Several horns beeped but nothing hit them.

Nina held onto the car door as she was buffeted around and phoned Morag. This time, she didn't get put through to a warzone.

"Hey, Nina."

"Where are you?"

"The Think Tank. With Kathy. Why?"

"Shit."

"Language," said Mrs Fiddler.

"What's the matter?" said Morag.

"Right. Don't freak out," said Nina.

"Er... Why would I?"

"What's she doing?"

"Who?"

"Kathy."

"Putting a circle of protection around *Polliqan Riti*. Um, wards. He's a fairly dangerous character. What exactly are you doing, Kathy?"

Nina thought for a second. She only knew *Polliqan Riti* from what Morag and Kathy had said. A creature of pure muscle and brain, a shapeless blob...

"*Polliqan Riti* is the same as *Crippen-Ai*," she said.

"Are you sure?" said Morag.

"Yeah, because..." Nina paused as Mrs Fiddler bounced across the junction with Newhall Street, ignoring the traffic lights. "I don't know what's going on. But Kathy knew about the *mi'nasulu* and no one knew about them except those Lunar Society guys or whatever they became. And the company that bought up the gunmakers, that's Kathy's family's company. Listen, I don't know how they got her a job with the mission."

"Ah," said Morag.

"Ah?"

Kathy held a gun in her hand, a small pistol.

Morag felt an inappropriate impulse to laugh. You just didn't see people carrying guns in the UK. Yes, Rod had a handgun, but he was different, ex-SAS, a mountain-shaped action man, the acceptable face of government sanctioned violence. But not other people. Not ordinary people. Not fun and curvy Dr Kathy Kaur. On her it looked ridiculous.

"What's going on?" said Morag.

Nina said something on the phone that Morag had let drift away from her ear. Morag lowered the phone but didn't end the call.

"Do you want to hurt me, Kathy?" she said for the benefit of Nina.

What's going on, mother? said her unborn.

Kathy gave Morag a deeply irritated look. "What did Nina say? You can turn that off, by the way."

Morag did as she was told. "Something about a secret society from Georgian times. I didn't fully understand. It sounded like some conspiracy nonsense to me but then..." She gestured carefully at the pistol.

"I'm not a fan of weapons but these bullets... Venislarn killers."

"It's a real thing?"

Kathy nodded. "I've just heard from our team down at the Mailbox. Rod let *Crippen-Ai* loose, which was a stupid thing to do. We're running out of time now. If *Yo-Morgantus* finds out that *Crippen-Ai* is in the city, he'll tear it apart to get to him."

"Because he's a threat to the Venislarn. He's toxic. And *Polliqan Riti* is like *Crippen-Ai* in some way."

Kathy moved to put the tank between her and Morag. "*Polliqan Riti* isn't like *Crippen-Ai*. He is *Crippen-Ai*."

"Yeah? You're going to need to explain that to me."

"Timelines," said Kathy. "The Venislarn don't experience time like us. *Polliqan Riti* came to us, came to the consular mission, as a refugee from some distant hell but he has a destiny to fulfil. We know it because *Crippen-Ai* told us." Kathy held out her hand, so it was barely an inch above the surface of *Polliqan Riti's* tank. A pseudo-limb rippled just beneath her but didn't try to touch her. "We have come to an understanding. I'm sending him home."

"And what do you get out of that?"

"*Crippen-Ai*. In the future. His future. Our past. Two hundred and forty years of his secretions. Enough to build an arsenal."

"You're seriously going to make war on the Venislarn? With poisonous goo?"

"We have to." She pointed with her gun at Morag's belly. "Doubly so now."

Is she going to hurt us, mother?

Morag put her hands protectively over her stomach. Kathy's face darkened. The mother of the anti-Christ showing that she cared for the monster growing inside her...

352

"While you flipping quislings just keep appeasing and appeasing and giving ground, some of us are actually prepared to fight," Kathy continued. "The war is nearly on us."

"Why are you telling me this? Do you plan to kill me?"

Kathy smiled, not an evil smile but the smile of someone who knows they're the cleverest person in the room. As smiles went, they were probably quite similar.

"I don't need to kill you, Morag."

Kathy passed the pistol from her good hand to the one in the sling. Then she pulled a wand from her pocket. Morag had seen it before, in the lobby of the Cube. It was the *yellis* wand, the mind-wiper.

"Wait," said Morag.

"*Hyet-pa!*"

Bright light filled the room.

Nina pointed at a coned-off lane.

"Here! Go here!"

"We're not allowed through here," said Mrs Fiddler but took the lane anyway. "I really don't know where I am. These roadworks have me all turned around."

"We need to go back up there," said Nina, pointing in the general direction of the Think Tank. "We've got to save Morag."

"I can turn at that roundabout there."

"Whatever!" said Nina impatiently.

Nina put a call through to the office to alert the security teams at the Think Tank.

With Skye and the building manager at his side, Rod pushed through a service door into the shopping centre atrium of the Mailbox. A film company security guard nearby whirled.

"What the hell, man!"

Rod ignored him, went to the nearest fire alarm point and smashed the glass. A strident alarm began to whoop.

Someone had evidently called a lunch break or something because the atrium was already full of production staff going about their business on the atrium floor and in the workspaces they'd built in the unused retail units. At the sound of the alarm, people looked up and around. No one made for the exits. In Rod's experience, no one ever did. They'd all wait to see what everyone else did.

He huffed and stomped towards the nearest Tammy-lite, grabbed the megaphone she was holding and addressed the building.

"This is not a drill. Your lives are in danger. Go to the exit. There! Now!"

People started drifting. Smart people started running. A couple of the security guys and one of the grips had moved towards Rod. They approached cautiously, like he was a dangerous nutter and about to kick off.

"This is real," he said. "There's a... gas leak. This whole place could go up. Help the others out." This last comment worked. They were the kind of guys who needed a job to do, who needed to feel they were part of the solution and not just helpless citizens. Rod waved at one of the security dudes. "The hotel. They've got to evacuate."

He turned to locate the building manager. "Hey!"

The man looked at him, stunned. Rod pointed to the back of the shopping centre, to the stairs and shutdown escalators. "All the restaurants, the bars. They need to evacuate."

"But what...?"

"What's going on?" said Taylor Graham.

The actor, dressed in the sharp suit of Agent Jack Steele, had jogged up. A gaggle of worried production staff were fussing after him.

"What are you doing?" said Rod. "Get out. Can you not hear the alarm?"

"Is this some Venislarn shit?" asked the actor.

"Jesus. Have you not learned your lesson from the last time?"

A distant person caught Rod's eye. He raised the megaphone to his mouth. "You! Put down the pastry! You're supposed to be running, not attacking the buffet!"

There was the explosive crumple of wood and the rolling blob that was *Crippen-Ai* slid onto the set. Its path cut across the main doors at the front of the building and the dozens of people who had not yet escaped that way fell back running and shouting.

"Jesus in heaven," swore Taylor softly. "What is that thing?"

"Bad news."

Jayda ran alongside *Crippen-Ai*, linked to it by a length of white goo-flesh.

"It's like the Marshmallow Man but, like, melted," whispered Taylor.

Skye grabbed Rod's arm. "I don't know what's going on, but I would like this to stop now."

"We can take it," said Taylor with far more confidence than the situation deserved.

"Punk ass bitch—ggh!—is going down," said Pupfish.

The samakha youth wore the motion capture suit and, over the top, his character's hideous coat.

"Agent Jack Steele could knock up some explosive devices no problem," said Taylor.

"You're not Agent Jack Steele!"

"Course not," said Taylor, offended. "But you are."

"Containment," said Rod. "This is about containment. Let's try not to make things worse."

"My lord!" bellowed a voice from on high.

Looking up, Rod spotted Langford James standing on a second-level walkway, naked but for a loincloth, his arms raised in praise. Next to him, clad only in a bikini and an improvised sparkly headdress, Khaleesi-*Qalawe* struck a dramatic Peter Pan pose.

"Lord! Arise!" shouted Langford. "It is I, your royal servant. Ggh!"

"*Sogho fer juriska!*" intoned Khaleesi. "*Shu'phro, rho-lergisko'l!*"

Rod didn't understand what she was saying but he saw the effect. *Crippen-Ai's* whole body rippled and flipped up, like a bouncy castle attempting the high jump. It hung in the air for a second, then the bulk returned to earth, smashing partitions and trestle tables.

"Okay, this is worse," said Rod.

Kathy was circling *Polliqan Riti's* tank, casting charms in Venislarn.

"*Yandi voors a-lakh.*"

Morag blinked.

The circle of symbols around the tank had turned a deep, non-reflective black – as though they had become gashes between this world and some far, lightless place.

Morag blinked again. She couldn't remember how she had gotten here, but she was certain Kathy was doing something 'important' and she ought to let her 'get on with it'.

Mother? said her bump and she realised it was not for the first time.

"Sorry, I think I drifted off there," she said.

Kathy looked up at her. "Ah. Now, where was I? Oh, yes, joining the consular mission. So, it was decided long ago that we really needed people on the inside with the consular mission to the Venislarn. We did have people working in lower level positions in most of the facilities but we needed to get close to the action. I was already a junior doctor at the time, at the QE even, but I needed to make the move to the Restricted Ward upstairs. I needed the consular mission to take me in as one of their own but without me having to approach them."

"Uh-huh?" said Morag, not sure what conversation they were having but not wanting to interrupt.

Mother, you need to listen to me.

"And what's the best way to get a job offer from the consular mission?" said Kathy.

Morag knew this one. "Survive an encounter with the Venislarn."

"Exactly."

Mother, that woman is not your friend. She wants to hurt you.

It was a silly notion and Morag ignored her baby. She would have shushed him but didn't want to be seen talking to him.

"We had a *granshak zex'l* in our cages at our main site," said Kathy, "so all we needed to do was take it somewhere remote enough and fake up a car crash with me in the car. We jazzed it up, gave me a bit of a starring role to show my qualities. My dad and I worked together on that project, our last one together."

"What happened to him?"

"The Winds of *Kaxeos*. That was more than ten years ago now." A bitterness swept over her face. "You can't tell me that death is natural. You can't tell me that this is the way it's all meant to be."

356

We need to get away from here, mother. She's going to hurt us.

"I'm not sure I understand what's going on here," said Morag.

"I'm a doctor. It's my job to fix things. Screw this palliative pussyfooting around. *As vanir'gi finarl beraayh-u!*"

The blackness in the magic circle spilled over from the confines of the writing, rose upwards, like ink through water until a black curtain of un-light surrounded *Polliqan Riti's* tank. And then, with a crack like static electricity discharge, the curtain fell apart. The gloop in the tank sloshed together, closing over the space where the Venislarn creature had been.

"Where's he gone?" said Morag.

We need to escape, mother. Please.

"He's gone to hell," said Kathy. "Home."

"I don't..."

An alarm started blaring. Red lights set into the ceiling flashed.

"Is it a fire?" said Morag.

"Nina more likely," said Kathy.

She put a hand in her jacket pocket and took out a wand. Morag had seen it before, in the lobby of the Cube. It was the *yellis* wand, the mind-wiper.

"Wait," said Morag.

"*Hyet-pa!*"

Bright light filled the room.

Up above, Langford laid on the thickest slab of hammy acting Rod had ever seen while Khaleesi waved her arms about self-importantly. She might as well have been a child directing a thunderstorm for all the actual impact she was having. But down on the ground floor, *Crippen-Ai* was throwing itself about with wild abandon, smashing lighting rigs, whipping power cables about, lashing out and snaring any humans who were too slow to get out of its way.

"We come!" said the possessed Jayda.

Trying to keep Skye, Taylor and Pupfish together and out of harm, Rod watched *Crippen-Ai's* progress from behind an on-set generator.

"How are we going to stop it?" said Taylor.

357

"We can't," said Rod. "We're not allowed to hurt it. It's a Venislarn."

Pupfish made a clicking sound deep in his throat. "Ggh! I dunno, man. There's something fishy about that thing. Ain't no *adn-bhul* Venislarn."

"Not Venislarn?" said Rod. "Just take a look at it!"

The *samakha* youth turned a huge golden eye on Rod. "You think all Venislarn look the same? You think cos it's some weird ass *muda* that it's one of ours? Ggh!"

"Isn't it?"

"You *adn-bhul* humans have got some weird *muda* of your own. You ever seen kangaroos? What's that *muda* about? It's a *doi* giant rabbit but with pockets."

"If it's not a Venislarn then— Move!"

Rod shoved Skye and the others out of the way of a growing tentacle of white flesh that shot across the ground like a tree root growing on fast forward. The four of them came to a stop behind a fake marble pillar.

"And naked mole rats. What are they all about?" said Pupfish.

"If it's not a Venislarn then what is it?" said Rod.

"Ggh! I dunno, dog. I is just tellin' you it don't smell right."

"It's fair game?"

"Is that what you call us when you're allowed to shoot us, man? That's some Rodney King *muda*, right there."

"There's a helicopter on the roof," said Skye suddenly.

Rod looked to her. Her eyes were wide with fear, darting with hypervigilance.

"The camera chopper," nodded Taylor.

"Not a bad idea," said Rod.

The main doors to the Mailbox were blocked by debris on this side and almost certainly by the emergency services on the other. The same would apply to the exits through the restaurant area towards the rear. If they could get to the roof and the helicopter was still waiting...

"We need a distraction or two to allow you to get to the roof," said Rod.

"I've got an idea," said Taylor and ran from cover and into the nearest empty retail unit.

"Wait!"

A white tentacle slapped around the pillar. The two humans and the *samakha* stumbled away. *Crippen-Ai* lashed out with a fresh limb. Pupfish put out an arm to block it and the tentacle grazed the back of his hand.

Pupfish screamed. The grey skin of his hand bubbled and steamed.

"*Adn-bhul shaska* Mr Blobby *bhul-tamade!*"

Rod hauled him back, still screaming and swearing, into the retail unit. As they entered, Taylor was shoulder-barging his way into the locked area at the back. It was Jayda's armourer's unit.

Rod spun Pupfish into a chair.

"Tend to him," he ordered Skye.

Skye stared. "But he's..."

"What?"

"He's not human!"

"Just do it!" said Rod and followed Taylor into the armoury. Taylor scanned the racks of Hollywood firearms.

"You know there aren't any actual weapons in here," said Rod. "No live ammo. It's all smoke and mirrors." And as he said it, he realised that smoke and mirrors might be enough. "You thinking to dazzle it with smoke and sparklers?"

"I'm thinking pipe bomb," said Taylor.

As Rod watched, Taylor picked up a movie prop fire axe and used its heavy metal head to break open a case marked with an explosives warning.

"I did a weekend course with the guy who taught Steven Seagal everything he knows," said Taylor as he cracked open an aluminium and chlorate compound and poured it into a nearby can.

Rod reached past him to pick up a small tin. "Ammonium nitrate."

"That's... um..."

"It's an oxidizer." Rod turned. In the corner was a plastic tub of cleaning grease. Rod grabbed it and read the label. "This will do it."

"Do what?"

Rod upended the ammonium nitrate into the tub.

"Blasting powder."

Just outside the door, Pupfish was whimpering and crying.

359

"This thing isn't a true Venislarn," said Rod.

"Good. So?"

"It means we can blow it to kingdom come," he said and looked around for something with which to make a fuse.

Morag walked along a corridor. She wasn't sure how she had gotten there but she didn't feel overly concerned. Kathy was next to her. Beyond was a glass barrier, escalators and a high central concourse, lined by several storeys of offices and open plan spaces. She was at Millennium Point, the Think Tank building. They were walking out towards the car park. She grunted to herself, glad she now knew where she was. Somewhere, multiple alarms were ringing.

Mother, put your hand on me.

Morag put her hand on her stomach.

One tap for yes, mother. Two taps for no. Do you understand?

Amused by the little game, Morag, tapped her fingers once.

Good. Well done, mother. You have to listen. Don't say anything. Understand?

She gave a tap.

Kathy wants to hurt us. She knows about me.

Morag frowned and she actually laughed. It was ridiculous.

"Everything okay?" said Kathy.

"Yeah," said Morag and coughed to compose herself.

"The car's just out here."

Morag drummed her fingers on stomach. One tap for yes, two for no was all well and good but what did you do when you wanted to say 'don't be silly, baby. She doesn't want to hurt anyone'?

She changed your memory, mother. Just like Nina changed your memory. She works for the bad people.

Morag didn't know what to do or say.

She has a gun, mother. It's a bad thing, yes?

Morag tapped once.

And she has a wand. That's bad too.

One tap.

The bad people work for something called Forward Management. They put the creature called Crippen-Ai under the place called the Mailbox. Rod who is a friend of yours has let it escape. It is the same creature as Polliqan Riti.

360

Morag took out her phone.

"You calling someone?" said Kathy.

Until that moment, Morag hadn't believed what her chatty little foetus had been telling her, but Kathy had spoken with such urgent abruptness that there could be no doubt something fishy was going on.

"Just Rod," said Morag as nonchalantly as possibly. "Just gonna check on him."

"You don't need to do that," said Kathy.

"Oh?" Morag didn't stop. She flicked through to her recent call list. Nina had called her, less than fifteen minutes ago. She didn't remember that call.

"Put your phone away for now," said Kathy. "We're nearly at the car."

"Just checking in," said Morag.

Kathy had something in her hand. Morag saw the metallic prongs of the wand and grabbed it before Kathy could raise it.

"*Hyet-pa!*" Kathy shouted but the angle was wrong, or she wasn't holding it right. The tips of the wand sparkled but nothing happened.

"You *teglau* bitch," said Morag, bashing Kathy with her whole body.

The women teetered and turned like drunken ballroom dancers. Kathy was taller and heavier, but for all her talk of exercise and martial arts training she didn't have Morag's energy. Morag stamped on her toes and attempted a headbutt but missed. In reply, Kathy grabbed at Morag through her blouse and gave a savage twist and pinch.

Morag gasped and almost lost her grip, but she knew that if Kathy got control the wand the bitch would win.

She used her lower centre of gravity to plant her feet and heaved Kathy back against the nearby up escalator. Kathy twisted and pulled but Morag did not let go.

"Traitor!" Kathy coughed.

"Me?" snarled.

Perhaps to make the point, perhaps because she had few moves left in the tangle of limbs, Kathy kneed Morag in the stomach.

Mother!

In horror and rage, Morag yanked Kathy's arm round and shoved hand and wand into the slim opening where the rubber handrail of the escalator disappeared back into the mechanism. Several tips of the wand jammed and caught and the whole thing was dragged into the aperture. Wire prongs bent backward, snapped and shattered and the wand was gone. A half-second later, there was a fatal crunching sound and the escalator stopped.

Morag stumbled in surprise as large chunks of stolen memory slammed back into place.

"Morag is pregnant with the anti-Christ!" yelled Nina suddenly.

"What?"

"And Maurice was knitting it booties!"

"Please stop shouting things while I'm trying to drive!" snapped Mrs Fiddler. She swerved to avoid a slow-moving van. "And make more sense, Nina!"

Rod came out into the atrium in a bent-kneed jog, carrying the tub bomb by its handle. The improvised fuse fizzed in the top. *Crippen-Ai* squatted massively in the centre of the atrium, limbs splayed, flesh leeched of colour by time and tide. Rod swung the tub round, underarm to get some momentum before lobbing it. *Crippen-Ai* still held Jayda and a dozen other individuals so, though Rod suspected they were already beyond saving, he attempted to hurl his homemade bomb into the folds of white flesh farthest away from the human captives. He hoped the many people still trying to flee would see what was happening and take cover.

At the moment he released the bomb, Rod was walloped with the sudden return of certain memories.

"I had sex with Kathy Kaur!" he shouted involuntarily.

"Er, okay," shouted Taylor, "but shouldn't you be ducking?"

The tub bomb disappeared with a plop into the soft flesh. As it did, Rod remembered something else, something that had been taken from him, something Kathy had said just before they'd had sex. Something about it having distributed intelligence, that any part of it was as clever as the whole.

362

"If you break the creature apart..." he murmured and then shouted in panic and self-recrimination. "Oh, this is bad! Very bad! Everyone, get down!"

"All praise our mighty lord!" yelled Langford James.

Rod sprinted back towards Taylor and Skye, flapping his arms with utter urgency.

"Get out of the splash zone!"

He leapt for the shelter of an overturned table as the bomb detonated behind him. Something—the blast front or a chunk of *Crippen-Ai*—caught his lower leg and spun him over and he landed behind the table shoulder first.

He rolled, coughing with the pain. "Buggeration."

He got to his knees and looked over the table. The walls, shop fronts and every exposed surface were peppered with blobs of thick white slime. Fat lumps slid down the walls and dropped, squelching, to the floor. People got up from where they'd fallen or hidden.

The design philosophy conceptualist (Jarmane or Charmaine, Rod had never been sure) turned over her hand to inspect the gobbet of goo-monster clinging to it.

"This is interesting," she said.

Jayda, whose arm was coated in a sleeve of the stuff, came forward. "So many new bodies."

Producer Tammy stepped up next to her. The whole of the left side of her face was hidden beneath a layer of white. "And a whole new world to explore."

"Very, very bad," Rod said to himself.

In the Think Tank, Morag disentangled herself from Kathy, tripped as she skidded away across the smooth floor and looked back. Kathy rolled out of the jacket that had gotten wrapped about her. She had lost the wand but now she had that incongruously silly pistol in her hand.

"*Bhul!*" said Morag and ran.

Kathy fired. The window front of a university careers office fractured in a crazy spiderweb.

Why does she want to hurt us, mother?

Morag didn't answer. She focused solely on escape.

The automatic doors were open. Morag sprinted. Behind her, alarms wailed, people shouted, there were screams and there was another gunshot and then Morag was through the door and outside. She jinked right, down the slope towards the car park.

"Morag!" screamed Kathy behind her.

Morag turned to look. Kathy was outside, dishevelled, pistol arm swinging round.

From the rooftop, *Shala'pinz Syu* dropped onto the ground, just missing Kathy but knocking her forward onto the floor. Morag could never imagine being grateful for the arrival of one of the August handmaidens of *Prein*, but *Shala'pinz Syu* was here and Kathy was down.

Shala'pinz Syu reared up over Kathy, raising a pair of spear-tipped legs to impale her. Kathy fired up at the alien crab-nanny. The handmaiden was huge. Bullets from the tiny handgun should have had as little effect on her as on a charging rhinoceros, but *Shala'pinz Syu* reared back at the first shot and screamed at the second. A creature with no natural voice was screaming, the pink-toothed mouth on her exposed underbelly a perfect 'o' of surprise and pain. Kathy shot a third time and *Shala'pinz Syu* tipped onto her back, dead.

"Fuck," whispered Morag.

You used the bad word, mother.

"Kind of justified in this instance, baby," she said.

Distant sirens joined the alarms going off in the building. Morag ran on, towards the multi-storey car park.

Twenty or thirty people had slowly drifted together in the central atrium. More were joining them, each carrying a chunk or smear of *Crippen-Ai* on their exposed skin. Rod was entirely out of ideas so he went to his usual default: polite conversation.

"Er, good morning," he said and then checked his watch. "Afternoon even. Um, how are you doing?"

Jayda tilted her head and looked at him. Her eyes flicked to the floor. Rod looked down and saw a fist-sized lump of *Crippen-Ai* slowly slithering towards his foot. Rod slid his toe under it and flung it away.

364

"What's going on?" shouted Langford James from the walkway above.

As Rod looked up, Khaleesi slapped a gobbet of slime creature onto her boyfriend's neck. The look of confusion on Langford's face vanished instantly.

Crippen-Ai spoke with a voice that bounced from person to person.

"You do not have—"

"—to worry, Rod. We aren't—"

"—going to hurt you."

"Oh, aye?" he said, backing away slowly. "They all say that."

"It doesn't hurt," said Producer Tammy.

"You can trust us," said Jayda.

"Well, you would say that. You're controlling their minds."

"This isn't mind control," said a guy in a caterer's apron.

"*Crippen-Ai* just tells us what he wants," said a Tammy-lite.

"And his needs are greater than ours," said Jayda.

"Right." A utility monster, that's what Kathy had called it, before she'd shagged him and betrayed him and wiped his memory with that wand. Rod suddenly remembered that dealing with this creature wasn't his only priority.

He realised his phone was buzzing in his pocket

"We all want to make him happy," said Charmaine (or Jarmane).

"Whatever it takes," said Tammy. With that, she stood tall, struck a pose and started to sing. It was a few moments before Rod recognised the words, as they echoed from many mouths in a confusing way, but the movements were unmistakable. They jumped to the left, stepped to the right and, as one, their hands flew to their hips.

"Oh, surely not?" said Rod. "The Timewarp?" It seemed unlikely that *Crippen-Ai* was a fan of *The Rocky Horror Picture Show*. Presumably, he wanted to demonstrate his control over the humans.

Rod kept his gaze well away from Langford James and Khaleesi, who would be thrusting their near-naked groins in time with the chorus. He ushered his group closer to the exit as the dancers all declared themselves 'insa-yay-ye-ye-ye-ane'.

"I've never been a fan of big musical numbers," said Rod.

"Philistine," said Jayda.

"And that guy at the back there definitely isn't keeping time with the rest of you."

"Everyone's a critic."

A slime slug crested the edge of an over-turned table by Rod. He flipped the table back, squashing the thing underneath it.

Skye and the others were almost at the service door.

"My goodness! Look at that! Wardrobe have brought you all sequinned boob tubes and tinsel suspenders!" shouted Rod and pointed off in no particular direction.

Most of the mind-controlled people turned to look, which was better than Rod could have hoped. He ran for the service lift.

"He thinks he can escape," said Tammy.

"He's going for the helicopter," said Jayda.

Crippen-Ai's zombies began to run after him.

Morag hunkered down between two parked cars and tried to regain her breath. She put her hand to her forehead. She was bleeding. Had one of Kathy's shots come too close?

"Are you all right, baby?" she whispered.

We're in danger, mother.

"I'm going to sort it," she said.

Morag peered over the bonnet of the car next to her and looked towards the pedestrian entrance to this level of the car park. There was no sign of Kathy. Police sirens were very close, but Morag wasn't in a frame of mind to risk things by running out towards them.

She phone Rod again. He eventually picked up. She heard clattering like he was running up stairs.

"*Crippen-Ai* has infected dozens of people in the Mailbox," he panted.

"Kathy is trying to kill me," Morag replied, feeling an instinctive if ridiculous need to compete.

"Nina was right about that secret society."

"They plan to make war on the Venislarn."

"Are you safe?" said Rod.

"No. We're not safe."

"We?"

366

She wasn't ready to break that news to Rod.

"I'm hiding in the multi-storey near the Think Tank." Morag closed her eyes a second. "Is *Crippen-Ai* still in the Mailbox?"

"Most of him. I mean all of him. Yeah. Taylor!" he abruptly shouted. "Watch out!" There was a scuffle and then a loud metallic thunk on the line and then Rod was back on. "That was close. Yes. He's still in the Mailbox."

"He can't get out," said Morag.

"We're trying to keep him here."

"No," she said with whispered insistence. "He *cannot* get out. If any of the local gods get even a sniff of him, there will be carnage."

"Does that make him fair game?"

"Absolutely," she said. She peered over the top of the bonnet again and ducked down immediately; there was someone by the entrance. She raised her head, slowly. It was Kathy. Even as a distant silhouette, Morag recognised those curves. Kathy's hands were together as though holding a gun.

"Shit."

Mother, you're scared.

She nodded. "I know, baby."

She crawled on all fours back between the cars, away from Kathy. When she looked at her phone, the call with Rod had been ended.

Rod looked at the floor number on the stairs they were climbing and tried to remember the internal layout of the building.

"It's through here," said Taylor and pushed through the nearest door.

"You sure?" said Rod.

"We just been filming on the roof, dog," said Pupfish. "We know."

Before Rod was through the door, something bowled into Taylor spilling him over onto the marble floor.

"Take him, my love," shouted Khaleesi.

Rod groaned. These clowns. On the walkway overlooking the atrium, Langford James was laying into Taylor with fists and bare feet. Taylor had his arms up protectively like a boxer and Langford's attacks were hardly the most devastating. Taylor was probably reeling more from the indignity of being attacked by an actor in a loin cloth.

"Don't let the creature touch you," shouted Rod.

Khaleesi charged at them. Again, the bikini-clad woman didn't offer that much of a physical threat, but *Crippen-Ai* was at the steering wheel and one touch from that slime would be a death sentence.

Skye ducked a clumsy lunge from Khaleesi. Pupfish danced around her, panicky.

"Ggh! I don't hit bitches," he said.

"Sexist," said Skye.

Rod bunched his jacket sleeve around his fist and walloped Langford James. The man was tall, but he was a lightweight bag of sticks and the blow sent him flying.

Khaleesi grabbed Pupfish's face in both hands. The touch of *Crippen-Ai* burned him like acid. Skye wrenched a fire extinguisher off the wall and whacked Khaleesi in the lower back. Khaleesi wailed in pain as she fell.

Langford leapt up, losing his loin cloth. *"Dirib lope'r sazchla ghos!"*

"I told you," said Rod. "I don't speak Venislarn."

Rod met the man as he charged, planting a kick in his solar plexus. Langford doubled over and Rod used his momentum to push the man into the wall. Nose and jaw crunched loudly as they broke.

Skye whacked Khaleesi again with the extinguisher to make sure she stayed down. Pupfish was reeling and swearing at the pain in his cheeks.

"You not get any on you guys?" Rod checked with the others. "Not a speck of this thing can leave the building."

Skye inspected her hands and arms.

The door from the stairwell swung open. Infected movie folk clamoured to be the first through.

"I got this!" yelled Taylor, "I can slow them down."

He disappeared into the toilets, there was a loud hammering sound, and then he came out holding a soap dispenser in his arms.

"Check this out," he said, "I know acting, and these guys are all walking like they learned it out of a book or something."

It was true, Rod realised. The advancing horde resembled a zombie army. Taylor pumped the soap dispenser and wove back and forth across the path.

"I'll save some for the stairs, it'll work well there," he yelled.

With a supporting arm around Pupfish, and Taylor dispensing soap behind them, Rod steered Skye toward the final stairs up onto the roof.

Morag squeezed between a transit van and the far wall of the car park.

I can feel your heart beating, mother.

"Yes," she whispered.

Are you frightened?

"It's fine. It's fine baby."

She turned her head to look at the narrow exit from her hiding place and focused on listening.

Does Kathy still want to hurt you?

She put her hand on her stomach and tapped once for yes.

I won't let her hurt you, mother.

Her unborn's voice was just a thought in her head but it had never been such a loud and angry thought.

I won't let her, he insisted.

"Shhh," she said, rubbing her belly.

I will come out and stop her if I have to.

"That won't be necessary, baby," she whispered.

"Morag?" It was a man's voice.

For a second, she struggled to place it.

"Malcolm?"

The consular mission security officer appeared round the front of the van. He had a hand on a holstered weapon and a concerned look on his face.

"You all right, Morag?"

She didn't automatically move.

"Kathy," she said. "Kathy tried to kill me."

"I know, I know," he said. "The police are looking for her now." He made a big deal of looking about him. "She's not here."

Morag nodded, understanding, and awkwardly slid out, brushing between van and concrete wall. Malcolm carefully took her arm when she was within reach.

"Careful now. Let's make sure you and baby are all right."

She looked at him, startled.

"It's okay." He smiled reassuringly. "We know. It's fine."

She stepped free of the van. Her knees were scuffed. Her forehead stung where it had been bleeding.

"Kids," said Malcolm. "We'd do anything to protect them, wouldn't we?"

"You have children?" she said.

"Little boy," he nodded. "Apple of my eye."

He looked round, scanning the car park, hand still on the holster of his weapon.

Rod, half-dragging Pupfish along with him, followed Skye out onto the roof. Taylor had emptied the soap dispenser and then hurled it down the stairs with a clatter. Gusty winds whipped across the roof, stinging Rod's eyes. Up here, it was possible to get a sense of the true scale of the building. The old post office sorting building stretched from the city centre at one end through to Gas Street Basin at the other. Inside, it was divided along its length into the shopping centre turned film set and then further sections of offices and restaurants. Up here, it was a long landing strip of a roof, interrupted at this end by a triangular prism of skylights.

Taylor Graham, who had spent the morning running (or pretending to run) its length being pursued by Vlad Botticelli's henchmen, started nimbly and confidently along the low edge of the sloping skylight towards the far end where—thank God—a helicopter waited. Skye stumbled after the Hollywood A-lister.

"Come on, mate," said Rod and pulled Pupfish after them.

The *samakha* gasped. Rod guessed the cold winds had brought fresh sensation to his burned and melted face. The pain seemed to wake him up and Pupfish found his feet with increasing confidence as they followed the others.

Rod heard the roof doors open behind them.

"Now, we definitely need to run."

"Ggh! What you think I'm doin', dog?"

370

Rod's eyes scanned the way ahead for anything he could use to swat *Crippen-Ai's* zombie slaves away with – a length of scaffolding, a steel bar. Heck, he'd even take a broom.

Shoes slapped on the sloping glass behind them. Rod pushed Pupfish forward, dug in his pocket and turned.

"Stop!" he shouted. "Or I blow us all to hell."

They actually stopped. Jayda, at the front of the charge, with Producer Tammy close behind, skidded to a halt.

"What's that?" said Jayda, jutting her chin at the small white globe in his hand.

"Grenade," he said. "I drop this, and your puppets are dead."

The infected were piling onto the roof behind the first wave. Rod just needed to hold them off, give those few with a chance of survival time to board the helicopter. He could hear Taylor shouting and—he hoped he wasn't imagining it—the whine of the helicopter blades starting to turn.

"That tiny thing?" sneered Jayda.

"It'll smash that glass," he said, nodding at the sloping windows they were standing on. "It's a long way down."

They looked. Jayda and Tammy and the others looked down. Another few seconds. Jayda looked at him, disbelief in her eyes. Rod hurled the white ball, smashing it on the glass at her feet. They flinched. Some tried to get out of the way.

Rod ran. Jayda yelled. It had taken her only a moment to realise that a sodium toothpaste bomb wasn't about to kill anyone, so Rod was running for his life now. The helicopter was starting up. It was a simple utility chopper, an old Eurocopter. It wasn't big but there'd be room for them all—just. There were two crew that he could see. One was hurriedly dismantling the camera at the door to make room. Taylor and Skye were waiting, crouched low against the rotors' downdraft.

Pupfish, clutching his injured arm as he ran, but running nonetheless, was not too far behind. Rod sprinted for his life.

Two police cars blocked the entry road into Millennium Point and the Think Tank site. Mrs Fiddler braked to a sudden stop. Nina was already opening the door.

"You can't come through this way," said a police officer.

Nina waved her ID at him. The man leaned in to inspect it.

"I haven't got time for this," she said and hurried past.

He made to grab her, but she shook him off and ran.

Police and fire crews were arranged around the pedestrianised area at the rear of the Think Tank building. There was a hell of a lot of milling about.

Attempting to orchestrate some of the chaos was Chief Inspector Ricky Lee. He was berating and directing uniformed coppers while, behind him, men in the dark uniforms of consular mission security attempted to cover the body of a dead August Handmaiden of *Prein* with a tarpaulin that was too small.

"Have you found her?" Nina said.

"Who?" said Ricky.

"Morag. Kathy. Both. Either."

"I don't even know what's going on here," said Ricky. "What's supposed to have happened?"

"She's in danger. Morag's in danger." She looked at the dead Venislarn. "We're all in danger."

"Sir!" shouted an officer over by the multi-storey car park entrance. Ricky hurried over, Nina right beside him.

The officer waved them through and pointed to where other officers stood by a parked transit van. They were looking down at the gap between the van and the wall. Nina pushed through. A mobile phone lay on the concrete floor beside a small smear of blood.

Nina crouched and turned the phone over. The background screen flicked on. It was a picture of a wide sea inlet. Nina had seen it before.

"It's hers." She looked up at Ricky. "This is Morag's phone."

Like an idiot, Nina looked round, expecting Morag to suddenly appear from somewhere. Ricky gave swift instructions to the officers around him and then spoke into his radio.

The helicopter rocked on the cusp of taking off. Skye was tucked into a far corner of the cabin. Pupfish and Taylor sat by the open door. Taylor was shouting something to the pilot. Pupfish was holding out a hand to Rod.

Rod shouted for them to go even before he had got to the door. The pilot needed little encouragement. The helicopter lifted.

Rod took Pupfish's hand and pulled himself into the cabin then rolled over to kick back at anyone who might be trying to follow him in. His heel connected with a face, but he didn't see whose.

The vehicle tilted slightly in its ascent. Rod grabbed a seatbelt strap for support and leaned out to check the skids for clinging zombies. They were clear.

Taylor whooped in elated relief. Skye made a noise that was half-laugh and half-sob.

"I don't understand any of it... any of it..." she said to no one at all.

Down on the roof, directly below them, a flash mob of *Crippen-Ai*'s servants gathered; they didn't claw mindlessly for the escaped helicopter; they were human beings, just human beings who knew, in their hearts of hearts, that *Crippen-Ai*'s wants and desires were far more important than their own.

The co-pilot waved and pointed at the headsets between the back seats. Rod moved to put one on.

"Seatbelt!" he shouted at Pupfish, above the roar of the engine.

He turned to say the same to Taylor Graham. The American was pumped up with adrenaline, grinning a wild and manic smile.

There was a glistening mark on Taylor's wrist, just a slick shine, but it caught Rod's eye. He moved his head, brought it nonchalantly lower to look further up Taylor's cuff. A finger-length of white wormy mass pulsated against his inner arm.

"What?" grinned Taylor, seeing him look. "What is it?"

"Taylor..."

Taylor's grin morphed into pleading and bargaining. "It's nothing. It's fine. Trust me."

Rod glanced out. They were still above the roof of the Mailbox. *Crippen-Ai* might be distributed among fifty to sixty hosts, but it was contained. There were emergency vehicles all around the building and consular mission staff would be on site. It would count for nothing if any fraction of *Crippen-Ai* escaped.

"You can't—" Rod began to say and then Taylor gave him a two-handed shove towards the open door.

Rod had hold of the seatbelt. He swung, feeling his grip slide along it. As he pitched back, he grabbed Taylor by his shirt and tie and let his momentum pull the actor with him. Taylor fell forward and collided with him, the seatbelt burned along the palm of Rod's hand and they fell back and out.

Reflexes kicked in. Rod lashed out for anything to grab, to save himself. His elbow bounced off the helicopter skid. His other hand missed it but found Taylor. Taylor had bounced off the cabin edge but managed to hook one arm over the skid arm and had latched his other hand to his forearm to lock his arms about it. Rod had a grip on Taylor's belt, nothing else. His legs swung over the long drop to the Mailbox roof.

The helicopter tilted at the weight shift. Rod looked up and saw Pupfish screaming. Skye clutched the far door for support. Taylor wriggled and kicked. He looked down, a strange, mad glee in his eyes and shouted at Rod. Rod heard nothing over the pounding thrum of the engine, no screams, no yells, no shouting.

Taylor's feet beat against his chest. Rod flapped against the man's back, the pen and pencil in his breast pocket jabbing him with each collision. Rod hauled himself up and hooked his hand over Taylor's shoulder. He didn't rate his chances of being able to climb up the other guy's body before Taylor lost his grip — Hollywood athlete physique or not, no one could support the weight of two men like that for long — but Rod had no other options.

Taylor continued to shout but it was all noise in the wind. Rod let go of the belt to bring his other arm up and then he saw the sliver of *Crippen-Ai* on Taylor's neck, oozing and stretching out towards Rod's uppermost arm. Rod couldn't move out of the way. It was the only hold he had. It would have him before he had established another grip.

Taylor was laughing now. Not a good sign.

The glass roof was below them. Against the spinning sky and a skyline of a city that would never be complete, Rod saw the odd geometric shapes that made up the exterior of the Cube. The Court of the Venislarn and the home of *Yo Morgantus*, prince of this city. Rod couldn't contemplate what *Morgantus* would do if *Crippen-Ai* was loose in Birmingham. And no way was Rod going to be taken over by the bad guy, turned against those he was meant to protect.

He snatched the taser-pen from his breast pocket and fired it point blank into Taylor's back. The two men were locked together and the electric shock, a powerful and total body cramp, convulsed

Taylor and Rod alike. Mind-controlling creature or not, Taylor couldn't hold on while his muscles involuntarily spasmed. His armlock grip failed and they fell.

Wild adrenaline fear surged through Rod. They fell, wrapped up in each other. Rod saw the sloped window roof of the Mailbox coming at them. If this were a movie, he thought finally, they'd go straight through in a spectacular blizzard of glass fragments.

"Sean fucking Bean," he hissed.

Nina stalked back towards Mrs Fiddler's car. It was still parked at the roadblocked entrance to the car park. Mrs Fiddler stood in the open car door, waiting.

"She's gone," said Nina.

"Your friend?" said Mrs Fiddler.

Ricky Lee jogged to catch up with her.

"You've got leads though?" said Nina. "CCTV?"

"Yes, we're already on it," said Ricky. "Listen, there's something else—"

"But it's really important. It's not just Morag." She didn't want to blurt out news of the pregnancy, about the *kaatbari* Morag was carrying. "I spoke to Maurice. He and Professor Omar—"

Ricky took her hand and held it tight. It stopped her dead. The two of them were experts at keeping their professional and private lives distinct and separate.

"It's Rod," he said. He squeezed her hand tighter. "I've just heard from the Mailbox. There was a fight, a fall or something."

She knew what he was going to say before he said it, but she let him say it anyway.

"He's dead, Nina."

"You've seen the body?" she said, which was a stupid kind of question, but she wasn't going to believe it otherwise.

"No one can get to him. The building's on lockdown but he fell... from a helicopter onto the roof. From that height..."

"No," she said. She wasn't ready to accept it. "We're going there, now," she said to Mrs Fiddler and broke away from his grip.

"I've got to stay here," he said.

She felt her face flush with anger. "Damn right. You need to find Morag. You need to find Kathy."

Mrs Fiddler got into the car beside Nina, swiftly turned them around and drove towards the main roads and the Mailbox. There was a cool detachment about her, a sudden new efficiency. Mrs Fiddler didn't say a word and Nina was grateful. Speaking now would be just filling the air with words.

Rod was dead and Morag had gone, taken by the Maccabees or Forward Management or whatever they called themselves in private.

It was a grey bright day over Birmingham. Middle of the day and the traffic was building but moving. The city hummed, alive and oblivious. Nina's phone buzzed as they entered the first of the Queensway tunnels. It was Sheikh Omar. She almost didn't bother answering it.

She answered but didn't speak.

"Nina," said Omar.

"Yes."

"Is it true about Morag?"

"They have her. She's been kidnapped."

"This is calamitous."

"I know," she said. "I know about the baby."

There was silence on the line for a long time.

"*Yo Morgantus* has summoned her," said Omar. "He wants answers. He might know what has happened at the Mailbox."

"What happened at the Mailbox?" said Nina.

Omar cleared his throat. "The creature... fragmented. Maybe Rod tried to blow it up."

"Is Rod dead?"

"I've seen footage from the roof..." He sighed. "Yes, he's dead."

They emerged from the tunnel. From here, Nina could see helicopters circling over the city ahead, in the general vicinity of the Mailbox.

"I also hear *Polliqan Riti* has vanished from the Think Tank," said Omar. "That's Kathy's doing."

"I'm going to kill her," said Nina.

"Not if I get to her first," said Omar coldly. "In the meantime, I will present myself to the Venislarn court. I will try to placate *Yo Morgantus*. What will you do?"

The question struck Nina hard. She had had no plan in her mind, only a fierce one-note desire to be where Rod had been, to make things anything but what they were. She had no plan until Omar asked her and then she understood exactly what she intended to do.

"I'm going to Soho House," she said and nodded at Mrs Fiddler to make it an instruction.

Mrs Fiddler gave her a momentarily querying look but immediately flipped her indicators from right to left to head up towards Five Ways.

"What are you going to do there?" he asked.

"I'm going to fix this. I gotta go."

She ended the call and put her phone in her lap. Mrs Fiddler's face twitched as they drove, like she was trying to comprehend a difficult puzzle, but out of respect for Nina's grief, said nothing until they had pulled into the Soho House car park.

"I think I know what you intend to do," she said.

"Good," said Nina and got out. "Are you going to try to stop me?" She hurried across the lawn to the house. "Do you have the notepad?"

Mrs Fiddler rummaged through her handbag and found the 'History is Fun!' notepad.

"You're going to send a message back through time," she said. "Something that will warn someone so that this can be undone. I don't know what kind of message that might be."

"That's not what I'm going to do," said Nina.

"Because I don't know how that would work, if at all. If time is fixed, then you know that whatever you're going to do won't work because it hasn't worked. If it's a bifurcating-trousers-of-time thing, then we'll still be in the world where your friends are dead and—"

"Morag isn't dead," Nina snapped. "Not yet. And trousers of time? What are you...?"

She huffed and zigzagged through the hallway, the door by the stairs and along the corridor. The door to the section of the house that hadn't existed until this week was still there. The sash barrier remained across the doorway, solidly doing more work than a sash barrier should be expected to do.

"I'm going to go back and change history," said Nina.

"Go back?"

Nina shoved the sash aside and hurried down the corridor.

"Wait, wait," said Mrs Fiddler. "*Go* back?"

They entered the room from which all their explorations of the past had begun. Nina picked up the oculus.

"Find me a time."

Mrs Fiddler stood there helplessly, staring. Nina grabbed her hand holding the notepad. "Find me a time!"

"But it won't work," the woman said quietly. "In everything we've done, the oculus only opens windows to a time period of maybe ten or twenty years in the late seventeen-hundreds."

Nina didn't care. "Boulton has an oculus. He built this one. It's the same oculus everywhere. *Everywhen*? If I can use it now to go back to Boulton's time, maybe I can use it there to come home, but at an earlier time."

"You don't know if it works like that."

Nina wasn't listening. "A one-way ticket to ancient times, and then a one-way ticket to last week, last month. I'll have the list of co-ordinates," she said, flipping the edge of the notepad. "I'll work it out."

"You don't even know you'll survive."

"I've put my arm through before."

"Look at it, Nina!" said Mrs Fiddler sharply.

The oculus, a set of concentric rings, was twelve inches across, if that. Nina held it low in her hands against her hips.

"One of my best qualities," she said. "I'm small but perfectly formed."

"You need to think about this."

"I don't want to think!" Nina snapped and she was suddenly crying but she wasn't going to let tears spoil her resolve or her big plan. She snatched the notepad from Mrs Fiddler, shoved it inside her jacket and turned the hoops of the oculus to what seemed an appropriate setting. A hum too deep to be truly heard rang out from the device and the light through the oculus changed.

"You'll die," said Mrs Fiddler.

"We all *adn-bhul* die, Julie."

Mrs Fiddler's face pinched and she went quite pale. She stepped back to give Nina room. "Language, Nina."

Nina looked through the oculus. The floor in the past was dark. It was night, as good a time as any to travel back in time. She held the oculus over her head – like it was a jumper she was about to shimmy into – and put an arm through.

The wind from nowhere sprang up. Nina's arm tingled and vibrated, and all sensation was driven out of it. The wind moaned and the room joined in, brickwork grinding, timbers creaking like a pirate ship in a storm.

"It's not happy," said Mrs Fiddler.

"Don't care," said Nina.

"You shouldn't be doing this. It's some sort of pressure differential, like a time valve."

Time valve, time trousers. Nina decided the woman was either far cleverer than she let on or was just making it up. Most teachers said confusing things to give them an edge on the schoolkids, but maybe Mrs Fiddler did know some things.

Nina pressed on, drawing the oculus down over her arm to the top of her head.

Somewhere, wood splintered. Dust was shaking out of the ceiling. Nina had experienced earthquakes before, and this was kind of the same. The fireplace gave a deep crunching bang and bricks fell into the hearth.

"The place is falling apart!" said Mrs Fiddler needlessly.

"Then get out!" said Nina. "Seriously! Now!"

She lowered the oculus over her head which was an unpleasant sensation, like being dunked underwater in a pool charged with low voltage electricity. She gasped and blinked and brought her other arm up and through.

Her upper body was in the silent house of the past. The air smelled of flour and wax and distant sewage. Her lower half was in the future, her present. The floor was shaking under her feet. She felt something very heavy fall beside her—a wall? timbers?—and unnatural vibrations pulsed around her.

Something smacked hard against her heel. Dying with her top half in Georgian England and her bottom half in the twenty-first century would be a stupid way to go.

"To hell with this!"

She fought the oculus down over her hips—she wasn't quite as thin as she thought she was—and then fell free and landed hard on the tiled floor.

There was a thunderous crash behind her and the hole and the oculus were gone.

She stood, groaning. Outside was a moonlit garden. She recognised it, even if the version she recognised was over two centuries into the future.

"Okay," she said to herself. "Find the oculus, open a window to yesterday and save the world."

Boulton's study and the oculus were just along the hallway.

"Stealth mode."

Nina took out her phone, switched it on as a torch and crept out into the hallway. She moved towards the study by torchlight.

A shadow flitted across the hallway ahead, but when she raised her light it was gone. It had looked human. Nina momentarily considered investigating. No, she was here for the oculus. She put her hand on the study door handle.

She heard the smash of breaking glass, a window. Somewhere close.

Suddenly, there were shouts throughout the house and a second later Nina saw a faint flicker of candle light on the stairs.

"Crap," she said.

THURSDAY... AGAIN

A hole appeared in the air less than a metre above the lawn of Soho House. It was not a large hole and would only have been noticeable to observers by the odd shadow it cast on the grass and then, some moments later, by the feet that appeared through it one at a time.

There was wriggling, huffing and puffing as the legs pulled themselves down through the hole. A short linen dress got momentarily tangled up with a long Georgian coat and then gravity pulled Nina entirely through and the hole winked out of existence.

She stood on the lawns of Soho House – modern day Soho House, half the size it once was, with new windows and guttering and the lines of telephone wires cutting through the sky behind it. The hole to the past was not visible from this side. She adjusted the three-cornered hat on her head.

"You okay, Steve?" she said.

Steve the Destroyer, a ragdoll with a top half made of rough sack cloth and a bottom half currently formed from cotton fabric printed with a bright floral pattern, freed himself from Nina's pocket and jumped to the ground.

"Steve the Destroyer is never okay," said the ragdoll, shaking himself back into shape. "He is always superb!"

"Good," she said. "Cos we've got friends to save."

Nina had spent far longer in the past than she had anticipated—long enough that, once the day was done, she wanted to spent two solid hours scrubbing herself in the shower and the rest of the week laid up watching Netflix.

She looked at her phone. The battery had died a long time ago – a long, long time ago. Like a fool, she looked at the sky to see if she could gauge the time from that. Naturally, she could do no such thing and so ran into the Soho House museum gift shop.

Tank Top was behind the till. She looked at the clock on the wall. It was nearly noon.

"*Muda*," she said. "Not enough time."

Tank Top had a newspaper crossword open in front of him, barely started.

381

"Five down is 'twister'," said Nina, without looking.

He studied the crossword. "So it is."

"Thursday," she said, reassured she had the right day. That was at least one good thing.

"Um, where did you get those?" said Tank Top, gesturing at Nina's clothes.

"Thursday at noon. Where was I?"

"You haven't stolen those clothes from a display, have you?"

She grabbed his knitted tank top. "Where am I right now?"

"Soho House...?" he offered in slow confusion.

She blinked furiously and tried to order her thoughts. "Not me! Me! Earlier. I don't want to bump into myself. Where did you last see me and Mrs Fiddler?"

She had him frightened, worried at least, but it seemed to speed him up.

"Er, er, you went into the house."

"How long ago?"

"An hour?" he guessed. "Two?"

"You're no use. I need your phone and your car keys."

"What?"

Steve the Destroyer leapt onto a display rack of novelty history pencils and, grabbing one embossed with the motto 'THIS MACHINE KILLS FASCISTS', vaulted over to land on the counter.

"Your phone and keys, you pathetic morsel," he sneered, stitched on mouth downturned.

Tank Top burbled in incoherent fear but was already passing them over.

Nina looked at the car keys.

"Is it an automatic?"

"What?"

"Your car. I can only drive automatics."

He couldn't take his eyes off Steve. "No, it isn't."

"Then we'll need you as well," she said and dragged him out.

In the Mailbox, Jayda and Skye approached Rod as he wandered across the set pushing his tea trolley.

"I'm looking for... something dangerous," he explained.

"With a pot of tea," said Skye.

"Has this got anything to do with that creepy ass Hogwarts door we found yesterday?" said Jayda.

"What Hogwarts door?" said Rod.

"The one on the train track."

Soon enough, they were following the route they had taken the day before, down the steps and into the tunnels beneath the building. Rod saw his own footprints in the filth but had no memory of making them.

"We came down here," said Rod when they stood on the narrow railway platform.

Jayda shook her head. "You really don't remember?"

"I don't know. It's odd."

"PTSD."

"No."

"Or a brain tumour," said Skye, and smiled to show she was joking.

Rod climbed down onto the train tracks, teapot in hand.

Tank Top's VW Lupo was not being driven with the level of urgency Nina required. Steve the Destroyer stood on the man's shoulder, one toy hand gripping the head rest, one gripping his novelty pencil-spear, and shouted exhortations in the man's ear.

"Faster! Faster! To the Think Tank, maggot!"

It was possible that Steve was doing more harm than good. Tank Top, drawing more and more into himself at each yell, seemed unmotivated by Steve's encouragements or by the occasional jab in the face with a pencil.

Nina, one finger thrust in her ear to keep the noise down, left a third message for Rod. Calls were going straight to voicemail. His phone was either off or out of range.

Rod's number was one of a select few she knew by heart. Her own phone was dead and although Tank Top had a phone charger in his car, it had some weird HTC connector that she could not plug into her phone. She called the consular mission switchboard to get a message to Morag. It occurred to her as the phone rang that if Kathy was working for the Forward company or the shadow organisation behind it then there could be others working for them in the consular mission.

The operator picked up. Nina didn't even give him time to speak.

"This is Nina Seth," she said. "I need to get urgent messages to Rod Campbell and Morag Murray."

"This is not your usual number," said the operator.

"You have to tell Rod to not let *Crippen-Ai* get loose and definitely not—"

"I will need to take you through some security questions first," said the operator.

"*Fer bhul kindu,*" Nina swore softly. "Urgent message, man! Urgent message!"

Jayda led the way from the railway tunnel into the secret chamber.

Rod shook the storage drums stacked along the wall. They were all empty. The lengths of hose lying curled on the floor indicated that something had been moved to or from those drums at some point. Rod crouched to investigate a blue shiny splodge on the floor.

Rod crouched before it.

"It's okay. It's solid," said Jayda.

"Some sort of residue or secretion," he suggested.

"That's what you said last time," said Skye.

"I was a clever and insightful chap."

He turned his attention to the containers in the alcoves on the other side of the narrow room. There were four of them, running up in size, weird nested containers lined with clay, glass, metal and a white crystalline powder that looked like salt. He moved along the line to the largest one.

"Increasing in size," he mused.

Jayda nodded. "Exactly. Getting bigger as they get newer. Like whatever they needed to store, there was more and more of it as time went by."

"Or whatever it was—this *Crippen-Ai*—grew and needed a bigger container."

Tea splashed over his hand. It was near to the brim.

"This is a bad place," he said.

"Ya think?" said Skye.

He tapped the largest container. "Is it still in here?"

"You checked," said Jayda.

She pointed at a sturdy plastic box and he realised that it was pulled into place so he could stand on it. In fact, he had stood on it. His inability to remember being here before was as perplexing as it was infuriating.

Rod stood on the box and peered over the top of the vat-like container. The lid was off at a slight angle.

His phone rang.

He answered as he felt around for his torch. "Campbell."

"Don't hang up," said Nina. "Don't move. This line is very bad."

"I'm underground," he said. "Under the Mailbox."

"I know. I know," she said and there was a peculiar restrained note of emotion in her voice. "Have you let it out yet?"

Rod shone his torch into the opening in the vat and tried to see inside. "Let what out?"

"*Crippen-Ai. Polliqan Riti.*"

"Why would I do that?"

"Because you will," said Nina. The line swirled for a second. "You'll do it because you did it," said Nina. "Just don't do it."

"You say the strangest things," said Rod.

Beyond the linings of metal and glass and crystal salt, the vat was evidently empty. Rod wanted to step down but that would probably disrupt the signal.

"And don't blow it up," said Nina. "And don't say you won't because you did. Don't blow it up. Keep it in one piece."

"This is all sterling advice, Nina," he said, "but there's nothing here. These containers are empty."

"What?" said Jayda.

"Whatever was in here is long gone."

"It isn't," insisted Nina. "The Forward company people used salt to contain it. It doesn't like being dried out. But somehow it broke the seal or maybe you broke it last time you were there."

"You didn't say it was empty last time," said Jayda. "Rod."

"Hang on, Nina," said Rod and turned to reassure Jayda.

"You tried the lid," said Jayda. "It made a noise, but you said it was secure."

"Right," said Skye.

There was a smear of blue on Skye's blouse.

"What's that?"

Skye looked at herself. "Urgh. Where did that...?"

Jayda shone her torch upward.

Crippen-Ai filled the ceiling, edge to edge.

Skye started to make a panicked panting sound.

Tea splashed in a constant stream onto the floor.

Rod looked at his phone. The signal had dropped.

"We should leave," said Jayda.

"Right," whispered Rod. He blindly set the teapot down to one side, pocketed his phone and, as he reached for his wallet and the emergency phrase cards with one hand, he reached into one of the medium-sized containers with the other and grabbed a handful of salt.

The very act of picking up the wallet caused key phrases to leap to his brain.

"*Skeild hraim yeq courxean*," he said reverently.

Jayda started to physically steer Skye out. Movement caused her panic to increase and her panting exclamations to go up in volume. "Oh... Oh..."

Slowly, *Crippen-Ai* bulged and reached down towards them.

"Hey," said Rod, trying to draw its attention. "Hey!"

With his fist mostly closed, he flung his hand up and sprinkled salt at it. The drooping limb recoiled momentarily. *Crippen-Ai*'s body rippled.

Jayda propelled Skye to the exit. Rod ran after. *Crippen-Ai* dropped to the floor, swelled and rolled after him.

"Quickly, quickly," he said to the women.

He all but barged Jayda out onto the railway tracks and turned to pull the door after him. It was stiff. Before he had it closed, *Crippen-Ai* had pushed itself into the gap and was working against him. *Crippen-Ai, Polliqan Riti*, whatever his name was—was all brain and muscle and Rod didn't have a chance against him.

He staggered back as the creature forced its way out. He scattered the last of the salt, not even a cupful, in front of the door. *Crippen-Ai* seemed to contemplate it for a second and then flowed around the wall, over and down and past it.

Rod waved Jayda and Skye towards the exit—"Go! Go!"—and then moved along the railway line in the opposite direction, trying to taunt and draw the creature to follow him. "Hey! Hey! This way, you great big spitball!"

Crippen-Ai ignored Rod's taunts and flolloped in the other direction.

Rod suddenly remembered the sodium toothpaste bomb in his pocket, his last one. Salt, sodium, if the thing was mostly liquid and didn't like the touch of drying agents...

He fished in his pocket, found the white ball and hurled it into the central mass of *Crippen-Ai*'s body. It smashed and fizzed and—by God!—he didn't like that.

Crippen-Ai reared up like a breaching whale and tried to angle its bulk to come down on Rod, but Rod was running, dancing ahead and calling to the bastard to follow him.

Morag entered the laboratory in the Think Tank. Kathy wascrouched, adding elements and symbols to the occult circle she had created. She looked up. There was a surprised, almost guilty look on her face.

"Catch you unawares?" said Morag.

"No one knocks in this place," said Kathy.

"What's this?"

"Contingency planning. *Polliqan Riti* here—*skep su'fragn*, my lord—is a valuable commodity but a dangerous one as well." She added punctuation to a *Kal Frexo* rune. "Did I tell you he tried to eat me earlier this week?" said Kathy.

"No," said Morag.

"Made the mistake of touching him. And then, because he's a utility monster with touch-telepathy, I felt an uncontrollable urge to let him drown me."

"How did you escape?"

"I'll tell you one day," said Kathy, smiling.

Morag moved closer to read the runes better. "Aren't those the lost runes of *Kal Frexo*?"

"Can I help you with something?" said Kathy.

"Oh. I wanted to ask you about the *mi'nasulu*."

387

"The one Nina claims to have observed in Georgian England through a supposed viewing device none of us have seen."

"You don't believe her?"

Kathy said nothing and added another symbol to her circle. Morag's phone rang. It was an unknown number.

"Hello?"

"Morag," said Nina.

"Ah, speak of the devil," said Morag and pointed to the phone for Kathy's benefit. "It's Nina."

"You're at the Think Tank with Kathy?" said Nina.

"Yeah, we were just discussing your reports on Georgian life and wondering if they were really true."

"True? Been there, done that, bought the... the pointy hat."

"Tricorn," said a man's voice on the line.

"What?" said Nina.

"It's called a tricorn."

"Quiet, you!" squeaked another voice. "Your attention should be on the road."

"Ow!" yelped the man.

"Don't snivel," said the shrill one. "It's only a pencil."

Morag frowned. "Is that...? It sounds like Steve the Destroyer."

"Yes, it is. Long story," said Nina. "Now, shut up and listen. You have to get out of there. Kathy works for Forward, for the Maccabees."

"She what?"

Morag looked at Kathy. She had returned to checking and adding to her ritual circle, but she was watching Morag now. Well, why wouldn't she be? Even hearing half the conversation, it probably sounded odd.

"She's going to kidnap you," said Nina.

Morag laughed at that. It seemed the perfectly appropriate response.

"She knows you're pregnant," said Nina.

Morag's hand went straight to her stomach. "How do you know I'm..." She looked at Kathy. Kathy was looking right back. "I don't know what you're talking about," said Morag in her best lying voice.

Kathy stood, struggling with only one good arm.

"Just act casual and walk on out," said Nina. "Do it. Do it now."

Morag found herself nodding.

"I think I need to go see what Nina's up to," she began to say to Kathy.

An alarm started blaring within the facility.

"What now?" said Morag.

"Nina?" said Kathy.

Morag saw the wand that was now in Kathy's hand. It was the *yellis* wand. She'd seen it before when Nina had used it at the Cube.

"Why've you got that?"

"*Hyet-pa!*" said Kathy.

The call ended abruptly amid the sound of sirens.

"*Muda,*" said Nina, staring at the phone.

"We're here," said Tank Top. "Do you want me to go into the car park. I haven't brought my wallet."

"Just stop," said Nina. "Let me out."

Very happy to be rid of her, Tank Top braked to a stop on the sliproad onto the Millennium Point car park. Nina opened the door.

"You're taking him with you, aren't you?" said Tank Top, eyeing the doll on his headrest fearfully.

"Come on, Steve," she said and ran for the Think Tank building, not even looking back to see if he was following.

"*Yandi voors a-lakh.*"

Alarms sounded. Red lights set into the ceiling flashed.

Morag blinked.

Mother? said her bump, and she realised it was not for the first time.

"You were telling me about your pregnancy," said Kathy.

"Was I?" said Morag. For the life of her, she couldn't remember how she'd got here or what was going on. Kathy was circling *Polliqan Riti's* tank, casting charms in Venislarn. The occult circle around the tank had turned a deep, non-reflective black – as though the glyphs had become windows to a lightless dimension.

Morag pointed at the red lights.

"Is it a fire?" said Morag.

"No, just a drill," said Kathy. "The pregnancy. Some man called Drew you were saying."

"Was I? Oh. So, I'm pregnant with the *kaatbari*."

Mother, you need to listen to me.

"You're going to give birth to the anti-Christ," said Kathy matter-of-factly.

"Yes. I guess."

Mother, that woman is not your friend. She wants to hurt you.

"*As vanir'gi finarl beraayh-u!*" intoned Kathy loudly. The dark magic in the writing on the floor poured outward and upward to make a cylinder of blackness around the tank. There was an abrupt crackle of energy and at once the cylinder vanished. The viscous liquid in the tank flowed back into the space where *Polliqan Riti* had been.

"Where's he gone?" said Morag.

We need to get away from here, mother. She's going to hurt us.

"He's gone to hell," said Kathy. "Home."

"I don't..." She frowned. Kathy was holding a *yellis* wand.

"*Hyet-pa!*"

Bright light filled the room.

In the career of any soldier who lived long enough there were bleak moments. Those moments might be on a cold wet Welsh hillside, in a bombed-out cellar, in a featureless desert, or in the ward of a hospital miles away from the field of conflict. When the dark moments came to Rod, he found it best to clear his mind and literally count his blessings. So...

One—he had wanted *Crippen-Ai* to follow him and *Crippen-Ai* had done just that.

Two—Skye and Jayda were safe and running in the other direction and hopefully raising the alarm.

Three—Nina knew he was here and what he was up against.

Four—They were deep underground and, therefore, firmly out of sight of *Yo-Morgantus* or any Venislarn who might take exception to *Crippen-Ai*'s presence.

Five—He knew it had an aversion to salt, sodium, and presumably anything that reacted with water.

Six—He'd been in tricky situations in dark tunnels before—it was almost his 'thing'—and he'd not died yet.

Seven—

"Seven..." he said to himself as he ran.

Away from the abandoned railway platform, the lighting quickly petered out. He was moving by the light of his credit card torch, high-stepping to avoid tripping on railway sleepers and rails. That limited his speed.

His mind was drifting toward the cons of his situation. He feared they significantly outnumbered the pros.

The tunnel ahead was going to do one of two things. The least horrible option would be that it would end in a wall or a mountain of rubble and Rod would be cornered. The other option was that joined one of the other railway tunnels under Birmingham and then Rod would have to contend with either trains or members of the public or both. Meanwhile, Rod had no salt or other substance to ward off the blob, no weapon to fight it with, and no plan. And he had no phone signal down here to call on the wisdom of his more resourceful colleagues.

He turned and shone his torch back down the tracks. *Crippen-Ai* filled the tunnel utterly. He'd offended the bloody thing with salt and minty toothpaste bombs and now it intended to scoop him up and have him.

"Aye, well you've got to catch me first," said Rod and ran on.

Torchlight picked out something ahead: a ladder to an access shaft in the tunnel roof. Climbing would be a welcome change from running. Rod's mind conjured images of manhole covers and access doors that might be blocked or that he could open and then seal safely between himself and his pursuer.

He sped up to give himself that extra distance, put the torch between his teeth and began to climb the rusty rungs.

Morag was walking through the Think Tank, along one of the middle floor levels above the central concourse, barriers and escalators to one side, university offices along the other. She didn't know how she had come to be there. Kathy walked next to her, perhaps she knew. There was a tense look on Kathy's face. Somewhere, alarms were ringing.

Mother, put your hand on me, said Morag's unborn.

Morag put her hand on her stomach.

One tap for yes. Two taps for no. Do you understand, mother?

Morag tapped: one.

Well done, mother. You have to listen. Understand?

She gave a tap.

Kathy wants to hurt us.

Morag frowned. It was a ridiculous thing to say.

She altered your memory, mother. Just like Nina did. She works for the bad people. She has a wand. I don't know what that is. But that's bad.

Morag tapped. She looked at Kathy Kaur.

"Everything all right?" said Kathy.

"Yeah. Sure," said Morag.

"The car's not far."

The automatic doors ahead slid open and a woman ran in. It took Morag a long moment to recognise Nina Seth. She wore a thick long coat with shiny silver buttons and, on her head, a three-cornered hat with a turned-up brim.

"Are you into historical re-enactment now?" Kathy called out with a clearly false jollity and raised the wand. She shouted something in Venislarn. Morag saw Nina throw her arms up in a counter spell gesture. Morag was dazzled by a flash of light.

Morag was running through the Think Tank. She had no idea why.

She was arm in arm with Nina.

Nina was wearing a peculiar long coat and a three-cornered hat and—Morag noticed very quickly—smelled strongly of something that could be most charitably described as 'horse and other assorted smells.'

"Where have you been?" said Morag.

"Seventeen seventy-three, mostly," said Nina.

"No time for questions, mortals!" snapped Steve the Destroyer and Morag realised she was carrying the possessed ragdoll in her hands. She had last seen him weeks ago, shortly before he'd fallen into hell with Vivian Grey. Since then, he'd apparently acquired new legs fashioned from cloth featuring a red carnation print.

Morag had more than a few questions.

The doors opened in front of them. Nina hauled her through.

"I don't know what's happening," said Morag.

"Oh, hang on," said Nina. She stopped, turned and rammed the *yellis* wand she was carrying into the concrete wall. Prongs bent, casing shattered and the many lights of the *yellis* wand went out.

Whole sections of memory that had been stolen from Morag dropped painfully back into place. She reeled as she remembered it all.

Halfway up the access ladder, shoulders brushing brickwork on either side, guided only by a torch clenched in his teeth and the sound of a grievously annoyed blob glurping up the pipe below him, Rod was suddenly slammed by a pile of recovered memories.

"I had sex with Kathy Kaur!" he shouted, dropping his torch.

He was now confused and without a light.

He forced himself upward and now, eyesight adjusting to the gloom, he began to see motes of light above. Square regular shapes, holes in a manhole cover perhaps... Daylight, almost certainly.

Something slurped below him.

He powered on up and struck the underside of the metal cover. It shifted a couple of inches and he worked with that. He pushed, levered and worked himself through the gap.

He crawled out into daylight. This wasn't where he wanted *Crippen-Ai* to be but in that instant, Rod's animal soul delighted in daylight.

Tarmac. He was on a road. He looked round for the bus or lorry that might mow him down and saw the road was empty. It was blocked off by construction barriers.

He was on Broad Street, down by Centenary Square. The building works that dominated the square were feet away from him. On the other side of them was the Library of Birmingham and the consular mission offices.

He rolled free, shoved the manhole cover back into place and then stood on it. He didn't think for an instant that it would hold *Crippen-Ai* down but, right now, he had nothing else.

The cover wobbled beneath his feet. White flesh, like links of squid sausage, extruded through the holes and the cover lifted up. He jumped clear.

Two builders at the open gate to construction area stared.

"Now would be a good time to run!" Rod shouted.

The men, waking to their situation, did just that.

In the construction zone that covered Centenary Square, where artful steps, graceful slopes and sunken lawns were being built, workers stopped at the sight of the amorphous and massive *Crippen-Ai*. The men at the gate ran and the good thing about running was that it was contagious. They abandoned their tools and their diggers, their cement mixers and their wheelbarrows, and ran.

Rod stepped back from *Crippen-Ai*. He couldn't just flee.

"Keep it here," he told himself. "Keep it contained. Kill it if you can."

The Venislarn monster threw out a tentacle limb to grab Rod. He jumped away and retreated into the building site.

"If you can," he said.

Nina and Morag hurried away from the Think Tank building. Nina didn't have much of a plan where they were going to; 'from' was kind of key at the moment.

There was a bang, a gunshot. Morag looked back. Kathy, blood on her face where Nina had whacked her against a wall, had come out of the building holding a pistol.

"Morag!" Kathy screamed.

Kathy fired again. Morag had no idea where that shot went but she guessed she probably wouldn't see the one that killed her.

Shala'pinz Syu dropped down the side of the building onto Kathy. It should have squashed her flat but only caught her a glancing blow. Kathy sprawled forward.

"What the *bhul*?" said Nina.

"My nanny," said Morag.

Kathy turned over and fired up at the handmaiden as it reared over her. It was a tiny gun. It should have been utterly ineffective, but the handmaiden recoiled at the first shot, began to scream and was silenced by a second fatal shot.

"Fuck," said Morag.

You used the bad word, mother.

"Kind of justified in this instance, baby."

Kathy was slowly getting to her feet, but her attention was still fixed on the dead Venislarn.

"Keep running," said Nina.

"Steve the Destroyer runs from nothing!" said the ragdoll in Morag's hands.

"We're not out of the woods yet," said Morag.

"And he is frightened of no woods!"

Together, the women ran to the nearest shelter, a multi-storey car park, and hurried in through the pedestrian entrance. There was another gunshot but they heard other sounds as well – alarms inside the building, distant shouts and screams, and the sirens of emergency vehicles approaching from all directions.

Morag and Nina didn't stop. By silent agreement they continued onward, seeking distance, seeking shelter.

Morag's phone rang. She glanced at it automatically. In the present circumstances, she didn't intend to answer it but the caller ID said it was Nina.

"You're calling me," said Morag.

"What?" said Nina.

Morag answered. "Hello?"

"Just ignore that," said Nina by her side.

"Where are you?" said Nina on the phone.

Morag stopped dead.

"It's you," she said to both of them, neither of them.

"That *was* me," said the Nina next to her. "Past me. Ignore her."

"Right, now don't freak out," said Phone Nina.

"Bit difficult not to," said Morag.

"Why have we stopped?" demanded Steve. "Are we going to make a stand at last?"

There was a noise on the line, like Phone Nina was in a car.

"I don't know what's going on but—"

"I don't know what's going on either," said Morag. She looked at the Nina with her, this strange individual in the outlandish cosplay outfit who stank like she'd been on a farm and not bathed in a month.

"We've got to go," said Stinky Nina.

"It's Kathy," said Phone Nina. "She knew about the *mi'nasulu* and no one knew about them except those Lunar Society guys or whatever they became. And the company that bought up the gunmakers—"

Morag heard footsteps. She looked past Nina and saw Malcolm walking towards them.

"Hey," she began to say. "Aren't you a sight for sore eyes."

Before Nina could turn to see who it was, something struck her in the back. Morag saw the filament taser wires and Nina jerked and spasmed and then fell unconscious to the floor. Malcolm lowered his weapon.

"Morag," he said in greeting.

"What's going on?" said Morag. "Are there two Ninas? Is she Nina?"

"It's complicated," said the consular security officer. "You need to come with me."

"Kathy tried to kill me."

"I know, I know," he said. "The police are looking for her." He looked around. "Now, let's get you and baby to a safe place."

She looked at him.

"It's okay. We know. It's fine." He smiled. "Kids, eh? We'd do anything to protect them, wouldn't we?"

Rod ran through the almost deserted construction site and headed directly toward the caterpillar-tracked earthmover parked beneath the cement silo at the centre of the square. Against a creature with no notable weak spots and no fixed shape, all weapons were equally useless but, if Rod had to fight the thing off (if only to keep it occupied until help arrived) then he wanted to do it from the seat of a bloody JCB.

He was now in the shadow of the Library building and confident that someone inside would have seen him by now. He wasn't sure how he felt about that. The thought of Vaughn Sitterson being able to watch him in the thick of things, perhaps silently appraising him whilst sipping a cup of tea, was oddly unnerving. If things went well, this should at least get him through this year's performance management review. If things didn't go well... then there'd probably be no performance management review to get through.

With that cheery win-win thought on his mind, Rod jumped onto the digger's track and into the cab. He'd never driven such a vehicle before, but the limited number of controls gave him some optimism. He turned an important-looking key and thumbed a button marked 'start'. Beneath him an engine rumbled and roared into life.

He found himself unaccountably mumbling in a high tone a tune with the words, "Rod the Builder. Can he fix it?" It seemed stupidly apt and kept some clearly useless parts of his brain busy.

Already, *Crippen-Ai* was nearly on top of him. The creature threw out limbs and hauled itself forward. It was an unnerving motion, like an octopus aiming for a land-speed record. Rod grabbed the lever controls, pulled them in an action that he hoped would rotate the cab and swing the front bucket into *Crippen-Ai* but, before the digger arm had even moved, *Crippen-Ai* slammed into the JCB, pinning the arm in place and rocking the cab.

Crippen-Ai's flesh and ooze pressed against the plastic window and squirted through the narrow gaps. The Perspex gave a fairly fatal groan. One part of Rod's mind—the coward, the inner child, Rod the Builder—wanted to stay at the controls but a wiser part over-ruled it and he pushed open the other door and leapt out, moments before the cab gave way.

He stepped down on the caterpillar tread and lowered himself into the narrow gap between vehicle and the cement silo. The silo was a thirty-foot-high steel drum, funnel-bottomed on a heavy-duty stand. Cement powder dusted the ground around the air.

Cement powder, he thought. He'd lectured Nina on its exothermic reaction to water. It wasn't sodium or a salt of any kind but it was—he couldn't remember exactly what it was—Lime? Calcium?—Whatever, it soaked up water and it burned.

"Hey!" he shouted. "You missed me!"

Crippen-Ai flowed over, around and through the digger. Rod ducked under the supporting structure and, lowering his head to avoid the bottom of the silo, stood next to the funnel opening. There was a valve opening mechanism at the bottom of the funnel.

"Rod the Builder..." he sang-whispered.

It looked like the opening could connect to pipe attachments but there was also a simple wrench-like lever at the side of it. If he was lucky, he could just pull it.

"Can he fix it?"

Crippen-Ai, unstoppable and covered in a gloss of Venislarn-poisoning slime, flowed under the silo. As its leading edge touched cement dust on the floor, it shifted upward to flow along the underside of the funnel.

Rod held his breath and forced the lever arm round. A dense column of cement dust poured out and, as it hit the ground, exploded into a rapidly expanding cloud. Rod saw *Crippen-Ai* flinch as it made contact and then he saw nothing more as the dust utterly clouded his vision.

Rod staggered backward. His foot caught on something and he fell, knocking the breath from him. Only by a deliberate act of will did he stop himself breathing in a lungful of the caustic substance. He crawled, eyes shut, until he came up against something solid, the side of a tall box with hard plastic walls. He felt his way up and realised it was a portaloo. He worked swiftly round to the door, let himself in and finally risked opening his eyes and breathing again.

There was cement dust in the air but not enough to cause anything more than an irritated cough. The stink of the chemical toilet at his feet was a cleansing balm. He could breathe, he could smell.

He took another deep breath and headed out again. He had to see what had become of *Crippen-Ai*.

The cement dust cloud was thick but dissipating across the square. At its heart was a heavy, sludgy grey shape. *Crippen-Ai* was covered with a thick layer of clagging wet cement covered by a heavy dusting of still-dry powder. The more the creature thrashed, the more of its own slime it worked into the cement and the thicker the layer became around it. It tried to extrude fresh limbs but whatever burst the crust of hardening cement was soon covered in a fresh shell of grey dust. Its overall volume had increased threefold, more cement than creature now, a giant squid drowning in a tar pit. And inside that wet but quick-drying shell, the lime or the calcium—lime, he decided—was baking the creature to perfection.

As he watched, its thrashing contortions slowed.

"Rod the Builder, yes he can," he said.

Nina thumped Tank Top in the shoulder.

"Here. Stop here."

She'd forced him to drive the wrong way up a roadworks diversion and now he stopped in the middle of Broad Street. He stared at the dust and chaos around the building site in Centenary Square.

"You did good," said Nina and opened the door to get out.

The swotty museum clerk smiled. He was probably just glad she was leaving. He still had the pencil tip marks on his cheeks Steve had given him. Steve was gone, taken along with Morag. Nina didn't know where they'd been taken, but she was a hundred percent sure who was behind it.

Nina slammed the door and walked over to the building site. Police and ambulance were already in attendance, a fire engine too. Fire crews seemed to turn up to these things more out of a fear of being left out than anything else. A police officer tried to block her way. She showed him her ID card and even though her clothes were two hundred years out of date, he couldn't argue with the ID.

She entered the building site and clocked the weird sculptural monstrosity at its centre. Curving, thrusting arms, still dribbling with wet cement, reached out desperately and imploringly.

"Some of my finest work," said a voice behind her.

Nina whirled, threw her arms around Rod's wide chest and hugged him as tightly as she could. It was a rare emotional gesture from her, and one entirely ruined by the fact that she got only a face full of cement dust in return.

"Ugh! You're disgusting," she said, quickly releasing him.

"You're not so pleasant yourself," he said.

"It's a new look," she said and cocked her hat at a jaunty angle.

"I meant the smell," he said.

"I practically had to invent the bath."

"What do you mean?"

"Long story." She stared at him, alive and whole, in silent wonder. "You're not dead."

"Didn't plan to be." He patted his filthy suit, producing a cloud of dust and making no difference to the suit at all.

"They've got Morag," she said.

"Who?"

"The Maccabees."

"Kathy."

399

"Her. And Morag's pregnant."

"She's what?"

"You don't know the half of it. We have to rescue her."

"Any idea how?"

Nina shook her head. "But we have to. Time is running out." She rummaged in her pocket and retrieved the 'History is fun!' notepad. It had become battered, smeared and dog-eared in the many weeks that had passed between this morning and now. She found the relevant page and showed the oculus markings she had transcribed there, only yesterday and two centuries ago.

"The soulgate," she said. "The date of the end of the world. I saw it."

"And for those of us who don't read Venislarn?" asked Rod.

"Tomorrow," she said simply.

"Tomorrow?"

"Uh-huh."

Rod forgot himself and futilely tried to brush the cement dust from his clothes again.

"The world ends on a Friday. Figures. We don't even get the weekend."

On the other side of the building site, Professor Sheikh Omar and Vaughn Sitterson approached the drying monster sculpture. One wore an expression of fascination, the other, an expression of horror.

"So," said Rod, "our organisation has been infiltrated by an enemy we never knew we had. Our colleague—our *pregnant* colleague—has been kidnapped. And the world is going to end tomorrow."

"And we need to rescue Vivian from hell."

"That too. Champion."

"You up for it?" she said.

Rod looked at her, filthy and dressed entirely for the wrong time period. He looked at himself, beaten, bruised and dirty. He shrugged.

"You only live once, eh?"

"Some of us," said Nina.

"What's that supposed to mean?"

"Long story, Rod."

After they removed Morag's blindfold, they put her in a clean white room with a hospital bed and bars on the windows. Dr Kathy Kaur stood at the door, close to the protective presence of Malcolm. Malcolm had removed his consular mission beret and epaulettes, a statement of sorts.

"What the fuck do you think you're going to do with me?" said Morag.

You said the bad word, said her unborn but she ignored it.

"We will care for you," said Kathy. "We will keep you and the *kaatbari* in good health. For now."

Morag couldn't believe how stupid the woman was being.

"*Yo Morgantus* will tear the world apart to keep this child safe," she said. "You don't let me go, terrible things will happen."

Kathy nodded slowly, understanding, or perhaps simply waiting for Morag to stop.

"You carry the key to the apocalypse in your womb, Morag. We now have that key."

Morag laughed and if there was a craziness in that laugh then it was well earned.

"You're going to try to bargain with the Venislarn? You think you can hold them to ransom?"

Kathy was indifferent. "They will either cede to our demands or we will—regretfully—terminate their anti-Christ."

The words 'over my dead body' sprang to Morag's mind and almost to her lips. Over her dead body was probably part of the plan.

"You can't stop them," she said.

"We have the weapons," said Kathy. She pumped the slide on her little pistol, releasing a bullet from the breach. It had a dark blue sheen, stone rather than metal.

"Weapons," whispered Morag in disbelief. "We're ants. We've only seen their fists so far and you think... You can't win."

Kathy's expression hardened. "At least *we* haven't already given up." She sighed, her anger suppressed. "Get some rest. We'll talk later."

Kathy backed out. Malcolm drew the door closed. There was the clunk of a very heavy lock. And Morag was alone. Well, not quite, not at all.

Mother?

"Hey, baby," she said, reached into the waistband of her trousers and pulled out Steve the Destroyer.

He wriggled free of her grip and fell onto the bed, his pencil spear in his hand. He bounced on the tightly tucked in top sheet.

They said they would terminate me, said her baby.

"I won't let them hurt you."

Steve massaged his limbs back into shape. "You should not concern yourself with them hurting me," he said.

"No, I'm not, I—"

"No one should be concerned about me," he said and, happy that his stuffing was no longer out of the place, threw a bold and manly pose.

"I'm not,"

"I forbid you to concern yourself, gobbet."

I worry about you, mother.

"Me? I'm fine," she said, and stroked her belly.

She walked to the barred window. Below, there was a courtyard, the beginnings of a simple access road and then nothing but trees and grass, wild woodland. They could be anywhere.

"We've got time to figure this out," she said to herself. The one advantage of carrying the doomsday clock in her womb was that she could be confident doomsday wasn't arriving just yet.

"If there is a figuring out to be had, you will leave it to me," said the ragdoll smugly. "If it's figured in, I'll figure it out. All I need is some sort of figuring blade..." He searched the plateau of the bed, for what exactly, Morag couldn't guess.

"Right now, you need to be silent and hidden," she told him. "You're my secret weapon."

Appeased with the role of 'secret weapon', Steve duly shut up and looked for a hiding place.

That woman, Kathy, wants to hurt you.

"I said, I won't let them."

For a kid who was not yet born, he was already worrying about his mum too much. In her experience, children didn't worry about their parents until it was too late to make any difference and that was the way of things.

I can protect you too, he said.

402

"It's fine."

If I come out, I can care for you.

"When you're big and strong" she said and shushed him.

I'll be good.

"I know you will."

She felt something stir inside her and then suddenly stretch with force enough to make her grunt.

"Wait..."

The lump inside her moved again, pushing another way and she grabbed the railings at the foot of the bed for support. "*Muda*," she grunted.

It's fine, mother. I'll be out soon. Just you wait and see.

Morag doubled over the end of the bed, trying to hold herself together. She gasped for breath and stared, overwhelmed by the sensations in her gut and her own foolish complacence.

Maybe she didn't have any time at all.

AUTHORS' NOTES

YES — Moseley Bog, located in the Hall Green / Moseley area of Birmingham, is technically a fen and is now a public park.

NO — Moseley Bog, though wet and boggy, isn't an ideal habitat for crocodiles, dragons or any other aquatic horrors.

YES — The young JRR Tolkien grew up in the area immediately next to Moseley Bog. Sarehole Mill IS the mill he references in The Lord of the Rings.

YES — There is a yearly Middle Earth festival held in the grounds of Sarehole Mill.

YES — There is a Donkey Sanctuary in Sutton Park.

YES — There is a parade of shops on a roundabout near Moseley Bog, featuring the 'Hungry Hobb' café.

YES — The Hungry Hobb café was once called the Hungry Hobbit café but they were allegedly forced to change the café's name to avoid copyright infringement.

YES — Pretty much everything Julie Fiddler says about Matthew Boulton and the Lunar Society is true.

YES — The Mailbox was originally the Birmingham Royal Mail sorting office.

YES — There are private railway tunnels running underneath the Mailbox. They are quite extensive.

NO — We weren't able to get access to them whilst researching this novel. We asked and spoke to some very nice people, but they are currently unsafe due to on-going electrical works.

YES — It was indeed said that many businesses would, on a Friday, mail their takings to themselves rather than deposit them in a bank, knowing that they would be held securely in the Royal Mail tunnels over the weekend.

YES — The Mailbox has undergone renovations on several occasions and is now a shopping centre with offices, hotels, restaurants and bars on various levels.

YES — Spielberg does love filming in Birmingham. Much of the movie Ready Player One was filmed in the city (or mapped for the CGI video game sections)

NO — Ricky Lee is wrong when he says Charlie Chaplin was born in Birmingham. A rumour persists that he was born to travellers camped on the Black Patch, but it is only a rumour.

YES — Soho House is a museum and generally as described and well worth a visit. Julie Fiddler's brief description of its history from Boulton's home to the present day is correct.

YES — Soho House contains fine examples of Boulton's work, including various pieces of ormolu and a sidereal clock.

NO — There are no magic corridors or mystery basements in Soho House.

YES — The Lunar Society was arguably the focal point of the English Enlightenment. Its members did indeed include Boulton, Erasmus Darwin, Josiah Wedgwood, James Watt, Benjamin Franklin, Joseph Priestley, James Keir, John Baskerville, William Small and Thomas Day.

YES — Amazingly, Erasmus Darwin did lay out plans for a hydrogen-oxygen rocket engine (that would have worked) a hundred and fifty years before anyone else thought to invent one.

NO — Matthew Boulton did not have a servant called Jonathan Angus. He is a fictional character.

NO — Forward Management Ltd does not exist.

YES — The arm and hammer logo of Forward Management does exist. It forms part of the Birmingham City coat of arms. The city motto on the coat of arms is "Forward".

YES — The Think Tank at Millennium Point is a real science museum and as described.

NO — The Think Tank is not home to the secret laboratories of the consular mission.

YES — Erasmus Darwin and other members of the Lunar Society were fascinated by the caves in rural Derbyshire and studied both the geology and the fossils of the area. They were some of the first individuals to show an interest in the commercial possibilities of blue john.

YES — The blue john stone is as described in the book and can only be found in certain caves in Derbyshire. It is in absolutely finite supply and therefore its value has risen constantly since its discovery.

YES — The story Producer Tammy tells Rod about Daniel Craig's gloves is true. Sort of. There is some dispute over which scene required CGI alteration due to his decision to wear them.

YES — The Reverend W. Awdry was curate at St Nicholas's church in Kings Norton at the time when he wrote the original Thomas the Tank Engine stories.

YES — Though some of the floors of the Cube are unused, there are several floors of apartments available to rent.

NO — None of the apartments are rented out by servants of unspeakable gods or staffed by monstrous nannies.

YES — Gas Street Basin used to be simply the point where two canals nearly met. Goods that were being carried beyond this point would have to be unloaded from a barge on one side of a spit of land and loaded onto a barge on the opposite side. The reason the canals weren't originally joined is probably because the two canal companies feared the other would take advantage of its water supply.

Printed in Great Britain
by Amazon